Catching Kyle
Football Heartthrobs Book One
Cliff J. Cavender

Cavender Books

Contents

1. Dedication   1

2. Prologue   2

3. Chapter 1   6

4. Chapter 2   12

5. Chapter 3   19

6. Chapter 4   26

7. Chapter 5   29

8. Chapter 6   33

9. Chapter 7   40

10. Chapter 8   47

11. Chapter 9   53

12. Chapter 10   61

13. Chapter 11   66

14. Chapter 12   73

15. Chapter 13   79

16. Chapter 14   87

17. Chapter 15   93

18. Chapter 16   101

19. Chapter 17   107

20. Chapter 18   112

21. Chapter 19   120

22. Chapter 20   127

23. Chapter 21   131

24. Chapter 22   139

25. Chapter 23   144

26. Chapter 24   148

27. Chapter 25   155

28. Chapter 26   162

29. Chapter 27   170

30. Chapter 28   178

31. Chapter 29   186

32. Chapter 30   197

33. Six Months Later   211

34. Chapter 31   212

35. Chapter 32   217

36. Chapter 33   227

37. Chapter 34   231

38. Chapter 35   242

39. Chapter 36   256

40. Chapter 37   263

41. Chapter 38   269

42. Chapter 39   278

43. Chapter 40   283

44. Chapter 41   291

45. Chapter 42   295

46. Chapter 43 — 302

47. Chapter 44 — 306

48. Chapter 45 — 308

49. Chapter 46 — 313

50. Chapter 47 — 316

51. Chapter 48 — 319

52. Chapter 49 — 322

53. Chapter 50 — 324

54. Epilogue One – Six Months Later — 330

55. Epilogue Two – One Year Later — 337

56. What's next? — 342

57. Acknowledgements — 343

Dedication

To my fellow gay men and anyone else who has believed themselves to be cursed with the inability to love or be loved—I'll tell you now: that's false, and you are definitely worthy of both

Prologue

Kyle Weaver

"How does it feel to be the best linebacker of the 21st century?" a woman asks.

"And the Sexiest Man Alive?" asks a man wearing button-up with the faces of Portland Tigers players all over it.

I chuckle as I stand in front of a bouquet of microphones and a crowd of reporters, a camera occasionally flashing. It's media day, and a bunch of key players from both teams are getting interviewed before the NFO Championship Game on the field of the Miami stadium.

I grin and stare at the man's shirt as I answer. "I've worked real hard for the first," I say, my Southern drawl strong. "Don't really know what else to say about the second."

The crowd of reporters laughs, and I'm feeling good. The Championship Game is this Sunday, and I have a feeling that the win is ours.

A short, round man comes to the front of my crowd, and I already feel my heart begin to race. Ricardo. The professional sports jokester, always asking players uncouth questions. Supposedly, he always asks in good faith, only meant to get a laugh out of the player and the crowd. He goes viral before every big game. But his questions, at least when asked to me, always feel barbed.

"Kyle! Kyle!" He shouts. I shift toward him. It's a cool sixty-five degrees out here on the field, but I'm already sweating. I thought I told my agent not to let him out here.

"How is it that the 'Sexiest Man Alive' is still single? At thirty-four years old?"

The crowd turns to me, and I have to take a deep breath to prevent my face from blanching.

"Just been busy working on my skills," I say, turning away, just how my agent instructed. Polite yet firm. I'm ready for the next question, hopefully about my playing and not about my love life.

"But surely there must be someone in your life," Ricardo continues.

I sigh through my nose loud enough to be picked up by the mics. "Any other questions?"

"Come on," Ricardo says. "You know what everyone's dying to know. Are you single because you're working on your skills? Or are you single because you're gay?"

The crowd gasps, and everyone stares at me, expectant. I stare down at my mic, mortified.

"I—" I cough and clear my throat. "I don't—"

When I can't answer, my agent storms onto the field.

"Alright, that's enough questions for now," he says when he reaches me. He nudges me off my chair, but it feels like my legs are filled with lead.

The crowd goes wild.

"Kyle, can you confirm Ricardo's words? Are you gay?"

"Is there a man you're currently seeing?"

"No comment," my agent says as he pushes me away.

Flashes blind me as mics are shoved in my face, and I want to do nothing more than bury myself into the field.

"I thought you said Ricardo wouldn't be here," I murmur to my agent.

"This is just as surprising for me," he says. "Keep walking."

A reporter steps in front of me and shoves a mic in my face. "There are rumors that you were part of the gay sex club at Miss U. Can you confirm?"

My stomach clenches as I remember all the players I slept with in college. "No comment," I say, and I disappear into the stadium.

* * *

It's Sunday, the score 21 - 26 with the Vanguards winning. The shouts are deafening. There are less than ten seconds on the clock, and both teams are out of timeouts. We're playing defense, and the Vanguards have three more downs. My team is depending on me to do what I do best: intercept and score a touchdown. But that means our win is all up to me. My last chance to honor my promise to my dead father.

I try to calm my beating heart as I crouch down in front of their towering center, but I can't help but blame myself for the current situation. My botched interview has put the Tigers all over the news. But they haven't been talking about our stats or players. They've been talking about potentially having a gay player on the team. And this embarrassing limelight has thrown many of us off our game.

The worst part is that if I win, they won't ask me about how it feels to raise the world record for linebacker touchdowns, or how it feels to honor my daddy's, former Coach Weaver's, wish to win the Championship Game. No. Instead, it will be speculation about whether or not a gay man can really handle a career in the NFO.

The center snaps the ball. The quarterback pretends to throw it out to a wide receiver to my right. But, just like I predicted, he jukes us and throws it to their tight end. Already running that way, I barrel to the spinning football. I jump high. And the moment I catch it, I run like hell. Just like my daddy taught me.

The color of our team's uniforms blur in my vision as I run, but I don't stop. There are screams. Deafening ones. But I can hear my heartbeat. Twenty yards away. Fifteen. Hands try to reach me, but I'm too fast. I'm going to win us the Championship Game.

But the question echoes in my mind again: 'How is it that Sexiest Man Alive is still single?'

I don't fucking know. Shouldn't I have some hot girl by now? What the fuck is wrong with me?

My speed falters. A hand grabs onto my thigh. Momentum yanks me backwards. The ball flies out of my hands. I collapse onto the turf, and the crowd goes wild. The Vanguards have won the Championship Game.

And I just broke my promise.

Chapter 1

Michael Cunningham

"THAT WAS SOME OF the best sex I've ever had."

I roll my eyes as I wash the lube off my hands in my bathroom. That's what they *always* say before they high-tail it out of my apartment. I dry my hands, then walk into the bedroom. "You really think so?" I ask quite literally.

"Fuck, man." The beefy, six-three guy plops down on my bed, still completely nude. I have to admit, he was a good lay. But I have no interest in him pretending to care about me now that he's gotten what he wanted. I walk out of the bathroom and lean against the doorframe. The ring light and camcorder are still on. That's fine. I'll just edit this out before out I post it.

"It's like you're handcrafted from the gods or something," he says. "You practically pulled that orgasm right out of me. I can't remember the last time..." The man—I don't actually know his real name except for his twitter handle of 'PortlandBeefCake'—closes his eyes his eyes as if in blissful sleep.

"Hah," I say, searching for my briefs on the floor. PortlandBeefCake's ecstasy makes me believe that his words could be true. I pick up my briefs and slip them on. "Thanks. I'm flattered."

But the man didn't seem to hear. He lays spread on the bed, contented.

And *this* is why dating is fruitless. Guys are always so kind, so sweet, so *into* you. But once I get them off, it's like I no longer exist. It's been the same my entire thirty-one years. It's best that I post on OnlyFans. If I'm going to have emotionless sex, at least I can get paid for it.

I scratch my head, roughing up my ginger mullet that PortlandBeefCake almost ripped off when he was railing me. I glance at my alarm clock. Shit. I'm supposed to meet Amani for a drink in thirty. Guess we were going longer than I thought. I need to clean up before I meet her. I can't wait to hear what she thinks of my novel.

"Hey, man," I say. "I gotta..."

But then PortlandBeefCake starts snoring.

Great. Now I have to be an asshole.

I pick up one of the man's massive arms and drop it on his hairy abs. He startles awake and eyes me like a complete stranger. Then he comes to, realizing where he is.

"I'm going to have to ask you to leave," I say.

"Sure, yeah." He rubs his eyes and stands up, about three inches taller than me. He raises his hands for me to fist bump.

I return it with a sigh.

"Great time, man. Let's uhh..." He starts gathering his things, letting his fake invitation to see each other again fade into the air.

I turn on my shower, then walk out to see him off. "I'll get the video edited and posted."

"Sweet," he says, all his stuff in hand. He looks more handsome with his clothes on. "It was a pleasure."

And then he's gone, and I'm alone.

I hop into the shower before the loneliness swallows me up. But I have no need to worry. Once Amani tells me how amazing my story is, which it has to be considering how hard I've worked on it, I'll shed myself of the typical post-hookup blues. And who knows. Maybe this novel will finally be the one that gets me an agent. I hope. Because if it isn't, this may just be the last one that I write.

* * *

I get to my favorite pub five minutes earlier than Amani and I agreed to meet, which is typical of me. This gives me time to continue reading this gay romance series about hot firefighters, and I prefer to read in public places. It helps me be alone yet not lonely. The ideal.

An ad blares on the TV in front of me, one that I instantly recognize because I've watched it at least 1000 times. Kyle Weaver, linebacker for the Portland Tigers, fills the screen, and my chest immediately tightens at the sight. The Mississippi sweetheart. He's shirtless, after having been just doused with a bucket of water, holding up the beer he sponsors. He flashes the camera a seductive grin, then winks, and I swear to God I'm already like a quarter hard. And when he speaks in that Southern drawl, I just want to lean back and spread my legs. There are few videos that have gotten me off quicker. No wonder he was last year's 'Sexiest Man Alive'.

I'm usually not too insecure about my body, but mine pales in comparison to his. Where I'm only about 5'11", he's 6'5". Where my muscles are more defined, his are thick and beefy. He seems to have the perfect balance of fat and muscle. And where my red beard can never grow more than an inch, his jet-black beard grows all the way down to his chest, which he never shaves. He has a perfect head of wavey, black hair and a smile that crinkles his warm, brown eyes. It nearly knocks me out every time. I've been told, on occasion, that I'm handsome, with my big nose and hazel eyes, and I'm often fetishized because of my red hair. Yet I feel like an ugly duckling compared to the swan he is.

But the thing that draws me to him more than anything else are his charity efforts. He has donated tens of thousands of dollars to organizations benefiting children with cancer, as well as cancer as a whole. He's given so much that he's often asked why he's giving so much away and not spending it on, say, a family, which he's usually asked because he's the most eligible bachelor in the country. To which he responds: the kids need it more than me.

Ugh. Swoon.

"I swear," Amani says, walking up the table. She looks at Kyle Weaver just before the commercial changes. "That man could make me straight."

I look away from the TV to my best friend from college. "Yeah, he's a handsome guy."

As Amani takes a seat in the booth across from me, I blush. I know having a crush on one of the best football players in the country is nothing to be embarrassed about, but I made a promise to myself after I broke up with my ex: no more chasing after unavailable men. If I want to write a good romance, I need to make sure my own romances are not unhealthy or unrealistic.

"Sorry I'm late," she says, tying her dreads above her head, her One-Piece jacket bright and garish compared to the black booth. "My coworkers are incompetent coders."

"Well, if you stuck with your literary agent, maybe you wouldn't be putting up with them."

"Hey," she says, pointing a finger. "I didn't break up with her. I can still reach out to her if I want."

"And it makes no sense to me that you aren't," I say, shaking my head with a lilt in my voice. "I'd be utilizing the hell out of an agent if I had one. Content-writing sucks the soul out of me, and I'd do anything to get out of it. That and all the porn I have to make to get by."

She playfully whacks my arm, and then the waiter comes to take our order. I love Amani. She and I have been best friends ever since we took an essay writing class at UDub. She's a nerdy black lesbian more obsessed with anime than anyone I know. And she can write a killer fantasy. Too bad she's had no luck landing a book with an editor at a publishing house.

"So, I read your stuff," she says.

I perk up. "Did you like it?"

She ticks and tilts her head. "I definitely think there are some strengths."

I frown, not fooled at all. "So it wasn't good."

"It's not bad!" she says. She's trying to sound reassuring, but it just comes off as pitying.

"Well, what are your overall thoughts?"

"You've got an interesting romantic premise," she says. "I like the whole addiction component. Spices things up."

"Okay," I say, sitting up. "What else?"

She sucks on her lip. "All the pieces were there—a premise, good characters, interesting story. But it just fell flat to me."

My chest tightens. "Flat?"

She winces. "Like the romance wasn't there. Like it wasn't believable. I didn't feel invested enough in these gay men for me to care that they got together."

I have to resist crossing my arms. We have a rule about crossing our arms when receiving feedback. Too defensive. But I'm still pissed, and Amani knows it.

"It's still a work in progress, Michael. That's different than being bad."

I start tapping my foot. "I've been working on this novel for over a year, and you're saying it still needs work?"

"Yes," Amani says with a raised brow. "That's how this industry works. All writing is rewriting."

I grunt and finally cross my arms just as our food arrives, and I wallow as we eat.

This is so discouraging. I miss our college days where I could see how my writing improved with each piece, where every week I could get with my writing group and learn and grow with fellow writers. Growing up neglected, this was like finding an oasis in a desert when all I was used to was sand. I want to have this again—the sense of community that comes with writing. I see published authors, both big and small, developing intimate relationships with each other, the same kinds of relationships I cherished in college. But I don't personally have that anymore, and with how hard it is to find writing friends, it feels like the only way for me to get this again is by getting published. Amani's great, but she hardly has time to read my stuff, and it feels like she's all but given up her dream to be a published author. And with her feedback, the dream of finally having this intimate community again feels farther away than ever.

"You're getting that sad look," she says. "Your face gets all droopy and you get quiet. The one you make when you get feedback you don't like."

I let out a sharp laugh. "Well what's there to like? I don't even know where to start to make my romance deeper. And it's not like I'm chasing after unavailable men right now. So I don't know why my romance is so bad."

"Again," Amani says, finishing her fries. "It's not bad. It could just use some zest."

I laugh, hopeless. "What does that even mean?"

She reaches into her pocket. "I'm so glad I grabbed this." She puts a card on the table and slides it to me. There are butterflies, roses, and a straight couple kissing on it.

I pick it up. "This is...?"

"You know Ruckers?"

The cool new indie bookstore in Portland. "Of course I do."

"They have a romance book club that's so popular it meets weekly. And it's eclectic. You'll get your Nora Roberts fans, your Sarah J. Maas fans. The whole gamut."

I furrow my brow at her. "How did you know about this?"

She laughs. "I went the other day to pick up a book when they had their meeting. Their cackles resonated throughout the whole store. You know how some romance readers are. I bet most of those women are reading more than one a day. Didn't interest me much, but I figured I'd grab one of their cards."

I glance down at the card. In iridescent font, it has the address of the bookstore as well as some authors they regularly read. All authors I've enjoyed, many of whom write gay stuff.

"I love discussing books as much as the next, but you really think this will help?"

Her eyes widen as if I've grown a second head. "What better way to learn how to how to write compelling romance than from its biggest fans?"

I sigh, then shrug. The next meeting is this Friday, and the card says they're discussing Pride and Prejudice. "Sure, why the hell not. I'm always down for a Jane Austen reread."

"Who knows," Amani says, sipping the last of her drink. "Maybe you'll find a special someone."

I fake gag. "With my luck? It'll just be some fuckboy."

She shrugs. "You never know."

Chapter 2

Kyle Weaver

I'VE ALREADY BEEN WORKING out for almost two hours today, but it isn't enough. If I had been fast enough, I could have made it to the end zone. I could have won the Tigers a Championship Game. I could have kept my promise to my dad.

I push the sled to the end of the forty-yard lane in our practice facility, and I turn it around to do another cycle.

"Hey, man, you need to take it easy." Ezekiel says. My wide receiver walks over to me, shirtless, his sweat dripping down his dark-skinned abs. He pulls his dreads back and ties them up.

I wipe my sweat-drenched face with my towel, yet the movement just causes my sweat to drop through my beard onto the floor. I take a seat on the sled, still breathing heavy.

"You're still pissed," Ezekiel says.

"Of course I'm pissed," I say. "Wouldn't you be? I fuck up our chance at winning the Championship Game, and the media hasn't shut up about who I might be sleeping with. We were so close."

"I know," he says, sitting down on the turf next to me. There are some other guys working out nearby, but they're doing their own thing. "But it's not really your fault. You know that. We're a team, Kyle. It's on all of us."

I just grunt.

"Hey!" Ezekiel shouts. The five other players in the gym look up at us.

"Do you think that it's Kyle's fault we lost the Championship Game?"

A lineman shakes his head.

"No," says one of our offensive tackles.

"Man, fuck Ricardo!" Our center says. "And fuck the media."

Ezekiel looks back at me. "See?"

"But you know how it is. No teams wants to sign a gay person or even a person rumored to be gay. Too much drama."

"Well, are you gay?"

My chest tightens, and I glare up at him. "No, dude. I'm definitely not gay."

He throws up his hands defensively. "I'm just asking," he says. He jumps to his feet. "Just know that I would still support you if you were."

My phone lights up. I grab it to see it's an email notification. And it's not just from any email, but a very special email, one that's meant only for very *private* things. Excitement bubbles in my chest.

I put my phone in my pocket and zip it up quickly, then rise to my feet, a good three inches taller than Ezekiel. "Thanks, man. But I'm serious. I'm into women. It's just, you know—since my dad died."

"I know that's hard on you," he says. "Maybe that's what you can use to convince the media to stop asking about your love life."

I snort. "I don't think they'll be satisfied until they see someone under my arm."

Ezekiel shrugs. "That might be good for you to do," he says. "Might make it easier for the Tigers to re-sign you."

A pit forms in my stomach, and my shoulders tense. "You think they wouldn't re-sign me if I was still single?"

He shakes his head. "I shouldn't have mentioned it," he says. "You're the best linebacker the NFO has seen in decades. They're going to re-sign you."

My shoulders relax. "You're right."

Ezekiel walks over to a nearby treadmill and slips a shirt on. "Me and the guys are gonna get something to eat. Wanna join?"

I rub my belly. "For sure. I haven't eaten since breakfast."

"And you're working out that hard?" Ezekiel says. "You really need to lay off."

I laugh. "I'll be okay."

As we wait for the other guys to finish up, I pull my phone and check out the notification. And I was right. He released a new video.

I scroll through his page, and my chest lights up with excitement. He hasn't released a new video in a few weeks, so this is the rain during my drought. There are few guys that consistently get me off, and Peter Cummins is one of them. I love his red hair, his thick beard, his hairy muscles. I've been a fan of his for years.

Am I gay? I don't like the question. I think guys are hot. I've slept with guys when I was part of that secret little gay club at Miss U. But I'm not *gay* gay. Meaning I still like women. And I wouldn't call it bisexual either. I just think that some guys are handsome. When it comes to it, I'll find a woman.

"You ready?" Ezekiel asks, the guys ready to go behind him.

I quickly shut off my phone and pray none of my blood went south. That would be a nightmare. I shift my legs and breathe a sigh of relief. We're good.

Just as we're walking out, my phone buzzes again. Did he release two videos in one day? Hallelujah. But when I pull it out, it's not another email notification. It's a text from my agent.

"We need to talk."

It feels like I have heartburn. "Call later?" I send.

"No," he responds. "Now. At our usual."

I sigh, trying to hide the anxiety in my voice. "Hey, y'all. Gotta go meet with Timmy."

The guys just tell me to have fun, but Ezekiel stops and looks at me.

"I don't have a good feeling about this," I say.

"You wanna win a Championship Game," he says. "So just do what Timmy says. He's always had your back."

I pull on my beard, an anxious habit. "I just hope he has it this time."

* * *

Timmy and I sit in a dark, old-fashioned American restaurant. We're sitting next to a fireplace, but it's only just bright enough for me to see Timmy's face. We regularly eat here because you can't see anyone beyond your own table. Nice and anonymous. And a little romantic too, if I wasn't with Timmy.

After we order and exchange our pleasantries, Timmy leans forward onto the table. He hasn't been this serious since the Tigers were trying to walk back on one of my raises.

"What's going on, Timmy?"

"I think you know." He scratches his bald head and clears his throat. He's wearing a button-up with a suitcoat and jeans, while I threw on some slacks and a nice henley.

"I know my interview didn't go well," I say. "But I didn't think Ricardo would be there."

The waiter brings out drinks to the table: a whiskey neat for Timmy and an old fashioned for me. Timmy picks up the glass and drinks nearly half of it.

"This is bigger than the interviews," he says. He gulps the rest of the glass and sets it on the side of the table for our waiter to refill.

"Bigger?"

He clears his throat and moves his napkin from his lap to the table. "The Tigers don't want to re-sign you."

It's that goddamned heartburn again. "Don't play with me, Timmy."

"I'm serious," he says, looking around for the waiter. He wants more drink bad. "After your interview, Tigers players got more questions about what you do in the bedroom than they did about your gameplay."

"Yeah," I say, shrugging. "I did, too."

He shakes his head. "Do you know how serious this is? Your love life became more important than us making the Championship Game. Management thinks you're a distraction, Kyle. A dangerous one."

I shift in my seat, sweat forming on my forehead. "It's really that bad?"

The wait returns with another glass, and Timmy gulps it in one go.

"Bad?" Timmy says as he wipes his lips. "It's worse than bad. If this keeps up, the Tigers will turn into a joke. We'll be seen as the 'gay' team. Our players will move to other teams. Fans will take us less seriously. We'll lose our momentum. And then the Championship Game will be a distant memory."

A burn flares in my chest. I didn't just lose us the Championship Game when I got tackled. With my interview, I may have compromised the whole team.

"So what do I need to do?" I ask, leaning forward. I'm tempted to down my drink just like Timmy, but I want a clear head. And even though I sponsor all these beer brands, drinking isn't really my thing.

Timmy laughs down at the table. "Management says the only way they'll re-sign you is if can prove to them you're not gay," he says.

I flinch at that word. "What? Being the best linebacker out there isn't good enough?"

Timmy narrows his eyes at me. "What's the problem here, Weaver? Are you actually gay?"

I fold my arms. "I'm definitely not."

Timmy plays with his empty glass. "Then I don't see the issue. Why can't you get a girlfriend?"

"I just—" I sigh. I've tried dating women, but my mind goes all dark when I know they're expecting things to get intimate. Like an eclipse in my brain. So, I just avoid dating altogether. But Timmy can't know that. He might actually think I'm gay.

"It's my dad," I say, remembering my conversation with Ezekiel. "It's just been hard since he passed."

"Your dad has been dead for almost a decade."

I grimace as I remember him dying on that bed. I wanted to hold my dad, but he was in too much pain. I just held his hand. He was the one who instilled within me a love for football. I have such fond memories of the sport: autumn weather, Saturday games, maple bars, apple cider, chili, burgers, friendly scrimmages, laughter, hugs, beer. And he was a saint, always helping other boys on my high school team and then mentoring other guys when he coached at Miss U. He may not have been very accepting of the queers, but the world was better with him in it. My life was better with him in it.

"It's true," I say, not knowing what else to say.

Timmy rubs his bald head. "Well, regardless of the reason, you gotta get over it. Or you can kiss your football career goodbye."

I grit my teeth. "Fine. So I just need to find a girl. By signing day?"

He nods, looking at his empty glass. "By July 1st."

I chew on my lips. It's the beginning of March. Four months away. That's manageable—I can do that.

"Deal," I say.

"Oh no," he says. "It's not gonna be that easy."

I look at him like he's grown a second head. "What do you mean? I agreed to find a girl."

"No," he says, rubbing his brow. "You agreed to be *looking* for a girl. That means dates. Pictures. *Evidence*. Management needs to know you're keeping your word."

Our food arrives, and Timmy sighs with relief. But I just stare down at my steak, dumbfounded. I've lost my appetite.

"And I can help you with that," Timmy says. "Finding dates. It will be easier considering you are the most eligible bachelor in Portland."

I scoff. "I'm so honored."

"Hey, I'm not the one who screwed over the team in an interview."

I lean back and fold my arms tightly. It's not my fault football hates queer people.

"Look, I know it sucks to be forced to find love," he says. "But we can make some fun out of it. What if we did some speed dating?" He asks as he takes a bite of steak. "Could make you some money. Maybe even film it."

My face twists like I've tasted something sour. "Absolutely not."

"Reality TV show perhaps?"

"That's worse."

"You're killing me, Weaver," he says, dipping his steak in some potatoes. "Give me some suggestions."

I glare up at him. "Like what? A club or something?"

He takes a sip of his refilled whiskey. "As long as there are women."

I sit there and think. I have a thing for reading—was an English major in college. "What about a book club?"

He chews and squints, thinking. "Could work," he says, food still in his mouth.

I lean forward, galvanized. "I could find a nice fantasy—"

He sets down his fork with a clank, startling me. "Fantasy? No. If you want to meet a woman, you need to do romance."

I deflate as all hope leaves my body. "Romance? Are you serious?" That is the one genre I cannot understand. It's just for women who want to get off.

"But that's where you're gonna find women to date," he says. "My wife's crazy for that shit. Her and all her friends."

I shake my head. "This is ridiculous."

"Hey, it's this or no new contract," he says. "And that means no Championship Game."

I thumb lines into the condensation on my ice water. I want to win the Championship Game more than anything, both for me and my dad. He worked so hard at Miss U, only to be diagnosed right as he got a coach offer in the NFO. I promised to honor his legacy. And the Tigers are the only team that will get me to a Championship Game, so I have no choice.

"I'll do it," I say.

"Good," Timmy says, shoving steak and mashed potato into his mouth. "I'll find you a book club. And you're gonna go to it regularly to find a girl. I'll expect updates and proof you're going."

I grumble, but nod. This is the only way.

"Great," I say through gritted teeth. I'm gonna be a goddamn romance reader.

Chapter 3

Michael Cunningham

Due to limited space, I have to park far from Ruckers and nearly jog to get to the romance book club Amani recommended to me on time. I'm carrying my designer edition of Pride and Prejudice, and the brooding clouds over head don't bode well. I need to hurry. I don't want to ruin the book. I should have brought an umbrella.

I reach the edge of the bookstore right next to the window that looks into the cafe. The chairs and tables have been rearranged in a round robin style, and beyond the glare, I can see that nearly all of the chairs are filled.

And there's not one man in the room.

The heat of embarrassment flushes my cheeks, and I move away from the window to hide. Is this a women only book club? I pull out the card and scan it quickly. It says everyone's welcome. So why is there not even another gay man in the room? Would I even be welcome here? I feel like an intruder.

A cold drop lands on my nose, then another on my neck. Then, almost instantaneously, it starts pouring. I shove my book inside my shirt and, having no other choice, I bolt toward the entrance of the bookstore. By the time the door rings shut, it feels as if someone pulled a prank by pouring a bucket of water on me. Because the rain is falling lightly again, and there's even some sun, as if the downpour never happened. I hate spring weather.

"Welcome!" The front bookseller says. She's a tan, short-haired woman with an intricate chest tattoo and classy-looking septum ring. "Man, you got drenched."

"Hi," I say shyly. I nod my head, dripping water from my short beard onto the floor. A shiver shakes my body. "Yeah, unlucky me I guess."

"Oh, no," she says, walking from behind the counter. "I don't want you to get sick. We actually have T-shirts if you want to buy one. I can certainly throw on a discount."

A laugh sounds out from the group of women. A hearty, happy laugh.

"Thanks," I say as I take the T-shirt from her. "Let me change and I'll pay after."

She nods, and a couple of women enter the bookstore and close their umbrellas, laughing to each other.

"Oh, hey Amber!" The bookseller says. "You're just in time!"

They exchange more pleasantries, which gives me time to invisibly slip away. I find the bathroom, set down the book, and take my soaking shirt off. Luckily, my book didn't get too wet. After I change into a T-shirt that says 'I <3 Indie Bookstores', I walk back out, and I can hear the discussion just beginning. Maybe I could just leave now. They wouldn't know I was intending to attend. They would just think I was some random guy buying a book.

I pick a random book off the shelf—some gay romance I've been meaning to read—and slink over to the checkout. I set that and my copy of Pride and Prejudice on the counter.

"The shirt fits you well," she says with a smile as she rings me up.

"Thanks," I say, trying to hide my embarrassment as I pull out my wallet.

She takes hold of my books to scan.

"Oh, that one's mine," I say, gesturing to Pride and Prejudice.

"Oh, sorry," she says, sliding the book back to me. "Wait, were you here for book club?"

My chest tightens. "I—uh." I wasn't sure what I was supposed to say. I didn't want to interrupt what already looked like a close-knit group of women.

Amani's suggestion was nice, but I don't think this book club is for me. I can find inspiration for my book elsewhere.

So I just shake my head.

A boisterous laughter sounds out again, making me wince.

"Okay, you can put your card in whenever it's ready."

I look down at the price, and all I see is the price for the gay romance book. "What about the shirt?" I ask.

She shrugs. "You were in need. It's on us."

I glance down at her nametag. 'Kelley', it reads. And she's a manager, so she can make these sorts of decisions.

But I nevertheless shake my head again. "Let me pay. I always want to support indie stores."

She smiles. "Well thank you, but that's quite alright. And if you really want to support us, go sit in on our book club. We are also looking for new faces."

I glance over again. One black woman is sharing some of her favorite Elizabeth quotes, and she's beaming. Everyone is staring at her with rapt attention.

"Okay," I say, finishing my payment. At first glance, this group seems pretty inclusive. "I guess I can stay. Thank you so much for the shirt."

"Wonderful," she says as she hands me the receipt. "I'll get you a chair." She grabs a chair from behind the counter and gestures for me to follow her. She leads me up to the group of women, and I want nothing more than to sink into the carpet and disappear. But this is the way to support the store and pay back this woman for her generosity, so I am going to stay for this book club. No matter what.

She introduces me, and the other women make room for me to sit. I sit down, trying to make myself as small as possible, and introduce myself with shallow breath, clutching my books to my stomach. I don't know what my deal is. I can have wild sex with pretty much any male stranger behind a camera. But I can't even sit in a chair and talk with other women about one of my favorite books? Something is definitely wrong with me.

"Alright," somebody says on the far side of the circle. I recognize her as another bookseller. "We've had enough miscellaneous discussion, so let's jump right into our first discussion question. Originally, Jane Austen titled this book *First Impressions*. Was she right to change or title to *Pride and Prejudice*? Or not?"

My stomach jumps, not from nervousness, but from excitement. I wrote a paper on this very subject for my historical English class in college. I raise my hand slightly, then lower it quickly. My point is probably obvious. I doubt I would contribute anything to this group of tight-knit romance fans.

The bookseller calls on the first person, an Asian woman with long hair, and the discussion goes from there. People raise good points, and I'm surprised that there are some who argue for the original title. But when no one brings up my desired point, I sheepishly raise my hand again, hoping but also not wanting to be called on.

"Michael, was it?"

I freeze as all eyes lock on me.

I look up at the bookseller. "Yes?"

"I saw you raised your hand. Did you want to share?"

I shift in my seat awkwardly, grimacing at the set already dripping down my sides. "Sure, uh. Yeah. Hi, I'm Michael—he/him. Uhh…" All eyes continue to stare, and I just decide to look at a random point in the wall and share what I want.

"This title is beyond it's time. Jane Austen was one of the first writers to execute a two-layered plot in a compelling way. We know that we have the overall plot to get the women married, but we also have Elizabeth and Darcy's inner journeys: overcoming prejudice and pride, respectively. By choosing this title, Jane Austen sets up a promise that we will understand both pride and prejudice and their roles in love by the end of the story, and not just see two people agree to a marriage. And she does just that. I can't think of a novel during that time that tells two stories like this in a better way. I thus cannot imagine another title."

My ears ring by the time I'm finished, but as sound gradually returns, I hear many verbal assents and see heads nodding.

"Wonderful insight," the bookseller says. And several hands shoot up after.

The next woman, one with hair the exact same shade as mine, piggy backs off of my comment. I'm worried she'll argue, but she respectfully qualifies my response by adding her own insight. And suddenly, it feels like I'm back in college again, discussing books and having the hope that others will one day be discussing my books. Gradually, I melt into my seat and let the discussion take my attention. I feel confident enough to raise my hand again, but I'm slightly relieved when the topic moves elsewhere and my point becomes irrelevant. I'm still decompressing from sharing my first insight.

Before I know it, the discussion is over, and I feel more energized than when I walked in. Somebody next to me thanks me for my comment, and I thank them for theirs. We all laugh and chat, and despite how scared I felt before, I feel safe now. Welcome.

We all put our chairs away, and I think about making my way to the bookshelf to buy our book for next week. I'm definitely coming back. This is the closest I've ever been to that feeling of effervescent writing excitement in college. I have a lot of things I want to try on my romance novel to make it better.

"Michael, do you have a moment?"

I turn to see the bookseller carrying just the book under her arm, *Montana Sky* by Nora Roberts.

"Sure," I say. "Did I say or do something wrong?"

She looks at me with a furrowed brow, then laughs. "Oh, no, you're fine. It was so wonderful to have you here today. I hope you come next week."

I blush. "Thanks—I'm planning on it."

She beams. "Wonderful. I was also wondering. We have another book club member who wasn't able to make it today. Sent us an email saying he wasn't feeling well but wanted to get the next book and come next week. He already paid for it, but he's not able to come to the store this week, and it won't ship out in time. He wanted somebody to deliver it to him."

"Oh, okay," I say scratching my head. I look around at all the other women here. "Why me?"

"Oh," she says, lightly tapping her forehead with her palm. "Forgot to mention that he requested a man drop it off. Not sure why. I just offered that he get the following week's book mailed and come in then, but he turned it down. Said it was urgent."

I shift on my feet. "So you want me to deliver it to him."

She shrugs and smiles. "If you wouldn't mind. We were tempted just to ignore the request, but he really wants to come to the book club. He said we could come by anytime this weekend to drop it off."

I pick at my beard as I think. There's no reason to be opposed to this. Plus, it's a guy. I had a wonderful time here, but it would be nice to have another man here besides myself. Plus, he could be gay. He could offer unique perspective that could help me enhance my novel.

"I can do that. Where's the address?"

She exhales, and her shoulders relax. "Oh, thank you. I didn't know how we were going to do this otherwise. He's over in the suburbs, Villanova area. I can email you the details."

"Sure." I provide her my contact info, and she sends me his address.

I squint down at the screen. "Does this guy have a name?"

She squints down at her screen as well. "I thought it was in his email, but it's just Tigersfan89."

"So he doesn't have a name?"

She harumphs. "I'm sorry if this is weird. We can just—"

"It's fine," I say. "Villanova's a nice area, so it doesn't seem shady. He might just be shy. I know I was nervous to come."

She relaxes again. "Well don't be. I loved your comment. Your insight is really welcome. I hope you continue attending."

My chest warms, and I press my hand against it. "Thank you. I definitely will."

She walks behind the bookseller counter, and most of the other book club goers are walking around, chatting about books on the shelves. I thought most would have left by now. But they're sticking around like it's their second home.

"I should be thanking you," she says. She hands me the book in a paper bag. "I'll tell him to be expecting some to drop it off. He wants it left at the door. Let me know when you do. I just want to make sure there's no trouble."

"Sure," I say. "You can tell him I'll be there tomorrow around noon."

Chapter 4

Michael Cunningham

VILLANOVA HAS SOME OF the largest homes that I'd ever seen.

There are houses bigger than my apartment complex downtown. Hell, there are *driveways* bigger than my apartment complex. What sort of jobs do people out here have to afford houses like this? What sort of generational wealth? My head hurts just thinking about it.

As I drive down the street, wide yet winding, I keep looking between my phone and the houses around me, making sure I'm not missing my stop but also trying to take in the view. There's a freaking stable out here!

The sky is overcast, but there's no chance of rain to my knowledge. Which is good. I hate Portland traffic, but during a downpour, it's a nightmare. Fingers crossed that it stays dry.

Thankfully, while I'm distracted looking at the center of a roundabout, my phone tells me that I've arrived at my destination. The house I'm looking for—the home of Tigersfan89—doesn't have a fountain or a stable or even that big of a driveway. It looks more sleek and modern, lots of straight edges and neutral colors, which makes it look just as expensive as some of these more regal looking houses.

I pull into the driveway, paranoid that I will accidentally run over some of the lights around the rim or hit some other expensive thing I can't see. I park my car and quickly get out and search around it just to make sure. Once I'm sure I haven't ruined anything, I grab the Nora Roberts book from the passenger seat and make my way up to the house.

I ring the doorbell. I know the bookseller just said to drop it off at his door, but I want to stick around. This guy could be gay—and the only other man at the book club—so I want to introduce myself. Let him know he's not the only gay man so he won't chicken out.

Looking at how massive this house is, I wouldn't be surprised if this guy is gay. I don't know why, but it always seems like gay people are crazy rich. Like they're always doctors or lawyers or some high up corporate executive. It's like we're trying to prove to the world that we're *just as* good as straight men, like it's some desperate attempt at proof that being gay isn't weird or even normal but a virtue in itself.

Yet I couldn't feel more out of place around these types of gays. Here I am, just some corporate peon trying to make it big as an author. Besides my body, there's nothing impressive about me. That's how I felt around David at least. Whenever I was around this ex and his friends, it felt like I had to fight just to be heard. And once I was, it was like I was being tested—popular enough? Driven enough? Wealthy enough? They did think I was hot, which is the only reason why I think they kept me around for so long. Even David. I'm just glad that relationship is over.

But it hasn't been easy since. The only time I feel comfortable with other men is in bed, 'straight' or not. Before I came out, I was so scared to be around straight men. So when I finally accepted myself, I was eager to jump into a community that loved me for who I was. But so much of the time, these gays feel just as exclusive. The only time I ever felt like I had a home was around fellow writers in college. Once I'm published, I hope I find a similar community. I just want to belong somewhere.

I glance down at my watch. Two minutes have already passed.

His email *is* Tigersfan89. What gay person likes the Tigers but is also avidly seeking to be a part of a romance book club? The Venn diagram has a small intersection. Too small to be believable.

This guy isn't gay. Maybe he just wants the book for his wife or something, so he wouldn't want to talk with some rando man. I'm wasting my time here. I better just go.

I set the paper bag down by the glass window and turn toward my car. But just before I step off the porch, the door opens.

"Sorry," I say, turning around. "I wanted to wait to introduce myself. I'm—" But when I lay eyes on him, my stomach sinks to the porch. Suddenly, the patter of rain sounds out from the driveway, and I'm trapped under the porch of The Sexiest Man Alive.

It's Kyle Weaver. Shirtless.

And I can see his hard cock through his shorts.

Chapter 5

Kyle Weaver

I COME INTO MY kitchen through my garage having just finished up at the gym, still sweaty as hell. I set down my gym bag, which is in desperate need of washing, and hobble to the fridge. I peel my shirt off, throw it on the floor, and pull out a bottle of Gatorade. As I drink, it drips onto my sweaty chest, but I don't care.

This past week has been hell.

Ever since that conversation with my agent Timmy, my mind has been a tornado. He told me the name of the bookstore where this romance book club was, but I had to figure out the rest myself. And not only does their damn romance book club meet *weekly*, but they also read things I would never be caught dead reading. My house is filled with fantasy and sci-fi books by the greatest. But this romance book club? I don't even know the authors. And it's a bunch of covers filled with pink, purple, orange, and other garish colors. The book for yesterday's meeting was Pride and Prejudice, and the only thing I hate more than romance is regency romance. I know Timmy said I gotta find a girl, and that there has to be proof, but I had to miss out on this one. I just had to.

For the next session, I asked if a man could drop off the book. I didn't want to just stroll in and let the whole world I'm attending this book club before I have to, and I don't want a woman knowing where the Sexiest Man Alive lives. I've had my address leaked to female fans before, and I almost had to move because of this. But a man likely won't care. The store emailed back and said someone would drop it off today, so I'll read it this weekend and hopefully have enough courage to attend next week.

Once I finish the Gatorade, I toss the empty bottle into the recycling and grab another from the fridge. I make my way to my giant living room couch and plop down. Management has said that being single is the problem, but I can't help that my skills need to improve, too. Especially my speed. So I've been upping my cardio and restricting my food, which has only made this week more hellish. I'd kill for a burger right now, but I gotta keep my calorie count low. Thanks, sugar-free Gatorade.

I set down my drink and reach for the remote, and then I pause. In all the commotion of this week, I had forgotten about the notification I received when I was working out with the other guys earlier this week. Peter Cummins—he released a new video. And I haven't watched it yet. I'm already a quarter hard at the thought.

I pull open the app and slide down my pants. As soon as I see Peter's handsome face, I get that warm feeling in my chest. Not heartburn, but like a warming of my heart. I love his thick thighs, the globes that he has for an ass. He's got a perfect torso, and that ginger mullet drives me wild. And it might sound weird to say, but he's got these gorgeous hazel eyes, and every time there's a closeup of him where I can gaze into them, I have to look away. It feels too personal.

I start the video and start stroking myself. I skip past all the foreplay stuff—not my style—and get right to the action. Peter is getting railed by PortlandBeefCake, someone who doesn't really get me off, but whatever. All I need is Peter. I love how enthusiastic he is, how he just knows what to do to get the other guy off. It's like he lives to serve, that all he cares about is what makes you feel good. But this doesn't feel like it's weird or obsessive. It feels like it comes from kindness.

Jesus, I'm already so close. I think I'm gonna—

Somebody rings my doorbell. My phone flies out of my hand onto the floor. I stuff my manhood back into my gym shorts and drop to the floor to grab my phone, the one still playing the video. I hear Peter moaning, and I can't help but blush. It slid underneath the foot table, so I have to press my cheek to the cold marble floor to retrieve it.

When I grab the phone, I lift my head too soon and bang it against the table. So now that's throbbing, and Peter is still moaning at full volume. I raise to my feet and finally turn my phone off. I make my way toward the door, and that's when I realize that I'm still rock-hard. This is what going a week without getting off can do to you. I rest against my staircase, trying to think about things that will make this boner go away faster: Timmy, my girlfriend Rachel from Miss U. Coach Johnson. That asshole Ricardo.

Wait. This is probably someone from Rucker's dropping off the book. They're likely just dropped off the book. So I don't need to worry about anything. My dick still hard after watching Peter Cummins, I slide in my socks over to the door as I hear drops of rain fall on my roof. I always like reading when it storms. Maybe this will make for a cozy Saturday.

I pull open the door, expecting to see the book on the porch, but what I see makes me feel like I need to take a bottle of tums.

It's him.

I'd recognize that mullet anywhere, and his ass is just as gorgeously round as I've seen it. As Peter Cummins turns around, it takes all my strength to keep my wobbly knees from taking me to the ground. What on God's green earth is he doing here? He's wearing form-fitting gym clothing, and it looks like he just got back from a workout. He has a jacket on, but dark red chest hair pokes out from his tank top.

"I wanted to introduce myself," he says. "I'm—" And then he freezes like he's about to be tackled.

His eyes drift my chest down to my dick. Shit. That's still hard. I shove my hands in my pockets and tent my shorts out so he can't see, but I swear my face is going red. What the hell is this beautiful man doing on my doorstep?

"Can I help you?" I ask, my accent coming out strong. That only happens if I'm angry, horny, embarrassed, or drunk. And right now, I can't tell which emotion it is.

"I, uh—" He clears his throat and points near my feet. I look down to see a small paper bag. "Your book."

I look down at the bag, then back at him. "So you're from that bookstore."

"Ruckers," he says. "I don't work there. I just volunteered to bring it to you."

"I asked them to just drop the book off," I say, annoyed. And confused. Tigers management says I have to find a girl, and the universe brings the man who makes me question my sexuality right to my doorstep. This is some cosmic irony.

"I'm sorry," he stammers. "I just thought—you know what, I better go." He steps off the porch into the rain, and then it starts hailing. He steps back onto the porch already drenched.

I rub my eyes. I don't want to be an asshole to this guy, but I can't let him into my house either. Not when I was just jerking off to him. I still don't understand how or why he's here.

"Look," I say, putting my hands on the door, ready to close it. "Thanks, but—"

A strong gust of wind blows water onto my porch, knocking Peter backward. He trips on my welcome mat, then turns and falls face first into my hairy belly. My knees still wobbly, he knocks me back, and I land on my back with a thud.

And then his wet face is pressed into my hard dick.

Chapter 6

Michael Cunningham

I JUMP UP FROM Kyle as fast as I can.

"I'm so sorry," I say, helping him up.

He grunts as he gets to his feet. "It's fine." The rain pouring outside, he grabs the paper bag with the book and ushers me inside. He slams the door behind me.

And then I'm standing in front of Kyle Weaver.

Kyle *fucking* Weaver.

Am I hallucinating? Am I really standing in front of the Sexiest Man Alive? The man whose wink sends me to my knees? Whose body I've fantasized being wrapped around mine more than I can count? *Whose hard penis may have just rubbed against my cheek?* And the way his torso glistens—I know I got some of his sweat on my face when I fell on him. Hallelujah.

"I'll get you a towel and some clothes," he says. "Stay here."

He barrels up the stairs with the bag I left at the door, and I'm too bewildered to speak.

'Look around. Point out five things you can see', my Al-Anon sponsor always says to do when I get anxious.

I take a deep breath and look around, trying to prevent my body from shivering. Unlucky for me to get poured on twice in the same week.

Marble floors. One.

Wooden staircase railings. Two.

I crane my neck to see into his large living room.

Leather couch. Three.

Large fireplace. Four.

And bookshelves. Five. So many bookshelves. They're filled to the brim, but I'm too far away to see any titles.

Kyle comes back down the stairs—still shirtless, my god—and hands me some clothes and a towel. Sadly, his boner is gone. But I look away quickly, not wanting to creep him out.

"Bathroom's around this corner," he says. "If you want to shower."

I nod and rigidly walk over to the bathroom, feeling like a freezing idiot. But inside the bathroom, he has one of those showers that's big enough for a threesome. I clean myself off, welcoming the warm water, and try to process what the hell is happening.

I just met Kyle Weaver. And now I'm showering in his house. *And I touched his dick.*

I grab the towel and dry myself off in the shower. I then reach for my old clothes that I set up on the rack to try, but they're still soaking.

So now I'm going to have to put Kyle's clothes on.

I slip on his sweatpants and an old T-shirt, both too big for me, and I catch a whiff of him. An earthly, almost sweet scent with a hint of vanilla. A mixture of his cologne, detergent, and him. I hope he lets me keep these.

I come out of the bathroom, and there Kyle is sitting on his living room couch. To my disappointment, he has a shirt on now, so I can't take in that beefy hairy body. But I stared long enough for it to be burned into my brain.

"Still raining hard," he says.

"Sorry to bother you," I say, as if the rain was my fault. Like I planned this whole wacky encounter. Which I didn't.

"Not a problem," he says. "Got you some water." He gestures to a glass of water on his coffee table, and suddenly I'm reminded not just of his looks but all that he does for others: his donations kids and adults with cancer. That sweet Southern charm that comes through every one of his commercials. I truly wonder if I've died and gone to heaven, and this is the angel greeting me at the gates, taking on the form of the most desirable person I can think of.

"You're free to sit," Kyle says. "You don't need to stand there."

"Sorry," I say, and I shuffle over to the seat on the couch farthest from him. I pick up the glass and take a sip, which feels nice after the hot shower.

"No need to apologize," he says. "So you're part of that romance book club."

"I am," I say, setting the glass down. "Just had the first meeting. My name's Michael."

He looks at me like I've just sworn at him.

"What?" I ask, embarrassed.

"Your name's Michael?"

"Yeah," I say, looking around shyly. "Michael Cunningham."

He stares at the ground, his brow deeply furrowed. Then he nods. "And you... you're part of this book club?"

I nod. "You are too?"

He sighs. "I guess I am now. I have to be."

I frown. He 'has to be'? I'd ask, but I barely know him. Even though my face was just in his crotch.

We sit in awkward silence. He pulls out his phone. A very brief but very cacophonous sound comes from his phone, and he shuts it off quickly. He looks like he's seen a ghost, which is weird. I figure he just had some YouTube video playing. No need to be embarrassed.

"So it's cool to meet the famous Kyle Weaver, I guess," I say. I listen to the rain, wondering when it will stop and this will be over. But it's going as hard as ever. Driving home will be a nightmare.

He sighs through his nose. God, from here, he looks so ruggedly handsome. His beard and hair combo is just perfect.

"You knew who I was?" The fear from earlier is gone, and he flashes me a grin. A seductive one.

I look away. "I mean, yeah. You're a huge deal here. And in football in general." And the Sexiest Man Alive, but that would be a strange detail to cling to. Kyle Weaver is definitely straight, and I don't want to make him uncomfortable.

"Didn't take you for a football fan," he says.

I can't help but scowl at him. "What's that supposed to mean?"

His swagger dissipates, and grimaces slightly. "Sorry, just—just didn't know guys like you were into football."

I scoff. *Guys like me.* Well, I'm not ashamed that it's easy to clock me as a gay. I'm over that. I'm just surprised that Kyle Weaver of all people was able to clock me so fast. It's like he already knew. But I can't complain. He's not being a dick about it.

"And I didn't peg you as a reader," I say, gesturing to all the bookshelves. I can see some titles now, mostly sci-fi and fantasy.

He winces, and my face reddens at my use of the word 'peg'. Why can't I just be normal around straight guys?

"Yeah," he says with a shrug.

"...but you want to join a romance book club? Why?"

He glares at me. "I can ask you the same question. Aren't these romance book clubs just for women?"

I scowl. I was already insecure enough staying at that first meeting. I'm not going to let Kyle, regardless of how hot he is, bully me into thinking I don't belong.

"I'm an author," I say.

He laughs. "Oh, really?"

I recoil. "What?" I ask, almost offended. "I work as a content writer by day, and I'm trying to be a romance author on my own time." And I also make porn, but there's no reason for him to know that. "This group will serve as inspiration. I'm trying to make my writing more compelling. I want to make it big as a writer."

He perks up. "A romance writer, huh? So that means you know you read a lot of romance?"

I fold my arms. "Mostly, yeah. What does it matter to you?"

He leans forward and starts stroking his beard. God, his forearms are toned. And his upper arms are almost as big as my thighs. I just want him to wrap his arms around me and—

"I've got a proposition for you," he says.

My chest tightens. "A proposition?"

He nods. "I don't want to be going to these book clubs, but I have to. The reason why is none of your business."

Sheesh. Alright. I guess if you're this hot you can talk to people anyway you want. He may be a giving guy, but I feel like I'm being manhandled when he talks to me. And you know what? I don't hate it.

"You've already come here. You know me. I want you to come by and drop off whatever book they're reading next and tell me how the meeting went. I need to be able to prove that I'm going to these things."

I fold my arms tighter. "Why?"

"Again," he says, that drawl coming out. "It's none of your business."

I have to shift in my seat to stop myself from being aroused.

"Sound good?" He asks.

"Good?" I let out a sharp laugh. "You expect me, some guy with a job and a life, to drop everything to cater to some rich football player? Why can't you just go to the book club yourself?"

He grits his teeth. "I just can't," he says. He saddens. "I just don't want to, alright? Is that a good enough answer?"

I see pain there in his brown eyes, and I pull back. I don't have to agree to help him, no matter who he is, but I don't want to turn him down right now either. Not with how much he seems to want this.

"Do I get anything in return?" I ask.

He's leaning forward onto his knees, shaking one of them. "I can give you whatever you want."

Whatever I want. God, there's so much I'd like to do with this man.

"You said you're writing," he says. "I can help."

I raise an eyebrow. "How?"

"I can be your sounding board," he says. "You can show me your work. I can give you feedback. Day or night, you can use me. 'Cause you're doing me a huge favor."

Day or night I can use him. Fuck.

"What do you say? I'll pay you for gas, feed you, and honestly give you however much cash you want. Just until July. We can meet at this time every week."

If I agree to this, I'd be seeing Kyle Weaver—the Kyle Weaver—on a weekly basis. I'm not sure why he needs my help with the book club, why he can't just attend or even pick up the books himself. But he seems dead set on not telling me why, so I won't argue.

He would also help me with my own writing. He doesn't have writing credentials, but it's honestly hard enough to get Amani to read my stuff with how busy she is, and she's the one who's willing. I don't know where else I could find a critique partner who will devote endless time to reading and helping me improve my work.

My sponsor and I have talked at length about my tendency to date men who are just unkind to me. It has to do with the low self-esteem after growing up with alcoholism in my family. But I'm not dating Kyle, as hot as that would be. We'd just be helping each other until July. I've worked on myself enough to the point where I don't fall for straight guys anymore, and I'd be benefitting just as much out of the arrangement. I don't want to take Kyle's money; I'd rather earn that on my own once I get published. But I would value non-biased feedback, and getting compensated with food and gas money is just a cherry on top.

"Fine," I say. "I can do that. You got the book?"

He leans back into the couch and sighs, and I wish I could just straddle him. God, he is such a specimen.

"You don't know how much this means to me," he says, sitting up. "And yep. I put the paper bag upstairs." By now, the rain has stopped, finally granting me freedom.

"It's no problem," I say, rising to my feet. "Now that you have the book, I should probably get going."

"Oh, and one more thing if it wasn't already clear," he says, rising to his feet as well. "Do not, under any circumstances, tell anyone that you're doing this for me. Or the deals off. Understand?"

I nod. *Goddamn*, please keep talking to me like that. "Understood."

He laughs to himself. "It will be our little book club."

Chapter 7

Kyle Weaver

"Ma! I'm home!"

"Kyle!" She exclaims.

I stand in the small foyer of her cozy Mississippi home as she rushes to put her arms around me. I've insisted on buying her a bigger place, but she always shoots me down. She moved here to Glamour Springs from Fordsville, where Miss U is, after she divorced my daddy. The smell of vanilla from her baking fills her home. Nothing like the jasmine incense she used to burn when she lived with my dad, but it's just as good.

She pulls back, a good foot shorter than me, and grabs my cheeks. "I missed you," she says, reaching up on her toes. I lower for her to kiss me on the cheek.

"Oh, my boy. Did you drive? Fly?"

"Fly," I say, laughing. "I can't last so long in a car. You know that."

She laughs, no doubt remembering our family road trips down to the coast. "Don't I know it. Come on in. Sit down. I have some leftover cookies. I woulda made them fresh if I knew you were coming." She bolts into the kitchen, and I plop down on her oversized couch.

After all that happened with Timmy, and then meeting Peter Cummins—who is actually Michael Cunningham—I needed to get out of Portland and visit my ma. Now that Michael's agreed to keep me up to date on book club, I can easily fake my attendance to Timmy. I'll still read the books so I can more easily lie that I'm going, but now I don't have to go and find a woman. I mean,

I'll eventually have to in order to get a girlfriend. But I can procrastinate it longer now. And that means Michael—the pornstar I've been watching for years—will be coming to my house weekly, and I'll be reading his writing. I don't see any problem with this.

Scratch that. There's a whole lot wrong here, which is why I left town—to decompress from the stress I'm about to cause myself. But what choice do I have? I can't date women. All that dark sadness that swallows my mind every time I try to get intimate with a woman? Better enjoy my single life while I can. And my time with Michael while I'm at it. We'll just be friendly, though. No funny business. I almost had a heart attack when I opened my phone with his porn playing right in front of him. Thank God he didn't recognize it.

My ma returns with a plate of small chocolate chip cookies, and my heart leaps at the sight. I miss these so much. I may be trying to slim down and speed up, but this is vacation time. Calories don't count now.

I grab three and set the plate on the coffee table close enough that I can lean over and grab more, because I definitely will, and Ma sits across from me.

"Now tell me," she says. "Did they fire that awful reporter who questioned you before your big game?"

Ricardo.

I sigh. "No, ma. He's still around. He probably got an even bigger following after that whole fiasco."

She shakes her head and grimaces downward as if she squashed a bug. "Using you to further his career? Now that's just low."

I finish off the last cookie and grab two more. "That's just the business of it."

She scoffs. "Well this whole business gives me a headache." She stands up. "I need some wine. Can I get you anything, love?"

I shake my head and laugh. "These cookies are good enough."

She nods and prances off to the kitchen while I indulge myself on the best sweets ever.

I love being with my ma. Even though a huge part of my brand is my Southern charm, I still tone down the accent, especially in public settings. But with my ma, I can let it go. I can be myself. I always feel like she has my back, and my whole life, she's never given me trouble for whether I'm dating or not. Even now, she's bashing Ricardo for invading my privacy rather than asking the same question that he and everyone else are asking—and no, I'm still not gay. My only wish is that she and my daddy could have stayed together. I still don't really know why they ended things. It hurts my heart to think about it.

My mom walks in with a glass of wine in her hands as I pick up another cookie. "Kyle Theodore Weaver, have you eaten anything else today?"

I look at her with wide eyes and a full mouth. I shake my head.

"You darn boy," she says. "Come on. Let's get some lunch."

I swallow, and despite all these cookies, my stomach grumbles. "Jimmy's diner?"

She looks at me above her reading glasses. "Where else?"

I rise to my feet, already salivating at the thought of Jimmy's double steak burgers. "Let's go. I'm starving."

When we get there, I'm immediately recognized, and the entire diner is in an uproar. An older couple that lives near my ma asks how life is a star in a big city. One of my high school friends, now a waitress, tries to tell me about all the drama that's gone on as my Ma drags me to my seat.

"Jimmy!" my ma shouts. "Your NFO brother is here!"

A burly man with a surprisingly well-kept beard longer than mine—I don't know how he manages it—barrels out of the kitchen wearing a dirty apron.

"Well if it isn't the best linebacker that the NFO has ever seen," he says. He swings his hand out and I shake it, and he's damn near stronger than me. A patch of his dark chest hair pokes out of his shirt, and he smiles at me, his eyes bright.

Jimmy's a few years older than me, and we became good friends when my mom moved here. He's practically my brother now. With how confident he is being gay, I've wanted to ask him so many questions. But I've just never been able to for some reason.

"I don't know about best," I say with a shrug. "Not after our last game."

By now, the entire diner is crowded around us as I stand and talk with Jimmy. Ma sits patiently in her seat looking over a menu.

"Pfft," he says, swatting his hand at me. "The fact that the team relied on you for that just shows how good you really are." He pulls out my chair. "Have a seat."

I tap him on the arm. "It's good to see you, buddy," I say.

He pulls me into a bear hug. For a second, I let myself melt into him. This touch is nice. Then I pull away.

"Now y'all need to give them some space," he says, addressing the crowd. "We may have a celebrity here, but he's a person like all of us."

At that, the crowd reluctantly goes back to their seats.

Jimmy looks at my mom. "The usual?"

She sets down the menu and takes off her reading glasses. "Please."

He looks to me, snapping and tapping his fists together. A small grin forms. "We got something new on the menu," he says. "Spicy triple steak burger."

I roll my eyes in ecstasy. "You're killing me, Jimmy. I'm tryna slim up." I grunt. "Just gimme two."

He taps my shoulder and laughs. "I'll give you extra lettuce for your conscience."

And then he saunters off. I forgot how welcome I've felt here, how loved. Sure, a lot here worship me as a celebrity, but it feels more familial than anything else.

"So," my mom says, leaning forward. "Anyone special in your life right now?"

I deflate slightly.

"I'm sorry," she says, knowing my signs well. "It's just—I couldn't help wondering as well after that interview."

"Ma!"

"Oh hush," she says. "I'm not out here harassing you about who you love. We don't have to talk about it if you don't want to."

I don't have that burger yet, but I already have heartburn. Probably from all those cookies. For a minute here, it almost seems like I can open up. Tell my Ma that it's been hard seeing women. That my mind always go dark whenever I need to be intimate with one, emotionally or physically. Like it goes real dark—my heart beats really fast, and I can't help but think I'm just some weirdo that was made up all wrong. Daddy always said to avoid these emotions—that these sorta negative emotions were for the women and queers. A real man didn't let these dark thoughts get to him. So I just avoided what always brought these emotions out: women.

But I can't tell my ma that. I don't want to talk poorly about Dad, even if they are divorced. Without him, I wouldn't be living my dream. And I certainly don't want to tell her about how I need to find a girlfriend in order to get re-signed with the Tigers. I'm here to enjoy myself, not stress.

"There's no one," I say, tying my paper straw in a knot.

"That's alright," she says. She reaches out and holds my hand. "I think you're amazing all by yourself."

"Thanks, ma," I say. She gets distracted by a text and looks down at her phone. I pull on both ends of the paper straw, tearing it in half. The knot stays intact.

And my mind immediately goes to Peter.

Well, Michael—that's his real name. They say that when the knot stays, someone is thinking about you. Does that mean he's thinking about me? My stomach tingles at the thought, or maybe it's just the cookies. Either way, he's on my mind. And I kinda want to be on his.

I was able to read nearly all of that Nora Roberts book on the plane, and I loved it. I've been to Montana before—stayed in a cabin with some buddies. But, dare I say it, the whole setting was very romantic. And reading a book about it unleashed a part of my mind that always wanted some cowboy to whisk me away to his ranch and tell me I was handsome and valid and awesome.

Just a fantasy, though.

And in a few days, I get to discuss this book with Michael. I know I'm supposed to be going to this book club to meet some girl or whatever, but I just can't stomach that. I don't want to feel all that darkness in my head again. But I didn't get those dark thoughts with Michael, and I'm actually kinda eager to hear what he has to say about it. That's also when he's going to give me a little of his book, and I'm curious to see what a gay romance is really about. Just curious though. I know it will be about love between two gay guys, but I can't help but wonder how that will all play out...

Yikes. I guess I sorta lied to my ma. There *is* somebody in my life. I wouldn't call him special, but he certainly isn't nobody.

My heartburn flares again just as Jimmy brings our food out.

"Jesus, Jimmy," I say, marveling at him. "You got a roadrunner in the kitchen or something? I feel like I haven't even blinked."

He sets down my ma's Caesar salad and my burgers and fries. I gawk down at the greasy masterpiece, already looking forward to the glorious nap after this, my heartburn be damned.

"What can I say?" Jimmy says with a shrug. "I'm good at what I do."

I take a bite of the steak burger, and it's like heaven pouring into my mouth. The juiciness of the burger complemented by a little ketchup and his thousand island sauce—I'm throwing this diet to the wind.

"Jimmy, you're not killing me—you have killed me, and I've gone straight to heaven."

Both he and my ma laugh.

"Thanks, Kyle," he says. "Now you both enjoy."

"We will," my ma says.

And as we eat, I can't help but notice bright orange and pink dip into my periphery. As I'm savoring the last bite of my first burger, I turn to see that the building across the gravel road as a gay flag in front of it—a lesbian flag if I'm not mistaken.

"That," I say, nodding my head to it, still swallowing my food.

My mom turns to it as she takes a bite. "Oh, yes," she says, light in her eyes. "That's a lesbian owned bookstore and coffee shop, The Book Corner. It's spectacular."

My chest burns again, and I press my hand against it. "Lesbians?" I ask, letting out a small burp. Even though I came here to stay with my mom often as a kid, I never noticed that Glamour Springs was this inclusive.

"You wanna know why I choose to live here, Kyle?"

I wipe my hands with a napkin and nod.

"Because it's like a little oasis in a tempestuous sea," she says, emphasizing each syllable of the thunderous word. "People are accepting here. Kind. And it's where I want to spend the rest of my life."

I gaze back over at the flag that blows in the wind. Some people walk by, but they don't pay the flag any mind. It's almost like it just belongs there.

I start on my second burger. "That's cool," I say. "I have to leave tomorrow morning, and there's some people I'd like to see while I'm here. But maybe next time I visit I can check it out."

"It's wonderful," she says. "I think you'd enjoy it too."

We finish the rest of our meal in companionable silence, but my mind keeps going back to one thought, one curiosity: What would Michael think of this lesbian owned café?

Chapter 8

Michael Cunningham

BECAUSE THIS STREET IS always somehow busy, I have to park far from Ruckers, and I'm already late. "Come on, come on," I say to myself as I parallel park. And miraculously I get it on my first try. I deserve an honorary straight badge for doing that under stress.

I rush to the bookstore in the blazing sun, already five after six when it's supposed to start. I want to get the most out of this discussion for myself—talk last week generated so many ideas within me for how to improve my story. But I also want to make sure I get all the details for Kyle when I see him tomorrow.

Kyle fucking Weaver.

I had my face pressed up against the man's dick for Christ's sake. And I'm going to be seeing him weekly to discuss these books and my own writing. Not sure why he can't come to the book club on his own, but he's adamant about it. And hey, I get a free critique partner, and I get to spend time with one of the most handsome men I've ever seen. He even offered to pay me anything, but I don't need much. And honestly, I feel like I should be the one paying to see him. He's so goddamn gorgeous.

I do need to keep my emotional distance, though. Even though I've grown a lot in my three years of recovery, I have a history of falling for guys who can never love me in return, gay or straight. I would be surprised if he was gay, but even if he was, I doubt he would be emotionally available. I'm not a football guru, but last time I checked, the NFO isn't very welcoming toward the LGBT. I doubt any gay person in such a position would really have a solid sense of themselves. What am I talking about? The Sexiest Man Alive is definitely not gay, so there's nothing to worry about. I'll just admire him from afar. That sounds safe to me.

I reach the bookstore and quietly open the door. All the other members are quietly sitting in the circle as Kelley, the bookseller who gave that free T-shirt when I was soaked, leads today's discussion. I pull up a chair and some women move their chairs aside so I can sit.

"So sorry," I say, my face reddening in shame. I always feel so bad about arriving places late. But work was hell today—given way too many articles this week for one person to write, so I had to rush through them all today.

"It's no problem at all," Kelley says. "We're glad you could make it."

Hearing the sincerity in her voice, my own inner critic quiets just a tiny bit. As she talks, I try to relax my shoulders. 'It's okay,' I tell myself, looking at all the women around me. 'You belong here. Late or not.'

And that's when my eye catches someone I didn't see last time. She's wearing a cute orange sundress with her hair tied up above in a bandanna, and she has a chiseled jaw. My first guess is that she's a transwoman, but I try not make these snap judgments anymore. She is just a woman.

We begin our discussion of *Montana Sky*, a Nora Roberts book I had not had the pleasure of reading until now. And I have to say that I loved it. There's something about small town romance that gets me all excited. I've heard that some queer people don't like it because they can't imagine themselves feeling safe in such a setting. But I can. All fiction is fantasy—a fantasy I can bend to my experience. So where is it better to imagine the quaint and cozy small town feel that is also queer friendly besides fiction? I pretended that I could have been any of the three sisters on this farm and had a similar experience—well, maybe without all the danger. I try to find ways to belong in the books I read so I can enjoy them. The story is in the hands of the reader, not the author, once it's published, after all. Reality is a place that's hard for me to fit into, but there's always space in books.

"Our next question," Kelley says. "Did all of these sisters truly get their happily ever after in the end?"

Oh, I have *thoughts* about this question. I shoot my hand into the air.

"Michael," Kelley says, remembering my name.

"Michael, he/him. And I just have to say: Nora Roberts did a fantastic job weaving together the love stories of three very different women. And I was just as impressed at her use of POV. I could always tell through whose eyes I was looking, and there wasn't a character I didn't like. Coming from the perspective of a romance writer myself, this book is a masterclass. As for the ending, I would have to say..." I express my one small frustration with the end of the book but describe how it was outshined by the harmony that the sister reach. "I just wish there was a sequel," I say sadly.

"Amen," Kelley says as other women nod in assent.

The woman in the orange dress raises her hand, and Kelley calls on her. "I agree with Michael about his point regarding POVs. Nora Roberts has definitely helped me with my own writing. As for the sisters each receiving what they deserve, I disagree..." As she explains her point, I listen in fascination. Her point about the ending, though the complete opposite of mine, is compelling. She comes at it from a writer's perspective, analyzing the promises of the book at the beginning and how well Nora delivered on those promises in the end. And I feel like I've learned something about structure after she finishes.

The discussion goes on as it normally does, and I make mental notes to share with Kyle tomorrow. I wonder what he thought of this book. Did he find the romance compelling? What's his type of girl? If he liked this romance, what others could he like? He reads a lot of fantasy—has he ever read any fantasy romance?

Like last time, we reach the end of the hour in what feels like two minutes. It's definitely not long enough, but I count this as one of the things to be grateful for. I was not expecting a romance book club to be so insightful, let alone enjoyable. I can't wait to get to writing after this.

After I put away my chair, I step out of the way of the others and pull out my phone. I shoot a text to Amani telling her that she's a genius and that this book club is the best thing ever. She shoots back a kissy face emoji, and I smile as I slide my phone back into my pocket.

"Michael, right?"

I turn to see the voice of the more gravelly female voice. It's the woman in the orange dress.

"Yes?"

"I'm Skye. I hope this doesn't come across as weird," she says, stepping slightly closer. "But you mentioned that you were a writer?"

I raise my brow. "Yes, I did. And you said you also have writing experience?"

"I do," she says with a shy shrug, lifting her shoulder bag with it. It's covered in multi-colored pins of bands, political slogans, shows, and books. "I'm new to the city, and I'm trying to make new friends. I came from a small town in Kansas, actually, and I could never really find a group of writing people. You mentioned you wrote, so I wondered if you had any sort of club or knew of one."

My shoulders sag slightly. "Ever since I graduated years ago, I've been search-ing for the same thing. It's hard. I had a group in college, but they've all since moved on to other things. I have one friend who still writes, but she's too busy to meet at all. I actually joined this book club as the next best thing."

She brightens. "Well, would you be opposed to starting on, you and I maybe? We could start as critique partners, potentially look out for others to join."

My chest warms. "I think that would be nice. I'm actually going to a coffee shop right after this to do some writing. You could join me."

Her eyes shine. "You wouldn't mind the company?"

I shrug, but there's an eagerness to the movement. "Writing can be lonely, and it'd be nice to have someone to talk to on a Friday night."

She claps her hands together twice and smiles. "Wonderful!"

After Skye and I purchase the book for next week—one of the new Kennedy Ryan novels—she and I meet at the coffee shop down the street. We get to know each other for a while we wait for our orders: a chocolate croissant and decaf mocha for me, chai latte for her. She grew up in Oklahoma but went to school in Kansas and wanted a big city experience.

"Me, too," I say. "I grew up in Minnesota with an alcoholic father and absent mother. And as religious as they were, neither of them liked that I was gay."

She winces. "Oof. I'm sorry to hear that. Glad you made it out."

"Same," I say. "And same to you." In one big way, my ex, David, was a blessing. His drinking was out of control, which led me to Al-Anon, the sister program of AA for loved ones of alcoholics. This continues to help me recognize how growing up in an alcoholic home affects me.

We then get to writing. I open up my first draft of my current work in progress. It's about two closeted guys that meet at Yale and, once they realize they love each other, they both abandon the stringent lifestyles they were raised in and move to California to open a small business. It sounds like a lot, I know, but it sort of mirrors the wanderlust I had in college. But there are a lot of logical errors that need fixing. And after hearing Skye's point about promises at the beginning of the book being fulfilled in the end, there's a lot I have to change in the beginning and end of my story to keep the tone consistent.

At first, the writing is slow, but I get into a rhythm. It also helps to have someone next to me working so fastidiously. And as I edit, I can't help but wonder what Kyle will think. I'm going to give him something tomorrow to look at, after all. Speaking of which, we never communicated how he'll read my stuff.

I pull out my phone and type in his contact in my messages. And when his name auto-populates, my stomach somersaults. I still can't believe I have *the* Kyle Weaver's number in my phone.

"I have my writing excerpt just about ready. How do you want me to give it to you?" I ask.

My experience testing David and other hot gays, I expect Kyle to give a delayed response. But my phone vibrates only a minute later.

"Paper," he sends. "Call me old-fashioned."

The corners of my mouth curl upward. But then it turns into a frown.

"Sorry," I say. "Don't have a printer. But I can figure something out."

I set my phone down and start chewing on the hair just beneath my lip. If I don't give it to him in the way that he wants, will he still want to read my writing? What if—

My phone vibrates again. "Not a problem. I have a printer here. Just email it—Tigersfan89@email.com."

I exhale sharply out of my nose, and Skye looks up at me.

"Sorry," I say. "Talking to another critique partner."

"That's some spicy critique partner," she says. "You've got a big smile on your face."

I blush, and my stomach somersaults again. "He's just a friend," I try to say as levelled as possible, wiping the smile from my face.

"Whatever," she says playfully, then looks back down at her computer.

I look back down as my phone vibrates one more time.

"See you tomorrow," he says.

And now I couldn't even stop the smile forming on my face if I tried. Here I am, writing after a wonderful book club with a new friend who also writes. And tomorrow I'm seeing the Sexiest Man Alive. I promised myself I would keep a distance, but I can't do anything about the butterflies.

"See you then," I send back.

Chapter 9

Kyle Weaver

I SNIFF MY ARMPIT one more time just to make sure it doesn't stink. It's not like I'm trying to impress Michael or anything, but the first time I saw him I had just gotten back from the gym. I want to put on a good impression. I shut my mirror cabinet in the bathroom just as the doorbell rings, and I get that light feeling in my stomach that I usually only get before a big game.

"It's just Michael," I say to myself as I make my way to the front door. "Or Peter Cummins, the super-hot pornstar." I feel my face go flush, and I have to pause and take a deep breath.

It's either this or go to the book club myself. Do I really want to go meet a bunch of women and get that dark feeling in my head again? No, this is much preferable. But I still don't know how I'm gonna find a girl if I keep it up this way.

Enough thinking. I can't keep Michael waiting.

By the time I reach the front door, I feel like I do just before kickoff. What the hell is wrong with me? It's just Michael. I open the door and try to still my racing heart by putting on a neutral face. He's wearing a well-fitting long-sleeved T-shirt with jeans that hug his legs quite well.

"Come on in," I say, my accent stronger than usual. I'm trying to look at anything but him.

"Here," he says, stepping inside. He hands me a book. "The novel for next week." The cover has a black woman with an afro on it.

"Kennedy Ryan," I say, reading the bottom of the cover.

"She's a romance powerhouse," Michael says. "Such good stuff. I'm excited to read her new book."

Powerhouse. I scoff to myself. Since when is anyone in the romance genre a 'powerhouse'?

"I've never said this before," he says, stepping into my foyer. "But your house is gorgeous."

My face reddens, and I scratch the back of my neck. I didn't build the damn house, so why am I getting all flustered? "Thanks," I say quickly.

We make our way into my living room.

"Uh, have a seat," I say, gesturing awkwardly to my couch. "Can I get you something to drink? A beer or anything?"

"Oh, I don't really drink," he says, sitting down. "Only occasionally." He holds himself tight, like he's afraid he'll spill himself all over my couch.

"Me neither," I admit to my own surprise. There's something about Michael that makes me want to be honest. Even though he hasn't been honest with me in telling what he *really* does for work. I just wish he felt more comfortable here. Unlike my dad, I don't hate gay people. They're people just like everyone else. I hope he doesn't think I hold some secret prejudice or something. I'd like him to feel safe.

"You don't?" He asks with a cocked eyebrow. He spreads himself out on the couch a little bit, but he stays inside his cushion. "Don't you sponsor like three different beers?"

"Yeah," I say, shrugging defensively. "Goes with my whole brand of being like a manly man or whatever." I scratch an itch on my chest, then feel my back light up. Did Michael bring in a load of pollen in here with him? Why am I so goddamn itchy?

"Interesting," he says, intrigued. "Water is fine."

Interesting, I think to myself as walk to the kitchen to get us both some water. Was my answer not convincing enough for him? I could have sworn I saw him smirk when I said that. Does he not see me as a manly man?

When I get back to the living room, Michael isn't in his spot. Instead, he's standing by a nearby bookshelf, assessing its contents.

"That one has all fantasy classics," I say, setting down our waters on the coffee table. "Published before 1980, that is."

"Huh," Michael says, as if he's more amused than impressed. He sits back down and picks up his copy of *Montana Sky*. "So what did you think of the book?"

I sit with my legs spread wide, melting back into the couch. The Southern hospitality in me is trying to convince Michael that he can relax here, that he doesn't need to be wound so tight.

"It was good," I say.

"Just good?" He asks.

I shrug. "It was—how do they say it?—cuuute," I say, drawing out the syllable.

Michael chuckles, and my chest gets all warm.

"Just cute?" He asks, looking at me with a furrowed brow. He's got a smile on, too, and I realize that there are few times when I've really seen him smile like that. I like it.

"I mean, yeah," I say leaning forward. I realize I've been pulling on my beard for a good minute, which is something I only do when I'm thinking. Or nervous. "You get these women on a farm and then these cowboy type men come in and court them. All very predictable, but very cute as they would say."

Michael laughs, but there's a sharpness to it. "Did you even read the book?"

There's that heartburn again. I feel like I've displeased Michael, but I don't know how. "Yes, I did."

He shakes his head. "Then we must have read different copies or something. Because the copy I read, I felt, really highlighted the autonomy of these three women in a setting that has traditionally been so restrictive to women."

I lean forward and drop my hand from my beard, leaning on my knees. I watch Michael. Fascinated. He talks faster, but he pronounces each syllable more clearly, as if this is some speech he's prepared. But I can tell this isn't coming from some paper he wrote. It's coming from the heart.

"A ranch in small-town Montana? That's as conservative as it gets. Yet these women defy the odds by continually making decisions that are best for *them*, following through on these decisions, and meanwhile having these 'cowboys', as you describe them, fall head over heels for them. And it's only when these women allow it do these men finally get what they want."

He finishes, and I'm just stuck staring at him. I have to remember to breathe.

"Sorry," he says. "I know you said you wanted to just go over the basic discussion we had yesterday at Ruckers. You don't need to hear all my ramblings." He pulls out a journal from his back, the one that presumably had all those notes.

"Hey, no, that's okay. I really like hearing what you have to say."

He looks up at me, there's a small sparkle in his eye.

I swallow and, not realizing saliva had pooled into my mouth, start coughing.

"Are you okay?" he asks when I don't stop.

I reach for my water and take a big gulp. I'm embarrassed when nearly a third of the glass spills onto my chest, soaking my shirt and dripping onto my stomach.

"Oh my gosh," Michael says, standing up. "Let me get you something to dry off."

I grunt. "It's fine." I grab the collar of my shirt and quickly strip it off. I take the dry bits and dry the rest of my torso off. And when I look up at Michael, he stares at me as if I ripped my own arm off.

And that's when it hits me.

Michael isn't being shy because he thinks I hate gay people or because I don't drink or whatever.

He's shy because he thinks I'm hot.

I'd recognize that look anywhere—I call it the sticky stare. When people's eyes seem to stick to you anywhere you go. Not to brag, but I see it every time I go out. I just didn't think the man I've been crushing on for years would think this about me.

"Let me go get another shirt," I say, even though I know he would much rather I stay here shirtless. I stand up as Michael remains frozen, and I pretend not to notice his gawking.

"Okay," he chokes out.

I make my way upstairs and find a replacement shirt, unable to keep the smile off my face. Michael—Peter Cummins—thinks I'm hot. Even when I was granted the title of Sexiest Man Alive, I was flattered, but not to the extent I am now. The gay pornstar that I have followed for years thinks I'm just as attractive. I don't know what to do with this information. But I like it.

When I make my way back downstairs, Michael is scrolling on his phone. His shoulders are tense, and he's shrunk himself inside the couch cushion again. Before, I would have been uncomfortable with his discomfort, but now I welcome it. He can think I'm hot all he wants. Now he knows how I feel.

He looks up at me when he sits down and quickly thrusts his phone into his pocket as if I were to chide him for having it out.

"We were saying?" I ask, unable to stop the smug, toothless smile forming on my face.

He looks down at his book. "Um, I was just talking about this book is just more than cute. It's inspiring. At least to me."

Ah, yes. His little talk that had me gawking at him just as he was me.

"I don't know if I would go as far as to describe it as inspiring, but like I said, it was good."

"Why is it not inspiring?" he asks.

I shrug, confidence oozing through me. "I mean, how inspiring can the romance genre be? It's about people falling in love. And often times it's unhealthy. Fantasy, on the other hand, is inspiring. Take Lord of the Rings. You take this little nobody from a backwater place and give him the directive to save the world. It's a bit overdone at this point, but the message never gets old: anyone, no matter how small, can change the world. Romance just gets people off."

When I finish, I expect him to ogle at me just like I did him. But he just glares at me, a half-formed scowl on his face.

"So you're saying that romance is the inferior genre because... it's porn?"

I recoil. Bold of him to say.

"No, I'm saying that fantasy has been, and always will be, the superior genre because its messages inspire us to be better people, while romance just gives in to everyone's basest desires."

Now his face has gone to full on disgust. I didn't think much of my words, but now I wish I could take them back.

"Romance does not give in to base desires any more than fantasy. Look at Game of Thrones. Would you say that fucking your sister is more inspiring or base?"

I shake my head. "That's not—"

"And let's compare that to, say, this Nora Roberts novel. Is defying gender roles inspiring? Absolutely."

"But you're comparing apples to oranges."

"You were the one to draw the comparison in the first place! Listen. I have nothing against fantasy. But I am against the idea that anything is superior to romance because all romance is just porn. *I*," he says, jamming his finger into his chest. "Love romance because it teaches me that love, even gay love, has room to thrive in this world."

He spoke with the eloquence of before, but there is a fervor now—a fire, just like my childhood preacher had. This is personal.

I raise my hands defensively, wishing we never went down this rabbit hole. "I'm just saying my opinion."

Michael huffs. "Then maybe you just don't understand romance."

I look at him. He has his arms folded, and he's frowning down at the coffee table. Michael seems like a smart guy, and even though he's a pornstar, it doesn't seem like all he cares about is sex. Clearly, the romance—not just the physical intimacy—is important to him in these books.

"I may just be wrong then," I say, shrugging.

Michael tilts his head at me as if that's the most confusing thing I've said all day.

"I used to think like you," he says. "I only read literary things. High-brow literature. It was like—have you ever watched SpongeBob?"

I recoil, the whiplash like a freight train hitting me. "Uh, yes?"

He laughs. "I'm sorry, but I promise it's relevant. Remember that episode where Squidward tries a Krabby Patty for the first time?"

I light up. "Yes! I loved that episode!"

Michael nods, that infectious eloquence animating him. "You know how he tries it and then goes crazy, how he says 'all those wasted years', lamenting how he missed out on all the times he could have been having one? That was me when I read my first true romance novel as an adult. It was *Beach Read* by Emily Henry."

"I think I've heard of her," I say.

"It was that book that taught me that romance was not only just as good everything else, but that it had its own strengths as a genre."

I nod. "I may be willing to take a look at what she's written then," I say. "Maybe I'll convert just like you."

A smile forms on his face, and it feels like my insides are a pot of warm stew being stirred on a Winter day. I don't want him to stop smiling at me. And damnit—that SpongeBob reference? He's funny, too.

"You wanna read on top of what you already are doing with the Ruckers book club?" He asks. "A book a week is already a lot of reading."

"I'm off season," I say shrugging. "There's only so much I can do besides working out. I can start with that book you suggested—*Beach Read*?"

He nods, leaning forward on his cushion. He's beaming like I did as a kid when I was opening presents on Christmas morning. God, I love how earnest he is.

"And you know what? Maybe I don't know fantasy as well as I thought. Why don't you give me a suggestion for a book I should read as well?"

A grin forms on my face, but this time it's not from being overconfident. "I read some romance, you read fantasy? I like it."

"And you're sure you still want to do the book club on top of this?"

I remember why I'm supposed to be in this book club, and my stomach twists. I need to be finding a girl, someone to get with so I can re-sign with the Tigers. Winning the Championship Game is still on the top of my agenda. So I gotta stick with this book club. Eventually, I'll go in person, and that way I can find someone. Then the Tigers won't have to worry about me being gay anymore. But that doesn't mean I can't have fun now.

"I'm sure," I say. "And you still haven't sent me your work. That was part of this deal too, remember?"

Michael deflates slightly, but his enthusiasm remains. He pulls out his phone. "I'll send that to you now."

"Can't wait to read it," I say.

He looks up at me, his eyes bright. "And I can't wait to read your recommendation."

Chapter 10

Michael Cunningham

A FEW WEEKS LATER, it's a busy night in Portland's gay district, and I'm shivering underneath a streetlight. Amani said she wanted to do something different, perhaps go somewhere else for our weekly catchup. Before I could throw out an idea, she suggested this street. I wanted to protest—I hate going out to the gay bars. I feel it's just a place where men eye one another and treat each other like sacks of meat. I've always wanted more than just carnality. That's why I write romance after all. It just sucks that a good relationship can only be fantasy.

Amani wraps her arms around me in a side hug, sending a satisfying wave of warmth through my body. "Thanks for coming out here," she says as she pulls away. "I know you're not a fan of the bars."

I spot a group of jacked, bearded men walking up to what is usually the busiest bar, and there's an uncomfortable tug on my stomach.

"Come on," Amani says, pulling my arm. "There's a new restaurant out here I want to try."

I feel as if I'm a tourist being swept through the streets of a foreign city. We slip through crowds of people and pass by multi-colored buildings and lights. It's been ages since I've been out here. I think the last time was when I was dating David. I shiver at the thought.

"Here we are," she says. I'm overwhelmed, but her excitement is infectious. She pulls me into this Japanese restaurant, one I never knew existed down here. And the walls are covered in anime.

"You have got to be kidding me," I say, the widest smile forming on my face. "Amani, this is your dream come true."

"Don't I know it!" She says as we approach the hostess. "Table for two, please!"

A Japanese woman wearing an elegant pink kimono bows and gestures for us to follow her. She takes us to a table just in front of Naruto slurping up a bowl of ramen on the wall.

"Isn't. This. Amazing?!" She says in a manic whisper as I sit down.

No longer moving, I have the bandwidth to look around. Banners with Japanese characters hang from the ceiling. To our left, there's a sushi bar with a ruggedly handsome man preparing sushi for several women eagerly watching him create their rolls. Each table is filled, and the sound of boisterous conversation buoys my mood.

"I'm glad you suggested this," I admit. I look up at the Naruto drawing again. "Though we could have gone with better seating."

She laughs. "Thanks for humoring me. I didn't know who else could tolerate my anime obsession."

We both look over the menu, and I've already decided. The katsu ramen sounds divine.

"It seems like it's more than just the restaurant. What's got you so happy?"

She looks at me above her glasses. "I've been thinking. You've been working with Skye—that critique partner you met because—" She coughs.

I playfully roll my eyes. "Yes, because you suggested I go to Rucker's romance book club. Thank you, Amani."

She swirls her hand and gives a mock bow. "You're welcome, you're welcome. And there's this whole mystery boy that you've been working with as well. I can see how it's affected your mood. And your writing."

My chest tightens. It's been a month since I started going to the Rucker's weekly romance book club and since I started meeting weekly with *the* Kyle

Weaver—the top linebacker in the NFO and the Sexiest Man Alive. It still blows my mind that I have his number and that he's actually reading my work. He says he wants to wait until he's read enough of my novel to give me feedback, which makes me nervous that he's just hoarding bad news until he can't stand to keep it inside.

But he has emphasized to me that he wants to keep his anonymity. That's why he doesn't go to the Rucker's book club himself, after all—he just has me bring his book and report what the discussion is about.

"I never told you he was a boy," I say.

"It can't be more obvious," she says. "You just seem more hopeful now."

"That's just because editing my novel has been easier," I say, trying to obscure the identity of this 'boy'.

"And your writing," she counters. "Has also been so much stronger. More compelling. You do realize that, right?"

The waiter comes to take our order, but I can't help but think that Amani is right. Writing has become easier. Skye and I have been meeting after book club every week to do our writing together, so it's nice to have an accountability buddy.

And then there's Kyle Weaver. When he took off his shirt during our first discussion, I thought I was going to pass out. And the look he gave in return somehow told me that he knew he had that effect on me. And he just swaggered on as if nothing happened, but I could see the lingering smirk there every time he looked at me. Like he was playing with me.

And I fucking loved it.

No wonder my romance seems to be improving. I have a real-time crush.

"Fine," I say. "You got me. There is a boy."

She pulls herself in and squeals. "I knew it! I can always tell!"

But as she congratulates herself, bitter dread pools in my chest. I can't be developing feelings for Kyle Weaver. I just can't. When I went through the twelve steps with my sponsor, I had to make amends in Step Nine, which included myself. I promised myself that I would never let myself fall for someone emotionally unavailable. Especially if I want my romance writing to keep improving. And a straight guy—a smoking hot football player of all people—is the most unavailable person on the planet. Even if he was the most mature person in the world, he could never like me back. So Kyle is not an option for me. I will nip this affection for him in the bud. My writing will thus improve because I'm not chasing an unhealthy affection. And then I'll get published and have my writing community back.

"But it's nothing, really. We're just friends. And it has to stay this way."

She pouts and sticks out her bottom lips. "Really?"

"Really," I say with a sigh.

In the nick of time, our food arrives, and both of us eat in silence. Amani and I came up with an agreement years ago. When one of us says something crazy or out of left field, and the other asks 'Really?', a response of the same word means it's really true. It has saved both of us plenty of breath.

"Well, I brought all this up to mention," Amani says, blotting her lips with a napkin. "That I contacted my agent again."

I set down my chopsticks. "Really?"

She nods. "Really."

"So you're writing again?"

She takes a deep, almost cleansing breath. "It's time. Seeing you blossom in your work has inspired me. I threw out an idea to her this morning. I hope to hear from her soon."

"That is so awesome, Ams," I say, my chest warming. "I'm so happy for you. What's this idea?"

"I can't jinx it!" she says. "Once I've fleshed out the idea more, I'll tell. I'd also like to join your little group with Skye."

"We'd love to have you," I say.

"Thank you," she says. "And thank you for the inspiration."

I feel heat behind my eyes. "I never thought I was inspiring, so that's nice to hear."

"Oh, hush," she says. "You are plenty inspiring."

As we finish up our food, I think back to my argument with Kyle several weeks ago, how he said that fantasy was the only inspiring genre. He and I challenged each other to read more of the other's genre, and I have to say that maybe that's also partly explains the improvement in my writing. He challenged me to read Brandon Sanderson's *Stormlight Archive*, which, in the main books alone, is over six thousand pages. Not wanting to seem like a coward, I took on the challenge. I was daunted at first, but I soon fell in love with each of the characters, so much so that hundreds of pages have flown by, and I haven't even noticed. I'm almost finished with the fourth book. But as payback for giving me so much to read, I've tasked him with reading the entire backlists of Emily Henry and Abby Jimenez, which, by the way, are *still* less than what he's making me read.

As long as I keep my emotions in check, I can make a good friend in Kyle. Maybe after this whole book club agreement is over, we can keep reading together. I just need to remember to not catch feelings.

"Besides coming out to this lavish establishment," Amani says, gesturing to the whole restaurant. "I did want to celebrate."

I raise a brow. "Celebrate?"

"Yeah, you know. Go to a bar. Take a shot or two."

I sigh but can't help but smile. She's convincing.

"You know I don't love to drink."

"Then you can just watch me. If not, that's totally fine. But hell, I'm happy for myself. I think I deserve this."

We pay our bills, and I chew over invitation in my mind. I don't love going to the bars, but this is a special occasion. Amani is writing again for Christ's sake. After she got that feedback from an editor, she never thought that she could make it as a black author again. But to see her excited—it makes me excited too.

Plus, maybe going out will get my mind off Kyle. And I don't need to worry about hooking up with someone. I can just let loose and have fun.

I rise to my feet, Naruto watching me from the wall. "Then let's go."

"You're serious?" She asks with wide eyes. "Really?"

I flash her a silly grin. "Really."

Chapter 11

Michael Cunningham

SINCE IT'S A WEEKNIGHT, I'm thinking the bar won't be busy, but I'm dead wrong.

A group of younger guys, mostly twinks, line the dancefloor, checking their phones periodically. The dancefloor is filled with both men and women—probably just as many straight women as there are queers—and they jump and dance to the thumping music. Older men sit at the bar as the shirtless bartender races from one end to the next, obviously stretched thin but belying his stress with a smile.

As we make our way to the bar, I spot Greg—a friend of mine I used to film content with. I wave to him, and he holds his drink up to me. He's got a receding hairline with a stocky build, and he's a monster in bed. We hooked up a few years back when I was still into that sort of thing, and then we started making content shortly after. He's a nice, down-to-earth guy, and I was immediately interested in dating him. But of course he was already married. Bill, his husband, is a wonderful man, but it always seems like I fall for the guys who are never available. Luckily, I don't have feelings for him anymore, and it's been a while since we've filmed anything.

"What can I do for you, baby?" The bartender asks Amani as she approaches the bar.

"One shot of fireball for me," she says, and she turns to me.

I grimace. "Fireball?"

Amani shrugs.

"Just an Aperol spritz for me."

He checks me out, then starts pouring our drinks. Three drag queens dressed to the nines with even larger personalities stroll onto the dance floor and make their way to the DJ's stage. They wear clashing shades of yellow and green, and I swear I recognize these colors from somewhere else. But it's not a good kind of familiarity. And looking around the room, nearly the entire crowd is dressed in the same colors. And I think I can even recognize some of the faces.

"What's going on tonight?" I yell into Amani's ear.

A guy leans over from the bar. "It's the gay rugby team's fundraiser," he says. "They're doing something every night all week."

And that's when my stomach sinks to the floor. It's the rugby team that David played on.

"Rugby," Amani says, pulling on my arm. "Does that mean David is here?"

My knees go weak. Memories of my ex flash through my mind. Sneaking away with one of the members from a visiting team and then lying about it. Him getting shitfaced, then angry at me for not keeping him in check. Promising he would stay sober and then caving in at the slightest provocation. Any and all rugby events were torture for me.

And I just walked right into one.

Though we broke up two years ago, the thought of us being in the same room makes me nauseous. He always knew how to push my buttons, how to make me anxious. He's the whole reason I went into recovery.

But I doubt he's here. I heard he moved a year ago.

"It should be fine," I say, trying to sound nonchalant. "There weren't enough guys to sleep with in Portland, so he moved to LA."

She squeezes my arm, seeing right through my bravado. "Are you going to be okay?"

I look at her, wanting to give her a reassuring look, but it just comes out as a wince.

"I'll take my shot, and then we can get out of here," she says.

The bartender hands me our drinks, and I slap enough cash for us and our tip on the counter. I don't want our cards holding us back when it's time to leave.

"No," I say, handing her the shot. I smell the cloying cinnamon gasoline drink and have to resist a grimace. "You supported me through that hell of a breakup. Now just let me support you. You're going to start writing again!"

She wraps her arm around me, then holds her shot up. "To making it big!"

I clink my glass to her. "To getting published!"

She somehow takes her shot in one go, while I just take a big sip of my spritz. The carbonation burns my throat, and I love the almost medicinal taste. It reminds of staying home as a kid from school and taking that liquid medicine from a cup. I know, it may sound disgusting. But God it was so nice to just have a day to myself as a kid. And an Aperol spritz is that feeling distilled into a drink.

"Okay," Amani says, wiping her lips with her sweater. She sets down the glass. "I'm ready to go."

With perfect timing, the DJ starts playing our favorite: Pink Pony Club.

I look down at her with a raised brow and pursed lips. "You sure you want to go now?"

As the bridge leads into the first chorus, Amani looks at the crowd, then back at me. Then she grabs my arm. "Come on!"

I laugh as she pulls me into the crowd just in time for all of us to scream the chorus on the top of our lungs. We dance together, and quickly, I forget about it all: David, my writing, even Kyle Weaver. I'm here to support a friend—to support myself—and have fun. I may not know how to write romance well, and I keep falling for the wrong guys, but at least I have this moment right now.

Toward the end of the song, someone taps my shoulder. Having lost sight of Amani, I turn to what I think will be her. But it's not.

It's David.

It's as if my confidence is punctured like a deflating Macy's Day Parade float. My mood gradually drifts to the depths as David grabs my hand and pulls me closer to him. He gestures for me to leave the crowd, to follow him, and I can't stop myself. Even after all this time, I've been curious: did he miss me?

When we reach the bar, I hope my ears are too shot for me to hear. But, just my luck, he somehow finds the quietest spot. And his voice, ever so soothing, is crystal clear.

"I didn't know you came out to the bars," he says.

I pause, hoping I've just conjured this all up.

He puts his hand on my upper arm, and that warm touch seeps through my sleeve. This is, unfortunately, real.

"It's good to see you," he says.

I sigh. "I thought you had moved," I say.

He laughs and puts his hand on the counter, flexing his arm in the process. Of course he's gotten more muscular.

"I did," he says. "But someone brought me back."

My stomach turns over itself. "Someone?"

He gestures, and this tall, hunky ginger man comes in and gives him a side hug. And stays there.

I want to melt into the ground. That's Steven. One of the guys David was sleeping with while we were dating. And he's like a more handsome version of me.

Pink Pony Club finishes, which couldn't feel more fitting. When I came out, I left my family's religion behind, the one where I could never belong. I thought I would immediately find love in the LGBT community. But it never seemed like I quite fit in there either. I was too feminine for David's friends, including Steven, and any other attempt at a gay friendship just turned into the other guy peddling for sex. Before long, I couldn't help but feel that either I didn't have a ticket to the Pink Pony Club, or it didn't really exist. Seeing these two guys together, though, makes me feel that the tickets are only sold to select clientele.

And I'm not one of them.

"Good to see you," Steven says.

I only nod back. Of course, Steven didn't know that David was in a relationship. Only because David lied to him about us. I know Steven's not to blame, but David has sucked up all my goodwill like the black hole that he is.

"So you came back to date him?"

David looks up at him admiringly, which is no different than him punching me in the gut. He used to look at *me* like that.

"Let me get us a drink," Steven says. He looks at me. "You want anything?"

I'm flustered. "I—"

"He doesn't drink," David says.

Steven kisses him on the cheek and leaves us.

David eyes me up and down. "You're looking good."

I roll my eyes. "You're unbelievable."

"What?" He asks, standing straighter, noticeably perturbed. "I'm just saying. Wouldn't mind getting in those cheeks again."

I blush, and it feels like one of those rugby events all over again. "David, you're already drunk?" He always knew how to hide it well. Until he didn't. But clearly now he's given up on sobriety.

He shrugs. "You know I can't resist you."

I scoff. "That's not happening. You have a boyfriend."

He wrinkles his nose and tilts his head side to side. "That's negotiable."

I shake my head. "And does he know that?"

David says nothing.

I turn away. "I'm leaving."

He reaches out and grabs me. I freeze.

"I am trying," he says. "To stop."

I don't turn to him. But I don't walk away either.

Stop what? I want to ask. *Your drinking? Lying? Being an asshole?*

"You know how hard it's been for me," he says. "And truthfully, I miss you."

My heart thaws a bit at the words I wanted to hear. I turn slightly to him. "Really?"

He nods, his eyes sparking. "Yeah."

Amani spots me from the crowd, then her eyes widen. She lets go of the girl she was dancing with and stomps toward us.

David looks toward the bar and lets go of me like I'm diseased. Just as Amani reaches me, Steven returns with their drinks.

"Here you go," the ginger Steven says, handing David his drink.

"Michael," Amani says, putting her arm on mine.

I glare at David, wanting him to say more. But his eyes are vacant, and he stares at nothing, as if he didn't just try and get in my pants. As if he didn't just try to apologize.

Some people wave to the two of them.

"See you around," Steven says to me, and he pulls David away—who doesn't even dare to say bye.

I clench my fists.

"Michael," Amani says, rubbing my shoulder. "I'm sorry, I lost you. Let's get out of here."

My phone buzzes. I pull it out as I rub my burning eyes.

It's a text from a number I don't recognize.

"If you want to see me, let me know – D."

And then my blood starts to boil.

I shove my phone back into my pocket.

"Michael, what's wrong?"

"David's what's wrong," I say, not even bothering to stop the tears.

"David lies," she says. "You said to tell you that whenever—"

"I know what I said," I choke out. "But I'm too goddamn stupid."

She shakes her head. "Michael, no. That's not—let's go home."

"No, I'm good," I say, looking for a particular someone I saw earlier. "I saw you dancing with someone. You've said how hard it is to find someone you like. Go back and dance with her."

"You don't sound good," she says. "I want to make sure you get home safe."

"I'm fine," I say, stepping away from her. "There's someone I want to see."

"Michael—"

"Really," I say, turning to her. "Really, Amani."

She sighs. She can't argue with me now. "Please tell me when you get home safe, okay?"

"I will," I say, wiping my eyes. "Just go have fun with that girl, please. Don't worry about me."

But I turn around before she does. And that's when I spot who I'm looking for. I march up to his group, not even caring how I may look or how they may see me. There's only one thing I want to do right now.

"Michael," Greg says when he sees me. "I was hoping to catch up with you."

"You wanna come over?" I ask. I don't have time for small talk.

He shuts his mouth, then squints at me, then smiles—surprised, confused, accepting. "Right now?"

I shrug. "It's you or someone else. And I'd prefer it was you."

He laughs, flattered. He sets his empty drink down on the table. "I'd be down for some fun."

When we get to my apartment, I send a quick text to Amani and clean myself up.

"Please be safe tonight," she responds. And I just send a heart back.

"You wanna record this?" Greg asks. "Could be cool."

I look at my camera and ring light standing to the side of my bed. I shrug. "Why the hell not."

And then we get to it.

Sex with Greg isn't as great as I remember, but that's probably because I'm sad. And furious. And so, so tired.

I should be over this. I shouldn't be hurt by the asshole that David is after all this time. It doesn't even feel like I've taken a step back. It feels like I never took a step forward.

I see the camera blink red as Greg rails me from behind. At the very least, I'll get paid for my misery.

Chapter 12

Kyle Weaver

Watch for the QB. Break the gap. Grab the ball. Run like hell.

These are the same instructions Dad gave me back in High School, and they've helped me since. I am the best linebacker of the century, after all.

Offense snaps the ball, and my senses heighten, and it's like everything's slow motion. The QB tosses to the wide receiver on the left. I spot a gap in the line and burst through, too fast for the lineman to stop me. Just before the wide receiver catches the ball, I jump and seize it.

And then I start running.

And the whistle blows.

"Damnit," I say through my mouthguard. "Come on."

I take off my helmet, which widens my vision. The bleachers are mostly empty except for a few of our team's officials. They're likely putting together a strategy for this next season. And determining what role their linebacker is going to play.

I jog over to the huddle, still pissed that we didn't do the whole play. Some coaches, along with my agent, are in those bleachers. I want them to see that I'm losing weight. That I'm getting faster. That I can outrun just about anyone on the field. Maybe then they'll forget about this whole girlfriend deal and re-sign me based on my enhanced skills.

That's what I'm hoping for.

"That's enough for today," Ezequiel says. Since he's the most senior player, he tends to call the shots. I'm old on the team, too, but I don't have too much to say of a say without an official contract. I'm just grateful that Ezequiel's even inviting me.

I kick my cleats into the turf and curse to myself. I damn well hope that someone saw me out there. I gotta prove that I'm worth the trouble.

"You did good," Ezekiel says jogging up to me.

"You think so?" I ask.

"Yeah, man," he says. Then he marvels at my slimming torso. "And you're slimming up."

I pat my belly. "I'm already missing it."

Ezekiel laughs. "I just can't wait until I can eat what I want."

I groan. "Tell me about it." Retirement is only a year or two away for us. But I'm winning that Championship Game first.

We make our way to the locker rooms.

"You wanna join us for lunch?" He asks.

I shake my head. "Y'all go ahead. Got an appointment with my financial advisor."

"Everything good?" Ezekiel asks.

I shrug. "He thinks we should discuss my charity donations now that retirement is coming up."

Ezekiel puts his arm on my shoulder. "They're gonna re-sign you. They'd be crazy not to."

I wipe the sweat off my forehead as we reach the locker room. We go to our lockers, which are thankfully far away from other team members.

"I don't know, man," I say, lowering my voice. Reporters are already here, asking the other players questions. "I just think it's wild that my job hinges on me having a woman."

He sighs. "I get it." I know he's just being nice, but I doubt he does. Even if Ezekiel left his wife of five years, he'd be able to find one in a heartbeat. But not me. I've been trying find a woman my whole life, and now I got a three month deadline? It's all bullshit.

"How's that going by the way?" He asks.

My heart burns. "If you're asking if I have a girlfriend, the answer is no."

"I knew that," Ezekiel says, which hurts more than I liked it to. "I mean your book club thing. Isn't that how Timmy thinks you'll find someone?"

Book club.

Images of Michael's smiling face fills my mind.

"It's fun," I admit. "I'm even helping out someone there with their writing."

Ezekiel beams and taps me on the arm. "There you go. See, maybe this is the one."

My stomach tumbles over itself at the thought. I'm not gay, but I've wondered what it would be like to date a man. And naturally, that man I wonder about happens to be Michael. He's so sweet, and these books he's having me read—I thought they would be boring, but damn do these women know how to write. I stayed up way past my bedtime reading that Emily Henry. She makes me want to kick my feet like a little girl. I'm no expert at love, but I just have this feeling that dating Michael would feel a little something like that.

Just a thought though.

The reporter makes his way to Ezekiel, which means it's time for me to go. Not even fully out of my practice gear, I grab my things and make my way out. In my hand, my phone buzzes with that particular notification, and I get a rush of adrenaline. Michael posted a new video.

"Wait, Kyle," another reporter says. "We have some questions—"

"No comment!" I yell out as I scurry the hell out of there. My agent said to not talk to the press until I have a girl, which means I don't have to talk to anyone yet. Thank God.

I fast-walk to my car. I throw open the trunk, toss all my shit inside, and get inside my car before any more reporters can harass me. I welcome the blistering heat, sweat dripping down my bare chest, and that's when I remember the notification.

My heart pounding, I open the notification and go straight to OnlyFans. I know it's risky opening it up here, but this is the first video he's posted since he and I started meeting. And I don't know if I like it.

I start the video, and there's no foreplay. They get right to it.

Heat surges throughout my body, and that stale car heat no longer feels good. I turn on my car and start blasting AC. "Come on," I say, hot and uncomfortable. "Cool me off already."

The guy railing him is one of his old regulars. Oh God. Are they dating? Have they been dating this whole time? I just assumed, since Michael has videos with so many different guys, that he was single. I should be okay with this. Michael is just some guy—a friend, nothing more. But then why do I feel like I'm burning from the inside out?

And his face. It's hardened, and his eyes almost look puffy. He's upset.

Someone knocks on my window, and I shout and throw my phone into the air. I quickly grab it and not only close it but shut it off. I pray to the god I've grown up with that whoever this is didn't just see me watching Michael.

I put my phone in the little cubby and turn to the person standing at my window. The sun shines off his bald head.

I roll down the window. "Hey, Timmy," I say.

"Scared ya there," he says, leaning on the window frame.

I force a laugh. "Just startled me is all. What's going on?"

"I wanted to follow up on how the dating's going," he says. "Haven't heard from you."

Even with the AC blasting, I just get hotter. "It's uhh... going."

"You are trying to find someone, right? Management still hasn't budged on their stance. They want to see you with a girlfriend, and only then will they consider. The sooner the better."

Great. Even with my improved playing, I'm still in the same place I was. "I'm trying, Timmy. I promise."

"Well gimme some details then."

I freeze up. I still haven't even gone, but Michael has been telling me what they're reading.

"Yeah, we've been reading..."

"I don't care about the books," he says. "Are you meeting girls there or not?"

That heartburn feeling returns. The only person I've talked to at book club is Michael. So, I just make up a lie.

"Yeah, I... I've been talking to this girl." If I had known Timmy wouldn't care about the books, I wouldn't have needed to set up my little agreement with Michael. But, in truth, I'm glad we are reading together. And I like spending time with Michael.

Relief melts his tense shoulders. "Alright, good. Tell me a little bit about her."

"She's..." I pause. I told Ezekiel I was helping someone with their writing. I can do the same thing here. "...a writer. I'm looking at the stuff she writes. It's real good. She's even having me read—"

"That's good," he said, tapping my window frame. "Good details. Send me a picture ASAP, and I'll talk to management. Hoping they soften their stance. Then we'll have a chance of getting you back on the team."

My stomach jumps so much it feels like I've been stabbed. I have to take a deep breath. At least by now the AC is doing its job. I've just dug myself into deeper into my lie. It means everything to honor my dad's legacy by winning the Championship Game, but getting there by fooling everyone around me just feels sleazy. Yet finding and committing to a girl in less than three months makes me even more nauseous. I want it to be true. Authentic. But now I either have to find a girl, and fast, and deal with all the depression that comes with that later. Or I just have to keep lying. And now, Timmy's expecting hard evidence, which of course I don't have.

Timmy taps my door and pushes away. "More updates like these," he says. "Keep 'em coming. Send that picture over quick."

"I will Timmy," I say. "I gotta go. See ya around."

He walks away as I roll up my window. The AC ice cold, my sweat now chills me, and I rub my bare arms. Sitting there, I turn my phone back on. I make my way back to the video and watch the rest with a frown on my face, not even aroused.

My life is a mess. But seeing Michael clearly upset like this triggers the protective Southern man in me. Is it because of this guy he's been seeing? Someone else? I need to know.

At the very least, I did tell one truth to Timmy: there is a special someone I'm seeing. One who is smart and kind and interesting—one who just happens to not be a woman. I can't bear to imagine what would happen to my career if this secret got out, but it would be worse to just stuff it all down and suffer through a relationship with a woman I couldn't bear to call mine.

So, I'll lie until there's a better solution.

And in the meantime, I need to know what has Michael so upset. And if this man fucking him is really his man.

Chapter 13

Michael Cunningham

I STEP ONTO KYLE's porch, our new books in hand. We've been doing our little book club for over a month now. Yesterday, we discussed a Beverly Jenkins novel at book club. It was a good book, and I knew I would have had a lot to say. But ever since I saw David, I've been in a funk. I could hardly pay attention while I was reading it, and I was so absent yesterday that Kelley asked what was wrong.

'Oh, I'm just a loser who can't seem to do better than his ex,' seemed like a remarkably self-pitying thing to say, so I didn't say it. But that's nonetheless how I've felt.

Kyle opens the door, and the sight of him makes me tingle head to toe. He's wearing well-fitting jeans with a light-blue button-up that makes his hazel eyes pop. His sleeves are rolled up, revealing his hairy, muscular forearms.

"You're dressed nice," I say, stepping inside. I try to sound enthusiastic, but even I can tell it's coming out flat.

"Thank you thank you," he says, chipper.

"Any special occasion?" I ask. Probably some date with a woman hotter than the surface of the sun.

"Just felt like dressing up," he says.

I follow him into his living room, unable to keep my eyes away from his perfect ass. He gestures to the coffee table, and it's covered with large brown bags.

"I took the liberty of ordering us some food," he says. "I remember you mentioning pad thai was your favorite."

I sit down on the couch and set the books aside, already salivating. Smelling hot, savory goodness reminds me that I haven't eaten at all today. I probably haven't been eating well at all.

"Oh!" He walks into his kitchen, and he comes out with a bottle of Diet Coke. "And I know how much you love this." He hands it to me, and my chest is alight with warmth.

"You didn't have to do all this," I say. "It's just me."

He sits down, his elbows resting on his knees. "Sometimes it's just nice to celebrate," he says. And then he winks at me, and I have to immediately look away.

Goddamnit, that sexy ass wink. The one that melts me into a puddle of goop. And he did it to me. *In person.*

"Everything okay?" He asks.

"Yeah," I say, clearing the saliva that's pooled in my mouth. "Just hungry."

"Well dig in," he says.

"I have to say," he says as I crack open the pad thai. The smell is heavenly, and the moisture of the food softens my hardened face.

"I have absolutely loved what you've been making me read."

I look up at him with a furrowed brow. "Really?"

He nods vigorously. "Oh yeah. It was—" He lifts his fist to his mouth and clears his throat. "I enjoyed it," he says, more subdued. "I may even have to concede and say that romance is inspiring."

I widen my eyes at him with a mouth full of noodles.

To my relief, he cracks open his food—some chicken fried rice—and starts eating too. I'm glad to not be eating alone.

"Now that's a win," I say. Being around Kyle has buoyed my mood just a little bit. "What had you convinced?"

"It's just..." He pulls on his beard and puts on his thinking face, accentuating all of his perfect facial features. "I never realized how deep romance can be.

It's like these authors dig into these character's insecurities, and they have to overcome these insecurities to be with the ones they love."

His words prick my heart, and heat trails down my torso like blood dripping from an open wound. "What do you mean?"

He shrugs. "I don't know. It's like—take Book Lovers. You have this accomplished blondie go to this small town. Her work is her life. Then she finds someone who makes her question these goals. Helps her see how she can slow down. But then she doesn't give up on these goals. She just adapts to be better version of herself. I think that's really cool. Definitely inspiring. I was expecting just blind affection. But these lovers don't get tied up in just physical attraction. It's emotional, too."

The air in the room thins around me. I swallow my food and stare blankly ahead.

"And you know, that makes me think," he says, nodding. "I think I'm ready to give you some feedback."

My chest squeezes. He told me he wanted to wait until he read enough of the book, but I just thought he wasn't reading at all. "Oh?"

"Your book—the premise is cool," he says. "But the attraction just feels more physical than it does emotional. I'm having a hard time understanding what really attracts these two besides their looks."

Nausea overwhelms me.

"I think if you looked at what these authors were doing—how they weave together internal issues with external problems—and tie that into the romance, your story would be stronger."

I grimace and set my food down.

Kyle notices me, and his face lengthens. "Did I say something wrong?"

"I need to use the restroom," I say. I make my way to the bathroom, the same one that I used the first time I came here.

"Can I get you anything?" He asks. "Tums? Pepcid?"

"I'm good," I say, then shut the door. I sit down on the toilet and collapse into my hands.

That insight. How is that I've been reading romance for years and have never realized this? Of course. It's so obvious. I even had a similar insight when I shared in that very first book club meeting about the title of *Pride and Prejudice*. But analyzing a text and writing are two different things. I didn't understand how such an insight could apply to my own writing until now.

These characters he's describing—they have *internal* problems that are then interwoven, seamlessly when written by the greats, into the larger narrative. So when the character goes through external problems, such as interpersonal conflict with their love interest, they are forced to grow internally as well. *That's* what makes a story great. Not just an interesting plot or a hooky idea, but relatable characters growing emotionally as they endure and overcome relatable problems.

Amani talked about my book lacking that spark. She didn't use these words, but my gut tells me that this is exactly what she was talking about.

And I couldn't be angrier with myself.

Kyle Weaver—just a football player with more money than I could dream of having—came to this conclusion after reading only a handful of contemporary romance novels. What does that say about me, someone who's been reading the romance genre for years? Shouldn't I know this by now? Or has my resolution to stay away from unhealthy romance weakened, causing my writing intuition to wane?

There's a knock at the door. "Michael, you alright?"

I raise my face from my hands. "Yeah, I'll come out in just a minute."

"Was it the food?" He asks.

"No. The food was great."

There's a pause. "Was it something I said?"

I want to say something, but I can't just tell him the truth. He'll just think I'm some insecure, emotional gay. Yet I don't want to lie either.

"It's just," he says beyond the door. "You're doing me such a huge favor, coming to me on a weekly basis. I told you I could pay you."

"That's not necessary," I say. I want to make my own money.

"See?" he says. "The best way I can repay you is by giving you the most honest feedback. I'm sorry if that hurts you."

I wrap my hands around my stomach, filled with butterflies.

And there's the Kyle Weaver that tips me over the edge. Not only is he attractive; he's kind. If he could pay me for what I'm doing for him, he would. So instead, he's pouring his heart into understanding a genre that he didn't even like before. All for me. He's so unlike David in so many ways.

I rise and approach the door. I take a deep breath, then open it.

Kyle stands just on the other side, his arm propped up on the frame. From here, I can see sweat beginning to stain his armpits, and I'm suddenly aware of what a man Kyle Weaver is. I look up at him, and he's standing slightly over me, his wide chest broader than my shoulders.

He doesn't step away. Instead, he comes a little closer. I hold my breath, our noses only an inch apart. Then his wide nose brushes mine, sending chills down my spine. My gaze trails from his chest to his brown eyes, and I just want to fall onto him. Being this close, it's like all my fantasies are coming true, the anger toward myself a shadow of what it was. We close the distance between our lips, and I close my eyes.

No. I promised myself I wouldn't fall for men who couldn't love me back.

My eyes shoot open, and I pull away just before our lips touch. Kyle straightens.

He shakes his head. "I—"

"Sorry," I say, but I try to act like nothing happened.

He winces slightly, hurt. I slip past him and make my way to the couch.

I don't know what just happened, but I do know this: Kyle Weaver is *straight.* He has to be. So, he is *not* emotionally available. I just discovered why my romance lacks zest. I can't just throw that all away by repeating my old, toxic pattern. I will not fall for a guy who can't love me back. Not again. I will write a solid romance, get an agent, get published, and get my community back. Kyle Weaver will not stand in the way of this.

I sit down, but Kyle's still standing there. He's expressionless. Frozen.

He takes a breath, almost gasping, and breaks from his stupor. "Oh, no worries at all," he says, trying to return to his affable manner. But I can tell the enthusiasm has waned.

"Are you sure you're okay?" he asks, returning to his seat.

I nod. "Just working through some things is all," I say. "I appreciate your feedback. I think you're completely right. My characters lack that internal conflict. I don't know how I didn't see it before."

"It's a pleasure," Kyle says, less pleasurably and more pained. "I'm glad I can help."

Both of us sit there and silence. Neither of us have returned to eating, and now Kyle's leg is shaking rapidly.

"Do you have a boyfriend?" he asks.

The question is a sharp cut to my heart, widening the wound from earlier that's making my chest tighten. "Why do you ask?"

He's chewing on his lips, staring at the table between us, his leg still bouncing. He opens his mouth to speak, then shuts it, as if revising his response.

"I'm wondering—" He shakes his head, then swears under his breath. I wince and lean back, already on the defense after all that's happened.

"Maybe," he says. Then sighs. His leg stops bouncing as quickly, so he must have figured out what he wants to say.

"I wonder if you were in a relationship, maybe that would help you understand how to get those internal issues down," he says. "Relationships aren't easy, but you could apply what you feel there in your writing."

My whole body tenses. "Are you saying that because I'm single I don't know how to write love?"

He perks up. "So you are single?"

Anger flairs in my chest. "Yes, if that wasn't so obvious," I say with gritted teeth.

"I'm sorry," he says, noticing my anger. "I didn't mean to offend."

I scoff. "So what? I have to have a boyfriend to write be a successful writer?" I ask aloud, as much to myself as to Kyle.

He grunts and rubs his forehead. "That's not what I'm saying. I'm—"

"And by that logic," I say, the heat of sweat prickling my forehead and back. "Because my ex still pushes my buttons—because I'm not over someone who clearly fucked up my life, that means I'm fundamentally incapable of writing good romance?"

He grimaces at me. "How the hell did you come to that?"

The disgust on his face lingers, which only adds to the flame in my chest. Now on top of him thinking I can't write romance because I'm broken, he thinks I've gone crazy.

I jump to my feet. "I need to leave," I say. I pick up the books I brought and start making my way to the front door.

"Michael, no," he says, standing and following me. "Let's talk about this."

"There's nothing to talk about," I say back. He already thinks I can't write romance because I'm single, and I know that I'll never be able to do it because I can't seem to let go of someone who treated me like shit. It all makes sense. In my resolution to never fall for unavailable men, I failed to realize that I still cling to David, the most unavailable man of all. No wonder my romance has been shit. It's like I'm cursed. Kyle's right. I'm fundamentally incapable of writing a good romance because I just can't love healthily.

I open the door, but Kyle puts his hand on the door. I turn and find him towering over me, just like before.

"Stay," he says. "Please."

I just stare at him, lost in those brown eyes again.

"You are not 'fundamentally incapable of writing good romance'," he says. "I shouldn't have said what I said. I'm sorry."

I think about how close our lips were, how the touch of our noses sent me into the stratosphere.

But Kyle Weaver is straight. I can't let myself develop feelings that he won't be able to reciprocate. It's best to leave now.

I thrust his copy of next week's book into his belly. "Here," I say.

He turns it upward, revealing the cover. "It's a Cat Sebastian book about a gay couple in the fifties," I say. "And I'll send you an email of bullets from yesterday's discussions since we didn't talk about it."

I move his arm blocking me and open the door again. I turn, and Kyle looks at me imploringly. God, he's so handsome. I have to look away before I get second thoughts.

"I'll see you next week," I say. I step outside and shut the door. I don't look back.

Chapter 14

Kyle Weaver

I DECIDE TO SKIP unofficial practice this week and take a red-eye home again to see my mama. I needed to get away from the city—away from anything and everything that reminds me of Michael. As I load my luggage into my rental, I go over all that I said to him, cringing the entire time.

I was a fool. A damn selfish one at that. I said I wanted to know what was bothering him, why he looked all sad in his latest video, but in reality it was just green jealousy. I wanted to know if that man screwing him was his boyfriend, and if not, if he had one. I didn't like the idea of him being with another man. So I asked him, in a roundabout way, if he had one. And of course, that idea exploded in my face—him saying that he's a failed writer because he doesn't know love. And it's all my fault.

By the time I reach my mama's home, the Mississippi sky is bright, but my mind is dark and stormy.

Mama, tending to the garden, stands when I pull into the driveway. I roll down my window

"Now this is a mighty surprise," she says as she's approaching me. "What brings you home, boy?"

I tap the frame of the window. "I fucked up, ma."

She sighs, not from exasperation I can tell but from understanding.

"Then come on in," she says. "I've got some leftover stew."

* * *

By the time I settle on her couch, clouds are already beginning to cover the sky, and they're darkening. A storm is on the way. My ma's hairless cat, Miss Beautiful, prances over to the couch when she sees me. She leaps onto my lap, purring all the way, and I have to set down my stew before she snags a piece of beef. She runs her head into my chin.

"Now tell me what's going on," Ma says as she sits down. She picks up her hook and begins crocheting.

I sigh. I can't just tell her about Michael. I have to say what I'm saying to everyone else.

"There's this girl," I say. Miss Beautiful has nestled in between my legs.

"Okay," she says, nodding. She's looking at me and robotically working her needles. Impressive, I must say.

"She's a writer, and—" I don't know how to explain all the details while telling all these lies. "Ugh, ma, I just made her mad. I said things, and I made her mad when I was only trying to help."

She nods, this time looking down at what she's doing. I think she's making some sort of hat. Outside, there's thunder, startling Miss Beautiful. I stroke her to calm her down. She settles again.

"Are you being fully honest with this girl?" She asks.

I get that heartburn again. I would say it's from the stew, but my ma's cooking is impeccable. I think it's from something else.

"I'm tryna be," I say honestly.

"You and I know that trying and doing are two different things in this case," she says. "Are you being honest or not?"

I rub the bridge of my nose as rain begins to fall hard outside. But I'm warm and cozy in here. I got Miss Beautiful purring in my lap. I'm here with my mama who I know loves me dearly. Dad's gone, but I know he would be proud of my career. So why do I feel so twisted inside?

Tears wet my eyes. "I could stand to be more honest," I say, trying to keep my quivering lip still. "It's just so damn hard."

She eyes me warmly as I let my tears fall. My mama has always been the only one I could do this with. Miss Beautiful looks up at me with sleepy eyes as I sniffle.

"I know it is," Ma says. "But you know what your father always used to say?"

I look at her all serious. She never talks about Dad unless she has to.

"He was always honest," she says. "No matter the price. He said that integrity was the most valuable thing we had. And if people didn't like us for that, that was on them."

I nod. I do remember him talking about honesty a lot, especially as a little kid.

"Kyle, search for the courage to be honest—and not just with this girl. But with yourself."

I wipe my eyes. "I'll try."

"Do is better."

By now, the quick burst of rain we got has subsided, and the sun is even shining through the clouds. Miss Beautiful rises from my lap, yawns and stretches, then makes her way to a ray of light on the couch. She settles into a loaf there and closes her eyes.

The sudden sunshine has me itching to get outside.

"Thanks, ma," I say, wiping my eyes one last time. I set the stew down and get up and stretch. "You mind if I go to town for a little bit?"

"It's a free country."

I can't help but grin. That's her favorite thing to say.

I go to the door. "Need anything while I'm out?"

She perks up. "Oh, yes. There's a book at The Book Corner that I need picked up if you don't mind."

"The Book Corner?"

"It was that bookstore right next to Jimmy's diner."

I raise my brow. That's the bookstore with the lesbian flag.

"Sure thing," I say.

"Thank you kindly," she says as I leave the house.

When I get in the car, I ponder the places I could go. This town has a ton of little touristy businesses that I could browse, but I'm not in a huge mood to be spotted in public. The lake is great, too, but this weather has me thinking that it could rain again at any moment.

I glance over at my backpack. "Shoot," I say, remembering. I open the small flap and pull out my copy of the Cat Sebastian book that Michael gave me. I said I would read it on the plane, but I conked out. On the cover, there's some nerdy looking guy with glasses standing next to a baseball player, and their outfits look old. A gay novel based on some time in the past, I gather.

I do need to pick up a book at The Book Corner for ma, and she said they had a little café. Maybe I could sit there and get started on reading this book for book club. I got nothing else to do after all. After what I said to Michael, I doubt he'll send me more stuff to read. God, I was so stupid. In hindsight, it woulda been less weird to just ask him if he had a boyfriend, not justify why I was asking him.

I sigh. Something tells me that bookstore might be the best place to go if I want to be in public, but discreetly—maybe besides a library. Not really my kinda fans in these places. But the closest library is at Miss U, and I'd surely be recognized there.

So the lesbian bookstore it is.

When I make it to the bookstore, the lesbian flag bats in the wind, almost like it's drying itself off from the rain. I pull into the gravel lot, and I'm surprised it's almost full. I manage to take the last open spot. Hopefully, with how busy it is, I still won't be recognized.

I shove the book inside my backpack, lest someone see that I'm reading a book with gay men on the cover. And then I make my way inside.

The Book Corner has shelves lining the walls, as well as smaller shelves in the middle of the floor. At the center of the shop, there's a circular counter. Behind it stands a young black woman checking out an older white woman, and there are three people standing behind her. Next to her, there's a red-headed woman helping her out. To my right, a sturdy, stocky man with a mustache is manning the café. When I glance at him, his eyes widen.

"I'll be damned," he says. "Are you...?"

I walk up to the counter, hoping he won't say it so loud. "It's me," I say. "Kyle Weaver."

He reaches his muscular arm across the counter. I smile and shake it back.

"Your mama's Linda Higgins, right?" he asks.

I look around. There are some people watching us, but not many. "She is."

"Sorry to bother, but that woman's my hero. I wondered when I'd meet her son."

I smile a little. She had told me about a young man around my age who moved here a few years back. Rough home life, she said about him. But he's found support here.

"She's mine too," I say. "You're...?"

"Silas," he says. "Sorry, can I get you something? Didn't mean to fangirl."

"All good," I say. I glance at the food behind the glass. "How bouta blueberry muffin?"

"Sure thing," he says. "Heated up?"

"Please."

I stand to the side and wait. The way he talks—he's Southern for sure, but there's a lilt there. One only gay men have. It sounds like he wasn't accepted back home. But my ma accepts him. That means she could accept me if I was like Silas.

"Good to meet you," he says. "I hope to see you around."

"Likewise," I say, taking the muffin. I notice someone get up from the comfiest looking armchair. It faces the window, its back to everyone else. Great place to read and be undisturbed.

I make my way over, set my take off my backpack, and plop down. I dig into the muffin, marveling at the sweet, cinnamon taste. Then, knowing I've procrastinated it enough, I take out the book and start reading.

And ho-lee shit.

The next time I look up, I'm halfway through the book. It's raining again, steadily tapping against the window. There are fewer customers than before, and most are different than the ones that were here when I arrived. It feels like I've been transported through time.

I look down at the book again, unable to believe that this random person named Cat is telling me my story.

This baseball player? He's me. He's struggling to keep up his reputation as a professional player, and even the conversations with his mother mirror the ones I've been having with my own. There's a reporter who both comforts him but also makes him question himself. Every time I read in this other man's voice, I can't stop thinking of Michael.

I dive into the book again before I overthink it.

As their love gets stronger and stronger, I get that familiar heartburn. But I don't stop. The more I read, the more I seem to understand: about myself, the world around me. How my whole life I've been living in the dark, and how this book is like a flashlight shining through the darkness.

By the time I reach the end, I'm teary-eyed, and my chest feels like it's on fire. For so long, I've attributed this sensation as something purely physical, as heartburn or sore muscles or whatever. But this is more than that. I can't pinpoint it exactly, but I know it has to do with the feelings I get when I think about Michael or being with a woman for the rest of the life. For a while, it all seemed disconnected, but now I understand it all orbits around one idea. One truth. And if I've learned anything today, it's that, just as mama said, that I need to be true to myself.

I close the book and look out the window. As it would be, the rain has stopped, and light now shines through the clouds again. Like God is telling me it's alright.

I breathe in, then breathe out.

I, Kyle Weaver, am a gay man.

Chapter 15

Michael Cunningham

AFTER AN AL-ANON MEETING, my sponsor, Susan, and I agree to eat at a nearby pizza place. Ever since my argument with Kyle, I've gone to at least two meetings a day. I've felt off since seeing David at the bar, and I'm trying to get my serenity back. But it's eluded me.

On the drive there, I bite on my knuckles. Susan will probably think that I was an idiot for going to a place I suspected David might be. Or she'll criticize me for staying and talking with David, or for leaving Amani behind. I know she'll definitely have something to say about how I reacted to Kyle.

Kyle. The gorgeous man I've been keeping a secret from everyone, including my sponsor. He's said to tell no one that we're meeting regularly, but I need to get what I've done to him off my chest. I guess I just have to speak in broad terms or anonymize him.

By the time I reach the pizza place, I'm simultaneously relieved and frightened. I no longer have to keep this all my head, but that means someone else will hear about what happened. Susan has yet to judge me harshly, but I always fear that this will be the time that I finally break her.

We take our seats and order our drinks.

"How was your week?" she asks, chipper.

I sigh. "Is it okay if I say it was bad?"

"Of course it is," she says after a sip of water. "That's how you feel. What's going on?"

My heart racing, I take a deep breath, and I spill what happened: drinks with Amani, running into David. Of course, with my luck, the waiter comes to take my order just as I'm describing how I had sex with Greg. I had to stop just before he arrived so he wouldn't hear the details. And, of course, I describe how I exploded on my anonymous friend—Kyle—for saying I'm a bad romance writer because I'm incapable of loving correctly.

"Oof," she says. "Sounds like you had a rough week."

I sigh. "Tell me about it."

A year ago, I chose Susan to be my sponsor. I heard her speak in a meeting, and despite what a harrowing childhood and life she had with her first husband, she smiled and laughed. She had a peace that I wanted, and since she agreed to help me work through the twelve steps, she and I have grown close. I now see her as one of my closest friends.

Our pizzas arrive—meat lovers for me, margherita for her—and I immediately dig in. Even the act of just saying all that out loud has taken a burden off my shoulders, but the effort alone left me famished. I just hope that Susan takes pity on me and isn't too harsh.

"So," she says after taking a couple bites from her pizza. "What really bothered you about seeing David last week?"

I shrug, still hungry after gobbling down two slices. I pick up my third. "It was like, shouldn't I be better than this by now? Shouldn't I not be so swayed by my ex? I should be over him right now."

She clears her throat, and I'm worried she's about to answer in the affirmative to all my questions.

"Stop 'shoulding' on yourself," she says, the 'should' sounding like 'shit'. "There's nothing you 'should' be doing at all."

Tension melts from my shoulders, and I lean back into my chair. "You're right," I admit. And, as usual, what she actually says is far kinder than what I anticipated.

"But you say you 'shouldn't have feelings for David'," she says. "*Do* you still have feelings for him?"

I furrow my brow as I chew on my pizza.

When we first broke up two years ago, I missed him often, jerking off to photos him for months on end. But then one day, attraction for him just faded away. And after that, it was easy to remember what an asshole he was. So pretty soon I didn't miss him at all.

"No," I answer honestly. "Not at all."

"Interesting," she says in her 'we're onto something' tone. "Then tell me. What *actually* bothered you about seeing him?"

And here's the reason why she continues to be my sponsor. She knows where to dig, like my brain is a muscle and she's the masseuse, massaging out my poor thinking.

"I..." I picture Stephen, that ginger he cheated on me with, how *jealous* I was when I first discovered the affair. I remembered how David was almost more animated around Stephen and his other friends, and how every time I tried to be a part of their group, they would deflate a little, like it was a drag to have me around. And seeing David's face when this happened—it was like he was embarrassed of me.

"I think... over the years, I wanted to understand why David did what he did, and eventually I just concluded it was because I wasn't good enough for him. But I still *wanted* to be good enough. I wanted to prove I was worthy enough to be dateable by winning him over. So I think seeing him was so hard because I was hoping for him to finally see me as equal to him and his friends—to finally have this proof. But he didn't. I was hoping he'd have changed, but he was the same old David."

"Is David somebody you can change?" She asks.

I let out a heavy sigh. "No. Step One says I'm powerless over anything but myself."

"So even if you were to change—to be this person that you think David likes—do you think David would like you?"

I play out a scenario in my head of me becoming the version of myself I think he'd respect. I can't imagine a positive ending. I try another. The same thing. Eventually, I exhaust all possibilities.

"I don't think he would," I say.

She nods softly. "Yeah. I think you're right."

There's a weight pressing on my chest and bitter taste in my mouth. Everything feels dark all of the sudden. If I can never be good enough for someone like David, then what hope is there for me?

I grimace slightly. "I can accept this, but why does it feel so bad? I thought accepting what I can't change was supposed to be relieving. But I feel like shit."

"Because it's loss, dear," she says. "And you have to acknowledge that. You lost what you hoped to have with David. And that grief is just as real as any other."

My eyes water, and I take a shaky breath. I grab hold of my third slice of pizza, but I'm not hungry enough to take a bite. I don't even feel sick or anything—just numb.

For so long, I tried to ingratiate myself with David and his friends, hoping that in doing so I would finally be that 'cool' gay, the one that everyone hits on, that everyone wants to sleep with. That's how I saw them, and with David, it seemed achievable. And once I achieved this, I would be worthy. And the acknowledgement that this is no longer sound logic makes everything around me look ashen.

"If chasing David and his friends is no longer a viable way to feel worthy, then what is?"

Susan smiles. "What a great question. Have you ever considered that you already are worthy? That there's nothing you need to do?"

"That's what I keep hearing in meetings and from my therapist," I say. "But it's not sinking in. How do I get it to sink in?"

She thins her lips and squints down at her hands clasped on the table. She looks up at me, her curly black hair immaculate. "You've spent so long thinking about what David and his friends would think of you. Let them go. Focus on yourself. Ask yourself: what do *you* think of you?"

The question makes me want to curl into a ball. "I... I don't know."

She leans back and crosses her leg. "Then you have a wonderful opportunity. You get to discover yourself."

I try and chew on the question, 'what do I think of myself', but it's as sturdy as a chicken bone.

"What if I don't even know where to start?" I ask.

She nods slowly. "Are there people in your life that you feel you can be your complete authentic self with?"

I lean forward and start eating that third piece of pizza, my hunger steadily returning.

My mind jumps to Amani, as well as some of my other writing group friends from college. But I don't keep much in touch with them anymore. There's Skye, my new writing friend, and she's awesome…and then there's Kyle. Which doesn't make any sense. I'm trying *not* to have feelings for him.

"My friends Amani and Skye," I say. "You as well."

The waiter comes to take our check, and Susan leans forward onto the table, nodding. "Learn from them, from me, from other people you trust. Look at how they see you. Learn to see how you're lovable. Pretty soon their love for you will become your own.

My chest warms at her words. They feel true.

"Thanks," I say, my mood becoming a tad brighter. "I think you're right."

"It's my pleasure," she says. "So do you still think you're incapable of loving the right way?"

I frown, thinking. "Well, no. Because I still don't love David. I just…wasn't loving myself." I'm surprised the words are coming from myself and not her.

She nods somberly. "Exactly."

My body relaxes, and things aren't looking so ashen anymore. I'm not cursed after all. I just had to dig deep into my feelings to discover what was really wrong.

"Is there anything else?" she asks.

I suck on my bottom lip. "I think I need to make an amends," I say, thinking of Kyle. "To my friend I blew up at. As well as Amani."

"I think is a kind thing to do," she says. "And remember you are also making amends to yourself. Think about the way you've been treating yourself all this time, trying to be someone you're not. That hurts. Give yourself that kindness you deserve."

I feel as if I've been swaddled in a blanket just out of the dryer. "I think I will."

* * *

The next day, I meet up with Amani and Skye after book club for writing group.

Amani pulls me aside before I sit down. "Are you okay?" She asks me in the corner of the coffee shop.

I give her a tight hug. "I'm fine," I say, pulling away. "Just dealing with some trauma is all."

Her shoulders relax. "You seem better, though."

I reflect on my conversation with Susan. "I am. I'm sorry I ran off from you that night."

She laughs. "It's okay. At least you got to have some fun."

Flashes of the sex I had with Greg run through my mind. "I guess it could have been worse. But what about you? Did you and that...?"

She nods, unable to hold her grin back. "I got her number. We're going out to dinner this weekend."

I squeal and hug her again. "You get it, girl. I'm so happy for you."

"Hey!" Skye says from a nearby table. "I know I haven't known Amani long, but I wanna hear the good news, too!"

Amani and I laugh and sit down with Skye, giving her all the details.

"Sounds like your ex is a dick," she says.

"Tell me about it," I say.

And then we get to our critiques. Even though I blew up on Kyle on Saturday, I did take his advice to heart. I went back and looked at my novel with a critical eye toward internal conflict. I read up and watched a bunch of videos on it too. And then it started to make sense. I built character profiles for my two main love interests, really digging into their internal workings, and rewrote the first two chapters of my book. That's what I'm sharing with Amani and Skye tonight. I hope the romance is much more intimate now.

Amani shares some scene sketches she has for her new fantasy novel, and both Skye and I love it. We give her advice on how to weave it into her outline.

Skye shares about a romance she's writing between two transgender characters at university, and her banter is publishable quality.

And then we get to me.

As I read a portion of my first chapter out loud while the others read along, my nerves overwhelm me. What if this is somehow worse than before? What if I have to scrap this whole idea? Or worse: what if my writing is somehow worse, negating everything I learned yesterday with my sponsor?

"Holy shit," Amani says when I finish.

"Yeah," Skye says, nodding, twirling her blonde hair with her finger. "You hit with this one."

I lean back. "Really?"

"Really," Amani says, looking at me above her glasses.

"It's just so much more compelling than what you've brought in before," Skye says. "Like I'm so invested in your main character. I need to know what happens next."

My chest lights up with excitement. "Oh, my god. Thank you."

"Where did this come from?" Amani asks. "This is the zest I was talking about. It's finally here."

I remember Kyle's genuine advice before I fled to the bathroom. "My other critique partner," I say. "I got this comment from him."

"Oooo," Amani says, winking to Skye. "His 'other' critique partner."

"He's gonna run us out of business with the advice that he's giving," Skye says.

And as they give the rest of their feedback, I try to really internalize all the kind things they say about me, just as Susan instructed. It's uncomfortable at first, because for so long, I've been attaching strings to my worth. As long as I do x, I will be worthy.

But this is different. This is me just learning that I am worthy—that I am good, learning through how others see me. It's crazy that there's really nothing I need to 'do'. I just need to be.

And what's even more wild is that if it weren't for Kyle, I wouldn't have gotten all these praises tonight. Not that Skye and Amani needed a specific reason to say good things about me, but applying Kyle's advice definitely brought out genuine adulation. I'm a little nervous that he'll be upset with me after what I did to him last week, but more than anything I'm just excited to see him. As it turns out, I'm not fundamentally incapable of writing good romance. I know he didn't say that, but I projected my insecurities onto him. So, tomorrow, I'll apologize. And I can't wait.

Chapter 16

Kyle Weaver

I'M IN THE FOYER of my home pacing back and forth waiting for Michel to arrive, anxious as hell.

When I was back in Glamour Springs, I said the words in my head. I admitted that I liked men. That I was gay.

I pause to look again at the cover the Cat Sebastian book we had to read for book club, the one that made me come to my senses back in that lesbian bookstore. Since that day, I read it again, and it hit just as hard the second time.

Me. Kyle Weaver. A gay man.

I start pacing again.

All those feelings around women finally make sense. It's not that I get all moody and down around them because I'm a misogynist, or because I'm mentally unstable or something. I just don't swing that way. Like at all.

But I'm terrified for what this means now. All this talk of me being single for so long, the speculation as to why—it's all true. It *is* because I'm gay.

What does this mean for my new contract? For the NFO? For the Championship Game? My promise to Dad? Sure, some players in the NFO have come out in the past, but none have been as established as I am in my career. Plus, my whole goddamned reputation is the Southern heartthrob gentleman. How would me being gay change that? I'm getting my heartburn again thinking about it—no, these are emotions. I think this is anxiety.

Michael is gay. I'm thinking I can tell him about this. My whole situation. My agent Timmy is the only other one who knows in detail, but he doesn't know the gay part. I need someone else on my side.

I freeze. But I *can't* tell Michael. With how many videos of his I've jerked off to over the years? Sheesh. If I were to break this secret, what's stopping me from telling him that he's the most handsome man on this planet? That I've fantasized about plowing those globes he has as ass cheeks? I may be able to say I'm gay but no more than that. I don't know what to do about my football career, but I sure as hell am not ready to give it up just for some hot redhead with a mullet.

My doorbell rings, and I just about throw the book into the air. My heart is racing just like it does before kickoff. *Breathe, Kyle.* What did Dad use to say? He said things always work out for those who try. But Mama also told me he said integrity was the most important thing we have. And I definitely don't have integrity the longer I keep this secret. *Gah!* I can't keep teetering back and forth. I gotta just open the door and deal with what's coming. Which sure as hell won't be me and Michael. *Damnit.*

I open the door, and Michael's there holding one of those big grocery tote bags. It looks like it's filled. Now what the hell is—

"I wanted to say that I'm sorry," he says, his shoulders curling into his chest, which he does to make himself small. I used to like it—I thought his shyness showed how into me he was. But it just makes me think he doesn't like himself. And I hate that.

"Sorry?" I ask.

"For how I acted last week," he says. "I was a total jerk."

Jeez. After all that's happened, last week feels like a year ago. I have a hazy memory of him getting upset after I gave him the feedback about his novel.

I scratch the back of my neck, already damp with sweat. "That's nothing to worry about, Michael. I understand how hard getting feedback can be."

He sighs, tension melting from his shoulders, and part of me thinks it was me saying his name that got him to relax like that. If I had him in bed, how else would he react to me saying his name?

No, Kyle. Focus.

"It wasn't just the feedback," he says. "Lots of other things too. But thanks for understanding. Can I come in?"

"Oh, what am I doing? Of course," I say, pulling the door open for him. "That bag looks so heavy. Sorry to keep you standing."

Once we're inside, I take the bag from him and carry it to the coffee table. I peak inside and see some containers with the Clucker's logo on them.

"What'd you bring?" He asks.

"Well," Michael says, drawing out the vowel as he walks into the room. "I brought some food as an apology. I was thinking of flowers instead of food, but then I remember how we usually eat, and I was wondering what use a football player would have for flowers. I figured you eat a lot of protein, so I got us both a lot of chicken tenders."

The words spill out of like they're burning his mouth, and I just stare at him with my mouth open, a grin forming on my face.

I want to go over, kiss him on the cheek, and call him babe, just like real couples do, but I can't. Damnit, I feel just like that baseball player—confused inside, unable to accept what I want. What would Dad do? He would definitely be against doing anything gay. And ma? She would say to be honest. But right now, those are at odds with each other.

"Are you okay?" Michael asks. "You're staring into space."

I shake my head and blow air out my mouth. I clap my hands and rub them together. "Just hungry," I say. "Let's eat!"

I hand a container to each of us. When I open mine, I'm intoxicated by the scent. It's filled with chicken tenders and crinkle cut fries.

"I know I'm supposed to be dieting, but damn am I excited for this," I say.

Michael smiles shyly. "I'm glad."

We both dig in, and I manage to convince myself that maybe I was acting weird because of the hunger. Because now I feel a lot better. I don't even remember if I ate after my workout this morning.

"Sorry again. I appreciate you being so understanding about how I acted," Michael says, finishing off a fry. I peer over at his container, and it looks like he's hardly made a dent. Me, on the other hand...

I finish off a chicken tender, and I'm sad that there's only one left.

"I got some extra," Michael says, pointing to the bag.

I look him dead in the eye. "You are my hero, Michael Cunningham."

He blushes, and I get chills at the sight. How in the hell am I supposed to have this man over every week and not leak that I'm into him? And on top of this, I still have to find a girlfriend. Luckily, with the book club info that Michael's been giving me, I've been able to keep Timmy at bay. He thinks I've been faithfully attending. But what's going to happen when July 1st comes? All I have to show is a schoolboy crush on a hot gay pornstar.

"You got nothing to worry about," I say, referring to his apology. I dip my last chicken tender in their special spicy sauce.

"Thanks," Michael says. He's holding himself small again, trying to pull in his large frame, and it looks unnatural. It looks like he's got something on his mind. Maybe he wants to talk about this.

"If you don't mind me asking," I say, closing my container and opening up one of the extra ones. Inside, there's another whole load of chicken and fries, and I offer a silent prayer of gratitude to God.

"Yes?" Michael says. He's sitting on the edge of his seat, making me think he'll answer anything I ask him. I wonder if this obedience extends to other areas...

Kyle, stop it. For fuck's sake.

I clear my throat. "What got you so upset anyways? You said it was more than just the feedback."

He leans back and rests his elbow on the armrest, propping his head up. He sighs, ready to explain. "Your feedback was deeper than you realize," Michael says. "A few years back, I started dating my ex, David."

Just the mention of his ex makes my heart burn. I don't like the idea of him being intimate with someone else.

"He wasn't good for me in a lot of ways, and he really wore me down. Our relationship was mostly superficial. And his drinking was crazy, which led me to recovery in Al-Anon. I slowly discovered parts of myself there. One of those big things was that I like to write romance. Because I only came to such a conclusion away from my ex, I figured that my best writing would be done as a single man, away from the distraction of any unhealthy relationship."

I marvel as he speaks. This man—he knows himself so well. It's like his mind is a freaking snake and he's got a flute, charming the snake and making it dance however he likes. And the way he says it out loud... he's so damn smart. I can't describe what's going on inside my head like he can.

"But I still haven't been able to land an agent. Hearing you come in and so clearly break down my writing weaknesses—which, thank you so much, by the way—was illuminating. To say it was because I was single made sense, but it went against everything I knew about myself. For years, I thought that being away from a relationship was making me a better writer. Now I had to be in one? And hearing this news after I had a horrible run in with my ex at the bar?"

My heartburn worsens. He *saw* his ex. Does he still like him?

"But I was able to work all that stuff out with the help of my support network, mostly my sponsor," he says. "And you didn't deserve me running out on you like that." He shrugs. "In short, I took my insecurities out on you, and I'm sorry. Hope that all makes sense."

I exhale through my nose. Make sense? I woulda never guessed this was how he felt if he didn't say it so plainly.

"Well you clearly have a talent with words," I say. "Because you made something really complicated make total sense. Thanks for explaining. And you have nothing to worry about."

"Thanks," Michael says, blushing again. "You're welcome."

Goddamnit. I have to look away from his gorgeous face before I say or do something I regret.

"And you have a way of critiquing," he says. "Your feedback was spot on. I went and applied it to my writing and—holy shit—you were right. I shared it with a couple of writing friends, and they said it was the best of mine they had ever seen."

Pride swells in my chest. "I was just being honest. And for all that you're doing for me, you deserve my honest help. I can't wait to see your next installment."

He leans forward and starts eating again. "You'll be getting it soon. Can't wait to hear what you think."

I resume eating as well, finally feeling satisfied, both in terms of hunger and my feelings. I'm glad that Michael and I are good again, and I'm glad that he's happy. As long as all this is going well, it will be a little easier to finally get a girlfriend. And, I have to say, I'm happy he's truly single.

I lean back into the couch and rub my belly, contented. "Glad you're doing good," I say. "'Cause when I saw your latest video, you looked so sad. You had me worried."

Michael nods, chewing, and then he freezes entirely.

And that's when my body goes as still as stone, as cold as ice.

He looks at me with wide eyes, mid-chew.

I want to sink into the couch and disappear.

I may have just revealed that I watch his videos.

Chapter 17

Michael Cunningham

I SWALLOW THE FOOD that feels like cement in my throat, unable to fathom what I just heard.

"What did you just say?" I ask, gripping the armrest of Kyle's couch.

Kyle's as pale as a ghost. "I said I can't wait to read your next installment."

"No," I say, firm as ever. "What you said after that."

Kyle audibly swallows. But says nothing.

"You referred to my video," I say, leaning forward on the couch. "What video?"

He runs his tongue along the inside of his lip and looks around.

"What video, Kyle?" I ask.

My heart is nearly beating out my chest. My latest video—if that's what he really said, which I'm nearly 100% sure he did—is of Greg fucking me. And he's right: I did look sad in that video. But the only way for him to have known about that...

He leans forward, pulling on his beard, staring into space. Saying nothing.

"Kyle, I'm getting uncomfortable. You're going to have to tell me or else—"

"Something happened this past week," he said in a voice more devastatingly serious than I've heard from him. "Something back home."

"Are you okay?" I ask. For a second, I thought he was trying to change the subject. But this feels like he's providing an explanation.

He looks right at me, his hands steepled just below his chin. He grabs the Cat Sebastian book from his armrest. "This book," he croaks, his voice warbling. "This book helped me see things I've never been able to see before. In myself."

My insides warm, and I lean forward in anticipation. I get the feeling Kyle's about to tell me something deeply important and personal.

"My whole life, I've never been able to be myself around women. It was like this dark storm cloud formed in my mind every time I was alone with one. My dad—bless him—was often there for me, but he said I had to push through it. So I tried. And it only made things worse.

"For so long, I swore there was something wrong with me. Like I had some illness or whatever. I told myself I couldn't have been queerness—I played football, and I was damn good at it. And I was masculine as hell. The queers I were seeing were all skinny and small and dressing up in frilly colors. That wasn't me. There was something else—something else I needed to do to get over this problem."

As Kyle talks, tears have been pouring from his eyes. I take napkins from the bag and slide them his way. He grabs them with one of his bulky, hairy arms, and wipes his red eyes.

"But I couldn't keep my eyes off men," he says. "And in college, I even hooked up with other guys at Miss U in secret. We all fucked like crazy."

My insides twist around themselves. The image of Kyle fucking somebody else—other football players for Christ's sake—is an image my mind does not have bandwidth to render.

"But when I signed pro, I had to give that up. I couldn't stomach dating women. So, I stayed single, focusing on my skills. And that's when I turned to porn."

My stomach churns. So that means...

"I eventually found your content, and—" he sniffles "—I'm sorry if this sounds creepy, but I just couldn't keep my eyes off you. You are just such a goddamn beautiful man."

Warm trickles from the top of my spine down to my toes, like stepping into a hot shower on a cold day.

This entire time, Kyle Weaver has thought I'm just as hot as I think him. And I get chills when I think that he's probably watched most of my videos at this point, if not all.

He shakes his head and rubs his bear arms, still crying. "Awh, man. What am I going to do. What am I going to do."

And I do the only thing I can think to do—the same that was done for me by my high school English teacher when I came out to her.

I stand up, walk around the coffee table, and sit right next to him. Before he can lift his head to look at me, I wrap my arms tightly around him and give him the biggest bear hug that I can.

He stiffens for a moment, then melts into my embrace. And that's when he starts to sob, and his entire body shakes. I hold him there as long as my arms can take, stroking his hairy upper arm with my knuckles.

"Cry it out," I say. "Just let it out."

Eventually, he lifts his head, and I unwrap my arms. We both make eye contact, his eyes red and swollen from crying. He looks slowly between my eyes and my lips.

He moves his arm around me, forcing me to fall into his chest. His hand slides down to the point just above my ass, and my mind is screaming for it to continue downward.

He pulls me closer, and I don't resist. Our noses touch again, sending electricity down my spine.

I can feel his warm breath on my lips. Then our lips touch just briefly, as if we're both just testing this whole thing out.

Then his lips press harder into mine, and his warm tongue extends, begging to break through my lips.

This is ecstasy. Or at least it should be—kissing the sexiest man I know.

But it's wrong.

I put my hand on his huge leg and push myself away from him. He releases his arm and looks at me, mortified.

"Kyle, this isn't a good idea."

"Do you not want this?" he asks, confused.

"I—of course I want this," I say, shaking my head. I push myself slightly farther away so I'm not tempted to let him put his arm around me again.

"Jesus, you know I've thought the same about you?" I ask. "For years, I've jerked off to whatever pictures or videos of you I can get. You're fucking sculpted by the gods, Kyle."

Though he just wept his eyes out, he manages a smile. "No wonder you lost it when I took my shirt off."

I laugh, wiping away my sympathy tears. "No shit," I say.

Then he frowns. "But why not?"

I slump back. "You just came out, Kyle. This is a sacred moment for you, and you have no idea how vulnerable you are. I'm not going to take advantage of you. God, I shouldn't have even kissed you."

Kyle falls back into the couch, slightly annoyed. "So what now then? I come out but then I'm not able to celebrate it?"

I want to get closer to him and rub his arm to comfort him, but that would just encourage what I'm trying to avoid.

"Of course you can celebrate it," I say. "But it's not healthy to just jump into having sex. You're fragile right now. I won't do that to you."

Kyle lets out a sharp laugh, as if someone like him could be fragile. He runs his tongue around the inside of his mouth, then sighs. "I see. You're a bigger person than me for holding yourself back."

I shrug. "It's what I'd want for myself."

For a moment, we sit in silence. And then he turns his head slightly to me. And God, from this angle, his handsome profile makes me almost want to go back on what I said. Almost.

"I'll tell you what," he says. "You give me a week to process this. And then I want you to come back at your normal time."

I relax into the couch. "Are you sure?"

He nods. "Positive."

Butterflies of excitement flutter around my stomach. I just kissed Kyle Weaver. And he's gay! He said so himself. But I need to give him the space he deserves. He probably has so many thoughts overwhelming him.

I have to admit I'm more than thrilled that he wants me back over next week. But he could change his mind. Lord knows how many times I've scheduled a date or hookup with some guy, only for him to cancel last minute or completely stand me up. That's how all these emotionally unavailable guys have been. But something about Kyle tells me he'll be different. He's always kept his word, and with how honest he just was, I can't help but think he'll be true to it.

Ah, who am I kidding. I shouldn't keep my hopes up.

"I better be going then," I say before either of us are tempted to go back on our forbearance. I pick up my leftover food, then pause. "You can have the rest of mine."

Kyle does a gesture of supplication, showing off his thick arms. "Thank you," he says.

I nod, then collect the rest of my things. I plop my own copy of the Cat Sebastian of my book, briefly marveling that one book had such an effect on Kyle. And then I make my way to the door.

"Oh, and I have one request," Kyle says.

I stop and turn, sliding on his perfectly polished floors. "Yes?"

He stares at me, the swelling around his eyes having reduced a little. Though disheveled, he looks free, like a weight is off his shoulders. Happier.

"Please don't post anymore content," he says.

I squint at him for a second, and then recognition quickly dawns on me.

"If you need the money, just ask, I just—" He leans his elbow on his knee and trills his lips. "The thought of you with someone else right now—"

"I think I can go a week without posting," I say, unable to hide my grin. Kyle Weaver. *Jealous.*

He nods dramatically, biting his lip. "Thank you."

And then, with his desire for me as intense as it could be, I leave, knowing that next week my greatest fantasy might come true.

Chapter 18

Kyle Weaver

BY THE TIME THE sun shines through the cloudy sky, I'm splayed out on the turf of the Tigers' practice arena, panting like a dog. Ever since Saturday, I've been coming here at the crack of dawn to calm my mind. The only time I've felt peace lately is when I'm working out or sleeping. And I've been sleeping hardly at all.

I rise to my knees, and then my vision swirls. I let myself collapse back onto the turf again—I'm too tired to keep going. It starts to rain outside, and there's a nice little patter on the roof of the metal complex.

At the time, I was annoyed that Michael rejected my advances. But now I couldn't be more grateful. Because I'm confused as hell.

I admitted I was gay after I was idiotic enough to leak that I watched Michael's porn. But that didn't solve problems like I thought. It only created a bunch more. What do I do now that what everyone is saying about me is true? That I am gay? And if management finds out, they definitely won't re-sign me. I still want to win the Championship Game. It's what I promised Dad, and my heartburn—anxiety? I don't know—goes crazy when I imagine ending my career so I can be someone he'd disapprove of.

I wish there was someone I could talk to, but who? Ezekiel said he wouldn't care, but admitting to a fellow teammate that I'm gay feels like shouting it to the world, no matter how close we are. Somebody will find out. I can't talk to Michael about it. I'd be too tempted to get between his legs, and that'd only make things worse. Ma maybe? She would accept me, but admitting it to her means I couldn't take it back. I need somebody to talk to where there would be no consequences.

My eyelids grow heavier as the rain gets stronger. For the first time in the last couple days, I actually feel sleepy.

I look around for something to cover myself. There's a pile of rope nearby. I reach for it and pull the entire coil over my body. It doesn't do much to warm me, but the weight pressing down on me relieves my aching chest. And soon, I'm fast asleep.

I wake to the sound of my phone ringing on full blast. The sun is out, and I hear someone nearby in the locker rooms.

I throw the ropes off me and crawl over to my phone, nearly faceplanting when I trip over them. My back aches from sleeping on the hard floor, but I won't complain. At least I slept. I reach my phone, and I check the caller ID. For a moment I'm hoping it's Michael. But my stomach sinks when I see the name clearly.

Timmy.

"Hello?" I say, plopping down on the turf. By now, Ezekiel and a couple other guys have entered the gym. They wave, and I wave back.

"Kyle," he says.

"Yep, that's me," I say, wiping my eyes. I check the time. I clonked out for a good three hours.

"A while back, I told management how you're dating this girl."

I'm silent. I don't want to ask 'who', but for the life of me I can't remember what I told him.

"The writer girl," he says.

My heart starts to race. "Ah, yes," I say, thankfully remembering. I basically described Michael to him but as a woman, and he ate it right up.

"What's the status there? They want to know."

I sit up straighter. "Oh, we'll it's going really well," I say, wanting to sound as convincing as possible. "I've been helping her with her work, too. She's really improving."

He sighs through the phone. "Good," he says gruffly. "Have that picture for me?"

The two protein shakes I downed this morning curdle in my stomach. "Right, the picture."

"What?" he asks, his impatience clear. "You know you need evidence of a girlfriend before signing day. If you want to play another year at least."

Signing day. Only two months away. But I have no pictures of this 'girl'. All I have is a confession hanging on the tip of my tongue and the fiery lust for a certain redhead.

"She's... private," I say. "And we actually don't have any pictures."

"Kyle..." he says, annoyed. "You know how this looks. Now it just sounds like you're lying to me."

"Timmy, I swear it. I'm not lying."

There's a silence, and I can picture him rubbing his shiny forehead. "Then what are we supposed to do here? I need something to show your bosses. Or I doubt they'd even consider re-signing you."

I'm rubbing the bridge of my nose, feeling a headache come on. I've had one every day for the past week. I can't do this alone. I need someone to talk to. Support.

"Gimme a week," I say to him, just like I told Michael. "In a week I'll get you that picture."

"Alright," he says. "And no longer. You hear me?""Loud and clear."

"Wait, one more thing," he says, when I'm about to hangup.

"Yes?" My stomach is already bubbling. I don't know how much more of this I can take.

"You'll be hearing from a reporter soon," he says. "Gave her your contact info. Wants to interview a bunch of Tigers players."

I grunt. "Is she legit?"

"She's from ESB," he says. "And I wouldn't complain. She wants to interview you about your relationship with your dad and how that led you to where you are now. Might help distract the narrative from your sex life."

Doesn't seem horrible. Talking about him actually might help clear up some of this confusion. "Fine," I say.

"Anything else I'm forgetting?" he asks.

I watch as Ezekiel spots one of the linemen at the bench press. He's told me about how he sees a therapist and how good it's been for him. I think Michael has one too. Maybe that's why he talks so eloquently about himself. And I bet talking to somebody more qualified than a reporter might actually be just what I'm looking for. In fact, this might be exactly what I need.

"Yeah," I say. "Would you mind helping me get a therapist?"

I can picture him balking. "A therapist?"

"I got shit to work through," I say. "With my dad and all." Which isn't a lie.

"I can get you set up with one," he says. "But this better not stop you from getting me that picture."

I sigh. "Don't worry. It won't."

* * *

I show up to this pristine office building downtown. Timmy's email tells me she's up on one of the top floors. Wearing a hoodie and sunglasses so no one notices, I make my way inside the building and into the elevator. By the time I reach the designated floor, I'm already sweating, and it's not just 'cause it's a balmy day and I'm in a hoodie.

Timmy was able to find me an appointment with a therapist a day later, but I don't know how I feel about this now. I was able to say I was gay to myself, and I could say it to Michael, but that's only because it felt weirder not to. But to say it to a stranger? Who likely only knows me as being the one of the best linebackers the NFO has ever seen? This is a bad idea.

I check in with the receptionist and sit down in a beige armchair. The room is filled with old looking pictures of mountains, lakes and rivers. There's a sign that says 'Serenity' with the serenity prayer underneath it in purple cursive.

My heart starts to race. I could leave now. Could say to Timmy that this would distract me from my dating. Then I wouldn't have to—

"Kyle?"

A young, Indian woman has her head poked out of the door next to the receptionist's desk. Unable to run away now, I stand up and follow her. She leads me down a hallway, a full window at the end giving a stunning view of downtown.

"Right here," she says, gesturing to an open door.

I nod to her, then step inside.

The room is a reddish orange, and there's a long, expensive-looking beige couch. At one end of the room, there's an even bigger window than the one in the hallway, giving a clear view of the Delaware river. On the other end sits a small Indian woman in a swivel chair wearing all red with an orange scarf. Next to her, there's some incense burning. Jasmine—I recognize it. My mom used it around the house growing up. It reminds me of heading out to hot summer practices with my dad.

"Go ahead and shut the door if you please," she says in a crisp Indian accent. "And feel free to sit down on the couch."

I close the door and plop down, air blowing out of the cushion in both directions. She turns around. She's pretty, probably in her sixties. She's got gray streaks in her hair, and she looks like she's got wrinkles around her eyes from smiling too much.

The wrinkles crease, and she extends her hand. "Nice to meet you, Kyle. I'm Neeti."

"Nice to meet you," I say, shaking hers. I retract it, all embarrassed—my palms are sweaty. But she doesn't notice.

She glances down at her clipboard and writes something down.

"Is there a certain way this all goes?" I ask. "Do I need to do anything?"

She looks up at me and smiles, setting down her clipboard. "Sorry about that, just needed a quick note to myself. No, there's nothing you *need* to do. In the first session, I just like to talk and get to know my client. So, tell me about yourself."

I shrug. "Well, I play football for the Tigers, but you probably know that."

She tilts her head. "Tigers?"

"Yes," I say. "Portland Tigers. The football team? We played in the Champi-onship Game last year." *And lost because of me*, I'm tempted to say.

"Forgive me," she says, giggling. "I'm not very knowledgeable about sports. My husband plays cricket, but that's the extent of my knowledge. So you play professional football, very cool."

"I guess," I say. I don't see how this woman can help me if she doesn't understand football.

"So what brings you in today, Kyle?"

I sigh and rub the bridge of my nose. Coming here was a mistake. I don't even know where to begin.

"I'm hoping to get my contract re-signed with the Tigers," I say. "My contract ended with them a couple months ago, but I want to play at least one more year. You know how contracts work?"

"I get this gist," she says, nodding. "You say 'at least one more year'. Why?"

"Why not?" I ask back.

"Well," she says, looking up at the ceiling. "American football is hands-on, and you are..." she glances at her clipboard. "Thirty-four years old. That's pretty old to play professional sports, no? Especially one so aggressive."

I shrug. "It's fun," I say. "And it's important to me."

Her eyes thin. "Important in what way?"

I shift in my seat, feeling that heartburn—anxiety, still not used to calling it that—in my chest again.

"Well, you know, I grew up playing it. It's my career and all. It's part of who I am."

She nods, then looks out her window, her hands clasped in her lap. She sits back and adjusts her scarf.

I breathe in the scent of jasmine, and suddenly memories of sitting next to my dad in that hospital bed hit me hard. His breathing was shallow, and his pale, skinny frame still haunts me.

I grabbed his hand. 'Dad, you're a strong man. You can hang on a little longer.'

He put his other frail hand on mine. He was cold, and his touch sent chills all the way down to my toes.

'Son,' he said, raspy. 'Promise me something.'

I leaned in. I was all ugly crying at that point, trying not to squeeze his hand too hard. I couldn't admit it, but I knew it was over.

'Carry on my legacy,' he said. 'Our family name.'

I felt like I got punched in the gut. *Legacy*? I wanted to ask. But I knew exactly what he meant.

I nodded. 'Absolutely,' I said.

He died four hours later, peacefully in his sleep. The next days, all through the funerals and the mourning, guilt weighed down my conscience like an anchor.

Legacy, he said. *Family name.*

Grandchildren. He wanted grandchildren. Posterity.

And here I was, his only son, fucking around with other players at Miss U. Doing exactly the last thing he wanted his son to be doing.

I had tried dating women. I couldn't do it. My head and heart hurt too much when it came to being intimate. I then decided to do the only other thing that could make the guilt go away. He always wanted to coach in the NFO and eventually reach the championships, but the pancreatic cancer got in the way.

So, I vowed to win the Championship Game in his honor.

Neeti uses her feet to pull her over to a box of tissues nearby. She scooches back and hands the box to me. I take it and use some tissues to wipe the tears off my face, but it's no use. They just kept coming. I'm relieved to blow my stuffy nose, though.

"Sorry," I say, wiping my eyes again. "I don't usually do this." Even though I had just balled my eyes in front of Michael only a couple days ago.

"It's good to let it out," she says. "Is there anything you'd like to share?"

I think back on what my dad said to me, what I promised in return. And what I've done all these years to compensate for failing to keep up that original promise.

"I do," I say. "Do we have time?"

She glances at the clock, then nods. "Tell me anything you'd like. I'm here to listen."

Chapter 19

Michael Cunningham

I SLAM MY FIST against my desk in my home office. "No," I mutter under my breath. "No, no, no, no, no."

I pause my Joe Abercrombie audiobook and read the email for the third time, still sweaty from my work out. I message a fellow content writer on Teams. "Did you get the same email I just did?" I send.

He replies immediately. "Yep. They're tossing us in the garbage. I knew this was coming."

"No," I moan one last time out loud. I check my email again, hoping it's somehow disappeared. But it hasn't. It just sits there, laughing at me.

I've been laid off, and my last official day is next Friday. I get a month of severance pay, but that's it. Then I'm on my own.

I stand up and collapse onto my bed, not caring that I'm soaking it with sweat. And I lay there for God knows how long.

This week had gone so well.

Instead of worrying about what Kyle's doing now that he's come out, or worrying about whoever David is fucking, I decided to take my sponsor's advice. I've been taking time for myself.

I took myself out to dinner. I went on a hike. I went to see a movie by myself. And no matter how much I've been tempted, I haven't followed up with Kyle about his coming out. I don't want to add extra stress to his life, and I don't want to feel clingy either. Besides, he and I are still having our normal meetup tomorrow.

But starting next Friday, a week from today, I won't have a job. I have my OnlyFans to supplement my income, but that isn't enough to fully support me. And I promised Kyle I wouldn't post again, for at least this week. I want to keep that promise.

How am I going to pay rent? The last thing I want to do is move back in with my parents in Minnesota. They would allow it, but I'd have to live a half-life, unable to date any guys or talk about my sexuality. So much for unconditional parental love. I wonder if Kyle could relate.

I lift myself off my bed and slump to my computer. "Is it because of AI?" I send to my coworker. "Don't need us writers anymore?"

"That might be what they say," he says. "But corporations are always looking for excuses to lay people off. I think is a long time coming."

I wipe my face and collapse my hand into my arms.

Now I have to look for a new job. How the hell am I supposed to write in the meantime? It took me four months of straight hunting to find this job, and that's when I was doing it fulltime. I couldn't write at all during this period. This couldn't have happened at a worse time. I was so hitting my stride with my novel. I wish, more than anything, that my writing could be my day job. I don't know if my soul can take another corporate position.

Eventually, after God knows how long, I lift my head and look out the window. The sun is shining, of course, as if nature is completely indifferent to my situation. Which, like, of course it is. But really, why does it always rain when I *don't* want it to, and why is it sunny now that I couldn't be more miserable?

While I've been whining to myself, I've received four emails. I guess they're having me work up until they nix me. Figures.

I eventually, I sit myself up and stare at my screen. If I want to find another job, I gotta start looking as soon as possible. But I still have to work this job now.

"Just for today," I say out loud, parroting what I've heard in Al-Anon meetings. "I can get my work done."

Before I check my emails, I join a random Al-Anon zoom meeting on my phone. And then I get to work. The entire day, I answer emails and do my writing, all while listening to others share their experiences. It strengthens me, puts it all into perspective. At least I'm not the only one suffering, and there's light at the far end of this tunnel. It just sucks going through it. I'm grateful to have this community as a resource, but I'd still like to be a greater part of the bookish community, one where I can bond, read works by, and share work with other book lovers. That sense of home I found in college can't be beat.

At lunch, I decide to continue on with my Joe Abercrombie audiobook while I eat. *Best Served Cold* is much more compelling than I thought it would be and just as good as the *First Law* trilogy. Hearing about all the shit that Monza is going through, comparing it to Logan Nine-Fingers, I get an idea for a romantasy: two knights in a disgraced retinue who fall in love and want to keep their fellow soldiers safe from bandits, other retinues, and the magical wild. Sort of inspiration from Brandon Sanderson as well. I *loved* reading the *Stormlight Archive*. I consumed those 6,000 pages like it was nothing. Even if this ambiguous relationship with Kyle Weaver goes nowhere, at least he challenged me to read outside my comfort zone. Just as he said, fantasy is inspiring.

But it's not something *I* can write. That's more for the straight men. Besides, I have the contemporary romance I'm writing, one that I'll be struggling to finish as I descend into unemployment. Even if I could write the fantasy, I wouldn't have the time to do it.

After eating and a little reading, I get back to work. During a lull in my day, I start looking at other content writing jobs, but the sheer idea of updating my resume, writing cover letters, and putting myself out there quite literally makes me nauseous. So I let myself wait until Monday.

By the time the workday ends and it's time to go to book club, I couldn't be more relieved. This week, we read Rachel Gillig's *The Knight and the Moth*. I loved the duology she debuted with, and this one was just as good. I love her writing for the same reason I like Joe Abercrombie: when characters encounter the dark, gritty, and hopeless, we get to see who they really are. And often, they are better than we would think.

Buoyed after a lively discussion with who I like to call my book club girlies, I make my way over to the coffee shop we use as our light night meet up. I was maybe a little too enthusiastic tonight in my comments, a little manic over the loss of my job, but nobody made me feel unwelcome. In fact, romance book club is my favorite place to be these days. A couple women after even approached me and recommended some places to apply.

But by the time I see Skye and Amani, I'm happy that I can just speak with no filter.

"You guys are not going to believe the shit I went through today," I say.

When I'm done with my tirade, my mind clears enough for me to realize that Skye brought a friend.

"I'm so sorry," I say, reaching out my hand. "I'm Michael."

"Josue," he says. "And I don't blame you. I'd be just as pissed if I was laid off with a week's notice."

"Right? God."

Skye laughs. "Josue's a writer, too."

"I write fantasy," he says. "I heard about your group from Skye. I know you all write romance, so I hope that I'm not cramping your style."

My stomach tugs when he mentions fantasy, but I'm not sure why. "Not a problem," I say. "I'm actually a big fan."

"Don't see how you couldn't be," he says.

We all find a table and sit down. Skye and Josue get up to grab a drink.

"I'm really sorry to hear about your job," Amani says. "Let me know how I can help. I'll see if my company is looking for content writers."

I sigh. "There were so few positions today that I could see," I say. "I doubt it."

"Well I'll check anyways," she says. "Are there more positions you could look for?"

I pause. "I don't know. I hate corporate life so much I couldn't imagine trying to pivot into something else."

"Maybe you don't go corporate then," she says. "Maybe you could work retail. Something mindless so you can work on your writing when you're off the clock."

Upon hearing the word 'retail,' I immediately think of Ruckers. Though I'm not sure why. I've never seen that the bookstore is hiring, and they have so many positions filled by enthusiastic people that I doubt they'd have room for me. Plus, I'd like a job where I can work from home and potentially write while I have down time.

"I'll think about it," I say.

Skye and Josue return, and she hands me a tall cup. "Decaf mocha for you."

"Awh," I say. "You didn't have to."

"You'll be unemployed soon," she says. "It's the least I could do."

I can't help but laugh. "How thoughtful."

And then we jump into our shares. Skye shares a brief excerpt of her romance when her two characters finally realize they love one another, and there's a cool magical realism element she's infusing into the story that allows us to look at the character's past and present at the same time. Amani's agent liked her idea, so she brought in the first five pages of her new dark lesbian romantasy, and it's fantastic. Josue has this really interesting fantasy heist idea that he's outlining right now, and I'm excited just listening to it.

We take a brief break, and I pull out my phone. All this fantasy reading and discussion has me excited to talk to him. Without thinking twice, I type out a message. "Hey, been reading some great stuff this week. Excited to talk fantasy with you. Are we still on for tomorrow?" And then I hit send. Amani then asks me a specific question about her writing, and I completely forget about the text.

And once everyone's back, it's my turn to share. I look down at my excerpt, and I can't hold back my frown.

I love contemporary romance, or at least I always have. But I just don't feel as excited about my original novel as I used to. I know I said that I would query this book, and that if it didn't get any traction, I would give up.

But I don't know if I feel that way anymore. At first, editing the novel was exciting, but now it just feels like monotonous drudgery. I know that editing is hard, but is it supposed to be *this* hard? Like 'bang your head against the desk hard'? I don't want to get 'grass is greener on the other side' syndrome, where the next project always looks better than my current one, but something feels off here.

"Whatcha got for us today?" Skye asks.

I sigh. "You know, I've been editing my novel, but I also had this really cool romantasy idea."

"What is it?" Amani asks. "I didn't know you were into writing fantasy."

"I didn't either," I admit. "But I want to give it a try."

"Well tell us," Skye says. "You've heard enough from us already."

I take a deep breath. "Alright," I say. And then I lay it all out. I talk about the two knights, how the retinue they belong to uses a specific magic practice that has now been outlawed as a result of a revolution. "So now they're all criminals," I continue. "But what else are they supposed to do? Their options are to turn themselves in for execution or fight back and become the barbarians they are painted out to be.

"Uhh," Josue says. "That's fucking rad."

I catch my breath. "You think so?"

Amani gives me that dead serious look she always does. "Really," she says. "And listen to yourself. I've never seen you so animated about an idea."

I look back, realizing how I was talking so excitedly that I wasn't stopping to breathe.

"I think you should write it," Skye says. "Give your current book a break. Start this one. If it's right, you can go back to it."

My phone vibrates in my pocket, and my stomach leaps, remembering the text I sent to Kyle. I wonder what he'll think of this new idea. I can't wait to tell him.

But then dread pools in my chest at the thought setting my contemporary romance down. "What if this is just a shiny object? What if I'm just not disciplined and this is a way to distract myself?"

Skye shrugs. "Then you can deal with that realization when it comes. But if you feel strongly about this, I don't think you should hold yourself back."

The dread in my chest turns to excitement. She's right.

"Then next week, expect to see my new story."

Amani smiles. "Can't wait."

As we wrap up, my feelings are all over the place. I'm most excited about embarking on this new romantasy journey. I can't wait to see what it's like to explore love in a fantasy world. But in a week, I won't have a job. And in a month, I won't have an income. If I want to resolve this, I have to start working as soon as possible. Which means no writing at all.

I pull my phone out, eager to see what Kyle said. Maybe he'll have some advice. Hell, he might even have ideas about where I could work. He's so confident, so talking to him always makes me feel a little more sure of myself.

When I check my messages, I expect to see his name. But instead, it's just a random promotional from a bakery I became a member of a couple months back. There's no response from Kyle. Nervous, I open up our messages and see that he still hasn't read it.

"That's okay," I say quietly to myself. "He's probably busy."

But as I make my way home, my mind goes to the darkest places. What if he's gonna ghost me? I can't name how many times it was going well with a guy and then I never heard from him again. Or worse: what if he's fucking someone else?

The image makes me queasy. I told myself I could never catch feelings for him because he is straight and therefore emotionally unavailable to be my partner. And this helped. It was like a wall between us. But now that he theoretically can be there for me—the facts that he *just* came out and is part of the NFO notwithstanding—the idea of him with somebody else ignites primal jealousy inside me. I can feel it stirring in my gut.

I check my phone one more time when I get home. Still nothing.

"Please," I say to the screen. "Don't be like all the others."

But as I get ready for bed, I prepare myself for the worst.

Chapter 20

Michael Cunningham

I CHECK MY PHONE first thing in the morning for a text from Kyle.

Still nothing.

My stomach in knots, I decide the best thing to calm my frayed nerves is a solid workout. Without even sleeping in, I throw on some scrappy clothes and head straight to the gym.

When I get there, I claim a bench press and get myself set up. I'm not usually here this early, so I notice some faces here I haven't seen before. There are a couple guys I've seen around the gay district, and there's even some from the rugby team. Luckily no one I feel obligated enough to greet.

I start lifting, and it feels good, having my mind focused on exertion. But the second I'm resting, my mind races again. Has Kyle gone back into the closet? Erased our relationship from his mind so there's no reminders of who he is? Or is he going on a bender now, having as much gay sex as he can?

I pull out my phone and go to the most popular gay hookup app here in Portland. I hardly go on here anymore—too stressful to manage—but I want to see if Kyle is on here at all.

I scan through the squares. Couple of the guys closest to me I recognize here. I go down further to see guys further out toward the suburbs, where Kyle would be. I see torsos and some 'not gay but will fuck' type profiles, which is crazy that these exist in Portland, but no Kyle.

My timer goes off, and it's time to go for my bench press PR. I scroll back up on the top, and that's when a familiar face catches my eye.

David.

My stomach curdles, and I feel all the strength leave my body. Of course he's on here. Did he and Steven already break up? Or is Steven just unaware?

I delete the app and lay down on the bench. I wrap my hands around the barbell and sigh.

I've been through this. I don't need to be thrown off by David anymore. Just like my sponsor said, he has nothing to offer me. I'm better than this. I'm not settling for him or any other emotionally unavailable guy. And I'm not cursed to keep falling for them either.

I take a deep breath again, and then I push the barbell off its hooks. I hold 265 pounds above me, and then I lower it to my chest. I keep it there for just a moment, and then I use all my strength to thrust it back up.

I'm wonderful just the way I am. I have the beginnings of a wonderful writing group, and I'm finding so much joy in this weekly book club. I may not have a job, and I may not know about Kyle, but I don't need those things to be happy. That will all work itself out.

Before I know it, the barbell is back up in the air, and I set it back down in its hooks with more ease than I thought myself capable. I let out a satisfying breath.

I'm tempted to look at my phone to see if Kyle's texted, but I know I don't need to. Whatever he does, I'll be okay. I am enough without him.

I go through the rest of my workout, not even bothering to check my phone except to occasionally pause the audiobook I'm listening to. I'm on the third book of the *Wheel of Time*, and I'm loving it. Fantasy is starting to feel like my thing, even if I'm just reading it right now. I can't wait until I get to writing.

By the time I'm finished, I finally do check my messages. Still nothing. I guess I can assume that whatever Kyle's chosen, he doesn't want me in it.

When I get home, I go to my dresser to grab some clothes. I come across the T-shirt and sweatpants Kyle gave me when I got rained out the first day I met him. That was crazy—showing up at the home of the Sexiest Man Alive. And then getting to know him. Flirting with him. *Kissing him.*

I shake my head and adjust my stance, already halfway hard. At the very least, I had a cool experience. Now that I'm not seeing him anymore, maybe I can finally tell Amani all that happened.

I close the drawer and spot next week's books on my dresser: a debut author who's coming to give her talk at Rucker's in a couple weeks.

Even though Kyle's ghosted me, he still did pay for this book. And I have no need for a second one. I may as well just go there today at our designated time and drop it off. Along with his clothes. It was fun while it lasted, but I don't want any reminders of him. It's all too bizarre to hold on to.

By the time I shower and eat breakfast, it's time for me to meet Kyle. If our meetups are still happening. I'll just set the stuff on his doorstep and be out of his hair. Then I can finally focus on myself: finding a job, writing my new novel, and hopefully getting another guy who is actually emotionally available. I'm done chasing guys who don't want me back.

On the way there, I take the time to drive slowly through his neighborhood, admiring all these houses one last time. These are definitely sights I'm going to miss.

When I pull into driveway, there's a pristine Cadillac sitting squarely in the middle. The garage door is open and empty, so it must be Kyle's. I've just never seen his car before.

Or it could be his date's, either a guy or girl. My stomach rolls at the thought.

"It's okay, Michael," I say out loud. "Kyle isn't yours, and you aren't his."

Sheepishly, I park to the side, out of the Cadillac's way—which I can do because his driveway is big enough—and get out of the car, his clothes and book in tow.

That's when Kyle's front door opens, and my heart skips a beat. This could be some other guy—or girl. Or Kyle himself.

I want to run and hide, but there's nowhere for me to go. I'm standing right in the center of his driveway.

Kyle steps out of his front door and shuts it behind him, and my knees go weak. He's wearing a black suit with the most crisp tie I've ever seen, a deep blue color that somehow makes his black beard and hair pop.

He looks at me, and I want to melt into the driveway. He smiles.

"You're all dressed up," I say. I don't know what the hell else I can say.

Without a word, he walks around the Cadillac. He opens the passenger door, then stands by it. Waiting.

"What?" I ask.

He gestures to the door. "Get in."

Something pinches in my chest. "Why?" I ask. "What's going on?"

He puts his hands behind his back and looks at me with the smile that crinkles his eyes. "I'm taking you on a date." He winks at me, and then all the lies I've told myself today become alarmingly clear.

Kyle's wanted me this whole time.

Chapter 21

Michael Cunningham

Kyle just stands there, that goofy, pants-dropping grin on his face. Then he gets a little more somber. "What's wrong?"

I realize I'm just standing there, frozen stiff. I haven't moved a muscle. I would normally want to get in the car with him. But I'm so confused.

"I didn't hear from you," I say. "I thought..."

He furrows his brows, then raises then in recognition. "Oh, my bad, Michael. I saw your text and didn't think to respond. I thought it was given you were coming over."

My stomach lifts. I overthought everything. Kyle was expecting me this whole time. But what does that mean about how he feels about his sexuality?

Kyle taps his foot patiently. "If you don't want to go, I won't make you."

I force myself to step forward, still nervous that he could reject me at any moment. "I want to go," I say.

"Good," he says, putting one of his hands in his pocket, which stretches the fabric around the side of his leg and shows just how muscular his thighs are. Just the sight of him gives my stomach the flutters.

I set the book and his clothes inside my own car and then rush to get inside Kyle's car, and the moment he shuts the door, all my thoughts race up to me.

Kyle Weaver, *THE* Kyle Weaver is taking me out. *On a date.* And how could I fucking forget that our lips touched? We kissed for Christ's sake. Did I enter the Twilight Zone?

He opens his door and sits down, and sitting this close to him, I'm overwhelmed by how much of a man he really is. His smell lingers over to me—earthly cologne with a hint of sweat—which tells me that he's a little nervous. For me, though?

Oh my god. He *has* been watching my videos for probably years now. If I had known that he was... I probably would have made all my videos especially for him.

"I'm taking you to one of my favorite places," Kyle says as we pull out of his driveway. He puts his hand on the back of my seat, and I just about melt into the leather. He drives in that confident, self-assured, and lazy way that men drive, keeping one hand on the wheel and taking cautious but modest glances to make sure he's safe. Our eyes catch just as he turns back to face the front.

"Awesome," I say, warmth building in my chest.

As we drive, I have a million questions. But I don't know which are appropriate to ask. He's one of best football players on one of the best teams ever. He can't just come out. I don't think I've ever heard of any professional sports player come out, let alone one that plays one of the most American sports ever.

And now I'm going on a date with him. I've said no emotionally unavailable men, but does this include Kyle now? Though he could be accepting his sexuality, how can I be sure that he's in a healthy enough place to be a good boyfriend? I'm tired of sex, of guys who just want something from me and then let me go once they have it, and then getting hurt in the process.

But here Kyle is, taking me out. He could have just invited me into his house, taken my clothes off, and fucked me right there. And considering he's my biggest fantasy, I don't know if I would have stopped him.

Yet here he is, dressed to the nines, taking me to one of his favorite restaurants. I glance down at my clothes and grimace. I'm wearing a gray workout shirt and bright pink shorts.

"Jeez," I say, glancing over at him then back down at my clothes. "If you're dressed that nice... I wish you told me. I could have worn something better."

Kyle leans back and puts his other hand on the steering wheel. "I guess I could have," he says. "Sorry about that. But there you don't need to worry. No one but our waiter will see us anyways."

I frown. Right, because Kyle taking me, a gay man, out on a date in public... that would surely mean outing himself. So that answers that. Yet he is taking me on a date, so he's had to come to some sort of acceptance about himself.

"So, what have you been up to this week?" I ask, after we reach the city. I'm curious. He went from crying on the couch about his sexuality to taking me on a date. There are some gay men who could never even dream of making that leap.

"I decided to get some help," he says. "I talked it out with a therapist."

I gawk. "After one therapy session, you felt confident enough with being gay that you asked me out?"

He winces slightly when I saw the word 'gay', and a pit forms in my stomach. But I ignore it.

"I didn't just meet with her once," he says. "I met with her several times—she happened to have a lot of openings that week."

"Wow," I say.

"And we got more meetings," he says, pulling onto a less busy street that I've never seen before. "We're gonna try to dig into my past."

"How do you feel?" I ask, looking up at the buildings. The facades have that old Western look, and something tells me that somebody without money like myself would never just find myself in a place like this.

He shrugs. "It feels shitty and great at the same time."

I reflect on my conversations with both Susan and my therapist. "You're right there."

He parks the car. "But enough talk. Let me take you inside."

The next moments are strange. He opens my door, and then a man dressed in a suit like Kyle's opens a nondescript door next to what looks like a fancy, New American restaurant. The man leads us into a dark hallway. Kyle's hand hovers just over my back, as if he wants to touch me but can't.

"Here's the private room for you and cousin," the man says, holding a door open.

Cousin? The pit forms again in my stomach, this time stronger. Kyle lets me walk inside the room first, and he follows. The man shuts the door, leaving us alone in a warm light. On the far end of the room, there's a fireplace going. There are several dim lanterns hanging from the ceiling, also candlelight, and there's one small table for two in the middle. Above the fireplace hangs a deer head, and I don't want to know if it's fake or real. The rest of the dark maroon walls are covered in landscape art. On the far wall, there's a small opening, I presume for the waiter to walk through. But besides them, we're completely alone.

Kyle grabs his napkin and sits down, covering his lap in white. He gestures to my seat and grabs his glass of water. "You wanna sit?"

After he called me cousin, I'm not sure. But I see no other option. I sit anyways.

"So it's true," I say. "You date your cousins in the South."

He chokes on his water and spits it back into his glass.

A waiter emerges from the curtain covering the opening in the wall. He's an older man, and he looks gay to me.

"Good to see you again, Kyle," he says.

Kyle brushes off some water from his tie with a napkin. "You too, Charles." After he cleans himself, he orders us some artichoke dip and drinks, and Charles disappears behind the curtain.

"I'm sorry," he concedes.

"Sorry about what?" I ask. "Lying to me that this is a date, or calling me your cousin?"

He grumbles and looks up imploringly. "This *is* a date," he says. "Can you just give me a break? I came out to you a week ago, and I barely did to myself before that. I'm not ready to tell the world."

"Then why do you wanna date?" I ask.

"'Cause—" he raises his fist to his mouth and seems to burp. He presses his hand to his chest, takes a breath, then relaxes his shoulders.

"Because I like you, okay? And it's not just because I've been watching your porn for three years."

"Oh man," I say under my breath. He's been watching me since I first started. "You like me?"

He scrunches his face and nods like it couldn't' be more obvious. "You're funny, and you're smart. And you're so driven. I've never met anyone who goes after their goals like you wanting to be an author. And it shows. Your writing has really improved. I read over your most recent draft."

I blush. "You really think this about me?"

He rolls his eyes, but he's smiling. "You want me to explain it all a second time? Because I can and will. You're a good guy, Michael."

Kyle quiets himself when the waiter arrives with our appetizer and drinks. After we order our entrees, I take some buttered bread and lather it with spinach-artichoke dip. I can't resist letting out a moan when I taste it.

"Good, huh?"

"This is the best dip I've ever had," I say.

"You ain't tried nothing yet," he says. "If you think this is good, I got a lot of places to take you."

I smile, but the pain in my stomach has risen to my chest. Of course, he's saying this now, but how many other places have discreet rooms like this? Where all Kyle has to say is that I'm his cousin or something so that nobody suspects?

"So tell me, Michael," he says, taking a sip of his whiskey on the rocks. "How's work been treating you?"

My stomach sinks to the ground. All this pomp had me briefly forget. "I was laid off," I say flatly.

He leans forward, his hairy brow forming a V. "Really? Are you okay?"

I shift in my seat, the concern on his face doing crazy thing to my stomach. "I have one more week of work, then a month of severance. After that I'm on my own."

He leans back and folds his arms, thinning his lips. His concentrated face is almost as handsome as his smile.

"And don't worry," I say. "I haven't made any more videos."

He lets out a heavy sigh. "Good," he says. "Thank you." His relief is palpable. I didn't know I mattered that much to him. "But I don't want you to go broke, and I don't want me to stop you from making money through your videos if they help."

"Well, they help, but I can't live off what I post," I say. I take a sip of my spritz, and I taste that nostalgia of staying home from school again, relaxing when I'm supposed to be working. And I've realized that this entire dinner has either been me skeptical of Kyle or talking about my shitty job that's about to end. If this is really a date like Kyle says it is, we should treat it as one.

"But enough of that," I say. "I'll figure it out. I have something else important to tell you."

He raises his brow, intrigued, as he takes a sip of his drink. This has only been his second sip, and the glass barely has a dent. I love that, at least so far, he doesn't seem to have a drinking problem. Unlike David.

I shrug, almost embarrassed. "I think I'm a fantasy writer now."

His face lights up. "No way. Did Brandon Sanderson finally get to you?"

I nod. "And not just him."

I list off all the fantasy books, explaining why I love each. And Kyle just stares at me, rapt. And when I tell him what I've been writing, he nods his head vigorously.

"Oh, yeah," he says. "That's a banger idea. Tell me what you have so far."

By the time our food arrives, Kyle and I are still talking so much about it that we barely dig into our food.

"Okay," he says. "Enough talking. Just for a minute though. We need to try our food."

I have half a whole chicken with rice pilaf, while Kyle got some gourmet steak burger.

"I would make fun of you for ordering off the kids' menu, but that's the best-looking burger I've ever seen. It looks better than what I got."

He starts cutting into it. "Then you gotta try it." He slices off a generous piece and puts it on a small plate, then slides the plate to me.

"Well with a piece that big, you need some of mine." I pull off the chicken wing and put some rice on a small plate and give it to him.

We both try each other's dish at the same time, before we even try our own.

"Oh my god," I say, setting down the other half of my piece of burger. "That's the juiciest burger I've ever tasted."

Kyle's silently chewing.

"Is it bad?" I ask.

He looks up at me, deadpan. "The only thing better is your idea."

I blush. "Oh shut up."

And he just smiles.

As we continue eating our own food this time, I realize that we haven't talked about Kyle at all.

"Let's talk about the elephant in the room," I say.

He looks up at me, almost worried.

"I mean that you're one of the top players out there," I say. "What's that like?"

He takes a big gulp of his water. "It's like any other celebrity gig," he says. "Except I get to play the sport I love."

"It hasn't gotten old?"

He furrows his brow and shakes his head. "Football never gets old. I love the rush, the strategy, the skill and endurance required. The camaraderie, how it brings everyone in the nation together. It's awesome." Then his face darkens, and he sighs. "But I might never play again."

I set down my fork and look at him. "What do you mean? Is this your last season or something? From what I know about football, you're like essential to the Tigers. And you're one of the best players the NFO has seen."

He laughs. "You would think so with how many touchdowns I've scored."

"Then what's the problem? If you want to play, what's stopping you?"

He sighs. "People are... talking. Don't know if you saw my press interview before the Championship Game."

I shake my head.

"Bless your heart," he says. "But let's just say that after that, people started to wonder which team I play for, if you catch my drift."

I don't. "You mean the Tigers?"

He blows a raspberry. "No. They're wondering if I'm gay."

My stomach sinks. He meant *that* team. Besides his therapist, I think I'm the only one who knows he's gay.

"My team's management says that if I don't find a girlfriend, I won't be able to play with them next year. And they're my only real shot at winning the Championship Game." He throws his napkin on the table and wipes his face with his hands. When he lowers them, his face looks haggard and worn, as if he's aged a year in this admission alone. "That's why I wanted to go to the book club in the first place. It was the plan I came up with my agent—to find a girl there." He chuckles to himself. "But with your help I got out of that."

My chest tightens. His plan is to find a girl—our weekly little one-on-one book club was his way out of this. But Kyle *is* gay, right? He admitted it to me. Or is he going back in the closet to preserve his career? If he's going back in the closet, then isn't this date a phenomenal mistake? Dread pools in my chest as the realization sinks in. I promised myself no emotionally unavailable men. But I may be sitting across from the most unavailable person in the country.

"So what are you going to do?" I ask. "I mean, me helping you dodge book club can only last so long."

He looks up at me, his shoulders sunken in defeat. "I don't know."

I don't know. Not 'I'm gonna find a girlfriend', but not 'I'm gonna come out' either. I sigh to myself. I was a fool to think any of this could go anywhere.

Before either of us can say anything else, Charles returns with our check. "Is there anything else I can get for you?"

Kyle looks at me, but I just look away. Kyle shakes his head.

"You ready to get going?" he asks once he's paid.

I shrug, unable to process the bomb that Kyle just decided to drop at the end of dinner. "Yeah, I think it's best that we go."

Chapter 22

Kyle Weaver

As we take the highway back to my place, the sun is setting. Oranges, pinks, reds, and purples dance across the sky. God, I love sunsets. I want to talk to Michael about what I'm seeing, but he's acting all depressed like Eeyore. He's just slouched in his seat, staring away from me like I'm the last person he'd like to see, giving me one-word answers.

"Are you upset?" I ask.

He straightens a bit, adjusting his hot pink shorts that make his legs look goddamn perfect. "No. Why?"

Finally, a two-word answer. "You've been acting all sad ever since I told you what management's making me do," I say. Making me find a girlfriend. Sheesh. My new therapist, Neeti, agreed that it's bullshit. Business, but bullshit all the same.

He doesn't answer. He's just playing with his fingers.

"Hey," I say. "I asked you a question."

His head whips toward me. "Is it not obvious?"

I get that anxious feeling in my chest. Neeti says this is normal. I just gotta breathe. "Obvious how?"

He scoffs. "You have to find a girlfriend to keeping playing for the Tigers," he says. "And you just took me on a date. Don't you see how those two things are at odds?"

I take another deep breath, the pain in my chest getting worse. "I told you I don't know what I'm doing."

"But you want to play football again next year, right?"

I tighten my grip around the steering wheel. I told Neeti, my therapist, everything—how my dad asked me to continue on the family name. How I compromised and decided to win the Championship Game instead. That was the only way I could think to honor him then, and that hasn't changed.

"I do," I say. "I made a promise."

He shakes his head and folds his arms, looking out the window again, his gaze as far away from me as possible. "Seems like you already made your decision."

I huff out a breath. "I haven't made it fully yet," I say. "Michael, I like you. I wanna keep seeing you. Isn't that enough?"

He lets out a sharp breath this time. "Okay, let's say we continue seeing each other. In secret like we just did. What happens when you decide you need a girlfriend so you can continue playing? What happens to us? To me?"

I release one hand off of the steering wheel and press my aching chest. I gotta keep remembering to breathe. Neeti said that the choice was mine, regardless of the pressure from outside. Regardless of Dad.

"I don't want to let you down," I say. "But this is all new to me."

"It's great that you came out," Michael says, wiping his face. "But I can't be a casualty of the process. I've been hurt enough."

I picture his douchebag ex and tighten my grip even harder around the wheel 'til my knuckles get white. "I won't treat you like him. I promise I'll be better."

He sighs. "I don't think that's a promise you can make."

The rest of the car ride home goes in silence. Because he's right. I can't promise him that I won't hurt him. And out of all my problems, I think that I hate that the most.

Storm clouds come out of nowhere, blocking the fading sunset and giving us a light drizzle. The patter on windshield begins to loosen my tightened chest.

When we make it to my house, I see Michael's dented up little Acura, and the pain returns to my chest. This might be the last day I see it in my driveway.

I park in the garage, and Michael can't get out fast enough.

"Careful," I say before he shuts the car door. "Don't want the rain to—"

But he slams it before I finish.

I get out, and he's walking to his car.

"Damn rain," I hear him mutter. It's coming down harder now.

I make my way to my front porch. "You can stay," I say. "Until it lets up. I know driving city traffic is bad when it's wet."

"I'll be fine," he grunts. He reaches his car and opens the door, but he's soaked now.

All the fantasies I've had of us—both in bed and in real life—flash before me. I never get that dark feeling around him, and I feel so seen by him. He's so kind. And now I feel like he's running away. Will I see him again?

"Michael," I say.

He hesitates before he gets in the car.

"Thank you for bringing me all the books, for showing me how inspiring the romance genre actually is," I say. I reflect on that Cat Sebastian book I read at the lesbian café. "Because it definitely has inspired me. No matter what I choose, I'll always be grateful for that."

He pauses, rain coming down hard now. His mullet is soaked to his neck, and water drips off his chin. He stands there leaning on his car door, still, and I can't read his face. For a moment, I think he might come to me.

But then he gets in his car and shuts the door.

My eyes get all hot as he starts his car. I make my way through my front door and slam it behind me. I prop myself up on my banister and hold my aching chest.

What kind of God is there that brings the man of my dreams to my doorstep and then has him go? Sure, I discovered part of my true self because of him, but is that it? Can't there be a little more?

Rain is falling hard now, and I'm tempted to text Michael, or even call him, to be safe. But I don't think I can do that anymore.

I swear under my breath and untie the noose of a tie around my neck. Some tears even stain my cheeks. I hate how damn much I'm crying these days. I throw the tie on the ground and keep myself held up by the banister, needing it more than ever to keep myself up. When I get my bearings, I sigh, and then I make my way upstairs.

There's a crash of thunder that almost sounds like a knock. I stop myself. That can't be...

I turn around and look at my door. Just out the side window, I can see a flash of bright pink, the same color as his shorts.

I race down the stairs and open my door.

And there he is.

Michael, completely drenched.

And he's holding a book and some of my old clothes in his hand.

I stare at him, my jaw heavy and hanging. "What are—" I don't even know what to ask.

"Sorry," he says, shrinking into himself like he always does.

"Don't say you're sorry," I say.

He wipes rain—or tears, I don't know—away from his eyes. "I thought about what you said, and—"

Lightning crashes, followed quickly by earthshattering thunder. A gust of wind blows rain onto the porch. Without thinking, I grab the handsome man on my porch and pull him into the house before he gets even more soaked.

I hold him his wet body against me, probably ruining my suit, but I couldn't give two shits. I slam the door with one hand, but I keep my other wrapped tight around him.

He gulps so loud I can hear it. "I—"

"Why did you come back?" I say, pulling away and looking into his hazel eyes. My lips are dangerously close to his.

He looks at my lips, giving me all the answer I need. But I wanna hear him say it.

"Tell me," I say so low it shakes us both. I rub my nose against his, and I feel him shiver, so I hold him tighter. I'm hardening down south, and I can feel he is too.

Good. After years of watching him, I might just get him to myself.

His lips pull away from mine slowly, and for a second, I panic. Does he want me to let go? Did he really just want to give me my book and then go?

"Because you're too much of a good guy to let go," he says. And then he presses his lips against mine, and my worries drip off me like rain.

Chapter 23

Michael Cunningham

I drink in Kyle like he's water.

I press my lips against his, and he cups the back of my head, and he kisses back with a force that tells me he's even hungrier for me than I'm thirsty for him.

After I set his things on a side table, I trail my hands up his belly to his wide, perfectly broad chest, and I fondle him through his shirt like I've fantasized doing for so many years. He recognizes what I'm doing and stops kissing me.

"Sorry," I say, pulling my hands away. "I—"

He presses a huge finger against my lip. "Shhh," he says. "No apologies."

Shivers run down my spine, and I'm tempted to suck his finger like I mean it. He steps back and starts to shimmy off his suit coat. And he's struggling.

"Your shoulders are just too wide," I say.

He smirks up at me as he gets one arm off. "Just means I look better in a suit," he says. "Wouldn't you agree?"

"I would," I say, blushing.

He throws the suit coat on the floor next to his discarded tie, and then he starts with his top button. Oh my god. I'm about to see Kyle Weaver shirtless. And this time it's on purpose.

"Wanna help?" he asks.

I step forward and start on his bottom button. My knuckles graze the hardness in his pants, and I almost lose my breath. He's *big*.

He manages to get to the next button, but I'm still struggling with my first.

"Sorry," I say. "Hands are wet and—"

He grabs my hand. "What did I say?"

My mouth goes dry. "No apologies."

"Right," he says. He looks down at his shirt and shrugs. "I don't need this shirt anyways."

He grabs an opening with his pointer and middle fingers and then rips his shirt open. Fabric tears, and buttons fly everywhere, leaving his hairy, perfectly sculpted dadbod out for me to see.

I must be gawking because Kyle's giving me that smug look, the same one he gave the first time I saw him shirtless.

"Oh, come here," I say as I pull him toward me.

My hands run along his bare torso as we kiss, feeling every hair, every muscle, every crevice. I cup his huge pecs, his nipples like warm chocolate chips in my palms. I love exploring his body like this. It feels like I'm a kid at a sandbox enjoying the way the texture of the sand flows through my fingertips. I don't want this to end.

He pulls away and gestures with his head to the stairs.

My eyes widen. "Really?" I ask. *Am I about to have sex with Kyle Weaver?*

"Yes, really," he says, almost saying it like Amani does when she's dead serious.

"I'm STD-free," I say. "No HIV either. You must be wondering since, well, you know."

"And I haven't had sex in ages. So we're good there."

Good. Because the thought of Kyle's seed inside me makes my hole twitch.

He grabs my hand and pulls me up the stairs, down a long hallway, and into his bedroom. I pause when we reach it, taking it all in. A king-size bed sits in the middle of the room, illuminated by two dim lights on either side of the bed. There are two tall windows beyond the lights, their curtains slightly parted. Outside, rain is still falling, the sun nearly set beyond the dark clouds, bathing the room in a navy glow. The bed is neatly made, and the floor is spotless. I'm surprised how well-kept his room is. But when the AC blasts me, I realize how cold I am.

"You're shivering," Kyle says, putting his hand on my arm.

"I was just out in the rain, so yeah," I say, my arms crossed against my wet body.

I had stood with my car door open in the soaking rain, thinking about what Kyle said. He might not know what he's going to decide to do about his sexuality, but I can't just let him go. Though there is a possibility he won't be available in the future, he's emotionally available to me right now. And that's what matters. And I like him too. I want to give this a chance. If there's a fallout, we can deal with it later.

"My bathroom's over here," he says, turning on the light. "You can take a shower."

I walk over to the pristinely tiled and well-lit bathroom that probably costs more than my yearly salary. Or what my salary used to be. In a week, I won't have my fucking job.

"Thanks," I say, making my way inside.

He smiles and kisses me. "I want to keep doing this," he says, planting another kiss on my nose. "But I don't want you to freeze."

"Me too," I say. "I'll be quick."

I look at the shower. It has a nozzle that I can use to clean myself with—prepare myself for some fun. If Kyle really means it.

I turn to him. "Weird question—do you have lube?"

He furrows his brow at me. "Why would that be weird?" He opens his nightstand drawer and there's a full bottle of silicon lube. "I bought it just for this."

I laugh. "You knew this would happen?"

"I've watched your porn for years," he says, laying back in the bed, showing up his tree-trunk arms. "I had my hopes high for this."

I smirk. "Cocky. Don't ruin your chances when you're so close."

"Oh," he says, sitting up. "Are you saying you don't want to do this?"

The worry on his face is so genuine that I'm tempted to abandon my shower and jump in bed with him right now. He may be forced to decide between his sexuality and his career, but I can tell he meant every word back there. He really does like me. He does want to give this a real try.

"I'm joking," I say. "Just give me some time to thaw."

He relaxes, laying back down. "Don't scare me like that," he tries to say playfully, but it comes out more serious than not.

"I'll be quick," I say. "Don't worry."

I hop in the shower, welcoming the steamy warmth. He has one of those flat-heads with like a hundred little spouts that covers me in water, and somehow, the water pressure is still fantastic. I guess this is what an NFO salary pays for.

As I warm up and clean myself, the situation hits me. I'm about to have sex with Kyle fucking Weaver. My dick hardens as I play through all the fantastic scenarios I've put together while thinking of Kyle. And since he's watched my videos, I know he's fantasized about me, wishing he could have done to me what so many others have. It's also been a couple days since I've gotten off, so my sex drive is high.

My entire torso lights up with excitement. I have an opportunity here. Maybe having sex will help him come to a decision. If I show him just how good our sex can be, maybe he'll see no other option worth taking besides coming out.

I dry off, then wrap the towel around my waist, my resolve fully strengthened. I'm going to bring Kyle Weaver to the altar of my body and give him pleasure so exquisite that he'll have no choice but to continue wanting me.

Chapter 24

Kyle Weaver

WHEN MICHAEL OPENS MY bathroom door, he's wearing one of my navy towels around his waist, his torso completely bare. His dark body hair creates a thick line from his waist to his belly button, from there to his chest and then flared out onto his pecs. He's got a toned belly with some muscle lines, and I just want to squeeze him and press my face into him, getting his natural scent all over me.

He approaches the bed, and neither of us say a word. He leans against it but doesn't get any closer.

I raise my hand to stroke just above his waist. "Are you sure you still want to do this?"

He looks over me. I'm shirtless, but I still have my pants on. I wanted Michael to take them off.

He meets my eyes and nods.

"Good. And Michael? I'm glad you came back."

With that, he leans down into the bed and kisses me on the forehead, then my nose. He exhales a warm breath over to my ear, and I have to hold myself from physically convulsing.

"I came back because I think I trust you," he whispers into my ear. "I want to give us a try." He pulls away and strokes my hair. "Not just this," he says, gesturing to the bed. "But us. Dating. A relationship."

I reach my thumb up and stroke is beard. "That's what I want too. And thank you."

"For what?" he asks.

I clear my throat. "For not taking advantage of me last week. I didn't realize it, but I wasn't ready to do anything then. It's very big of you to wait for me."

He kisses me gently on the lips. "It's what you deserve," he says.

Deserve. My hand strokes his hairy chest, the other one his beard. I deserve this. Love. Intimacy. I don't need to jump through hoops to make it happen with a woman. I can get it right now. With a beautiful and kind man.

And that's when he falls into me, but I can't tell who went first: me pulling him down or him falling into me. But it doesn't matter. I wrap my arms around his strong back and squeeze him against me, our lips melting together. He straddles me, loosening the towel around his waist.

I buck up into him, and his ass presses down against my already rock-hard cock. God, I can't wait to be in between those cheeks. I've seen others grab hold of them while they ride him, but I can't wait to feel them for myself.

I reach down to his waist to pull off his towel. "May I?" I ask.

But then he grabs both of my wrists and pins them above my head.

I look at him, bug-eyed, almost startled. He's got some strength in him—not more than me, of course. But still.

He settles himself onto my dick, and I can't help but groan. I need my pants off now.

"There we go," he says. "You've wanted this for a while, haven't you?"

I nod, and I try to hold it back, but a whimper comes out. He rubs himself against me again, and I swear I'm going cross-eyed.

"I'll tell you what's going to happen," he says, lowering one hand to stroke my hair. His voice is hypnotically low. The only time I've heard him talk this way in his videos is when he takes full control.

"You're gonna fuck me, and then you're gonna give me a load I know you've been saving just for me," he says. "Understood?"

I nod, warm chills going up and down my body. My stomach is fluttering like it has a horde of butterflies inside. How does he know that I've dreamed about this moment for years?

"And then you're getting me off," I say.

"God, yes," I say. I try to wiggle my arms free, but he's got his whole weight pressed down on them. I could resist, but I don't want to hurt him.

He lets my hands go, trailing his finger down my arms. He takes his time when he reaches my chest, my stomach. And when I hear the clink of my belt buckle, my throat goes dry.

He rubs his ginger-bearded face against my cock still in my pants like a dog, and I nearly yip like one. Then he pulls open my pants, revealing my spire of pleasure to the room. There's a shine of precum off the top, reflected by my lamps, and Michael marvels at it.

"God, that's bigger than I'm used to," he says, licking his lips. "Fucking pipe for a dick. It's more perfect than I imagined."

"Show me you really mean it," I mutter.

And Lord almighty does he.

And he doesn't just put his mouth around it and suck it mindlessly. He takes his precious time, as if I'm the sweetest thing he's ever tasted. He uses his whole tongue to lick it up and down. He spits on it, both of us watching his saliva drip down, and then he laps it up as if it's been made divine for having touched my dick. Tired of my pants, he yanks them off and tosses them aside. Then he wraps his hand around the base, engulfs the top half with his beautiful face, and gets to sucking.

I swear I see stars as he's going. I've never felt anything like this, not from any woman or guy from Miss U. And it's not because women can't do something like this. I think it's because he's Michael, and I'm Kyle, and this is what we're meant to be doing. Or something. I don't know. I'm not thinking straight because all the blood from my brain has gone straight to my dick. I glance down at him, and his towel's fallen off. His gorgeous ass sticks into the air, begging for me

.

"My god," I say, marveling at his ass, the first time I've seen it in the flesh. "You have me so close."

He releases his grip on me and gently laps at it with his tongue. "We can't have that, can we?"

He crawls up me. To kiss, I presume. Part of me hesitates. He was just sucking my dick. But by the time he reaches me, pressing his lips to mine is all I want. We sloppily kiss each other, almost like I'm trying to taste myself on his tongue. God, I must be a pervert or something. Because this is so fucking hot.

"The lube?" He asks.

I nod and reach over to the dresser. I grab it with one hand, but he's lifted my other arm into the air, revealing my sweaty, hairy pit to the room.

And then he presses his face into it.

I grab his mullet and pull him away. "I haven't showered since this morning," I say. "I stink."

He rolls his eyes. "That's the point, Kyle." He removes my hand from his hair. "I want to smell *you*. Not your deodorant or your cologne. You."

He presses his nose into my pit and takes the biggest whiff. And then he exhales, moaning in ecstasy.

My dick, somehow, gets harder. This is supposed to be weird. But Goddamn. I fucking love it.

Michael rubs his face into my pits, sniffing and licking like he's been in a desert all day and I'm his water. Watching him, I use one hand to get some lube onto my hands and apply it to my dick. Michael notices what I'm doing, then reaches over to squeeze lube onto my hand. Then he pulls my hand past my dick right to his ass.

The ass I've been wanting for years.

"This is what you want?" I ask, rubbing some of the lube on the surface of his hole.

He bucks and nods vigorously, still rubbing his face into my pit.

Mimicking what I've seen in porn before and my memories of Jeremy, I stick a finger inside. He stops his licking and moans audibly.

But I can't help but frown. "I didn't say you to stop," I say.

"Sorry," he says, getting back to my armpit, more vigorous than ever. It's like I'm his air and he can't breathe enough of me in.

I grab him by his mullet and pull him away from my armpit. "What did I say about apologies?"

He's about to say sorry again, but he stops himself, staring at me imploringly.

I stare at his beautiful face, his beard disheveled from rubbing himself against me for so long. "I know you said you were in charge," I say. "But I think the tables have turned to me this time."

I press into his asshole deeper, and he tries to buck, but I hold his hair to keep him in place.

"Yes, sir," he says, and that sends an electrical current down my spine.

"Keep calling me sir," I say gruffly.

He nods as much as he can with me holding him. "Yes, sir."

"Good boy," I say, parroting what I've heard in his videos before. I don't know what else to call him, but it feels right. And clearly, Michael loves it too. Because his back is arched higher than before, and he's pushing himself back into my finger.

"Get back to it," I command. And he goes back to sniffing and licking my armpit, moaning in delight.

Once I think he's got enough lube on him, I apply some more to my dick. And that's when I think I'm ready.

"I want you to sit on it," I say.

With gusto, he removes himself from my pit and straddles me. Then without my help, he guides my dick to his hole.

"You sure you—"

"Are you ready—"

With both interrupt each other, then laugh.

"Yes, I want this," I say. "Do you still?"

"Yes," he says, nodding.

He guides my shaft to his hole, then slides the tip in. Pleasure rings throughout my body.

"God almighty," I say, as his hole slowly engulfs my dick. "You feel—Christ that's good."

He grimaces for a moment, taking my girth, then relaxes and smirks. "Looks like the tables have turned again."

I let out a shaky laugh, the tightness of his hole making me dizzy. "That's what you think—gnah,"

He lifts himself up, then presses himself down as deep as he can. He stretches upward like a cat, and both of us moan in pleasure as my dick reaches the deepest part of him.

He looks down, and I stare up at him, defeated.

"Yeah," I admit. "You've got me beat."

He grabs both of my pecs like handles. "Doesn't surprise me."

I furrow my brow. "Surprise? Ahhhh."

He cuts me off with another buck of his ass, but I can't complain.

"Let me take it from here," he says.

And I couldn't even protest if I wanted.

Michael raises his ass up and down, using my chest as his handles. My pleasure is so great I have to clench my fists to keep myself from cumming. I can't let myself go that fast.

He gazes deep into my eyes, and I surprise myself by staring right back. In the past, I've usually looked away or had my eyes shut during sex, especially with women. I needed to conjure my own fantasies to get off.

But I don't even think I'm blinking. There's not a drop of Michael I want to miss.

He lowers his face to me, still fucking himself with my dick. When he's just above my face, we both hit an angle that makes pleasure shoot through my body like lightning.

"Oh my god," I say, wrapping my arms around his shoulders. I pull him down onto me, adding to his own force. "Don't you stop."

He smiles and presses his lips against mine. Then he doubles his speed, and I nearly lose my breath.

"I'm gonna suck that load right out of you, Kyle Weaver," he rasps out.

"Oh man," I say, euphoric heat blazing in my groin. "I can't hold it back."

He kisses me deep, his tongue searching my mouth.

And then I explode into him, practically wailing into his mouth. And the climax itself feels like an eternity. I shake, my fingers digging into his shoulders, pressing him as far down onto me as I can. I want to make sure every bit of me is inside him.

He pulls away and wipes away some of my sweat-soaked hair off my forehead. I take a deep breath and take in all the musk in the room. Damn, we made the room stink.

Michael slides himself off and then burrows himself into my side. I wrap my arm around him and stroke his belly.

"I'll give you a little break," he says. "But it's my turn now."

I rub my tired eyes, feeling like I just had a brutal workout even though Michael did most of the work. He starts kissing my chest, then nuzzles my armpit again, making my dick jump.

"You're insatiable," I say, kissing his forehead. "Whore."

He pulls back, his face stoic.

"I'm sorry," I say. "It just came out. I—"

"Sh," he says, pressing his finger to my lips. "No apologies. Remember?"

I chuckle, lowering his hand and kissing his knuckles.

"I'm a whore for you, Kyle."

I grin. "Prove it."

Chapter 25

Michael Cunningham

"Sit on my face."

Kyle looks at me like I said '*shit* on my face'. "What?"

"You heard me," I say, stroking his hairy belly.

"But I'll crush you."

"Again," I say. "*That's the point.*"

"But I stink."

"What?" I ask. "Are you one of those 'straight' guys who don't wipe?"

He scowls. "Who do you think I am? Of course I clean up. I'm a freak about that stuff."

I shrug. "Then what's the problem?"

He wipes the sweat off his neck. "I'm sweatier than I am after most practices," he says. "I'm not gonna smell like roses."

I almost swoon. "What part of 'that's the point' don't you understand?"

He rubs the bridge of his nose, and if it wasn't so dark, I could see his face going red.

"I won't pressure you," I say. "I can get off another way."

"No," he says. "I want to do it because you want to. But I just don't want to gross you out. Or scare you off."

Kyle always knows how to prick my chest. Everything he says and does makes me believe more and more that he wants a relationship with me. Why else would he care so much about keeping me around?

"I don't get it, anyways," he says.

I prop myself up on my elbow to see him better. "Don't get what?"

"Ass eating," he says, scratching his big thigh. He places his hand on my thigh, and the sheer size of it almost spans the biggest muscle of my body.

"What's there to get?"

He gently pulls on some of my hairs. Rain is still falling steadily outside, like an applause. "I don't know. It's really intimate. Getting up in somebody like that. I know your videos have a lot of it, but it's just like... 'hey, I'm up in the part of your body that's the grossest. And I like it'."

"Yeah, I get it," I say. "Like I said, we don't have to."

He tightens his grip around my thigh. I glance up at him, and his face has hardened. "I told you I want to do this."

I roll over, laying half my body on him. I kiss his nipple, then rest my head on his pec. "Then tell me what's holding you back."

He's silent.

"Is it that it's 'too gay' and doing it is like the last step to admitting it to yourself?"

His chest shakes with a short laugh. "I know I'm gay, Michael."

I gently nod, joy suffusing my body in the form of butterflies. I give his pec a gentle kiss. At the very least, he's not in denial. Which gives us a solid chance.

"You said earlier that you trusted me," he says. "Letting you inside me that way means that I would trust you."

My heart feels like it's coiling up in my chest. "Do you think you can't trust me?"

He looks me in the eye and strokes my drying hair. I practically rub into his touch like a cat being pet.

"I think I can," he says. "But I want to make sure."

My chest still coiled up, I hold my breath for his answer.

"I know my situation sucks," he says. "But if we're going to do this. Not just have sex but date. Get to know each other. Have a partnership. I want to give us—*you*—the chance we deserve. I don't know what I'm doing yet—if I'm coming out or sticking with football—but I won't give up on you just when it gets hard. I'll be with you until I absolutely cannot be, if we have to split at all." He sighs. "I need the same commitment from you."

I put my hand around him, pulling us closer together. He puts his hand on my shoulder, pulling lightly on some of the hairs there.

I can't deny it anymore. Kyle wants to be in a relationship. And he's going to try. To demand an answer about our future from him now would be unfair. And with how much I like him, it would be unfair to myself to say 'no' to this. I promised myself I wouldn't date emotionally unavailable men, but Kyle is being the most available he can possibly be. And that's enough.

I prop myself up higher so our faces are level, and my hand traces up his stomach, past his chest to cheek. I rub my thumb through his beard. I close the distance and plant a gentle kiss on his lips. And he physically shivers.

"As a pornstar I worried you'd be all physical," he says. "But you can make my whole body electric with just a kiss. That's magic."

"There's more to love than sex," I say, enjoying the smoothness of his beard.

He places the back of his hand on my chest and strokes my nipple with his knuckles, which feels almost as good as it is intimate.

"And there's more to this," he says, gesturing between us. "Than love. Meaning even with love we might not work out. But if it does, we'll need to be committed to each other. Supportive. Understanding. Monogamous—old-fashioned, I know."

I smile. "It's what I prefer, too," I say. "I can give up OnlyFans for you."

He kisses my forehead. "Thank you," he says earnestly. "The thought of you with someone else feels like someone is pouring lava on my chest."

"Ouch," I say, kissing his cheek. "I don't want that."

He sighs contentedly. "So what do you say?"

I trace my hand down his belly, twirling a patch of long hair around my finger.

Every relationship has risks. Any relationship can go south. I mean, look at me and David. I thought he was my soulmate, and he nearly tore me to pieces.

The risk in this relationship with Kyle is no different. He may decide to continue on with his football career. Or he may decide to stay with me. It's fifty-fifty, at the end of the day. Those aren't the best odds, but Kyle Weaver is so much more than a hot guy or nice philanthropist. He's a sweet, thoughtful man who loves to read and is willing to love what I read. He's willing to have hard conversations, and he's willing to treat me far better than any other guy I've ever dated. And he's got a killer dick.

"Let's do it," I say.

Kyle turns and reaches his arm over me. I fall into the bed, and before I know it, he has his entire weight on me, his lips pressed against mine. And I'm in heaven.

He slowly stops, then rolls over onto my side, his arms still wrapped around me. Like a giant teddy bear.

Contended, I close my eyes, ready to...

"Hold on," he says.

I shoot my eyes open. "What's wrong?"

"We still gotta get you off," he says.

A smile widens on my face, and my stomach flutters from excitement. "You're right," I say. "Are you sure you still want to do it?"

"Now that we trust each other, hell yeah," he says. "Only think I've had my ass eaten once or twice though."

I widen my eyes. "I'm not the first? Damn."

"Yeah, it was another player in college," he says. "But if you eat ass as good as you suck dick, there's no competition."

I lick my lips. "Well let's show you how good I am."

He grins, sitting up. "How do you want me?"

I lay down flat on the bed, then tap my shoulders. "Face that way," I say pointing toward his bedroom door. "And don't literally crush me. But be generous."

He laughs, and this time I can see his blush. "Alright." He stretches one leg over me, giving me a perfect view of his hairy ass. One of his ass cheeks is bigger than my head alone, and his thighs are even thicker. Then he lowers himself onto me.

In between his cheeks, I inhale deeply. "Oh my god."

He pauses. "Are you good?"

"Now I'm literally in heaven," I say. I take another deep breath, taking in his musk, sending chills down my spine. I used to be ashamed of how much I like 'dirty' smells, like ass or armpit. And then I got over myself. Better to spend a life happy than ashamed for no reason. Man smell—especially this man's smell—arouses me more than anything else.

"You really like that," he says, relaxing onto my face. "Don't smell too bad?"

I sniff, then pull away. "It literally couldn't smell better."

He chuckles. "Good boy."

"Yes," I nearly moan. "Do that."

"What?" He asks. "Treat you like the little slut you are?"

"Yes," I say, and I bury myself into his hairy ass. I stick my tongue out, lapping up his perfect manhole. To think this asshole has run across dozens of football fields. And I'm one of the two who's been able to give it the attention it deserves.

"That's right," he says, his huge back arched. "Show me how much you love it, whore."

I lick harder, faster, wanting to clean up all the sweat he worked up fucking me. My dick throbs, and I'm not even touching it.

He leans back, and I look up his glorious, hairy back.

I pull my mouth free—or as free as I can make it. "Can you flex your arms for me?"

"You mean like this?" He flexes his arms in an L-shape, showing up his thick trunks of arms. His back flexes with it, and I swear he is the finest specimen of man to ever exist.

'Yes, amazing' are the only words I can utter.

"You are my little slut," he says. "All mine."

I tongue him deep, in gratitude, and reach down to my dick, only gently holding it. I fear if I grip any harder I'll orgasm, and I want more time to enjoy this.

"I wanna swallow it," he says, still flexing.

"Please, sir," I say.

He lowers his upper half, showing just how round his ass is. I devour it happily.

And then I yelp as he closes his mouth around my dick.

"You're going to keep enjoying my ass," he says. "And I'm going to swallow your cum. You understand? But only when I say you can."

I murmur my assent, almost feral as I lap up his hairy hole.

And that's when he sucks. His tongue swirls around my dick with an alacrity I didn't think a star football player had. It's just not something I imagined. He's giving just as much attention with his tongue as he is the suction. That's high-level blowjob stuff.

I'm so distracted by Kyle's mouth on my dick that I have to stop licking and just take a breath. And that's when I take in his sweaty stench and moan.

He stops. "That's right," he says. "No more licking. Just breathe in. I'll tell you when you can lick."

I take several quick breaths with my nose, trying to take in as much as his scent as I can. "Yes, sir," I say. I can't get enough.

When he adds his hand to the mix, I know I'm a goner. I moan loudly.

"Keep breathing me in," he says. "I'm your air. You need me to live."

"Yes, sir," I say. I grab onto both of his cheeks and take him in. I swear I've fucking died and his cheeks are the gates of heaven.

"God, you're such a man," I say, unable to contain myself. And without thinking, I stick my tongue out.

"Ah," he says, like an owner punishing a dog. "No licking."

Remembering I can't apologize, I comply by sniffing loudly.

"That's a good boy," he says.

I can't believe this is happening. I've fantasized about this moment for years. And I have it. And it's even better than I imagined.

And because we're dating, we get to do this. Again. And again. And again.

"Lick it," he commands.

And I do like a fucking dog as his tongue teases my dick.

"I can't hold it longer," I say.

He lets out the sexiest chuckle. "Then cum for me."

I shoot my load into his mouth as I tongue his hole like my life depends on it. I make beastly noises as I release the rest of myself, my tongue bathing his hole. And once I'm all out, my head collapses onto the bed. And if there weren't a nearly 300-pound man on me, I'd fall right asleep.

Kyle gets off me, stands up, and stretches his legs. Part of me panics. I'm so used to guys just leaving or completely changing their personality when the sex is over. Will Kyle walk back on everything he said? Make me drive home is this dark rain?

But then he turns back to the bed, lifts the covers, and shimmies himself inside. He then lifts the covers open. "Get over here," he says.

Unable to hide my grin, I slide up until I'm pressed right against him, already cold from the blasting AC. He lowers the covers and wraps his huge, bear body around me, holding him tight against me.

He kisses me on the forehead. "That was amazing," he says.

"So you liked it," I say into his furry chest, loving the way it tickles my face.

He lets out a low grumble, vibrating my entire body. "I don't know what you're made of, Michael Cunningham, but it has to be divine. I didn't know something could feel this good."

I nuzzle into his pecs and kiss his warm skin. I said earlier that I'd get him hooked on me, making unable to stop wanting me. And I think I was successful, but maybe too much. Because now I think I'm hooked on him, too.

Chapter 26

Kyle Weaver

I WAKE TO A warm body pushing against me. My eyes shoot open, and I see the vague outline of Michael's head just in front of me.

"Christ," I say, and squeeze him tighter, pressing my lips against the back of my head. Still asleep, he nuzzles himself into me.

And that's when I freeze.

I didn't try to push Michael out of my bed. I didn't jump out of the bed either. No. I wrapped my arms around him and pulled him *closer* to me.

How in the hell am I supposed to choose football over him now?

He stirs in bed, rubbing his ass into my dick. And after running my mind over all that we just did, I'm rock hard. Again.

Asleep, he shifts his ass so my hard cock goes right between them. And I get uncomfortable. I shift away from him. Not because I don't want to do what we did again. I absolutely want to do that again, and again, and again. But he's not awake. I won't do anything to him if he's not conscious to agree.

But then he reaches around, grabs my dick, and puts it right back where it was.

"I see you're awake," I say into his neck.

"Feeling *you* woke me up," he says, wiggling into me. God, I'm already so hard for him.

"Sorry," I say, wrapping around him.

"No need for apologies," he says, grabbing my hand and kissing it. And then he does the unthinkable and sticks my thumb deep into his mouth.

I groan and hump his ass, but this time he pulls away from me.

"That's your punishment," he says. "For saying sorry."

"You give your ass back to me," I grunt into his ear.

He starts sucking my thumb again, this time just like he sucked my dick. Using all my strength, I pull him close to me. And this time, he doesn't pull away.

"Put it in," he commands, his mouth still around my thumb. And he doesn't have to tell me twice.

When I feel his sweet tightness, I roll my eyes in pleasure. This could be mine. For life. The conversations. The sex. His sweetness. Everything.

I pull all the way out, then I thrust back in. He whimpers. He's still lubed up from earlier. From the silicon and my cum.

"Oh, I got you now," I say.

He sucks my thumb harder and nods.

I pull it all out again, then thrust it back in, relishing his moan each time. And I do it until I can't bear to not be inside him anymore. His arm is moving rhythmically, and I can tell he's stroking himself. Good. I love to know I'm pleasuring him.

"Good boy," I say into his ear. "Don't cum until I say."

He keeps sucking, but I know he's heard me.

I thrust harder, so hard that Michael lets go of my thumb.

"Oh, I can't hold it," he says. "I can't."

And hearing those words sends me over the edge. We both reach our peak, whimpering and groaning. He clasps my arms, almost distressed.

"I'm here, Michael," I say into his neck. "I'm here."

His hands relax, and he melts into me.

And both of us eventually fall back asleep.

* * *

When I wake up, I groggily stretch my arm over Michael's body. But I just meet empty sheets.

He's gone.

My eyes shoot open and I look around the room, the spring sun shining through my curtains. And that's when I see him, naked, standing in front of one my bookshelves looking at a book in his hand, his beefy silhouette making me desperate for him in my arms. God, he's such a specimen. I came in that man. Twice.

"What are you doing?" I ask, almost hurt. "Get back in bed."

"Didn't mean to scare you," he says, grabbing another book off the shelf and coming back to me. "Just wanted to see what you've been reading." He slides back under the covers, his back to me, and I wrap my arm around him and pull him snug to me.

He sets down the two books in front of him: *You Should Be So Lucky* by Cat Sebastian, the book club book that changed my life, and *The Love Hypothesis* by Ali Hazelwood.

"You're reading romance books that I didn't even recommend," he says. "Ali Hazelwood's the GOAT."

I chuckle and kiss his neck. "I've just read that one. It was good."

"I don't even think I've read this one yet," he says. "Unbelievable."

"Sounds like I'm a bigger romance fan than you."

He scoffs. "I will die before that happens."

I grin and wrap both my arms around him this time. Birds chirp outside my window, and I glance over Michael as he opens up my copy of the gay baseball romance.

"You've really shown this thing love," he says, thumbing through the roughed up pages.

"It means a lot to me," I say. "It was saying things that I had only thought up to this point. About me. My sexuality."

My stomach sinks when I say that word.

Sexuality.

Here I am, waking up with a gorgeous man in my bed. A gay one. If I was able to deny it before, I sure as hell can't now. I am a gay man. After what I felt last night, I can't go back into the closet. But I can't just give up on football either.

It's not just the promise I made to my dad, but it's also for myself. Winning the Championship Game is a big deal. How can I just give it up? Especially when I might have another chance?

Overwhelmed, I bury myself in the crook of Michael's back. I take a breath of his unwashed body, and I can see what he's saying about stink. There's a sweet and earthy, almost intimate smell to it. Like that's what he's like all raw. I like it.

I harden against him.

"Woah there, big guy," he says, stroking my thigh. "Gimme a second to prepare. I woke up sore from last night."

"Was I too rough?" I ask.

He turns his head over and kisses me, my Ali Hazelwood book open in his hands. "You could actually stand to rough me up more."

"Don't challenge me," I say. "You might just get what you're asking for."

"I'm so terrified," he moans. "We'll see if you can be as rough as you say you are."

I insert myself between his cheeks, the head pushing against the hole just enough to push through, but not. "Says the guy who needs a break."

"Bottoming is a skill," he says. "It requires patience and practice. Maybe you should try it some time."

Imagining Michael inside me gives me butterflies. I can still taste his load, and I feel crazy to say I want more.

"I'd like that," I say. "Maybe one day."

We lay there for a while as he starts reading *The Love Hypothesis.*

"You got any plans for today?" he asks me.

I sigh. I gotta call Timmy and explain to him how I don't have a picture of a girl yet. Jeez.

"I need to update my agent on my dating life," I say.

Michael sets down the book, and I can feel his heartrate increase. He turns around, our hairy chests touching.

"What will you tell him?"

I look into Michael's hazel eyes. I *want* to tell him that this girl I've been seeing is actually this wonderful guy with a red mullet who fucks like a siren and has an even bigger heart. But I'm not ready for that.

"I don't know," I say, wiping my eyes.

He sighs, disappointed I can tell, but he says nothing. After all, I did tell him that it would take time to make a decision, and I couldn't be pressured. He's respecting that. But that doesn't mean he can't be sad about it.

He starts playing with one of my hands, stroking each of my fingers, digging into my knuckles. Massaging them. But he does it so gently, like my hand is as fragile as a hummingbird.

I can't lose this man.

"Can I take you to breakfast?" I ask.

"Brunch?" he asks, light coming back to his eyes.

I chuckle. "Yeah, brunch. Is that what the gays call it?"

He rolls his eyes. "Breakfast is when you go to the cracker barrel at 8AM on a road trip. Brunch is for warm Sunday mornings after you've had the best sex of your life."

"That was the best sex of your life?" I ask, surprised. But honored. "I've only had sex with a few other men. And not that many women. I've seen most if not all of your videos. Your body count is stacked compared to mine."

He pouts. "Are you calling me a whore?"

I reach around and grab his ass. "Only if you want me to."

He bites his lip. "Yeah. Brunch sounds nice. We could maybe have some fun first," he says, his dick hard against me. "That will only make waffles taste better."

I frown. "Well, the only place that will have us is that restaurant I took you to last night," I say.

He looks like I've just popped a balloon right in his face. "The one where we ate in secret?"

I search his eyes for that excitement he just had, but it's long gone. "Yeah, is that a problem?"

He sighs and stops playing with my hand. "It's just that—we can't..." He doesn't finish, but he doesn't need to. I already know.

I stretch my leg around him, pulling him closer. I kiss him on the forehead, and he gazes foreword to my chest, his eyes busy. He's thinking. And I can guess what about. This bedroom is one of the few places we can be ourselves unless I decide to come out. And if I choose football, then we can't see each other at all. I'll have to find some girl. Michael's mentioned before how much he's wanted a legitimate, healthy relationship. Is it healthy for him to date me in secret? Only for me to potentially dump him for my career?

His dick has softened, and so has mine. But I still hold him close. Damnit. Why can't I just make him happy?

He turns away, and my chest sinks.

"Will you please hold me?" he asks.

And I do so eagerly, giving the back of his neck three small kisses.

He picks up the Ali Hazelwood book and starts reading again. I rest my head and close my eyes, letting myself drift off. At least here it feels like time doesn't exist. Nor does the outside world. I feel myself get sleepy breathing in Michael's scent. If only we could stay here forever—

"That's it!" Michael says, jumping up to his elbow.

I wipe my eyes and yawn. "What is it?" I ask.

He jumps up and faces me, sitting cross-legged. He's holding the book open, and he points down at the page. "Fake dating."

"Fake what now?" I ask.

He rolls his eyes. "Fake dating. That's our solution."

I prop myself up on my elbow. "Fake dating... isn't that the trope where the main character needs a partner, so they get someone else to do it?"

He nods eagerly. "And then they fall in love."

I blink at him, processing what he's saying. "But..."

"But what?"

"Forgive me... but doesn't fake dating only work when the partner is accepted by those around them?"

"Yes," he says like it's obvious.

I grunt. "Then how can fake dating help us, Michael? You and I aren't supposed to be together to begin with."

He slaps his forehead with his hand, a smile forming on his face. "Oh, no no no. Sorry. I should have been clearer. You're going to 'fake date' someone else. And then you and I can date in secret. That way you can play football for another year, and then you can come out after that."

I look at him, deadpan. "You're serious?"

He shrugs. "What other option do you have?" he asks. "This way, you can have both: you can 'come out' by dating me, but you can also still play football. It's a win-win."

I can't help but wince. "But there's so much that could go wrong. What about this person I 'fake-date'? They won't know it's fake dating. And the media would be on me like crazy. That would be a logistical nightmare."

His shoulder sags, and he starts twirling his beard. Then he lights up with another idea. "I know just the people who could help us come up with a plan. And they would keep the secret too."

I raise my brow. "Oh yeah?"

"I do," he says. He lays down next to me and starts stroking my thigh. Blood rushes to my dick, as if his touch alone can get me hard.

"But will you hear me out?" he asks. "Is this something you're willing to give a chance? Or would you rather just decide on your own?"

His question comes across honest, not pushy. If I were to do nothing, he and I would have a maximum of two months, and that's if I found a girlfriend at the last second. But Timmy's on my ass about finding a girl. I'd have to give up Michael practically right now if I chose football. And I feel like I'd be missing out on something big if I just forewent this next season. But if I went with Michael's plan, I'd get both, just like he said. And maybe we'd come out on the other end of the season still together. And maybe then I could officially come out.

"Alright," I say. "I'm willing to strategize."

He smiles. "Great. But this will require one thing."

I frown. "What's that?"

He sighs. "I'll need the help of my writing friends," he says. "So they'd know your secret. We can meet here to discuss it. Is that okay?"

I sigh as well. "Eh, what the hell. I trust you. Invite them over."

Chapter 27

Michael Cunningham

"YOUR MYSTERIOUS SEXY CRITIQUE partner is Kyle fucking Weaver?" Amani asks.

I gesture for her to be quiet as she, Skye, and Josue walk through Kyle's front door.

"We don't want his neighbors hearing," I say, shutting his door behind them. "Quiet!"

"This is fucking insane," she says.

"Yeah," Skye says. "You're fucking a football player? That's honestly so hot."

Josue laughs. "Write a romance about that."

I pause, thinking about what a crazy kind of story that would be, then shake myself from my stupor. "I know this is wild, but it's serious. Very serious. And there's a lot on the line. I need to ask that you be respectful and understanding."

Amani shakes her head. "Shit, I will be. But God, I wish you told me about this sooner! Coming from the man who thought he would never find love."

"Well don't say that too soon," I say, leading them down the hall. "Because I invited you all here to discuss how the hell we're going to do this."

Kyle's sitting on the couch wearing a sleeveless Budweiser shirt and some basketball shorts. I don't know if this or the suit is hotter. This man can make anything work.

He stands up, and Amani fangirls, making some high-pitched squeal that could either be the result of pure fear or pure excitement.

He wears this cute, boyish grin as he extends his hand to hers. "Kyle Weaver," he says.

She shoots her hand out. "I'm Amani," she says. "Super big fan!"

Skye introduces herself, remarkably calm as she shakes his hand, but Josue is shaking when he approaches him. I keep forgetting how famous this man actually is.

We all sit down on Kyle's couch, and then everyone turns to me. Right, I'm the one with the plan.

"So, as you all now know, Kyle Weaver has been the one I've been secretly meeting with for the past two months."

"Insanity," Amani says.

"Cool as hell," Skye says.

"Unbelievable," Josue says.

Kyle blushes. I glance at him, wanting his approval to move forward with the plan. He nods and leans forward.

"I'm kinda in a sticky situation," he says, pulling on one of his beard. "My contract with the Tigers ended this last season." He pauses for a beat, thinking. "Before my dad died, I promised that I would win him a Williams."

"Williams?" Skye asks.

"Championship Game trophy," Josue responds.

"Ah," she says, nodding. But still not really getting it. I love her.

"But the Tigers are threatening to not re-sign me unless I have a girlfriend."

Amani scoffs. "What? You have to be married to play or something?"

"Not everyone," he says. "But the 'Sexiest Man Alive'? Before the Championship Game this February, my team was getting all sorts of questions. Not about our playing or season, but about my sexuality. The most eligible bachelor, they say, has no reason being single."

"So they think you're tarnishing their image," Josue says.

Kyle nods. "And distracting other players. The NFO will say they aren't discriminatory like that, but they'll find a way to keep anyone gay off their teams."

"That's ridiculous," Amani says. "You're not even hurting anyone."

"But football is the paradigm of American masculinity," I say. "A gay player threatens this image."

"And so the problem is," Amani says, leaning forward, her hands in her lap. "You guys want to date. But you can't. Because the shitty NFO—no offense—is making you get a girlfriend."

Kyle laughs. "None taken," he says. "And that's pretty much spot on."

Amani looks at me. "And you had some bright idea?"

I chew on my lips, the idea not feeling as bright as it did this morning. Probably due to the post-sex high. But it's the only thing I got.

"Fake-dating," I say.

She tilts her head, then her eyes widen in recognition. "You aren't thinking..."

"I definitely am," I say, unable to keep in my laugh. "It's insane, but I can't think of anything else."

"Wait," Skye says. "Your idea is to have Kyle find a fake girlfriend?"

"And then you two can date in secret?" Josue asks.

"Damn," Kyle says. "How did you all get that before me?"

"Most of us are romance readers and writers," Amani says, patting him on the knee. "This is our bread and butter."

Kyle shrugs.

"But what I'm stuck on is how we do this," I say. I look at Kyle. "Who knows that your gay?"

He winces. "Well, you all now," he says. "And my therapist."

"She single?" Amani asks.

He gives her a vicious, but playful, side eye, his lip curled up. "She's married. And old."

She throws her hands up in defense. "Just asking." They both laugh, and a pit forms in my stomach. They're hitting it off better than me and Kyle did.

He sighs. "My ma doesn't even know," he says, shaking his head. "How am I supposed to find someone who I can trust to keep this thing secret? At least until the next season is over. I can't think of anyone."

The five us sit there in silence.

"Well," Josue says. "The five of us know."

We all look at him.

"Kyle and I can't fake date for... obvious reasons. Michael, you can't even real-date him. So that leaves..."

"I'm just saying, you and I would not work," Skye says, shaking her head as she lays back into the couch. "You're a gorgeous man, and I'm a beautiful woman. But I'm open and loud about being trans. And if they're worried about you being gay, dating a trans-woman wouldn't exactly cover up that reputation. It'd do the opposite."

I frown. It sucks, but she's probably right.

"So that leaves you, Amani," Josue says.

She looks around at all of us as we stare at her, waiting for a response.

My heart begins to race. "But that one Chinese woman—Angie? You danced with her at the bar that one night. You got her number, right?"

"Yeah," she says, frowning. "And she ghosted me."

"Oh. You never told me that."

"Not exactly exciting news to share," she says. "But I'll be fine."

"I'm sorry," I say, patting her on the knee. Dating has been tough for Amani the past couple years, so I'm sure she's more upset than she's leading on.

"That could work," Skye says, sitting up. "Amani knows that Kyle's gay. She can fake-date him without revealing the secret." She turns to me. "And that way, Kyle and Michael can date in secret."

"Huh," Amani says, turning to Kyle. "Fake-dating a famous football player."

Kyle blushes, and my stomach churns. This was a good idea earlier, but putting it into practice makes me uneasy. Though I don't know why.

"See?" Skye says. "They have chemistry. I'd believe it if they were dating."

My chest squeezes. "But that's a big commitment, Amani. You'd have to date for almost a full year. And you couldn't date anyone else."

"But it really wouldn't be dating," she replies. "It would be so *you* could actually date him."

"Yeah," I mutter. "In private."

"I think that will work," Kyle says. "What do you think, Amani?"

I scowl up at him, betrayed. It's that easy for him just to find someone to cover me up? He doesn't feel a little bit of shame about this whole thing?

"I think so, too," she says. "I'm gay, but I don't talk a lot about it online. So it's not like I could sabotage it. And I'm not currently seeing anyone either."

She looks up at me. "I think I'm gonna do this. Michael, you've been searching for something like this for a while. You deserve it." She looks to Kyle. "And I'm doing this for you as a fellow gay. You deserve to love who you love."

He blushes. "I appreciate it."

But I just sit there, chewing on my lips, my arms tightly folded.

"You look like you wanna talk," she says.

I sit back. "What's there to say?"

She sighs and turns back to Kyle. "Is there a place he and I can talk in private?"

Kyle innocently gestures to the kitchen far behind him.

Amani claps the couch and stands up. "Come on," she says, gesturing to me. "You got something on your mind, and we're not agreeing to this until you share it. At least with me."

I grumble, sitting up. "Fine."

I stand up and follow her into the kitchen, a headache coming on.

She puts her hand on the granite countertop right next to Kyle's giant stainless-steel refrigerator, one that could feed a family of five.

"You look like you wanna deck someone in the face," she says. "Spit it out."

I wipe my face, already exhausted from this whole conversation. "It's not ideal, but it will have to do."

"But how are you going to be comfortable with doing this if you have reservations that you're not sharing?" she asks. "Like you said, we'd do this for nearly a year. That's a long time to hold something in."

I cross my arms tightly and lean against the fridge. "Why are you agreeing to this anyway? There's not much you're getting out of it."

She scoffs. "Excuse me? I'm doing this for you out of the kindness in my heart. And for the poor closeted man in the next room over who has probably kept this secret his whole life."

I press my forehead against the cool fridge.

She crosses her arms. "You and I both know what this is really about."

I glance at her, my forehead still pressed to the metal. "Oh yeah? What's that?"

"You're jealous."

I grimace and turn to her. "Jealous? Amani, you're gay too. Why would I be jealous?"

"Not jealous that I would steal him," she says. "But jealous he'd have someone else to share this burden with."

I look away, the backs of my eyes burning.

"When you dated David, I know how much you wanted him to open up to you like he seemed to do with all his friends. To be vulnerable and mature about his feelings. He never did, and that broke your heart."

A tear falls, but I wipe it away.

"But the truth is, he never really opened up to his friends. Because he couldn't. And you were the one who chose to leave after that. That was your strength, just like your sponsor told you. He missed out on you and your maturity, not the other way around."

I wipe my wet eyes, still looking away.

"I haven't known Kyle for long—well, in-person, for long—but he seems different. He may have just come out, but he seems earnest. Like he wants this to work. I don't think this will be a repeat of David."

I wipe the fresh eyes from my tears and finally look at her. "Jeez, Ams. We gotta make you a therapist or something."

She lets out a laugh. "A lot of this I learned from watching you grow after leaving David, so you're the one talking. But I think you should give this a try, Michael. I think this could work. And I'm willing to help."

I let out a deep sigh I was holding in and wrap my arms around Amani. She presses her cheek into my chest, and I rest my chin on her dreads.

"This is why the 'L' in 'LGBT' comes first," I say.

She squeezes me and laughs, then pulls away.

"Thank you, Ams," I say. "You're right."

She shrugs and smiles. "I know."

"Are you sure you're okay with being off the market in a fake relationship?" I ask.

She shrugs. "I haven't been lucky finding anyone in the past couple years, so what's a few more months?"

I hear a light knock, and something catches her eye beyond me, and I turn around.

"Am I interrupting?" Kyle says, his lips pressed shyly together, making his beard a dark forest on his face.

"No," Amani says, rubbing my arm. "We were just wrapping up." She looks at me as if asking me if I want him to enter.

I nod.

"You two probably need to talk about this too," she says, stepping away. "I'll leave you to it." And then she leaves me alone with Kyle in his kitchen.

He reaches up and strokes my red cheek. "You've been crying."

"Yeah," I say, wiping away the last of the tears. "Amani just knows what to say."

He leans against the fridge. "What's going on?" he asks, concerned. "How do you feel about all this?"

"I just have baggage from my ex," I say, shaking my head. "Just worried that we'll grow apart through this whole process. That you'll be closer to Amani."

"Well, she is gay, right?" he asks. "Sorry, I overheard."

"Yeah."

He puts his hands on my arms and rubs them slowly. "Then you've got nothing to worry about. I'm choosing this because I want you along with my career. *You.*"

He keeps rubbing me, and soon I find my head in his chest buried between his thick pecs. The smell of his lingering sex-sweat intoxicates me. "For someone who came out late in life, you are very affectionate."

He chuckles, his chest shaking me with it, and I bury myself deeper.

"I think I get it from my mom," he says. "Last night you promised me that I could trust you, and that goes both ways. I will be my best for you. As available as I can be."

My chest warms, feeling the truth in his words.

I look at him. He leans down and gives me a kiss, holding it there. He pulls away and looks into my eyes.

"Do you really want to do this?" he asks. "If not, we can figure out another way. I can look more into my decision—"

"You don't need to give up football for me," I say. "I want to do this."

He smiles and kisses me on the forehead. "Good," he says. "Me too."

We make our way back into his living room, Amani and Skye chatting on the couch. Josue is looking at one of his bookshelves.

"You've got a killer selection, dude," Josue says. "Didn't think you'd be such a fantasy fan."

"Thanks man," Kyle says, smiling in that radiant way he does. "Might be the best genre." He glances at me. "After romance."

I laugh and teasingly push him. And that's when I realize how happy I am. I'm surrounded by people who love and want to help me. And that's making it easier to truly love myself.

"So what'll it be boys?" Amani asks.

"Yeah," Skye says. "Is this fake-dating a go?"

I look at Kyle, then at my friends. "I think so."

"Great," Amani says, rubbing her hands together. "Now let's work out the nasty details."

Chapter 28

Kyle Weaver

I THINK AMANI MADE an understatement when she called them 'nasty details'. Because figuring out this fake-dating situation has been downright disgusting. Don't get me wrong—I'm glad Michael came up with the idea. But hiding who I truly am for so long goes against everything both my ma and daddy told me about integrity. Yet it's my only choice if I want to play and keep Michael around.

I sit with Amani, Michael's best friend and my new fake-girlfriend, on my couch as we wait for my agent Timmy to show up. When I told him I wanted to introduce my new girlfriend, he jumped at the opportunity. I hate having him in my house, but giving him this 'evidence' he's been asking for will get him off my ass. And another contract with the Tigers.

But overall, I'm relieved. With any other woman, I'd have to at least try to be intimate, bringing back the storm of depression to my mind. But with Amani, I don't have to do that. And I get Michael at the same time. It's perfect. I do wish Michael could be here, but I don't want Timmy suspecting we're a thing.

"Think he'll like me?" Amani asks. She's rubbing her palms on her jeans.

"I don't even know if Timmy likes me," I say. "I just know that he likes that I make him money. But since you're gonna help me get re-signed, that means more money for him. So yeah, I think he'll like you. Just not personally."

"Ouch," she says. "Is this what professional football is really like?"

I sigh. "Not always. There's a couple guys on my team that I really like. Made good friends on others as well. But the business side can be brutal. Even with a contract, I'm not guaranteed anything. It's pretty cutthroat."

She leans back into my couch. "So winning the Championship Game is worth all this then?"

I run my tongue across my teeth. I can still hear the beeping in my dad's hospital room. The pain on his face. I couldn't promise him a family. All that left me to give him was football. Neeti, my therapist, and I have been digging into this more and more, but I'm frustrated. After our first session, I felt good. But talking about it has only become more painful. I thought this therapy shit was supposed to make things easier. Guess not.

"It is," I say. "The least I can do."

My doorbell rings, making my chest constrict with anxiety. "I'll get it."

I leave Amani to answer my door. I open it, and there Timmy stands, but there's also someone else. She's a short brunette women dressed comfortable, yet stylish.

"Timmy," I say, trying to sound enthused. "And you are?"

"Robyn," she says. "Reporting with ESB. I've been trying to reach..."

"Ah, yeah, sorry," I say, remembering how Timmy told me to be expecting to hear from a reporter about my experience with the Tigers. But I was too busy with therapy and handling my feelings for Michael that I didn't notice.

"Figured I'd bring her along," Timmy says. He steps inside, uninvited. "She can ask her questions once I meet this mysterious girlfriend of yours." He leans toward me. "And her article will definitely help your image."

I hold back a grimace and invite Robyn inside. At least she has manners, unlike Timmy.

I bring her into my living room where Timmy's already greeting Amani.

"You must be the long-awaited girlfriend," Timmy says, reaching out to shake her hand. He does so aggressively.

I can see Amani resisting a grimace. "Nice to meet you, Timmy."

Robyn introduces herself, and I sit down with Amani while the other two sit on the opposite side of the couch. I lean back and put my arm around Amani, and she leans into me. Just like we've been rehearsing. It's more natural to hold Michael this way, but I don't have that luxury.

"So you're a writer," he says, almost skeptically.

"I am," she says. There's some defensiveness there, but I don't blame her. I've told her enough about Timmy for her to understand how he can be.

"I also work as a software engineer in the daytime."

"We got a brainiac here," he says, laughing. "You might be able to provide for Kyle if he doesn't end up getting re-signed. Make him a housewife."

Amani stares at him, almost scowling, while I shift uncomfortably. Just one more season of doing this. I can survive.

"Anyways," Timmy says, unperturbed. "Glad to see you've finally found someone. If I can just snap a picture of the both of you, I can leak it to my contacts. Then we'll get the whole sports world talking about the two of you. Enough of that, and the Tigers will be convinced you're no longer a threat."

"Great," I say, trying to unlock my jaw. "Well let's get a move on."

Timmy pulls out his phone. Amani and I pull close, and I try to put on the biggest smile that I can. Also another thing we've practiced. It's not that I don't like Amani, but we both think this whole thing is ridiculous. Why can't the world just accept me for who I am?

Timmy snaps the picture, and I try not to pull away from Amani too fast so it doesn't look contrived.

"Perfect" he says. He stands up and brushes himself off. "Robyn, be sure to mention the two of them in your article."

Robyn nods and then looks at me.

Amani pulls on my arm and gives me a quizzical look. "I can't stay for this," she says. "I've got errands to run."

"That's more than fine," Robyn says. "I know I'm a surprise. I just need to interview Kyle though. You're free to leave."

"Wonderful," Timmy says. "Kyle, we'll be in touch."

"I'm sure we will," I say.

Amani waits until Timmy's left. She then stands up. I tug on her, remembering that we need to act like a couple when we're around others. She kisses me on the cheek, and I kiss her back. Then she makes her way to my garage.

"See you soon," she says. Which isn't really true. I don't know when I'm seeing her next. But Michael will be coming over tonight. Thank God.

"Love you," I say. I don't really feel that now, but I'm sure by the end of this thing we'll mean it. I know how much going through hell can bring people together.

"Thanks so much for your time, Kyle," Robyn says, crossing her legs. "As Timmy may have told you, I'm interviewing lots of the key players on the Tigers. Trying to paint a picture of the team."

"Yeah," I say, remembering Timmy's explanation. "What do you want to know?"

"Well, I'm hoping we can get it all done in today's session," she says. "But I may come back for more. I wanted to talk to you about your upbringing, how you got into football. Then we can go into the most recent Championship Game and your hopes for next season."

My heartrate increases steadily. I take a deep breath through my nose. Neeti has been trying to get me to talk about my upbringing, but I get too nervous. I end up turning the conversation a different direction each time.

"That's fine," I say, not wanting to be difficult. "Ask away."

She pulls out a notepad and leans forward. "Well, it might be obvious what I want to talk about first. Your father—Brian Weaver—was a legend in the college football space."

I nod. "It was watching him coach that go me so interested in football."

"Really?" she asks, somehow leaning more forward. "Can you tell me more about that?"

There's a weird pit in my stomach. "What do you mean?"

"You say you watched him coach. This got you interested. How? Why?"

I pause, and suddenly my body feels heavier. Like if I make a sudden movement, I might just lose my balance and fall over.

"I...I'm not sure."

She shifts back, a little flustered, but manages to keep her cool. "That's fine. Could you tell me—what was home life like having a professional coach as a father?"

I can tell this is just her first question posed in a different way. I don't want to answer, but it would feel weird not to, especially given how simple the question is.

"It was... hard."

"Hard?" she asks, surprised.

I nod. "He was gone a lot. Busy. I don't know if this is what all coaches were like, but it seemed like he just never had time for me and my mom."

She furiously scribbles down on her notepad, then looks up at me, thoughtful. I can tell this wasn't what she was expecting. Me neither, quite frankly. I haven't even mentioned this to Neeti yet. I've been avoiding it. But there's something about Robyn—maybe that she's with ESB—that makes me feel like I have to be honest. My childhood is verifiable, after all. If I lie about this, won't people suspect I'm lying about my dating life?

"Then..." she drifts off, then refocuses. "How did this inspire you to get into football?"

The pit in my stomach gets bigger, but the answer to her question becomes crystal clear in my head. "My dad, he..." I wipe my nose, feeling the back of my eyes heat up. But I hold back the tears. "I saw the way he looked at his players. The ones that worked hard, did well. There was a fire in his eyes then that he never had when he looked at me or my ma."

Feeling my lips quiver, I pause until I regain my exposure. I am not crying in front of this woman.

"So I figured the best way to get his attention was to be like them. To play hard. To be that player that would make him proud."

"Wow," Robyn says. She sets her notepad down. "How old were you when you realized this?"

I sniffle. "Middle school, I think. Thirteen?"

She sighs. "That's a lot on a kid."

"Tell me about it," I say.

She picks up her notepad and writes something down, and I panic. I just badmouthed my father to a reporter, and no matter how kind she's being now, this news will get blasted. I don't want people thinking I didn't appreciate my daddy. He was a good man. Sure, he was busy, but he did his best. It wasn't easy being a coach of a competitive football team.

"But that's not the whole story," I say, reaching out my hand.

She stops. "Oh?"

I swallow my spit, and it hurts going down. I want to have integrity, but I'm so confused about what that even means anymore. I just need to survive.

"As I grew older," I begin. "I saw how hard the job was on my dad. He worked hard to provide for us. He didn't have a good relationship with his dad, after all. My grandpa drank a lot—didn't provide for the family. My dad wanted to be the opposite.

"Once I started playing at Miss U, that's when my dad was diagnosed with pancreatic cancer. He and my mom were divorced by then, but it still hit everyone we knew like a freight train. Here Brian Weaver was, a tank of a man, only to be afflicted by something completely out of his control.

"At first, it looked promising. We thought treatment would take care of it. Any Weaver man was a trooper, after all. But when the cancer came back full-force, we knew it was a matter of time. And in those days, my daddy's priorities became crystal clear."

"And what were those priorities?" Robyn asks.

I chew on my quivering lip, but I'm not able to keep some tears from falling. At least I'm not blubbering.

"Family," I say, my voice a little shaky. "Family was what was most important to him. Up until then, coaching in the NFO was his dream. Getting to the Championship Game. And he almost made it before the cancer got him. But before he died, he held my hand and told me how much he regretted losing my ma and how much he didn't want to lose me. Said he had his focus all wrong his whole life. I realized he was always a good man, after all. So I told him I'd be by his side, that I'd do anything for him. And that's when he asked me to make a promise—that I would carry on our family name."

Robyn gives me a puzzled look. "But you were single for so long."

I nod. "It's because..." Goddamnit. I hate lying. But I don't know how to tell this story any other way. "I couldn't find the right girl to honor his legacy. I searched for years, but it wasn't until Amani that I finally found a girl that he would approve of."

"So all this time," Robyn says. "You just hadn't found the right one?"

Yes, I want to say. *But I think I have him now. And his name is Michael.*

But I just nod. "Until I found Amani."

Robyn nods, taking it all in. "So, you've found the woman of your dreams," she says. "But rumor has it you want to play at least one more season. You want to go try and win the Championship Game one last time."

"Especially after we were so close with this last one."

"Why, though?" she asks. "I mean, sure. It's the Championship Game. But there are plenty of players who retire just before their teams win. Why persist?"

I sit back and think.

And that's when the words break through my mind and land on me like steaming piles of shit.

Queer.

What my dad would call me when I wasn't playing hard enough.

Faggot.

When I was goofing off with the other guys.

Goddamned disappointment.

When my first ever girlfriend broke up with me because I wouldn't have sex with her.

So I played hard and put on a show of being a man all so I could be shielded from his scorn. But even after he died, these words have still haunted me, like whips thwacking against my hide every time I lay down to rest. These words remind me that no matter what, I'm always shy of the man that my daddy wanted me to be. And I'm realizing, just now, really why I've been pursuing a Championship Game win this whole time, and not just 'cause I promised my daddy on his deathbed. But a bigger reason.

"By winning the Championship Game," I say. "I'll finally be the man I want to be. I'll finally prove myself."

I think that answer will satisfy Robyn, but she still sits there, curious.

"Prove yourself... to whom?" she asks. "To you? Or your father?"

I sit back, my head and heart too exhausted to talk further. "I think I'm shot for today," I say.

She nods. "That's fine," she says, setting her notepad down. "We talked about a lot."

I look up at her, imploringly. "Please be kind in your writing," I say. "I don't even remember all that I said."

"I'll send you a note in the next week with a draft. You can tell me what I can or can't include."

"That's kind," I say. "You don't have to do that."

She grabs her things and stands up. "And you didn't have to be so honest," she says. "I may reach out with more questions, but if you want to talk more about this, please let me know."

"Sure thing," I say.

And as she's leaving, I mull her last question over in my mind. Am I playing to prove myself to me? Or to my father? By the time I shut my front door, there's a sharp pain between my eyes, and exhaustion sweeps over me. Truth is, I have no fucking clue.

Chapter 29

Michael Cunningham

BY THE TIME BOOK club rolls around, I'm officially unemployed. My last day of work was today, and now all I have is the revenue coming in from my old OnlyFans videos. Now that Kyle and I are officially dating—well, officially yet still secretly together—I'm not making them anymore, per our agreement. I've never been one for open relationships, and besides, the sex with Kyle has been too good to pass up. I forget how wonderful sex can be when you have it with someone who has your heart.

Since it didn't matter now that I was laid off, I just went ahead and ended my day early. I got to Rucker's an hour before our weekly meeting so I could work on my new romantasy about two magical and disgraced knights who fall in love. I'm already 20K words in, and that word count is climbing higher every day. With all the fantasy that Kyle's been recommending to me, paired with the romance I'm reading for this book club, I'm getting a really solid understanding of how to weave the two genres together.

Finally having a boyfriend who is emotionally available has been so helpful too. All the tingles I get from a good conversation with Kyle, the warm chills I get when he runs his hand down my back in bed—all these experiences give me a lived understanding of how romance develops. This is what I've been looking for. I'm no longer distracted by the unhealthy love I had for David. The romance coming out of my fingertips feels organic, inspiring, and hopeful.

After I've been writing for a bit, Skye arrives and sits down across from me in at a small table in the café.

"Howdy howdy," she says, setting her stuff down. She's wearing a pink dress and a rhinestoned cowboy hat.

"You look like you're going to a Chappell Roan concert," I say.

"Thank you," she says.

I chuckle. "You're welcome."

"So tell me," she says, opening her laptop covered in stickers. "How's the fake-dating life going?"

I think back to the last time I saw Kyle—a couple days ago. "Honestly, better than I expected," I say. "You-know-who and I just spend time at his house a couple times a week. We don't go out in public, but that's not too bad. You should probably ask Amani how it's going." I lower my voice. "She's the one acting as his beard."

"Cool," she says, beginning to type. We write in silence for a while, and I mull over what I just told Skye. Spending time with Kyle—now as his boyfriend—is really nice. And I'm spending the night tonight. But it sucks that we can't be open. If we stay together past the next football season, we won't have to worry about this. There's a lingering, annoying feeling that tells me that time won't solve everything about this. But I try to just chalk it up to worry.

"I'm curious," Skye says once we wrap up our writing. Book club people are showing up, and we know it's a matter of time before it'll get too loud to focus.

"What's up?" I ask.

"Why is you-know-who so dead set on playing this next year?" she asks. "Like, hasn't he been playing for forever?"

"Yeah," I say, almost defensively. "He's wants to win the Championship Game."

"I get that," she says, putting her laptop in her bag. "But what I don't understand is how he's willing to put his life on hold for just a season, one game even. I would get it if he was young and had his whole career ahead of him. But he's been, what—playing for like almost a decade now?"

I put my computer away and fold my arms. I think back to that moment he came out to me, how hysterical he was, and all the times I've seen him since. He's told me that he made a promise to his dad that he would win a Championship Game for him, which made enough sense to me. I'm not close to my dad, but I know how emotional those relationships can be.

"His dad," I say. "He made a promise to his dad that he'd win the Championship Game for him."

Skye nods, but something about her face tells me she's not fully convinced. And then my heart starts to race, and I get that uneasy feeling in my stomach.

When I was dating David, I also thought that everything was fine. Even when he was rampantly cheating on me behind my back. Could there be something bigger here that Kyle isn't telling me? There has to be. This relationship we have is too good to be true, anyways. He has to be hiding something.

"I'm sorry," she says. "You're getting that distressed look you get when you don't like the feedback you're getting."

I blush. "Sorry."

"No, I'm sorry if what I asked was too personal."

"It's fine," I insist.

Kelley, one of the booksellers, comes to our table and asks if we can set it aside and put our chairs in the circle for book club. And as we're moving the table, I get that sinking feeling in my chest, the same one I get when I think about all that David did behind my back.

Skye grabs my arm. "Are you okay?"

I just let it out.

"What if you're right?" I ask as people take their seats around us.

"Right about what?" she asks. "Michael, I just asked why Kyle wanted to play this last season."

"Yeah, but you were insinuating that maybe Kyle has something to hide."

She shakes her head. "I wasn't insinuating anything. You've said yourself how Kyle is so much better than your ex. How he's honest. I was just curious, anyways, not suspicious. Playing to keep a promise to his dad makes sense."

"But should I be suspicious? He was closeted for so long. What if there's something else here?"

"Okay," she says, pulling me out of the gathering people. "Let's talk about this."

She pulls me toward a quiet corner of the bookstore. She's rubbing my arms, and she tells me to take a deep breath. Once I do, I feel a little better. Enough to talk without panicking.

"What's going on?" she asks.

"I'm just worried," I say. "Your question—it got me thinking. What if there's some other reason Kyle has to play? Or what if there's some other secret that he's kept hidden?"

"Have there been any secrets that Kyle has kept from you so far?"

I pause for a beat. "Just that he was gay. And why he was in book club."

"And he eventually told you, didn't he?"

I nod.

She sighs. "Then it sounds like he is honest. It just might take him some time. I think you're letting your fear from your last relationship get in the way of this one."

Her words echo off of something similar my sponsor told me a while back. "Yeah," I say. "I tend to have a tendency to self-sabotage. Kyle is nothing like David."

Skye chuckles. "Well don't do that to yourself! It sounds like Kyle really likes you, and he's been honest with you so far. And if you're worried, talk with him. I think the truth comes out regardless, anyways. You don't need to stress about it beforehand."

By now, my heartrate has gone back to normal, and I feel that exhausted, soothing feeling of having my exerted myself but now being able to rest.

"I'm seeing him tonight too," I say. "I think I'd like to ask him more details about this promise. But you're right. I don't think I have anything to worry about. Thanks for this."

She pats me on the arm. "Anytime." She eyes the circle of women. The discussion is about to start. "Come on," she says. "I can't wait to discuss this werewolf smut."

The discussion gets heated faster than any other book club session I've ever been to. Skye gets into a polite, yet bordering on aggressive, argument with someone else about the nature of 'knotting' and whether it was accurately described in this book. I manage to chime in how now that I'm unemployed, I'll have time to binge the whole series. When Kelley asks the question about whether or not this book is a good representation of the Omegaverse, I swear more hands are raised than are possible to answer. And with how long some of the explanations are, Kelley has to cut some people off. And when we talk about the scene where the vampire has to feed off the werewolf to survive, the room just about loses it.

In short, this is my favorite book club session yet.

Quickly, the anxiety I had to toward Kyle and whether or not he's lying to me about something dissipates. Like Skye and my sponsor have said, this is just a lingering fear that I have from my previous relationship. Nevertheless, I do want to know more about this promise Kyle made to his father. I'm just sure, though, that Kyle will be honest. There's nothing to be afraid of.

When the session wraps up, various threads of topics are still being vigorously debated by several others, including Skye. I put my chair away, and I'm about to pull out my phone when Kelley approaches me.

"Hey, can we talk a minute?"

My stomach clenches just like it did on the first day when she pulled me aside. But then I steel myself. I doubt I've done anything wrong.

"Sure, what's up?"

"I'm sorry to hear you lost your job," she says. "But we may have an opportunity for you."

My stomach flutters, but in the good kind of what. "Opportunity?"

"We've been hiring for a while," she says. "Specifically looking for more booksellers who would be willing to host more book clubs. As you can see, this one gets pretty big."

I gaze over at the dozens of women perusing the aisles, many of them joining the checkout line that stretches all the way to the front door. "No kidding."

"In this club, we've been reading all sorts of romance subgenres, but these other book clubs would exclusively focus on some of these subgenres. For example, a romance fantasy book club." She gestures to me. "An LGBTQ+ romance book club."

I put my hand on my chest. "So if I was hired, I could lead some of these book clubs?"

"Potentially yes," she says. "We'd have to go through the interview process with the store owner just to make sure, but we know you well at this point. I think you'd be a shoo-in."

I stand there, my hand on my chest, and a smile forms on my face.

For years, I've been searching for a bookish and writing community to call my own. I've started building that from the first day I walked into Ruckers. I met other readers, received inspiration, met Skye, got Amani back to writing, met Josue. And of course, I can't forget this is how I met Kyle.

"I'm super down," I say. "What do I need to do?"

"I'll email you with some dates and times to come in for an interview," she says. "After that, we'd be able to get you started quickly."

I exhale, relaxing my shoulders. I didn't realize how stressed being unemployed made me. I had some savings to live off of, but that wasn't going to last long. Sure, I could rely on Kyle, but I want to provide for myself. But now it seems like the universe has been looking out for me the whole time.

"Wonderful," I say. We exchange contact information, and my heart is bright and happy. I can't wait to share the good news with Kyle. I have a job!

I pull out my phone to text him that I'm on my way and that I have some very good news to share. But there's a text from Amani on my screen.

"Hey," it reads. "I don't know if Kyle told you, but he met with a reporter who interviewed him about his football career. You might want to look at this."

My stomach plumets, turning my excitement over my potential new job into flutters of fear. Kyle did not tell me about any such reporter.

I click on the link, and it leads me to an ESB article written by a Robyn Carter. At the top is a picture of Kyle and Amani with their arms around each other. My breath quickens, and I have to remember that this whole couple situation is fake—that in fact it was me who initially set up the idea. But it still makes me uneasy to see Kyle with someone else. Even if this someone else is my best friend pretending to be his girlfriend.

I step to a lonely corner of the bookstore and quickly read through the article. She discusses her aim to interview longstanding Tigers players to paint a portrait of the time over time—to trace their journey to (hopefully) winning the Championship Game next year. She brings up various facts about Kyle that I knew before I even knew him: his philanthropic efforts, where he went to school. But toward the bottom is where it gets interesting.

She starts the paragraph about his upbringing with a caveat that not everything is as it seems, then goes into describing his home life. And my jaw drops.

Kyle's father was... kind of a dick. She puts it nicely here, but I can pick up that he was a distant man, one who put his career over his family. It was only on his deathbed that he started reevaluating his priorities.

And this is where Kyle comes in, telling Robyn things I've never even known.

To win his father's approval, he tried to be the best player he could be. I mean, how else were you supposed to get the attention of a career-obsessed football coach? And she's a little less clear here, but I can tell that even this didn't win him the full affection of his father. It wasn't until his deathbed when everything came to a head.

Before Coach Brian Weaver died, he asked his son to make him a promise: to carry on his legacy. And we all know what that means: posterity, children, grandchildren.

My heart picks up speed as I read on. Did Kyle finish the story by coming out to this reporter?

But when I read his response, my chest folds in on itself.

Kyle said that after all these years, he's just been looking for the right one. And that person is Amani.

The rest of the article just talks about her thoughts on the subject and who she plans to interview next, but I don't read any of that. I just think about how I was right: there was so much more about the promise to his father than I thought.

And Kyle told me none of it.

"Uh oh," Skye says, approaching me.

"You got that look again."

"I need to go see Kyle," I say. "Right now."

"What's wrong?" she asks. "Is he okay?"

I show her the article on my phone.

"So he interviewed with a reporter," she says. "What's the big deal?"

"Read the bottom."

She takes my phone and scrolls through it, and I wait for her to have the same level of anger that I do.

Except she doesn't.

She hands back the phone, shaking her head. "There's nothing of importance here," she says. "You said he wanted to honor his father. This article explains why."

"Nothing of importance?" I almost squawk out. "If Kyle trusted me, he would have told me this. I didn't know any of this."

"You've known him for, what, a little over two months? You're still going to learn about him. I'm sure he wants to talk to you about this."

I rub my tightened chest, grimacing at the pain. Her words make sense, but they fall flat.

"I've got to go," she says. "Going out for some drinks with others. You can come if you want before you see Kyle."

"I should go see Kyle right now," I insist. We moved our writing group to another day of the week so we all had our Friday nights back.

She pats me on the elbow. "It's going to be okay," she says. "I can't tell why this is bothering you, but you'll figure it out. Relationships are hard, but you and I know they're worth it."

I laugh a little, releasing some tension in my shoulders. "That's why we write about it."

"Exactly," she says. "You'll be fine. Text if you need anything. I'll see you later."

She saunters off with some of her new Omegaverse friends, her rhinestone cowboy hat reflecting the setting sun.

I pull out my phone and send a text to Kyle I'm on the way, and he quickly responds telling me he got us some dinner. Which provides me some solace, though I don't know why. I want to understand why this whole situation makes me feel crummy, but I'm lost. Then I remember: there's one person I can talk to that will demystify the whole situation.

I wish Kelley a good night and hurry to my car. Once I'm inside, I immediately dial my sponsor. And when she answers, I set off to Kyle's, explaining the whole situation along the way.

"You've done this before," she says when I answer.

"Oh?"

"You find someone you like—romantic or not—and things are good for a while. But then you become afraid they'll abandon you."

Her words strike like an arrow in my chest. "You're right," I say. "But I don't know why."

"Well, I think it makes sense," she says matter-of-factly, but not unkindly. "Your parents were supposed to be there for you. But at most times, they weren't. So you learned from a young age that the people who were supposed to love you were also the ones who abandon you."

"But I don't think Kyle will abandon me," I say, driving on the highway. At this point, Kyle's given me permission to talk about him and us to people I trust, like my sponsor. So Susan knows everything now. "He's having me over tonight."

"Are you sure about that?" she asks. "Look at your interactions. Is there any evidence that's leading you to believe he will abandon you?"

Her words make me go over my interactions with Kyle more thoroughly. And I get stuck on the fact that he told this reporter all these details about his life and not me.

"There is one thing," I say. "The fact that he hasn't shared with me his upbringing."

She sighs. "I know how that can feel," she says. "When our loved-one doesn't tell us something important to them, it can feel like rejection."

"And abandonment."

"Exactly," she says. "But it doesn't have to be."

"How?" I ask. "How do I make this stop hurting? I don't want to be clingy or obsessive with Kyle like I was with David. I want to make this work."

"That's really up to you," she says.

I resist a scoff. "*That* answer."

"Yes, that answer. You said that you wanted to date an emotionally available guy," she says. "Is Kyle not immediately mentioning this to you a dealbreaker?"

I wince, thinking. "No," I say. I pause for a beat. "But it is something I think I would like. I want to talk to him about it. I feel like details like these are important to share as a couple. Keeping them secret goes against what I think is healthy in a relationship."

"There you go," she says. "You can talk to Kyle about it. But hear what he has to say. You may come to a mutual understanding and a strategy that works for both of you. But just be kind when you talk to him. From what it sounds like, he's not abandoning you. Trust that, trust your feelings, and trust that he's doing the best he can, too."

I sigh. It all feels clear now. "Thanks, Susan," I say. "I think I know what to do."

"Call back if you need to talk more," I say.

"Thanks," I say. "For this and for everything. I feel like I should pay you for this."

I can hear her smiling through the phone. "Someone did it for me, so I'll do it for you," she says.

I laugh. "Alright," I say. "Talk soon."

After I hang up, I still feel anxious to talk to Kyle. But there's undertones of peace there.

I didn't have great parents, and I haven't had very many good experiences with love, either. But that doesn't mean I need to keep expecting the same abandonment over and over again. I can break the curse of thinking those I love will leave me. And tonight, I can start by talking to Kyle, sharing my feelings, and listening to what he has to say.

Chapter 30

Kyle Weaver

WHEN MICHAEL SHOWS UP at my front door, I'm beyond relieved. It's been one of the longest weeks of my life, and I just want to hold my man in my arms. Between reviewing the article that Robyn wrote, showing my face in public with Amani, and waiting for updates from Timmy about the Tigers re-signing me or not, I can barely keep my eyes open. But seeing Michael lifts me up like helium in a balloon.

"Hey, you," I say. I lean forward and kiss him on the lips.

"Hey," he says, stepping inside. I may just be seeing things because I'm dead tired, but I swear that he's holding himself small and tight like he does when he's withholding something on his mind.

I shut the door. "You okay?" Michael is wearing those short shorts and a tank top that reveals how toned his arms are. I can't wait until his legs are spread and his arms are wrapped around my back.

"Uh, yeah," he says. "Just hungry."

I'm not convinced. But I take the bait.

"Well I got dinner for us right here," I say, leading us into my family room where I have some romantic candles going along with the fireplace. "I got your favorite."

His pad thai sits steaming on my coffee table, and there's a shadow of a smile on his face.

"Why don't you eat and tell me about your week?" I ask.

He nods. "Sure."

I sit down in my usual place, and he sits right next to me. He's still acting like an echo of himself, like he's scared of me or something. I hate it when he acts like this, like he's afraid I'll inevitably hurt him. I don't want to do that. I just want him to be comfortable with me.

"So you're officially unemployed," I say. "How does it feel?"

He digs through his pad thai with chopsticks, stirring up the noodles. He doesn't look at me, but a grin forms on his face.

"About that," he says. "Got some news."

"Right," I say, tapping my forehead. "You said so in your text."

He looks at me for the first time. "I may not be unemployed after all."

My face brightens. "You found an agent?"

He laughs. "No," he says, as if that was impossible. I still don't understand the publishing process well, but after reading so much of his writing, I wouldn't be surprised if he found one any day now.

"Ruckers may hire me," he says.

I turn my full body to him. "The bookstore that brought us together?"

He nods. "Maybe. I still need to interview, but it's looking strong."

The first thing I do is wrap my arms around him and give him a big bear hug. He wraps his arm around mine, and I kiss him on the cheek as I pull away.

"That's awesome," I say. "I know how worried you were."

"Yeah, thanks," he says, looking down at his food. Again, not at me. There's something here he's not telling me.

"Is there something else going on?" I ask. And then I just decide to say it. "Because you're doing that thing where you act all distant."

He looks at me, hurt. "Am I really?"

"Yep."

He sighs. "I try to keep my emotions to myself, but they just spill all over my sleeve. I'm sorry about that."

I put my hand on his thigh and squeeze it. "No unnecessary apologies," I say. "Tell me what's going on, babe. I want to hear it."

He sucks on his lip, then gives me a determined look, one that tells me he'll be completely honest.

"I read that article where you came out," he says.

"You did?" I say, exhausted just thinking about it. "I'm hoping that Robyn doesn't reach out to me again. I don't want to have to answer more questions."

He's chewing on his lips again, like he doesn't know what to say.

"What?" I ask. "Was there something in there you didn't like?"

He shakes his head. "Your dad—I didn't know he was so..."

"Yeah," I say with a sigh. "He wasn't the greatest."

I freeze for a second. I don't think I've said anything negative about him so matter-of-factly before. I thought I'd feel guilty, but I don't. I feel okay.

"I just—" he pauses and fidgets with his fingers. I rub his leg, waiting for him to get his thoughts in order.

"Growing up—" he sighs. "Sorry, this is hard. Growing up, I wasn't close with my parents. I was sort of neglected. Mom and Dad would just come home and do their own thing, leaving me to my own devices, quite literally. So much of my childhood was spent playing my GameCube, by myself, for hours and hours. It got so lonely."

I go from rubbing his leg to gently massaging it. His finger traces the hair along my arm.

"I sorta learned that... well," he blows a raspberry. "As I grew up and got to know kids in other families, I learned how mine was... different. How my dad drank more than usual. How my mom would cover it up, never let me bring it up to anyone. Not even her. I started spending more and more time at friends' houses because I felt better being away from home. And that was good for a while. But once I got to high school, I started to wonder why things were the way that they were—why my dad always drank, why my mom never let me talk about it. But being the isolated, neglected little kid I was, I did the only thing I knew how to do. I blamed myself."

I look up, expecting tears, but his face is stoic. Not rock-like stoic, but poised. Like he's got a handle of himself. Which impresses me. Because if I were telling this story, I'd be blubbering. Like I always do when I talk about my daddy.

He chews on his lips, then continues. "And I believed that for... years. When I finally came out, I kept letting myself fall for straight men who could never be available. And even when I got over that, I would fall for other gay men who were not ready for a relationship, David being the latest example."

My heart still lurches when I hear his name, but I keep it cool for Michael. I know he's going somewhere with this. His talk always makes sense; he never fails to have a point.

I lean back and start running my hand up and down his back. He's hunched over, talking to me yet looking at the table. But I know he's being as open as he can. I've told Neeti about Michael, and she thinks he's a solid guy. I do too.

"It wasn't until I went into Al-Anon recovery and looked at my past that I realized the pattern. I learned I was worthless because of the abandonment I received as a child, so I continued to seek out people who would abandon me as partners."

There's a tightening in my chest. It's not anxiety—I don't feel anxious talking to Michael. But something else. Something like guilt.

"Do you think I'm going to abandon you?" I ask.

He turns fully to me, a shine in his eyes. "That article—you were so deep in there. With this random reporter. But then you also had to lie about you and Amani. And that's when I asked myself—was he lying? I couldn't know. Because all of this is new information to me. You never told me anything about your dad, your upbringing. It hurt for me to discover this from a news article. I wish I heard it from you."

I stop scratching his back as the tightness in my chest shifts to my stomach, and I stare down at my coffee table. Then I get hot. Uncomfortably so. I think my fireplace and the candles are the culprits, but I'm also frozen in place. I couldn't get up to extinguish any of the flames if I wanted to.

Michael puts his hands on my knee, sending a shot of warmth up my leg. Not the bad kind of warmth, though.

"What's wrong?" he asks.

"You're hurt that I wasn't vulnerable with you," I say.

"Yeah." He frowns. "Yes," he says, more firmly.

I imagine myself playing in the cold mud all day, dried blood caked against my arms after getting cut up defending the ball carrier, and then losing. Coming back into the locker room after a defeat and looking at myself in the mirror for the first time—dirtier and more haggard than I expected. Muscles worn, joints sore, skin chaffed. Tired, cold, dejected.

That's how I feel right now.

Because I've heard it all before.

Every woman I've ever tried to date has told me something similar: I'm too closed off, there's a wall between us, I hurt them with something I did or didn't do. I've chalked this up to so many things in my lifetime: them being petty, me being cursed in some way, or that I was gay. The first reason I realized was just misogyny. The second one I eliminated when I came to accept who I truly was.

But the third? I've accepted I'm gay, but here Michael is, the perfect man, telling me the exact same thing. I can't attribute this problem to women anymore, nor can I lump Michael in with the women. Because I see so plainly that I'm the only common denominator. So the second reason has to be true.

I am cursed.

Cursed with what? I don't know. But with all the slander daddy threw at the queers, I can only think that my sexuality is at the root of it all. But that can't be it, can it?

"Hey, talk to me," Michael says. "You look upset."

"How did you do all that?" I ask.

"What?" he asks, leaning back.

"I'm sorry," I say. "I'm just—" I choke up, then curse at myself. Why can't I do any of this without crying?

"I'm sick of feeling trapped inside my own head," I say, tears just flowing. "It's like my feelings storm inside me and try to break out through my tears or my heart or my stomach. I want to be like you. I want to spit it out like a goddamned A-plus essay. God, I wanna know myself like you do, Michael. Because everything you're telling me is true. It always has been. I have a hard time opening up because, truth is, I have no goddamned clue how. As you can guess, I couldn't talk to my goddamned daddy. And even with my mama, who

I knew would listen, I just didn't know how to say. The truth would just get tangled on my tongue and then slip back down my throat like a goddamned le ech."

I take a big, shaky breath. Then I look at him. I expect him to look disgusted. Afraid.

But he's focused on me, leaning in. Like he doesn't want to be anywhere else.

"You promised when we got together that you would trust me," I say.

"I do," he says.

"And bless you for it," I say, holding back a sob. "But what good is that if I can't trust myself to be honest? I don't know how, Michael. I don't."

We sit there in silence, but I can practically hear Michael thinking.

"Do you want to be?" he asks.

"What?"

He swallows. "Do you want to learn how to be honest?"

I almost scoff, but it comes out as a laugh. "Of course I do," I say, wiping my eyes. "Why do you think I'm all worked up about it now?"

He grabs my hand and starts rubbing my knuckles. I watch as his thumb gently pulls my knuckle hair taut, then lets it go.

"Then you can," he says, looking up at me.

"But how?" I say with a sniffle.

"You've been going to therapy?"

I nod. "A ton," I say, laughing. Or sobbing. I can't tell. "But it's not working."

"Not working?"

I think back to all my sessions with Neeti, and my chest aches. "It hurts like hell," I say. "Every time. I thought it was supposed to get easier." I exhale through pursed lips. "Can you help me?"

Michael frowns and shakes his head. "I'm not qualified. Even if I was, I'm too close to you. And Kyle,"

God, I love it when he says my name.

"This is your journey. Only you can go through the pain. Only you can come out the other side. Nobody—not me or your therapist—can do it for you."

I sigh. "So you're saying it's supposed to hurt?"

"It's not 'supposed' to be anything," he says, adjusting himself to sit cross-legged and face me squarely. "It just *is*. Sometimes, this work of digging into who you are is euphoric. Eye-opening. Transformative. Other times, it's like wading through mud. Painful. Exhausting." He sucks on his teeth. "And sometimes, it's mundane and boring, and we see no progress whatsoever. But it's important during all these times just to keep going."

I grimace. "Why?"

He grabs my shoulders and tilts me so I'm squarely facing him, too. I comply and move one of my legs to the other side of him so he's sitting right between them.

"Because *you're* worth it," he says, poking me square in the sternum. "Because there's a little kid inside of you yearning to express himself. To be free. Authentic. To live a life of integrity."

Integrity. I feel like I've been sacked on the field. My dad said that to have integrity is the best way to be, and that was one of the few things that he and my ma agreed on. And now Michael's saying that I can have integrity by digging into who I am.

"You deserve that life," he says. "And so do I. It's why I do all that I do."

I gently grab hold of both of his hands and look into his eyes. And then I pull him close. When his lips press against mine, a jolt of electricity more powerful than anything I've felt before surges through me: more powerful than our first and even when we made love for the first time.

"Sorry," I say when I pull away. "I just had to." More than anything, I want to pull him back in and taste him again. Push him over right here and fuck him senseless. But I want to see this conversation through.

"No unnecessary apologies," he says, holding my hands and rubbing them. We sit there for a minute.

And then I take a deep breath.

"I'm going to learn how to be honest," I say. "For us."

He squeezes my hands. "Do it for you, Kyle. That's the only way it will last."

I think back to that last question Robyn asked me: Do I want to win the Championship Game to prove myself to my dad? Or myself?

"I'll do it for me," I say.

He smiles. "And we'll both benefit."

I lean forward into him, my head on his shoulder, and he rubs my back. I can smell his sweat, so I deliberately breathe in his odor. I want all of him.

"We'll need it," I say. "For better and for worse, this fake-dating gimmick is really working. From what Timmy is telling me, it looks like the Tigers will re-sign me. That means like eight more months of this... secret. Assuming we make it to the Championship Game again. Is that something you can do?"

He exhales his warm breath down the back of my neck. "I think I can," I say. "Let's continue to be open like this. Do what you need to do work on trusting yourself better, becoming more honest."

"I will," I promise. "Starting right now. And I'll contact my therapist tomorrow. But I can't always promise to be perfect."

"Neither can I," he says. Every syllable he speaks vibrates my whole torso.

I look up at him, our faces inches apart.

"Then let's come up with something," I say. I kiss his cheek, then rub his face with my beard, and he moans.

"When I'm having a hard time articulating myself," I say. "Opening up. I'll say..." My mind goes blank.

Michael shrugs. "What about 'it's too hard right now'?"

I shift my legs and look down, realizing the double-meaning. My dick is about to burst out my pants. "It's perfect," I say.

Michael chuckles, but he's still focused on the conversation. "And remember," he says, lifting my chin. "You're worth it." He kisses me on the nose. "Even if all else goes wrong, that will remain true."

I fall forward and kiss him on the lips, holding it there. God, he is so sweet. So divine. So perfect.

I pull away. Words are bubbling up inside me, but I don't know how to say them. So I say the words that are clear in my head.

"I really wanna make love right now," I say. "So bad."

Michael grins and reaches down to my crotch. He feels me, and his eyes widen. "Oh my," he says. "We have to take care of that."

We fall into each other, our lips dancing, our tongues lapping against each other.

Michael takes off my shirt. He kisses my sternum, then traces his tongue up my chest, my neck, my beard, to my lips. I'm leaking so much precum that it's probably staining my pants.

He teases me with his tongue, and I growl. He likes to play with me, to see just how far he can get me until I lose control. But not tonight. Tonight, I'm calling the shots.

I push him down on my couch, and he looks up at me with a smirk.

"Take everything off," I command.

"Yes, sir," he says.

By the time I stand up and manage to shimmy my pants off, he's in just socks and a jock strap.

"How do you want me?" he asks.

"Hands and knees," I say.

He gracefully flips over and presents himself to me, and my cock is already twitching for him.

I come up behind him and trace my big hands down his muscular back, feeling every curve, patch of hair, and bulge of his body. Worshipping him like the divine man he is.

When my hands reach his ass, I stop and marvel. I have big hands, but even I can't wrap them around the orbs he has as ass cheeks. I spread his cheeks wide and feel myself salivate as I stare down at his pink hole, adorned by dark blonde hair shining golden in the candlelight. Like Midas himself had the opportunity to touch his gem.

Hungrily, I lower myself until my face is inches away from it. I've only eaten his ass once, and then I was too nervous, so I stopped before long. But after this conversation, Michael's gonna need a crowbar to pry me out of here.

I take a deep breath, then moan as I press my entire face into his ass. "Fuck," I say. "Michael, you are so perfect."

"It's all yours," he moans.

I kiss his ass cheek, long. "Say it again."

"It's all yours, sir," he says.

I take in another breath, relishing his scent. "Good boy," I say, intoxicated.

And then I dive in. My tongue digs into his hole greedily, selfishly tasting what's mine. Michael's moaning, trying to talk but uttering nonsense instead. Good. I want him incoherent *and* unable to walk when I'm done with him.

"I need you in me," he manages to say.

I lift my head and pull up close behind him, letting my dick rest between inside his plump ass.

"Of course you do," I say. "Because you're a filthy whore for this dick."

He pushes back into my dick, sending a jolt of pleasure all the way up my spine.

"I'm gonna destroy you," I say, almost growling. "And you're gonna beg me for it."

"Oh, please, sir," he says, reaching down to stroke himself. "Please, I need you. Please. Please."

My dick resting on his hole while he pushes back against it, I reach down under the coffee table and pull out some lube. I don't regret stashing a bottle everywhere we like to fuck. I lather myself up, then him, stretching him out with one finger. Then two. Then three, gradually spreading them inside him.

"God almighty," he says, banging his fist against the couch, followed by desperate, rapturous mutterings.

"Oh, you know I'm bigger than this," I say.

He moans and pushes himself up, his back arched, showing me just how big his ass really is. "Then put it in me," he says. "I'm ready. I deserve it."

I chuckle. "Sure you do," he says.

"Please," he begs. "Please, sir."

"There we go," I say, kissing him on his back. He always loves it when I take charge like this. He's been requesting it more and more lately, turning into an insatiable gremlin when I finally do. And I can't complain. I love watching him grovel.

I insert myself into him. Slowly. Torturously slow.

"Oh, fuck," he says, collapsing into the couch. It's only halfway in. "You fucker. Come on."

"Arch that back for me," I command.

He erects himself and holds himself taut, his back muscles flexing. My dick twitches inside him at the sight.

"That's right," I purr. And then I slide the rest in.

His whole body shakes delight, and I have to let go of his ass and take a deep breath. I don't know how long I can last. I take another breath, steeling myself, and then I pull all the way out.

Michael gasps, and the silence after is so thick I can taste it.

And then I insert it slowly back in.

Michael yelps and has to grab the back of the couch to hold himself up.

"Easy," I say, stroking his back. He gets back in position, and then I pull out again.

I lean down and kiss him on the neck. "You good?" I ask.

He nods. "Harder."

I smile and sit back up. And then I thrust it inside him.

He grunts, but he stays completely in place, his back and arm muscles visibly taut.

I do it again, and again, and again, until I can't bear the thought of not being inside him. And then I turn into an animal.

I prop one leg up as I rail him, using his waist as my handles. I use all my strength to both pull him onto me and thrust myself into him. When that's not enough, I grab hold of his mullet like I always like to do, and he moans with pleasure. I spank him with my other hand as I thrust, and he's letting out as steady, almost inhuman groan. He turns his face to me, and he looks like he's died and gone to heaven. Pleasure fizzes throughout my body, and all I can hear are Michael's joyful incoherent mutterings and the clapping of his cheeks.

There's something special here, something different than before. I'm not sure what it is.

But it's not enough. I want more. More of him. I need us closer.

I press my hand against his back. "Get down."

He lowers himself and spreads his legs so his ass is pointed to me and only me. Almost frenzied, I stick it back in him, my whole body already dripping with sweat.

Again, I feel that bubbling in my chest, like there's something I need to say to bring Michael closer to me. Closer than before. I lift my leg to get a better angle, to go deeper. Michael, facing my foot, grabs it and pulls it to his face. He attacks it with his lips and tongue, flashing me the most seductive side-eye. I thrust somehow harder and faster than before, watching him go feral for my huge foot. Needing more balance, I press my foot against his face and pound him harder. He whimpers in delight.

I feel myself getting close, but there's that bubbling in my chest again. I need him closer. Closer.

I retract my foot and pull out.

"On your back," I say. "Now."

He flips over and pulls his legs back, presenting his gorgeous pink hole to me. Feeling out of breath, and like Michael is my air, I put myself back inside him, sighing with relief.

He wraps his legs around my back, pulling me onto him. My hands on either side of his head, I hold myself over him and continue to thrust.

I'm so close, but I don't want to cum yet. I can't. I feel like I need to do or say something, like it's something I've forgotten. That's what the bubbling in my chest is. But I don't know.

A drop of sweat falls from my beard onto his face. He wipes it with his finger and then sucks on it, groaning as his eyes roll back.

I pound him harder, nearly ripping the couch apart. "You fucking slut," I say. "You can't get enough of me, can you?"

That's when he reaches his hands up, strokes my sweaty chest down my belly, then wipes his face with it. He does the same with my armpits, and I think I'm gonna go crazy.

I think Michael loves me. He's patient with me. He listens to me. And he accepts the parts of me that aren't great, like how I can't communicate well. And here he is, still covering himself with my nasty sweat like he can't get enough.

"You're gonna stroke yourself," I say. "And I'm gonna watch you cum."

He nods. He picks up one of my hands and places it on his cheek. Then he sticks my thumb in his mouth and sucks it like it's my cock.

"Fuck," I say. His legs falter a bit, and I command him to keep them wrapped around me. He holds me against him, almost not letting me pull out, and my dick throbs. I know I'm past my point of no return.

He uses his other hand to wipe down my sweaty chest, then reaches down to stroke himself, using my sweat as lube. God, that's fucking hot.

"Yeah, that's right," I say, keeping a fast, steady rhythm. "Cum for me."

He stares into my eyes, his face contorted in desperation, ecstasy, as he slurps on my thumb. In all the videos I've seen him get fucked, he's never looked this happy. My chest bubbles more than ever with something, something I need to say. But it's still unclear.

"You're gonna make me cum," he says.

And those words set me off. As white hot semen shoots out of him all the way up to his neck, I release into him as well. I roar like a bear, flooding his gorgeous ass with my load. The pleasure lasts three seconds, five, ten—so long that my body convulses, and I have to close my eyes and brace myself against the couch so I don't collapse and crush Michael.

When I open them, I look down and find Michael staring up at me in wonderment. And suddenly, my orgasm clearing my mind of confusion, the source of the feeling in my chest becomes crystal clear.

I slowly lean down, and caress Michael, kissing him wildly, our hairy bodies glued together with his cum and our sweat.

"Please, don't pull out," he says. "I want to stay like this forever."

I pull away to look into his eyes and laugh. "I'm not going anywhere."

He nuzzles into my sweaty neck, gently kissing my pec, and I have both arms wrapped around him.

"Michael," I say.

He comes out of his burrow and looks at me.

"I think I..." The bubbling in my chest returns, momentarily scaring me, but then I realize I'm fine. It's actually giving me confirmation about how I feel.

"What?" he asks.

I kiss him on the nose, then pull away. And I'm ready to say it.

"I love you," I say.

Suddenly, I look away, the bubbling in my chest turned to painful tightening, like all the bubbles have tripled in size, and I fear I may have just ruined everything. I shouldn't have said that.

He grabs me by the chin and makes me face him again. Then he raises up to kiss me.

"I love you, too," he says.

And then it's like all the bubbles in my chest pop, providing me sweet release from the pain. I did the right thing.

"Thank God," I say, laughing. I don't know what else to say.

He laughs too, and we lay like that for a while, me on top and inside him. As I look at him, the feeling swells in my chest again.

"God, I love you so much," I say. And the swelling subsides.

He moves his hand through my sweaty hair. "And I love you."

I let my forehead collapse into his chest, and I take a deep breath, taking in our sweat and the earthy smell of sex.

So, this is what being honest with myself is like. What integrity is like. Michael strokes my hair, my heartrate calms, and I feel myself rock hard again. I'm so goddamn happy.

I lift my head and wiggle inside him, already hard again. "Ready for round two?"

He nods. "Vulnerability turns me on."

I grin. "Well, from now on, there will be plenty more of that." I gently thrust into him, and he moans. I laugh. "And much, much more of this."

He wraps his legs around me again, pinning me against him. "What are you waiting for?"

I chuckle. "Just getting started."

Six Months Later

Chapter 31

Michael Cunningham

AFTER THE HUSTLERS'S FIRST down, Amani and I can't take it anymore. We stand up from our seats and hover close to the ledge. The sun has just set, and snow is beginning to fall. Bright lights shine down on Portland's football field. The Tigers are hosting the Hustlers on this cold November Sunday.

We're at the end of the final quarter. The Hustlers are down six, so if they score a touchdown, we go into sudden-death. The Tigers have gone undefeated this entire season, but the Hustlers might end this streak. Yet if the Tigers win this game, their spot in the playoffs is guaranteed. And then we'll be one step closer to the Championship Game.

The Hustlers snap the ball, and their quarterback throws it to their wide receiver. I see Kyle running to intercept.

But he misses.

Amani and I scream, fearing the wide receiver will break away. But he's tackled by someone else just as he reaches the ten-yard line.

"Fuck," Amani says. And I can't help but laugh at her.

At the beginning of the season, she and I knew nothing about football. Kyle had to explain the basics to us repeatedly. But even then things didn't really make sense until we started watching games ourselves. Now I can watch a game and understand almost everything. And I have to say, this has definitely earned me my 'straight-card'. I'm like in the top tenth percentile of gay men who understand sports well.

The Hustlers are now less than twenty yards from a touchdown, and their downs have reset. I reach my hand to my mouth and start biting my nails.

"Look at us," Amani says, her voice muffled by the scarf over her face. "A couple of football chumps turned fans."

I grin. "Honestly, I feel like I've been missing out. This is fun."

Nearby, an older man swears at the Tigers. "Do your damn job, defense," he says. He spits, then takes a sip of his bear. "Fucking faggots."

I bristle at the word. Back in July, the Tigers re-signed Kyle for one more year after they were convinced he was straight—that is, no longer a threat to the Tigers' reputation. And since then, he's been inviting Amani, his fake-girlfriend, and me, her gay best friend, to all his games.

I love watching Kyle play, but it's not all great. In public, he and I have to pretend like we're only acquaintances, and even then it's risky. Timmy, his agent, became wary of me when he found out I was gay. So I just try to give Kyle all the space I can in public, especially when Timmy is around. Luckily, though, he hasn't suspected our whole ruse.

In entering Kyle's world, I expected that we would have to be extra careful. But what I didn't expect was how hostile the football environment would be to people like me and Amani. I mean, sure, gay people aren't banned from being here, but I hear at least one slur every time I come to a football event. No wonder Kyle has been closeted for so long. He'd have been met with nothing but scorn if he was an out player.

The Hustlers snap the ball, and one of the Tigers' linemen breaks through the offensive line. Everyone around us gasps, then exhales in relief when he manages to tackle their quarterback.

"Think we'll win?" I ask Amani.

"Don't even ask that," she says, clutching her lucky anime pendant in her hand. "Don't jinx us."

"Fine," I say, throwing my hands up in defense with a nervous smile.

My stomach is in knots as all the players get into position. Even from here, I can see Kyle's perfect bubble butt, and blood threatens to swarm my groin. I hope we get some intimate time tonight.

This football season has been hard. He's either practicing, out in public with Amani, or preparing for a game, let alone all the travel he has to do for an away game. I hardly get to see him once a week, and I'm lucky if I'm able to sleep over. I wish we could have some sort of vacation, just the two of us. Even if it's just a day.

On the bright side, Kyle's has been trying to be as open as he can about what's going on in his head. Mostly, I feel close to him. But there is one thing I don't understand. Any time I bring up the Championship Game, his jaw locks and shoulders tense. He doesn't look me in the eyes, and he'll bounce one of his legs furiously.

I try to ask what's wrong, but he uses our safe phrase we came up with, 'it's too hard right now'. Out of respect for him, I don't inquire further, but the tension always lingers after that, sometimes ruining the little time we have together. So I just don't bring it up anymore. But my concern only grows the closer the Championship Game comes. What is on his mind?

The Hustlers snap the ball again, and the quarterback manages to throw it. Luckily, Kyle's able to tackle their tight end before he takes off too far. Amani puts her hand on my shoulder to collect herself.

"These games are gonna take years off my life," she says.

"That and this arrangement," I say. "The Championship Game can't come soon enough." Once we're past that, we won't have to live our lives in secret anymore. Plus, he'll have no reason to be tense about the Championship Game anymore.

"Amani!"

I turn around and see Ricardo, the very same reporter that tried to out Kyle last year before the Championship Game.

Amani turns, sees him, then snaps right back to the game. Timmy has instructed her to not speak to Ricardo unless she absolutely has to. He knows how to get people into embarrassing, potentially career-ending binds.

"Amani," he says again, coming down the stairs to us.

"Ricardo," she says without looking at him.

"How is it being a football girl?" he asks. "Dating the Sexiest Man Alive." I glance over at him. He's wearing a coat over his all black suit, a Hustlers tie hanging from his neck.

"It's fun," she says with a smile, still looking at the game. "I've come to love the sport."

He smiles, but there's something on his mind. Something devious. "Tell me," he says. "How is it you two met again?"

Amani's smile falters, and I look right back at the game. I don't want to blush, breathe heavy, or give away any inkling that I'm invested in the conversation. But I'm worried the fact that my tongue intimately knows Kyle Weaver's asshole, that he's seeded me more times than I can count, will somehow betray that I'm the one very much in love with Kyle Weaver.

"At a book club," she says.

"Ah, yes," he says. "Ruckers, was it?"

My stomach sinks. Kyle never went once to that book club. It was only me coming over that gave him the knowledge of what happened so he could prove to his agent that he was going. If Ricardo finds that out...

"Yes," she says. "And if you'll excuse me, I'm watching the game."

"Apologies," he says. "I'll let you and your friend keep watching." And then he disappears up the stairs.

"That was smooth," I say, my heart racing.

"That's one thing I'm looking forward to being over," she says. "I'm done talking to sleazy reporters."

Both of us resume our watch of the game. Two plays have happened, and now the Hustlers are only ten yards from the touchdown line. They could go for a field goal, but they need a touchdown to tie.

The players get into position, and I steadfastly watch Kyle. When the game comes down to a wire, he has a tendency go into beast mode.

The ball snaps, and the quarterback steps back to throw the ball out.

Amani and I hold our breath.

And then it's like Kyle can tell the future.

The Hustlers quarterback looks like he's throwing it to his tight end to his right, but he really throws it to the left. The same direction that Kyle is already running.

The quarterback sees him too late. The ball already in the air, Kyle leaps for it.

And he catches it.

The crowd goes berserk as Kyle runs toward the opposite end of the field, almost unopposed. Amani and I scream his name, and my chest is hot with pride. That's my man.

The timer just about to reach zero, Kyle runs out of bounds just as it hits zero, ending the game and securing the Tigers a win. Now they're in the playoffs.

Amani and I scream and hug each other. I kiss her cheek, and then we see ourselves depicted on the giant stadium jumbotron. I pull away from her quickly. I don't know what's worse: showing everyone I'm gay or doting on the Sexiest Man Alive's girlfriend.

Blurry words appear at the bottom of the screen. When they come into focus, they read 'Weaver's lucky girl'. She cheers and waves, and my stomach curdles.

I know this whole situation is fake, but it hurts my heart every time. Why can't it be me? That jumbotron should be focused on me. It should say 'Weaver's lucky man'.

This season can't end soon enough. I need some sort of reprieve, a vacation. Thanksgiving is coming up. Some teams do play then, but I don't know about Kyle. Maybe I can ask him if we can have alone time. I think I'll need it to make it to February.

The jumbotron focuses on something else, and Amani sighs. "Gosh, that's exhausting," she says, but she's still smiling.

Exhausting is right. I wish I could fault her, but she's the one making a sacrifice for me. And I'll always love her for it.

"Come on," I say, putting my hand on her shoulder. "Let's go greet your boyfriend."

We shuffle up the steps and make our way down the stadium. I console myself with the thought that, at the very least, I get Kyle all to myself tonight.

Chapter 32

Kyle Weaver

IN THE LOCKER ROOM, I'm so swarmed by the reporters that I can't reach my stuff. Ezekiel gets some of them to back off me, but once security gets between us, I'm finally able to shed my sweaty and stained football clothes and grab some fresh ones.

They're all calling my name, trying to talk to me about the game, how it went, how I feel about going to the playoffs. I don't say much until I get one question in particular.

"Kyle, what would your dad think of you now?"

I sit down in my undershirt and take my cleats off. I wiggle my free toes, almost rolling my eyes in relief.

"He'd be proud," I say.

"Do you think you'll win the Championship Game?"

A grin forms on my face. "Let's just say I think I'll keep my promise I made to my dad."

The reporters all blurt out other questions, but security manages to get them out of my face and out of the locker room, leaving me in peace with my team.

Ezekiel sits down next to me. "That was some crazy shit," he says. "I've never seen you go that hard."

I exhale sharply through my nose, taking off my pants. "Me neither."

"I'm glad you got re-signed," he says. "Dunno how we'd make it to the Championship Game without you."

I take off my undershirt and grab my towel for the shower. "It's not just me," I say. "It's all of us contributing."

"Of course," he says, swatting his hand at me. "But you're what's bringing us to the top."

"Well let's just keep it that way," I say, walking to the showers. "Because I only got one chance to win the Championship Game."

"I'll hold you to it," he says.

By the time I'm alone in the shower, there's a bubbling or heat in my chest. I can't really tell anymore. But I know the discomfort comes from guilt.

I can talk about the Championship Game with anyone. But once Michael wants to talk about it, I freeze up. I have to keep telling him 'it's too hard right now', but I can't do that forever.

But I don't know if I can keep up this secret relationship forever, either.

Back in the locker rooms, I got dozens of questions about my playing, my dad, Amani. And none of them were about my sexuality. I never realized how much having a girlfriend shielded me from that sexuality shit. It's like I'm actually normal, and I can finally focus on playing.

And I hate to admit it, but sometimes when I'm practicing, or when I'm playing in a game, I like to pretend that this is my real world—that I really have a girlfriend, and that I'm really carrying my team to the Championship Game and honoring that last promise to my father. And I'm ashamed to admit that this means, briefly, forgetting that Michael exists. There's relief that comes with fitting in, with not being gay in a world that needs me to be straight.

Not to mention the guilt I feel about lying about this whole relationship. Both Mom and Dad talked about integrity. How honorable is it of me to hide a man that I'm fucking? Sure, my dad would be proud of me for making it this far. But would he be proud of me for dating a man in secret? Would he be proud of me for dating a man at all? Abandoning the family legacy?

My chest aches badly, the guilt getting stronger. Because all this means that I'm turning my back on the kindest, smartest, and gentlest man I know.

I turn off the water, hoping my thoughts will turn off with it. They don't, but that doesn't matter. I gotta get dressed and meet Amani. And Michael.

When I get to our designated meeting spot, Amani emerges from a horde of people. I put on my biggest smile for the flashing cameras, and we kiss deeply.

Once we release, I spot Michael staring at me from the crowd swaddled in warm clothing. He's looking at me passionately, like he wishes it was him kissing me instead. We wave to the cameras, then disappear into the crowd, led by security. The three of us stay silent until we reach our area of the parking garage and are completely alone.

"Well you were amazing," Amani says.

"Thank you thank you," I say with a mock bow.

Michael smiles lukewarmly, holding himself small like he does when he's upset. Fuck, I hate seeing him like this.

"So the usual plan?" Amani asks.

I glance at Michael. She comes to my house, drops Michael off, then goes her own way, then Michael slinks off with his car the next day. I want Michael over, but at the same time, I don't. God, we're only halfway through the season. Can I do this for another three months?

"Sure," I say, looking down at the ground.

Without another word, we go our separate ways. Once I'm on the highway, I replay the game in my head, thinking on how I can improve. But I keep seeing Michael's hurt face. When he's asked what's wrong, I've told him I'm not ready to talk. Yet I can only do that for so long. Sooner or later, I'm gonna have to say something. I just have no idea what I want to say. I can't give up this season. But I sure as hell don't want to give Michael up either.

I get home, and Michael and Amani arrive shortly after. She pulls into the garage, drops him off, then slips away before anyone sees. I drop my bag in the laundry room, take his stuff, and carry it up to my room without a word.

I set everything down to the side, and Michael sits down on my bed. He looks up at me, expectantly.

"That was a fantastic game," he says. "I was able to follow everything."

God, I love how earnest he is.

"Yeah?" I say, unable to stop the grin forming on my face. "I'm glad you both are taking a liking to football."

Months ago, I would pin him down and place and start kissing him. But it feels wrong to do that tonight after all my daydreaming of living a straight life. So instead, I strip my clothes and slip into bed beside him. I open up the covers for him to join me.

He looks at me, curious as to why I've skipped our normal step. But he says nothing. Instead, he gets into bed and snuggles up next to me. I wrap my arms around him.

"Is everything okay?" he asks.

"Yeah," I say. "Why wouldn't they be?"

"You just seem... distant."

I frown. "I'm just tired," I say. "The game took a lot out of me. My knees are sore, and I know I should be putting ice on it. I'll have to do that tomorrow."

"I'd stay and help," he says. "But I have my shift at Ruckers tomorrow."

Too tired to respond, I let my eyes drift shut. Then Michael moves, startling my eyes open. He turns around and looks at me, my nightstand lamps giving his face an orange glow.

"I should have said this sooner," he says.

My stomach sinks to the floor. Is he breaking up with me? But if he was, that would solve all my problems. Why do I feel sick to my stomach then?

"I think the stress of the season is getting to both of us," I say. "Maybe you and I should take a vacation. Together."

The pain in my chest subsides. He's not breaking up with me.

"A vacation?"

"Yeah," he says, talking a little more excitedly. "Like between one of your games and practices. We can get away from the city for a little bit."

"I don't know," I say. "It would have to be brief."

"It doesn't even have to be more than a day," he says. "The holidays are coming up. I know the Tigers aren't playing on Thanksgiving."

I chew on my lips. "You wanna do Thanksgiving together?"

His brow curls. "Why wouldn't I?"

More than I want to push him away, I want him to pull away himself. I can't bear to see him hurt, let alone be the one to hurt him. But he knows this can't work long term. Doesn't he? He has to. If I've learned anything playing in the NFO with a secret relationship the past sixth months, it's that this is not sustainable. Someone's gonna find us out sooner or later.

"I usually spend it with my ma if I'm free," I say.

He waits for a beat, then deflates. "I see."

"Come on," I say, rubbing his hand. "We can talk more about this in the morning."

Michael turns around without saying anything. I wrap my arms around him, but he doesn't hold them like he usually does. He's even holding his body away from me, as if I'm made of thorns. Guilt floods my chest again. I mean, I practically am made of thorns right now, aren't I? Making my words and demeanor all prickly like this?

Eventually, he drifts off, and the pain in my chest subsides enough to let me sleep.

My dreams are frenzied. I'm at a game. On the field. I need to score. But I also need to find Michael. Something tells me that he's far, far away. With some guy? Probably. I run and run, but the turf just expands beneath my feet, keeping me in place.

Then I'm tackled. Another guy piles on me, then another. And suddenly, I'm swallowed up, unable to breathe. I hear my daddy's voice. Nothing specific. Just angry. Yelling.

"Michael!" I choke out.

And then I startle awake. I'm laying on my belly, so no wonder I can't breathe. I get back on my side and reach out for Michael.

But he's not there.

My eyes shoot open, and I look around. Rain is falling outside, pattering against the window. I hear the sound of water trickling in the bathroom. Then it stops.

"Michael, where are you?"

I hear the toilet flush and the sink run. Then Michael comes out of the bathroom.

"Right here," he says.

I feel my eyes heat up and my lips quiver. I open my arms. "Come get in bed."

He comes and gets under the covers, and I wrap myself around him tightly. And I never want to let go. I thought he was gone, but I'm so happy to have him back in my arms.

"What's wrong?" he asks, stroking my hairy arm gently.

"I'm sorry for the way I'm acting," I say. "I don't know how to explain it all. Neeti is trying to help, but like you said." I pause and let some of the tears fall. "Sometimes it's just hard."

He turns to me and starts rubbing my chest. "I know it is," he says. "Thanks for telling me."

I press my forehead against his. "I'm sorry you gotta deal with a lug like me," I say. "I know this isn't easy for you, me being so guarded and all."

"It isn't," he admits, which brings on more tears. But I'm glad he's being honest.

We hold each other there, and I feel myself hardening. There's a lot I don't know, but I think I know one thing for certain right now.

I do not want to lose Michael Cunningham.

"I got an idea for a vacation," I say.

Even in the dark, I can see Michael's face brighten. "What's that?"

There's only one place I really love to go when it's fall. It's practically winter up here in Portland, but down south, the weather couldn't be better. The trees are all multi-colored, and the air has that crisp smell of fire burning.

"Glamour Springs, where my ma lives, is beautiful this time of year," I say. "People know me there, but it's isolated enough where you and I could walk around. Together. How does that sound?"

Our chests so close together, I can feel Michael's heartrate speed up.

"That sounds perfect," he says. "We'd be spending Thanksgiving with your mom, right? Does she know about us?"

Us.

My ma does not know about my secret boyfriend. I've never really told her that I'm gay, either. But something tells me that she knows. I've been reluctant to say anything to anyone I know, lest they get interviewed and out my secret.

Best to wait until after the Championship Game. Nonetheless, I can't think of anyone better for Michael to spend the holiday with. And I think I'd like her to meet him.

"She doesn't," I say. "But that doesn't matter. I want you to meet her anyways."

Michael's face dampens a little, making my chest tighten. He's disappointed.

"Sorry," I say. "I just haven't told many people I know. I'm waiting until—"

"It's fine," Michael says. "I get it."

We lay there silently, my arms around him and his fingers running through my chest hair. By now, both of us are too alert to fall back asleep. My erection has been pressed hard against his leg, but I steadily feel his harden against my belly.

"We don't have to if you don't want to," Michael says, shrinking into himself. He always does this when he feels bad about something, and it hurts me.

"Michael," I say. "I don't want you to feel bad about talking to me about these things, or even asking me when I don't want to talk about it. It shows you care. And that's what I love about you."

He sighs and nuzzles into my chest. "I know," he says. "Sometimes it's just hard."

I kiss him on the top of his head. "I know, baby. I know."

We lay like this until he's so rock hard that he's dry humping my belly.

"I've given you enough grief," I say, unwrapping my arms. "Let me take care of this."

"What?" he asks, almost bewildered.

But then he moans in relief as I wrap my lips around his cock.

I suck him thoughtfully for a while, his hands feeling all over my body.

I release his dick from my mouth. "I know what you need," I say. I hoist one of my legs over his head and hover my ass just over his face.

"Oh, yes," he says, desperately. "Oh, fuck yes."

"Eat up," I say as he buries his face in me. "I know how much you like my post-game ass."

He lets out an agonized moan as his tongue probes me and his nose takes in my scent. "It's divine," he says. "It gets better every time."

And that's when I get to sucking. I want to get my hand involved, but I don't want to lose my balance and break Michael's flow. I want to give him all the pleasure I can.

"So close," he says.

I let go. "Already?" I ask in a playfully mocking tone. "You've barely even started."

I engulf his dick with my mouth once more, and he loses it. His hot load floods my mouth as he goes feral for my hole, like I'm the only thing he's eaten in days.

I keep him in my mouth until I've swallowed every drop and his dick goes limp. His head relaxes, and unmount myself. When I lean up onto my knees, I realize how engrossed I was in Michael's pleasure. Because I'm just now noticing how I'm rock-hard and dripping precum.

"I want it," Michael says.

"You want me to fuck your face?" I say. "You think you've earned it?"

"Please," he says, squirming. "I need it, sir."

I smile. "Of course you do."

I reach down and pin his arms above my head. Then I place my knees on either side of him, pinning his arms in place. I put one of my hands on his wrists to keep them clamped down for good measure.

And then I put my dick into Michael's hot mouth.

He starts sucking, but he doesn't have much mobility. And I know how much he loves it when I take control. So I grab hold of his hair and pull him back and forth.

"My little fleshlight," I say, smirking.

He moans, almost gagging as I move his head, my dick going in and out of his mouth.

I had seen him and other guys do this position in videos, but I had never imagined I would be doing it. And the first time he requested it, I felt bad. Like

I was hurting him, taking advantage of him. But after much of his insistence, I gave in. And seeing how turned on he gets, it's now one of my favorite positions.

"I don't think you really like it," I say.

Michael moans and starts moving his lips and tongue more, doing anything he can to make my dick feel good.

"That's what I like," I say. I let go, lean forward, then thrust my dick into his mouth. He gags, his hands squirming. But he hasn't used our safe signal—three taps against the bedframe—so I know he's loving it.

I glance behind me and see that his dick his hard again. "Greedy boy," I say. "You want to cum again? With my dick in your mouth?"

He stops and nods with the most determined expression I've ever seen.

I lean back, and he sits slightly up. I free his hands, and they clutch my thighs as he starts moving his head back and forth on my dick. I reach back and start stroking his dick.

We stay in this equilibrium for a while. My eyes adjusted to the dark, I stare down at him as he greedily swallows me. His hands run up my thighs, my belly, my chest. He clutches my pecs, then starts thumbing my nipples.

"Oh, my god," I say, frozen.

And he smirks up at me, still sucking.

"You've found my weak spot," I say. "Holy shit."

I lean forward and thrust into his mouth, letting go of his dick and taking full control.

Michael Cunningham, the man who knows how to turn me on. Who knows what to say. Who is always patient with me. Kind with me. There's no way in hell I'm letting him go. Hell, I might even just quit in the middle of the season. Just so I can be with him.

No, I won't do that.

But I will make it to the end. 'Til after the Championship Game. And then we won't have to be a secret anymore.

"I'm gonna fucking cum," I say. "Don't fucking stop."

He keeps fiddling with my nipples, his tongue and mouth pure ecstasy on my dick.

And then I let out the fattest load.

I pin Michael's sweaty forehead down as I thrust my spurting dick into his mouth, letting out a low, inhuman groan.

Once I'm all out, I sit there on Michael's chest, my own chest heaving and sweat dripping down my body. I would get up, but Michael now has his arms wrapped around my thighs, holding me in place, with my entire shaft down his throat.

He moves one of his arms under my leg, down to his dick, and starts stroking. He looks up at me, my cock still deep in his mouth, his eyes shining with pleasure. I pull my cock out for a moment, and Michael balks at me.

"Patience," I say. I take the spit and cum on my dick, lean back, and lube Michael's dick up with it.

And then he greedily puts my dick back into his mouth like it's his pacifier.

"Now cum again for me," I command.

And it doesn't take him long. Once he's finished, I grab a towel and clean us both up. Then, both of us sufficiently exhausted, we get back in bed and I hold him tightly in my arms once again.

I kiss him gently on the neck as I feel sleep taking me on.

"I can't wait for Thanksgiving," he says.

I breathe him in, then sigh contentedly. "Me too."

Chapter 33

Kyle Weaver

Since Michael had to work at Ruckers up until Thanksgiving, I fly down to Glamour Springs a couple days earlier to get everything in order and help my ma out.

"For the last time," my ma says while I hover over her shoulder at the stove. "I'm good. I prefer to handle all the food anyways. You know that."

"I know, ma, but sheesh." I gesture to the kitchen counter covered in nearly a dozen different aluminum containers. "Do you plan on feeding the whole town?!"

She shrugs. "I make extra to give away," she says. "And I'm having Jimmy over, along with Silas from the bookstore."

So Thanksgiving dinner is going to be me, Michael, my ma, Jimmy from the diner, and Silas. "I met Silas, I think. The guy with the linebacker build at the bookstore?"

"That's the one," she says. "Martha and Llewellyn are headed to Jackson to see Martha's parents. They'll be leaving Thanksgiving morning, so I wanted to give Silas a place to eat."

"Well that's mighty kind of you," I say.

"You know what would be mighty kind?" she asks. "Clearing out some boxes in the guest room so you and your friend won't have such a cluttered room."

I cringe at the word. *Friend.* Michael isn't my friend, but she doesn't know that.

"Wait," I say, confused. "We aren't sleeping in the same room. He's gonna stay there. And I'll be on the couch."

She looks at me like I'm the dumbest person on the planet. "You're one of the most important players in the NFO, and you want to sleep on a couch? You have any idea what sleeping on that thing will do to your back? Believe me, I've tried it, and it's not good."

My ma's hairless cat, Miss Beautiful, prances into the kitchen, meowing up a storm.

"Oh no you don't," Ma says. "You're not getting any of this food."

Miss Beautiful whines as she purrs and rubs herself against my ma's leg. All three of us know that my ma will cave in eventually.

"Well, we're not sleeping together," I say. "We're..." I let myself trail off. Calling him my friend myself feels like betrayal. Yet betrayal might be fitting. I've been nothing but cold to Michael the past few weeks, despite what I said in bed a weeks ago. Every time I get scared about the future, I go back on my promise to be more open and push him away. I've been a rotten boyfriend. And I know he knows it.

She turns me and eyes me above her reading glasses. I almost wither under her glare. She has to know the truth, or I'm not a gay linebacker playing for the Tigers.

"Well, whoever he is," she says turning back to the stove. "He deserves to sleep in a clean room. I know you don't care, but I care about my guests. Take all those boxes and put them in the hall closet. Please and thank you."

"Aye aye," I say. "Yes ma'am."

I shimmy past my luggage in her living room and make my way to the guest room. This is where I usually stay when I visit, but I've never cared about the clutter. Ma always likes to make sure that the house is presentable to guests.

There are a couple of boxes open next to the bookshelf, and glancing at it, I never realized how big a romance fan my mother is until now. It's filled with Nora Roberts, Danielle Steele, and Nicholas Sparks books. I wonder what she would think of the romance book club that brought Michael and I together. Soon enough, I might tell her the whole story.

I crouch down to pick up one of the boxes, but I spot something familiar inside. I open it up, and I'm assaulted by the smell of dust and memories. Just inside, there's a cyan blue jersey with my name on it, the very same jersey I wore when I played football in high school.

I pick it up and hold it to my face. The texture is as coarse as I remember, and I swear I can still smell my old sweat and the scent of grass. God, this brings me back to those hot Saturdays, the ones where I'd play with Ma and Daddy watching from the sidelines. Ma was always so encouraging. Daddy was harsher, pointing out my flaws first. Sure, he helped me get better. But I don't know if it was worth all the hurt.

Underneath the jerseys, there are several old photos. One sticks out to me in particular. It was just after our homecoming game, I remember. Ma wanted a picture. I agreed, but Dad was being all grumpy about it. Eventually, we took the photo. I have my arm wrapped around him, but he's just frowning.

Suddenly, something hits me. My nose tickles, and my eyes heat up. I think it's just the dust, but my lip starts quivering. Goddamnit, I'm tired of all this crying. But I just have to remember what Neeti, my therapist, told me: our feelings aren't good or bad. They just are. I have to let them pass.

I stare down at the picture—at my father who left this earth so many years ago. That game, I scored my first touchdown through an interception, what would soon become my trademark thing. But Dad wasn't impressed. He said he'd seen guys who had done better.

Of course he had. He coached at Miss U. But I was just some sixteen-year-old. Sure, I improved with his coaching. But I needed love more than anything. And I never got it. And sitting here, letting my tears fall, I realize what Neeti has been trying to tell me for so many months now.

I was never good enough for my father.

Even on his deathbed. He made demands of me—demands that he likely knew I couldn't keep.

Even if I did win the Championship Game this year—even if I did carry on the family legacy by marrying and having children—I'm not sure I would have satisfied him.

I set the picture down back into the box, and then I put my old jersey over it. Whenever the conversation has turned to my dad, Neeti has asked me what I've done that *I'm* proud of—not my daddy, Timmy, my ma, my fans, or even Michael. Me. And for whatever reason, my mind would go blank whenever she asked me. I had no idea.

But now I think I can start answering that question. For myself. And the first thing that comes to mind is that I've somehow landed the kindest, most handsome man as a boyfriend. And he's flying in later today.

So I'm going to stop being a rotten boyfriend and make the most out of our time here. Regardless of what my dad might think if he was around. I'm tired of hiding. Of living up to other definitions of integrity rather than my own. I don't know what I'm doing about the rest of the football season. I enjoy the sport, and I may want to hold out until the end just because I want to, not for my dad. But I do know that when the time is right, I'm telling the world about me and Michael. And no one's going to stop me.

Chapter 34

Michael Cunningham

As I stand outside the Memphis airport waiting for Kyle to pick me up, the fall sun warms me, but dread pools in my stomach.

This may be the trip where I end my relationship with Kyle. For good.

This might seem abrupt, but hear me out.

A few weeks ago, Kyle promised we'd go on vacation together. And we are, which is awesome. But everything after that has been awful.

Kyle still won't talk about what we'll be after the Championship game, and the few times I've asked him just about the game itself, he hasn't just been cold. He's been mean.

And that's happened the few times I've actually been able to see him. Even though he's been in town for a majority of this month, he's blown me off most nights, making up excuses he's never used before, like how he's had mandatory team-building sessions with the Tigers or one-on-one training sessions.

Even when I'm with him, it's like he's a shadow of himself, just like how David was when he drank. But Kyle doesn't drink. So I don't know what's wrong.

After all this, he still bought me a ticket down to Glamour Springs, but that doesn't undo all the damage he's done. This relationship is starting to feel like it did with David. I made a promise to myself to not date emotionally unavailable men, and right now, Kyle's as emotionally unavailable as they come. I'm currently querying my romantasy about two gay knights, but I've been having writers block with my next novel, and I suspect that my failing relationship with Kyle has something to do with it. I'm not letting immature men stymie my creative process anymore.

But Susan also suggested not to do or say anything too soon. Kyle and I still had this trip planned, so I figured this would be the perfect opportunity to see how I really feel about us. I'll try to enjoy it, but I won't hesitate to end our relationship if it feels right.

Speaking of which, a man more handsome than I can stand pulls up to the curb. I trot over to the trunk, plop my bags inside, then get in the passenger seat. I shut the door, and Kyle's wearing these old aviators that make him look like a hot daddy.

"There's my man," he says. He leans over the console and kisses me.

I freeze. "There are people around," I say, pointing to the college students also waiting on the curb.

He swats his hand. "They don't see it's me," he says. "And besides, you're worth it."

A warm feeling brews in my chest. This is the true Kyle Weaver. Before he went cold.

"You ready for turkey day?" he asks as we make our way out of the airport parking lot.

"I am," I say. "Excited to meet your mom."

He smiles. "She's excited to meet you too."

I'm tempted to ask if she knows about us yet, but I don't want to be disappointed. So I keep the question to myself.

On the drive, we catch up with what we've been reading. Even though Kyle doesn't need to be in the romance book club, he still asks me to bring him his weekly copy. And somehow, on top of his NFO schedule, he gets the reading in. Before, he hated romance, but now he gobbles it up. I don't know how, but it makes me believe he's more emotionally available than I think. Why else would he read a bunch of romance for fun?

Ugh. This is confusing.

Because on top of all this, I love Kyle. I love talking about nonsense, hearing his thoughts about what he's reading, about his gameplay. I love it when he asks about my writing. David sure as hell never did that, and I only have a few choice friends that do. Right now, he feels like a boyfriend—the same man I fell in love with. I feel guilty for even wanting to break up with him.

By the time we reach Glamour Springs, just outside of Miss U, I'm convinced that Kyle's frozen heart from this month has thawed. Something's changed in him.

We pull into his mother's gravel driveway. It's one of those small, postage stamp houses, but the front porch is surrounded with flowers I didn't even know could bloom this late in the fall. It is warmer down here, but still. The house is painted a bright red, and there are bird feeders and windchimes hanging all around the porch. A ways behind the house, there's a hill that leads down to a placid looking lake. On the far end, there's a big wooden building with a dock attached, and then a bunch of small wooden cabins surrounding the lake. It's idyllic.

Kyle gets out of the car and hurries around it. By the time I've unlocked my door, he's opened it for me and holding it out wide.

I thank him and step out to smell the crisp fall air. The air also feels fresher down here, and I'm surprised how quiet it is. All I can hear are Kyle's feet crunching the gravel as he pulls our bags out of the trunk. I then hear the metal creak of a door opening, and I turn to see a petite woman with a gray bob walking out onto the porch.

"I finally get to meet him," she says. She hugs her orange cardigan tightly around herself as she walks down the porch stairs.

"Ma," Kyle says, dropping our bags next to me. "This is Michael. Michael, this is my ma."

"Call me Linda," she says, coming to us. "Welcome to Glamour Springs." She wraps her arms around me with a force I didn't think a woman of her size could have. I try to hug her back with the same fervor, but I swear I'm weaker. There has to be something in the water down here.

"So nice to meet you," I say, able to breathe when she lets me go. "Thank you so much for having me in your home."

"About that," she says, eyeing Michael then me like she's got a spicy secret. I like her already.

"What, ma?" Kyle asks. His accent was noticeable before, but it's now taken on a life of his own. It's like his mom brings out his true self.

"I've got a surprise for both of you," she says. She turns and gestures for us to follow. "Come inside."

I reach to grab my bag, but Kyle blocks my hand. He picks up the bags himself, showing just how big his arms have gotten this season.

"Welcome to my home," he says. "Well, sorta. My ma's. But it's my own." He kisses me on the lips, and I hold it there. This is the Kyle I love, the one who's present and available and kind and thoughtful. The one who has been fading away over the past few months. But he's here now. And I don't want him to go away.

"I'm happy to be here," I say.

"Come on inside!" Linda yells. "The brownies will get cold."

We get inside, and I relish the scent of lavender. A large, hairless cat with a blue collar comes up and rubs her leg against me, jingling the bell on its collar.

"Miss Beautiful," Kyle says. "You be nice to Michael."

I laugh. "Miss Beautiful?"

"Hope you're not allergic," Linda says from the kitchen. "She can be a real devil."

Kyle leans into me. "She's the sweetest thing to walk the earth," he says. "And my ma knows it."

I smile as I crouch down to pet Miss Beautiful. She purrs like a truck engine, nearly knocking me over as she tries to scratch her back against my leg.

"Come on," Kyle says, walking into the kitchen.

I stand and follow him into the kitchen. Both the counter and table are covered with all different sizes of aluminum containers.

"Sheesh, Linda," I say. "You went all out."

"Thanksgiving's my favorite holiday," she says, putting on an apron. "And I still have to bake some pies. Here." She puts out a plate of decadent looking brownies with orange goo on the top, likely caramel, and small salt flakes.

"Ma, you made these?" Kyle asks, widening his eyes. He stares down at the plate, nearly drooling. "It's been years since I've had this."

"It's my surprise on this special occasion," she says, looking between the both of us. "Try it!"

I pick up one of the brownies and take a generous bite. Warm caramel oozes into my mouth, and I can't stop myself from moaning.

I put my hand on the plate. "Can I just take this whole thing home with me?"

Linda laughs. "Oh, you. I'll make some more to take before you leave. Better eat them before you get on the plane!"

"Ma," Kyle says as I finish up the delicious brownie. "This is so nice of you. You didn't have to do this."

She shrugs. "It's not every day that your only son brings a wonderful man home."

My stomach clenches, and I glance over at Kyle. He's blushing, almost embarrassed. Does his mom know about us? She's talking as if it's obvious, but it looks like Kyle hasn't said a thing.

"Is there anything we can do for you?" I ask. "To help?"

"Oh, you're sweet," she says, shooing me. "But I love cooking and this time of year, giving away the food. It's like meditation."

"Yeah," Michael says. "And if you try to help her, she'll whack you with a wooden spoon."

She holds up a wooden spoon and wears a menacing expression, then laughs and relaxes. She goes up to Kyle and kisses him on the cheek. Then she squeezes my arm.

"I'm so happy you're here," she says. "You're welcome any time. I'm happy you're here with my son."

Something sticks in the back of my throat, and I have to clear it. She pulls away and starts gathering ingredients for what looks like a pumpkin pie, but I'm still reeling.

I can't remember the last time my own mother held me like that, like she loved me. And Kyle's mom is already treating me like one of her own. I know I said that I might break up with Kyle on this trip, but how could I after this? I could have a loving family with Kyle.

Kyle brightens. "I know what we can do," he says. "I'll take you to The Book Corner. It's a lesbian-owned coffee shop."

I raise my brow. "There are lesbians out here? In small town Mississippi?"

Linda starts measuring some sugar. "Glamour Springs is a wonderful little progressive dot. I love Mississippi, but it has its flaws. Living here is like having everything I could want."

I glance at Kyle, judging his reaction. He doesn't seem bothered by what his mom is saying at all.

"And that sounds like a great idea," she says. "See Martha and Llewellyn before they skedaddle tomorrow."

"I would like to get some writing done," I add, glancing back at my bag. "Could I do that there?"

"Right," she says, pouring the sugar into a bowl. "Kyle said you were a writer."

"I guess so," I say, shrugging.

Kyle puts his hand on my shoulder, sending warmth down my torso. He squeezes it. "Kyle's not just any writer. His stuff is good."

"You better send me something when it's done," she says. "You write romance?"

"Fantasy romance," I say, feeling shy like a little kid when all the attention's on him.

"Oh! Even better."

"I'm trying to find an agent now," I say. "Fingers crossed."

"You're in my prayers," she says, smiling at me through her reading glasses.

"Let's go check it out," Kyle says.

We get in his rental car, and he takes me down up the road, through some dense trees, to their town center. In the center, they have a municipal building all surrounded by shops I don't recognize. Ma and Pa shops, likely. Catty-cornered to the center is a large diner, and across from that I spot our destination: The Book Corner.

"This is where I read that Cat Sebastian book," he says as we park. "The one that helped me see I was gay."

"No way," I say as we get out.

When we enter the store, I take a deep breath, and I feel at home. All bookstores—Barnes & Noble to your used bookstore—have that distinct smell. It makes me want to sit down and read, write, and talk to other book enthusiasts. It inspires me honestly, making me feel like I could do anything I wanted. And that includes getting an agent.

I peruse the shelves, awed by how large their collection is despite being in such a small town.

"Welcome in," a woman says. She's black with her hair tied in a bandana above her head.

"Llewellyn, right?" Kyle says.

She nods. Then her eyes widen. "Oh my gosh," she says, her accent coming out. I love the way people sound here. "You're Kyle Weaver."

He shrugs with a smile. "The one and only."

"Silas told me you visited the other day, but I didn't—my goodness. Martha!"

A redheaded woman at the counter looks up. Then her jaw drops. "Sweet Jesus, he's back!"

She rushes from behind the counter and greets us. "Sorry," the redheaded woman—Martha—says. "I know you were here a few months ago, but I couldn't believe it. When I checked out that book for you, I nearly—"

"It's okay," Kyle says with a laugh. "I'm glad to be back."

"And I'm so glad you stopped by before we got outta town," she says. "How's your mama?"

"Good as can be."

Martha turns to me. "And who's this handsome man?"

I blush. "I'm Michael," I say. I glance at Kyle. How should I introduce myself? Friend? Boyfriend?

"He's visiting from Portland," he says.

"Very cool," Martha says. "Well, make yourselves at home."

"Can I get you guys anything from the café?" Llewellyn asks.

I suck on my lip. He didn't say boyfriend. But not friend, either.

Kyle looks at me. "You want an apple cider?"

"Yes" I say. "Sounds heavenly."

"If I don't see you again," Martha says as Llewellyn heads to the café. "You all have a wonderful Thanksgiving. And thank you for taking Silas in. It really means a lot to him."

"You probably know my ma by now," he says. "She'd take care of the whole world if she could."

"That's right," Martha says. "You boys enjoy."

"Alright," Kyle says, a grin on his face. He seems so natural here.

I sit down at one of the café tables and take out my laptop.

"I'm gonna look around," he says. "I'll find something to read and join you."

I nod to him and crack my computer open. As it's booting up, I watch as Martha and Llewellyn giggle behind the café counter. Llewellyn says something I can't hear, and Martha grins and kisses her on the cheek. Warmth tickles my chest.

I didn't know such a place existed, in Mississippi of all places. It's giving me inspiration to how we could be more inclusive to queer folks up at Ruckers. And to think that this is where Kyle considers home. For months, I've been afraid he's too afraid to accept me. But being here makes me think he clearly does.

I start writing while Kyle checks out a book. I open up to a scene that has been giving me grief for days. I try to write every day, but in the past week I've only gotten a few words in. I just can't seem to figure out the chemistry between the two gay magicians in my new work-in-progress. Is it grumpy-sunshine? Or second chance? Nothing feels right.

Our ciders are ready, and Kyle picks them on his stroll back. He hands me my drink.

"Thanks," I say. I blow on my drink. "What did you get?"

"Cat Sebastian's other mid-century book," he says. "Silas had a note written by it that it was just as good as the baseball one."

"Then it must be wonderful," I say.

He nods and sets the book down. He's laying back with the drink in his hand, his arms crossed, making his biceps, triceps, and chest bulge. The title of his book is *We Could Be So Good*, and I can't help but disagree. Kyle and I *are* good—it's not a hypothetical. So why am I thinking about ending this at all?

"How's the writing going?" he asks, taking a sip.

"It's not," I say with a sigh. "Can't figure out the dynamic between my love interests, which is like the entire point of a romance novel."

He leans forward, resting his elbows on the table. "I'm sorry, babe. But I know you'll get it. I've read plenty of you're writing. You know how to write connection well. It might be hard now, but you'll get there."

My chest swells. "You think?"

"I *know*," he says, nodding. "Plus, I feel so connected to you. That could count for something, right? As inspiration?"

I could swoon so hard that I fall off this chair. Where has this Kyle been? This is the man that I like—*love*.

"I love you," I say.

"I love you, too," he says.

I take a sip of my apple cider, then sigh, contented. "Now to writing."

He reaches over and pats me on the arm. "You got this."

He starts reading, and I start writing.

I start writing.

Holy shit. Of course. They're not grumpy sunshine or second chance. They're unlikely lovers. Just like me and Kyle. One's a magician trained in the order, the other orphaned and destitute. Yes. And as the experienced one trains the other one, they grow closer, similar to my first book. That's exactly it.

The inspiration has been in front of me this whole time. Literally. It's Kyle.

I get into that flow state where all I can think about are the words coming out of my fingertips, the kind that makes anyone with writers block jealous.

This is why I decided against emotionally unavailable men when I broke up with David years ago. I could never conjure up such intimacy if I was busy trying to win the attention of a man who didn't or couldn't love me. But now it's easy, and I think I know why...

I'm in love with someone who's actually emotionally available.

In what feels like a blink of an eye, Martha announces that the store will close in fifteen minutes.

"Already?" I ask, looking around. Besides a few customers at the checkout counter, we're alone.

"Yeah," Kyle says, rubbing his eyes. "How is Cat Sebastian so good?"

I glance over my computer and see he's already halfway through. "*That* good, huh?"

He shakes his head. "It's like she can read my mind." He checks his phone. "Shit, Mom's called three times."

"That's not good," I say, closing my computer. "We should head back. Sorry, I got lost in the flow."

"Don't worry about it," he says as we start making our way out. "Probably just telling us about dinner."

When we get back to Linda's, the house smells like chicken and vanilla, which is a surprisingly appetizing smell. She's on the couch in her pajamas. She's reading her kindle, and Miss Beautiful is curled up beside her.

"Was hoping you boys would eat with me," she says. "But figured y'all were busy. And I was hungry."

"Sorry, ma," Kyle says, shutting the door. "We'll clean up."

"That would be darling, thanks," she says.

"Why don't you go eat?" Kyle says. "I'll get your bed set up in the guest room."

Your bed.

Was everything I experienced just a lie? He can be my sweet boyfriend, but when it comes down to it, he'll sleep in a different bed?

"Oh," Linda says, slapping her forehead. "I forgot." She reaches over to her side table and picks up a small key chain. "Here," she says, handing it to Kyle.

"I wanted you boys to be comfortable while you were here," she says. "So I got you a cabin down by the lake."

"A cabin?" Kyle and I ask in unison.

"Yes, a cabin," she says like we didn't hear her. "Glamour Springs has a tradition of putting a little show on the water on Thanksgiving evening. Wanted to give you boys a front row."

Butterflies flutter in my stomach. Now that sounds romantic.

I steal a glance at Kyle. He's chewing on his lips, and I can practically hear the cogs turning in his brain. Is he upset? Angry? Sad?"Thanks, ma," he says, almost sounding relieved. He takes the keys from her.

She looks up and pats his arm, and there's more love and knowledge in that gesture than meets the eye.

She knows, and she wants the best for us.

He looks at our luggage, then at me. "Let's eat, then make our way over."

"Perfect," I say.

Chapter 35

Kyle Weaver

A cabin.

My ma got and me and Michael a motherfucking *cabin*.

Did I somehow tell her that we're boyfriends? Did it slip out of my mouth when I least expected? Or can she read minds now? Knowing her, the latter makes the most sense.

As Michael and I drive our stuff down the cabin, my chest tingles with something warm. Not anxiety or fear. Not even excitement either. Nothing crazy. I think I may just be happy. We park without a word, but Michael's radiating this aura that tells me he's just as happy as I am.

Inside, the cabin is bigger than I expected. To our right is a kitchen with cast iron pots and a huge sink and fridge. There's a massive couch and two high-back chairs on either side facing a fireplace. There's a massive glass wall, and beyond that there's a porch that extends into the lake. Next to us, there's a staircase that leads upstairs. To a bed. Singular. Where Michael and I will be sleeping. In the town where I spent half my childhood.

"The fireplace is going?" Michael says, approaching it. He sits down next to it, mesmerized. Outside the sun is setting, and none of the lights are on. Pretty soon this fireplace will be the main source of light.

"My ma probably got it going before we got here," I say. She set this whole thing up. She knows. She's known this whole time. Part of me feels ashamed that I haven't told her yet. About Michael. About me. But a much larger part of me finally feels safe. My ma accepts me for who I am.

I set our stuff down and approach Michael. I sit down next to him, our legs flush. I wrap my arms around his and rest my head on his shoulder. We rock back and forth, the waves of the lake gently lapping against the porch.

"This is amazing," Michael says, stroking a vein in my arm. "Your mom is amazing."

"I know," I say. "She's the greatest woman alive."

Michael turns to me and lifts my head. He kisses my lips, and I hold him there, wanting to taste him and only him.

"I'm pretty sleepy," he says. "What do you say we get in bed?"

I can't fight the grin forming on my face. Michael just gets me so damn giddy. "Hope you're wanting to do more than just sleep."

I feel his smile form as I kiss him. "Oh, I have plenty more I want to do," he says.

We fall into each other, our tongues and lips dancing. And that's when I realize I don't have the patience to climb all the way up to some random bed.

I grab him by the ass and hoist him up. He doesn't break from my lips and instead wraps his legs around me. I carry my man over to the couch and gently set him down. Then I get over him, ready to show him how much I love him.

Suddenly, he grabs me by the shoulders, and with a strength I *should* be able to resist but for some reason can't, he pushes me onto my back and pins me down. He straddles my crotch, my dick rock hard, and pins my arms to my side.

"I want to take control tonight," he says, his voice thick with desire.

I smirk. "I think I might let you."

"Oh, you're gonna let me," he says, twerking slowly on my lap. "And I'm gonna use your body how I want to get me off."

He stares down at me hungrily, making my breath go short.

"Have at it, babe," I say.

He nearly rips off my shirt, and I have to help him get my pants off before he curses at the buttons on my jeans. And by the time he's lubed up and riding me, I'm grateful he has the reins. Because goddamn does he know how to use them.

He rides me, up and down, but he looks like a wave, his muscled and beefy torso flexing in all the hottest ways. He moans every time my dick is all the way inside him, and my body locks up with pleasure. He's got his eyes shut, facing the ceiling. I have to say that I've probably seen all his videos by now. And I have never, ever seen him in this much ecstasy.

He adjusts himself to where my dick goes all the way inside him, sending a jolt up my spine. "That," I say. "Just like that."

He puts his arms behind his head, still facing the ceiling, his eyes shut in ecstasy. His pelvis thrusts back onto my dick, and he grunts with each movement. His movements get so passionate and my pleasure so exquisite that I'm convinced that without him, I'd starve. Without him, I'd suffocate. That I need him to live.

His gorgeous body hair reflects the light of the fire, and as I watch sweat drip down the curves of his muscles, I know that, without a doubt, I'm a gay fucking man who likes fucking men. And there's nothing anyone can do to change that.

"You're gonna make me fucking cum," I say.

"Good," he says, not stopping his thrusts. Goddamn, I don't even know how his body moves like this, rolling down on my dick like it's his business. Fucking snake charming, sirenic son of a—

"Fuck!" I shout.

I grab dig my fingers into his thighs and hold him down as I shoot my load up into him. My tongue hangs out of my mouth as I pant, pleasure rolling up and down my body like a wave.

Michael removes my hands from his thighs and goes back to rocking. "Good boy," he says. "Now it's my turn."

Michael eyes me as he keeps pressing himself back into my dick. He rotates his hips in a circle, back and forth, side to side, like I'm a joystick and he's putting in some divine cheat code that only he knows to win my heart. But that's not necessary. He's already got it.

He grabs one of my pecs and squeezes it as he strokes and fucks himself back and forth on my dick. I reach up and play with his nipples.

"Yes, like that," he says.

Pretty soon, I have him moaning and bouncing. And then, before I know it, his hot load shoots all over my hairy chest. I grin up at him and flex my biceps, wearing his cum like a medal. He laughs at me as he dismounts. Then he inserts himself right under my arm and rests his head on my chest.

"I'm glad we had this vacation," he says.

I kiss him on his sweaty forehead. "I'm glad I have you."

Just as Michael drifts off to sleep in my arms, I grab a nearby blanket and cover us. I watch the fire as my eyes drift, the sound of the water sending me to sleep. I was scared to let my mom know Michael and I were sleeping together. But feeling his warm skin against mine, his breath warming my neck, I wouldn't have it another way. And seeing what she's done for us, I'm grateful she knows.

The next morning, I wake to the sun shining on my face. But I'm not bothered by it. I got all the rest I needed. Plus, the sight of the light shining through the window above the kitchen, along with the sun hitting the surface of the lake, is a sight to be seen.

I glance over at Michael. He's managed to press himself further into the couch, and he's stolen nearly all the blanket. I chuckle to myself.

My stomach gurgles, and I realize how hungry I am. My ma makes chicken and waffles on Thanksgiving morning, and thinking about them makes me think I can smell them from here. I get up softly, not to disturb Michael, and go to my bag to slip some pajamas on. I'm gonna trek up to the house to get us some breakfast.

Outside, the grass is dewy, and there's a slight chill to the air. The trees around me are all in various stages of losing their foliage—some red, some orange, some brown. God, I forget how gorgeous it is down here.

I make my way up the hill to my ma's house. I shimmy inside through the side door that leads to the kitchen. On the counter, there's a plate with a heaping stack of waffles and a plate of fried chicken next to it. When the delectable smell hits me, I immediately start salivating.

In the other room, I hear the TV and more voices than one.

"Hey, Ma!" I shout.

"Kyle!" She replies. "You and Michael grab you some food and come watch the parade with us."

Ah, the Macy's Day Parade. How could I forget?

I saunter into the living room and see the handsome Jimmy on my couch.

"Jimmy," I say. "What's going on?"

"My little football player," he says, standing up. He comes and bear-hugs me. When he pulls away, I see he's lost weight, and his beard has grown.

"You turning into a dwarf for Christmas?" I ask.

He lightly thwacks my belly. "You know I grow it out for winter."

"And I'm just saying," I say. "You definitely give off Thor vibes."

He flexes, and I'm surprised how thick his arms are. "You think so?"

"I know so," I say. Jimmy's got a belly, but he's a looker, with his long black heard and bushy eyebrows. And add how muscular he is, he's a lady's man—well, man's man. "People at the diner get tired of you?"

"You know I don't get that many days off in a year," he says. "I deserve to relax."

"Where's Joe?" I ask him, wondering where his partner is.

"Me and Joe, uh..." He frowns. "We're not seeing each other these days."

"I'm sorry to hear that," I say.

"Me too."

"Where's Michael?" Ma asks. She's finishing off the last piece of her waffle.

"I was gonna bring him some breakfast," I say.

"Nonsense," she says. "Have him come here and watch the parade with us. He's part of the family."

My chest warms. I love how my mom is just taking him in.

"Alright," I say, smiling. "But it's early. Don't go and say anything too crazy this morning."

"Fine," she says, sighing. "I'll wait 'til dinner."

I leave and make the trek down the hill back to the cabin. Inside, Michael's up and reading a Nora Roberts book by the looks of it. Nearby, there's another bookshelf filled. Damn, my ma really likes Miss Nora.

"You're back," he says, looking up.

"Sorry," I say. "Wanted to get you some breakfast."

He smirks at my empty hands. "Well did you grab it?"

I smirk back. "Ma wants you to eat with the rest of us."

He stands up and stretches, showing off just how casually muscular he is. Seeing someone look the way he does without playing a professional sport baffles me. Like, you just like this because you can? I know he did porn, but damn. That's dedication.

"Hurry," I say, jokingly. "Or else the chicken and waffles will get cold."

He whips his head to me. "Chicken and waffles? Alright, I'm hurrying."

He quickly gets dressed, and we head over to the house. When we get there, Silas, the other bookseller at the Book Corner, has already arrived. He's wearing boots and a cowboy hat, his shirt unbuttoned low enough to show some chest hair.

"Well if it isn't my favorite football player," he says, reaching to shake my hand.

"Good to see you again, Silas. Glad you're eating with us."

With that, Michael walks from the kitchen into the main room, and all eyes fall on him.

"Well, who's this?" Silas asks, reaching out his hand to him.

The room is silent, waiting for me to answer. Michael shakes his hand, but clearly he's expecting me to answer the question for him. I take him in, his wonderful ginger mullet disheveled, his still-sleepy eyes only somehow making him look more handsome. I can still smell him on my skin, and I can still feel his unfailing kindness in my heart.

So I take the risk.

"This is my boyfriend," I say. "Michael."

Jimmy and Silas both look at me like I've grown a second head. But my ma doesn't even look away from the TV. Of course, because she already knows.

Silas breaks from his stupor. "Well it's a pleasure to meet you Mr. Michael," he says.

Michael blushes, sneaking a glance up to me, smiling. "Nice to meet you too."

The rest of the morning, we eat, talk about the parade. Silas and Michael, both gay booksellers, immediately flock to the couch next to my ma and talk feverishly about books, hardly touching their food because they're so distracted. Jimmy and I talk about the football season as we eat: teams that have improved, who's headed to the playoffs, and so on.

And I'm just surprised by how easy this is.

Whenever I'm at practice, or a game—or hell, anywhere else—I constantly have to act the part. To be manly enough, to give off that I'm attracted to women and not men.

But not now. As lunch rolls around and my ma pulls out Settlers of Catan, Michael finds his way to my side and leans against me. And I put my arm around him. And no one cares. Occasionally, my ma will sneak a glance, but I can tell she's giddy about the relationship and just wants to take it in. Though I can see how surprised Jimmy and Silas are to see me with a man on my arms, they don't question it. It's normal to them. They're both gay men after all, but still. It's so nice to just be normal.

When the sun sets, Ma says it's time for dinner. And boy is it a feast. The table is covered in plates and saucers, and so is the kitchen counter. After her blessing, she tells us to eat whatever we want and that the rest will be distributed tonight just before the show on the water.

"What is this show?" Michael asks.

"Oh, it's beautiful," Jimmy says, pouring more gravy onto his potatoes. "Everyone who's got a cabin around the lake lights lanterns and spreads them across the water. And then there's a little string quartet at that plays Christmas music on the community center dock."

"If I had a boyfriend," Silas says. "That's where I'd take him."

"Yeah," Jimmy says somberly. "Me too."

"Sorry, buddy," Silas says, rubbing his hand.

"I'll survive," he says. "Glad to be here with you all."

With the five of us, the conversation never seems to end. Ma will ask Michael something about his writing. Jimmy will get in on the conversation. And then Jimmy will talk about his aspirations, what recipes he's experimenting with and where he wants to travel. Then Silas will break in and talk about all the places he's been, and for someone only a few years younger than me, I'm impressed. Sure, it was born of running away from home, but it feels like Silas has lived more lives than one.

And this whole time, what makes me happier than anything, is that Michael is beaming. My boyfriend is beaming. And I'm grateful for it. I know he isn't close with his family at all. I'm glad that we can be his family tonight. And hopefully for a lot longer.

"So I gotta ask," Jimmy says, finishing off his beer and pointing the neck between us. "How did you two meet?"

I blush, and Michael laughs. "It's actually a crazy story." He glances at me. "Can I tell them?"

My arm resting on the back of his chair, my hand scratching his back, I smile and nod. I could listen to him talk about anything for any length of time, but this... I particularly want to hear him say it.

As he tells the story, he spares no detail. He gets them to laugh, to gasp. And that's when I'm reminded what phenomenal storyteller this man is. He has them eating out of the palm of his hand.

"And now we're here," Michael says.

"Holy shit," Jimmy says, looking at him, then me. "That's awesome as hell."

"Right?" Michael says.

My ma gasps. "All this good conversation and no dessert? What kinda host am I?" She pushes back her chair, but Silas stands up first.

"No," Silas says, putting his hand out. "Ms. Higgins, you've done too much already. I'll get the pies. You haven't even finished your food."

"But I—"

"No 'buts'," he says, wiping his face and setting down his napkin. "Let me have the honor of helping you miss. Please."

She scooches her chair back in. "Fine, fine," she says.

And I nearly drop my jaw and Silas makes his way to our fridge.

"I'm impressed," I say. "No one gets my ma to back down."

"You need someone just as stubborn," Silas says. "And I think I'm just her match."

"Hush," ma says, taking a sip of her eggnog.

Michael watches the whole thing with the widest grin on his face. God, I'm so happy that he's happy here. My ma asks him a question about his writing, and then they get wrapped up in some conversation.

Jimmy taps me on the shoulder. "Can I talk to you for a minute?"

"Sure," I say, putting my napkin down. We walk into the family room and stand on the far side.

"How are you pulling this off?" he asks, gesturing between me and the kitchen. He's asking about Michael. "You're one of the most recognizable NFO players."

"I have a fake girlfriend," I say.

Jimmy widens his eyes. He just watches the games. He doesn't know about the 'me being single' drama.

"Tigers management doesn't know about Michael," I say. "We've kept it a secret for this long."

He wipes his face and pulls on his beard. "Sheesh, Kyle. You've really fucked yourself with this."

My chest tightens. Hearing him say that reminds me how insane this actually is.

"But it's working."

He points to the kitchen. "I can see how much that man loves you," he says. "It pours out of him. He's bursting at the seams with it."

"Yeah," I say, blushing. "And I love him too."

"I'm sure you do," he says. "But what are you going to do if this secret is leaked? If they discover your girlfriend is fake? I don't think love will be enough in that case."

The thought makes dread pool in my chest. "I'm not sure."

He shakes his head. "Joe was the same way with me," he says. "All talk. He said he loved me, that he would always care for me. But when I was no longer convenient for him—when didn't want to tell his family about us—he found someone else. He cheated on me, then he dropped me like I was a scorpion in his hands."

I scoff. "But I wouldn't do that to Michael."

"Unfortunately, you don't know that. Kyle, this world you and I grew up in—the world that teaches that gay men like you and I aren't worth shit, that we're morally depraved and will burn in hell. That shit plays with our minds. It distorts our thinking. It makes us do things we would never otherwise consider doing."

I feel myself getting hot, and the collar of my shirt gets tight.

"So sure, you feel good right now because you're with people who love you." He pokes me hard in the chest. "I love you. Your mama loves you. Silas is newer to this, but I'm sure he loves you too. And that Michael—boy, he's got a bright, loving future. And you're lucky you have his love. But the second you go back into the world of football, hear all that talk of fucking women and talk of pussies and faggots and so on—you're gonna feel differently. Think differently. Maybe even do something you wouldn't do right now. I would know because it happened to me."

I run my tongue across my teeth, anxiety making my heart race. "So what do I do?"

He sighs and puts his hand on his hip. "I can't answer that for you," he says. "I don't know what coming out could do to you."

"They'll probably break my contract. They can."

"And what's alternative? Let's say your little secret girlfriend thing works. What happens then with you and Michael?"

"We'll become official after," I say. "Assuming we make it to the Championship Game, that's only a couple more months."

He folds his thick arms and shakes his head. "I don't know, man. Like I said, this homophobic world makes us do crazy shit. What does Michael think of all this? Does he trust you? I don't know if I would."

Heat flushes throughout my body, and I can feel my face get red. I didn't go through all my daddy's stuff, decide to choose Michael over him, and continually risk my career just to be told I'm not trustworthy.

"You don't know what I've been through," I say. "You don't get to judge me."

"I'm not judging you," he says. "I'm warning you."

I scoff. "I don't need your warning." I brush past him, then he grabs my arm.

"Look," he says, sighing. "I'm sorry."

I soften a bit.

"I've just... been through a lot these past months. You're right, I don't know what it's like in your shoes. You might do better than Joe. But just be wary, okay? If not for me, then for Michael. He trusts you. He loves you. Don't betray him."

I chew on my lips. Then I open my arms. "Come here."

I wrap my arms around the big man, and he does the same, patting my back.

"You're a good man," I tell him. "I'm sorry for getting defensive."

"No harm done," he says. "Let's get back to dinner."

When we get back to the kitchen, Silas is on his second slice of pecan pie, and Michael and Ma are still wrapped up in conversation. Ma looks up at us, then glances down at her watch. And then she panics.

"Oh, shoot," she says. "The show. It starts in ten minutes."

Jimmy puts his arm on my shoulder, his grip strong. "Guess we all got lost in that conversation." He winks at me, reminding me of all that he said. This homophobic world can make me do crazy things. Maybe, but I'm stronger. No one is going to get in the way of me and Michael. No one.

"Let's grab our lanterns and get to the community center," she says.

Michael stands. "How can I help?"

"You two have that cabin rented?" Jimmy asks. "I think you and Kyle should head there."

"Oh, yeah," Silas says. "This whole thing is real romantic. We wanna make sure you guys get the full experience."

Jimmy raises his eyebrows suggestively. "Alone."

"You boys are the worst," Ma says. "But yes, you two go on alone. Kyle, this is a tradition they recently started. You'll love it."

Michael looks at me. "You ready?"

Defiant, I close the distance between us and kiss him on the lips in front of my family. "Let's go." I won't betray him.

Ma hands us this giant cloth lantern and a lighter, then tells us to hurry on down. When we reach the cabin and look out the back porch, I'm surprised to see dozens of people crowded on the dock of the community center across the lake.

"What do we do?" I ask.

Michael holds up the lantern. "Your mom was telling me: we go on the back porch, someone at the community center will say a few words, we light the lanterns, then let them go onto the lake."

"Sounds easy enough."

On the back porch, the sun has just set, but there are lights from the community center that illuminate us, even here. Michael and I sit down on some wicker chairs. Then, a voice comes on over a microphone.

"Welcome to our annual Thanksgiving Lantern Festival," a female voice says. She explains how residents of Glamour Springs, as a way to build camaraderie, like to come together around big holidays. So, on Thanksgiving, they decided on a celebration where everyone thinks of one thing their grateful for and one wish they have. Then, they light their lantern and set it out onto the lake. Supposedly, rumor has it that the combination of water, wind, and smoke drifts your gratitude and wish to whoever can grant it.

When the moment is ready, Kyle and I kneel down at the edge of the porch and put the lantern between us.

"What are you grateful for?" he asks.

"You," I say, without needing to think twice.

He smiles. "You stole my answer. What about your wish?"

Looking at him, how happy this trip has made him, how happy he is with me—how happy I am with him. I don't think I can answer it.

"I have everything I need," I say.

"You sap," he says, laughing.

"What's your wish?" I ask.

He smirks. "That's private," I say.

I glare at him. "Come on. You asked me mine."

"If I tell you, it won't come true."

I reach out and hold his hand. "Fine," I say. "I'll let you do the honors."

Michael lights the wick in the center of the lantern. The flame ignites quickly, and the glow behind the cloth casts both of us in a deep yellow. We let our lantern go into the lake and push it toward the center. Around the lake, other cabins have pushed theirs in, and dozens of lanterns are being dropped into the lake at the community center.

As the lanterns drift toward each other, a chilly wind brushes by, and Michael and I snuggle up together. Soon, the string quartet my ma mentioned starts playing at the community center.

"White Christmas," Michael says.

Seeing how handsome he is, I take a selfie of us with the lanterns in the background. Then, I hold him close as the melody plays on, so grateful for this time with him. Grateful that he came to Glamour Springs, that I met him. Before I met him, I never knew that this was the life I always wanted: love with a man, a cozy night on the porch surrounded by twinkling lights and perfect music.

Inevitably, our lips find each other. Michael and I have made a lot of love, and we've tended to have a way of doing it. One of us takes charge, and the other obeys. But tonight, I wanna try something a little different.

I kiss him harder, and he wraps his arms around my neck. Something vibrates in my pocket—my phone, likely—but I ignore it.

"I wanna improvise tonight," I say. "I want both of us to call the shots. I want to listen to each other, a back and forth. Like we're dancing in bed."

"Has anyone told you how poetic you are?"

I smirk. "You, just now."

My phone rings again, and this time, Michael notices.

"You need to get that?"

I roll my eyes. "Probably my mom saying we forgot something."

"She gave us enough dessert to last us until the end of time," I say. "I think we're both good."

But when my phone rings again, both of us get uneasy.

"Maybe it's something urgent," I say.

"You're probably right."

I pull my phone out, and when I see the name, I regret not having made a wish. Because I could really use some courage right now.

"Who is it?" Michael asks.

I stand up. "Timmy," I say. "I'll handle it."

"I'll stay here and watch," he says.

I nod and make my way inside, my heart racing. I take a deep breath, then pick up the phone.

"Hey, Timmy. What's up?"

"You little shit," he says.

And my stomach sinks to the floor.

"You almost had me fooled," he says. "But I know everything now."

Chapter 36

Michael Cunningham

I WATCH THE FLICKERING lanterns until my eyelids get heavy. This trip has been nothing I expected and instead everything I wanted.

I can't remember the last time I've had a Thanksgiving where I've had so much fun. Where I've felt so loved. I had a great friendsgiving with my writing group friends back in college, but even that pales into comparison. Who would have thought that I'd spend the holiday with one of the greatest football players of his time, his mom, and two gay country men?

When I catch myself nodding off, I realize I've been alone for a long time now. Kyle had to take a call with his agent, but he isn't back yet.

I glance back in the cabin behind me, expecting to see him there. But he's nowhere inside.

I furrow my brow and stand up. I look all around, but I don't see him.

I open the sliding glass door. "Kyle?" I call out. Nothing.

I get uneasy. I pull out my phone and try to call him. It rings until it goes to voicemail. Maybe he's up at his mom's helping her with something. That would make sense.

I slip through the cabin and make my way up the hill toward his mom's house. I glance back at the lake and see all the lanterns floating peacefully about.

When I lit our lantern, I wished for a peaceful love with Kyle Weaver. Before I came on the trip, I thought that these would be our last days. But after this wonderful time, I don't see how our relationship could end. I'm hoping that wherever the wind takes the wish, it's fulfilled.

I reach the back door, and it's already cracked open. And that's when I get an uneasy feeling. I slip inside, and before I can even shut the door, I hear the front door slam.

"Honey," someone says. It's Linda, Kyle's mom.

"This isn't good, ma," he says, his voice shaky. He's crying. I would show myself, but this seems like a private moment, one I would disrupt if I made myself known. Yet I can't just leave. I have to hear this. So I stay in the kitchen and eavesdrop.

"Tell me what's wrong."

"Timmy's what's wrong."

"Your agent?"

"He knows everything, ma. About me and Michael."

My stomach turns over itself, and I have to brace myself against the counter.

"What do you mean he knows?"

"The NFO doesn't like queers," he says. "It's not like Michael and I were public. But he found us out. And now..."

Now what? I want to yell. Water drips onto my shoe, and that's when I realize I'm crying.

"How did this happen?" Linda asks.

Kyle sniffles. "He found my fake girlfriend on a date with someone else—a woman—and that's when he pieced it together. He got more intel from that reporter Ricardo about her and Michael's history as a pornstar, and then it was obvious."

My shock turns into rage as I grip the counter until my knuckles turn white. Amani said she would be faithful to Michael to not arouse suspicion. Did she just jeopardize this whole thing?

"Oh, baby," she says. There's silence, and I assume they're hugging.

"And now," Kyles says, and I can hear him suck on his lips to stop a sob. "We have to break up."

My chest caves in on itself, and my face gets white hot.

"If I'm to stay on the team, then I gotta find a woman. And I gotta win a Championship Game. So Timmy's gonna find me a real girlfriend this time."

My knees weak, I slump against the counter and let myself slide to the floor. Miss Beautiful finds me and starts rubbing against me, purring. She might be the only thing keeping me from losing it entirely.

"But honey," she says. "He's your boyfriend. You love him. Are you really willing to give him up just to finish out this season?"

Yeah, I say to myself, clenching my fists so hard they tingle. *Are you really willing to give me up?*

"You don't understand," he says. "When Timmy was talking to me, I swear it was like I was ten years younger, talking to Dad again. I swear I could hear his voice, and I remembered him saying what it means to be true to myself. What it means to have integrity."

"You think integrity is going back in the closet?" Linda asks.

"It's not living two lives, that's for sure," Kyle says. "I can't keep dating Michael if I want to live an honest life."

"Honest to who, though, Kyle?" Linda asks. "Because you're not being honest to yourself if you deny who you truly are."

Kyle groans. "You don't get it!" he shouts. "Michael is an amazing guy. You think so. Jimmy thinks so. But it just can't work between us. And he deserves someone who can make it work."

"No," I whisper to myself. "This isn't happening. No, no, no, no."

"So what now?" Linda asks. "Plan to tell your boyfriend you're leaving him after a wonderful Thanksgiving?"

There's a silence, and it feels like my entire body is filled with lead.

Listening here, I almost feel disembodied. Like I'm a ghost imagining this whole interaction. But if I move, then I remind myself that I'm corporeal. That I'm here, alive. And that I've just heard my boyfriend say he's breaking up with me.

"I'm going back to Portland," Kyle says. "I have everything I need with me." I hear the front door open, and it feels like my heart is tying itself in knots. He must have packed a bag while my back was turned to him. All while I thought how I was a fool to consider breaking up with him. And now he's breaking up with me, and he doesn't even have the balls to tell me.

"So you'll just abandon your boyfriend here?" she asks. "And leave me to clean up your mess?"

There's a beat long pause, and then…

"I'm sorry, ma." I hear the front door shut, and then Kyle's rental car starts.

"What's that?" Linda says out loud.

She makes her way to the kitchen to find me huddled against a cabinet on the floor, weeping into my hands.

"Oh, my sweet child." She lowers to the ground and wraps her arms around me, and Miss Beautiful scurries away. "Did you hear all that?"

I nod.

"My damned boy," she says. Her head rests on my shoulder, and I can feel her shaking it.

"I don't know what I did wrong," I say, lifting my face from my hands. "He had been so distant the past few months. But something in him changed. He was his old self again. Present. Before this, I even thought that I was going to break up with him. But he was so emotionally available that I let go of the whole idea. But now…"

Sobs pour through me, preventing me from speaking.

"My son is a troubled man," Linda says, rubbing my arms. "For the longest time, I've suspected that he was gay. He never told me, but I had that feeling. And seeing you was like seeing the light through the clouds. It was finally confirmed."

I let out a sharp laugh. "He never said anything about being gay? Or us?"

"He mentioned you were a friend, but I connected the dots."

Friend. Sheesh.

"I should have known this would happen," I say. "I always fall for guys who aren't emotionally available. And no matter how much I'm hurt, I keep coming back for more. I'm cursed. I'm a fuckup."

She shakes me. "Look at me."

Startled, I obey, and there's raw determination in her eyes.

"You are not cursed. You are not a fuckup. You are broken. Hurt. Betrayed. But that does not mean you can't bounce back from this."

"But Linda," I say, using all my strength to hold my quivering lip. "I *love* him. I'm in love with a man who walked out on me and didn't have the decency to say goodbye. A man that I tried to keep at arms-length because I knew he was emotionally unavailable. And yet I still let myself fall for him. I'm the least self-respecting man out there."

"And you listen to me, Michael. You and I have spent a lot of time together today. I've gotten to know you. There is a light within you. A bright one. And I won't have you sitting on my dirty kitchen floor putting yourself down like that.

"You're right. Kyle is not emotionally available, as least as available as I hoped he would be at his age. But that is not your fault. I can see that you're the kind of person who loves, and loves, and loves. But what you need to learn how to do is direct that love to yourself first and foremost. This is what I had to do when I left Kyle's father."

Her words sound just like my sponsor's right after I ran into David.

"I've been trying to do this for years," I say. "Why isn't it working?"

She releases me and leans against the cabinet just like I am. "Maybe it has been this whole time," she says. "And this was the push you needed to bring your self-love to the next level."

I sigh, taking her words in. They ring true, but my mind is too muddled and angry and sad to really internalize them.

"But I love him," I say, fresh tears falling. "And he's gone."

She grabs my hand and holds it. "But you're right here," she says. "You're all that you have." She squeezes my hand. "So, love that man first."

* * *

When I make it back to Portland, I'm in a sleepy haze.

Kyle left me. Without saying a word. He told his mom everything, and lucky for her I was eavesdropping, so she didn't have to be the bearer of bad news.

When I got back to the cabin that night, I tried calling him. Messaging him. But nothing went through. So I laid on that couch we made love on the night before, smelling his sweet skin on the leather, praying for sleep and to never wake up. Each time I glanced out the window and saw all those lanterns on the water, I wanted to throw up. So much for my wish coming true. Once the sun came up, Silas was kind enough to drive me to the airport.

"He's just figuring out who he is," Silas said on our drive. "I know how hard it can be when you're from these parts. He may come around."

I remember scoffing. "Yeah, whatever."

Now I lay on my bed, the sun setting through the window, and my chest feels like it's tearing itself in half.

I scroll through my phone. I could re-download a hookup app and get some shitty sex. But the thought of that just makes me feel worse. Already, I'm craving Kyle's body—his smell, his touch, his taste.

And I'll never have it again.

I'm mindlessly opening and closing the same apps, the same way you open and close the fridge, hoping something good will magically materialize.

I scroll through my contacts, looking for someone to talk to. I scroll past Susan's name and my stomach sinks. I'm not ready to talk to her right now. But once I hit Amani's name, all my aimless sadness compresses into white hot anger. I press on her contact and call her.

"Hey, Michael," she says happily.

"You sabotaged us," I say.

There's a pause. "What do you mean?"

"You know what I mean," I say. "You've been seeing someone else. And you've been caught."

I can practically hear her jaw dropping. "Oh no."

I sit up in the bed, unable to contain the rage in my body. "How could you do this to us? To me?"

"Michael, I'm sorry. Angie—that woman from the bar—she reached out and said she ghosted me because she had life things going on. She wanted to talk, so we met up. I was lonely, Michael. And we were discreet. I didn't think we'd get caught."

I groan, my chest tightening. "But you were caught, and you knew what getting caught would cost us. Why did you agree to being Kyle's beard if you knew you couldn't do it?"

"Because I also have a love life, and I couldn't shut it down when a beautiful woman came knocking on my door," she says. "I agreed to help because I could see how much you and Kyle loved each other, and I knew how much your past with bad guys haunted you. But I have a past that haunts me too. I deserve love and healing as well."

I breathe hot air out of my nose, my eyes stinging. I don't know what to say.

"I didn't foresee this all happening," she says. "There was no way to predict I'd get lonely or that Angie would reach out. But I was being careful."

"Clearly not careful enough," I say. "You could have just waited, Amani. But no. And now Kyle's broken up with me. His agent discovered the whole ruse. They're finding him a real girlfriend now."

Shock fills the space between us like a bad smell fills a room.

"Are you serious?"

"Yep," I say. "And now Kyle won't even talk to me. So thanks for ruining this."

"I'm sorry," she says, her voice shaky. "I didn't—"

"You know, I don't really want to hear what you have to say. I'm done with this conversation."

And then I hang up.

Amani tries to call me again, but I decline it. She texts, but I just delete the messages. Then, the sun finally setting, I burrow myself under my covers and shut the world out.

Chapter 37

Kyle Weaver

THE PAST MONTH HAS been a dizzy blur.

The day after I came home from Glamour Springs, Timmy demanded a meeting to discuss damage control.

He put me with Robyn and demanded we spin up some story that makes me look good and Amani look bad. The only story that he approved of was that Amani cheated on me, so I had to find someone else.

This someone else ended up being Jessica. Timmy and some of the Tigers' management hired an agency to get me a girlfriend. I met her the next day. She was slim, beautiful, blonde, and had a radiant smile. I liked her, but I couldn't love her. Because no matter what I did, I couldn't stop thinking of the man I truly loved. But that didn't matter anymore. I had to let him go.

Since then, it's been appearance after appearance, Timmy trying to convince the public that this relationship transition isn't abrupt or strange or unnatural but completely reasonable. And though our plastered smiles might make the world think so, I know deep down that this is not the true me. At the very least, I'm not hiding a taboo relationship anymore. Daddy would be proud of that.

I come in through the garage, and Jessica shuts the door behind me. We were just at some gala for a cancer charity I donate to, and per Timmy's instructions, we made sure to get in a lot of pictures. I throw my suit coat down and pull out my shirt from my tight pants, my head dark and stormy. Since Thanksgiving, I've been eating more than usual. I chalk it up to the weather, but I know my mood's been worse than ever. I may need to see Neeti again. Talk about depression.

"Sooo…" Jessica says, taking off her jacket. She's wearing this tight red dress that brings out her perfect blonde hair. She's an objectively attractive woman. I just wish she wasn't mine.

I start unbuttoning my cuffs. "What's on your mind?"

"Have you thought about Christmas at all?"

I sigh as I unbutton one wrist, letting blood flow back into my hand. Man, I need to get my shirts refitted.

"It's in a week," I say, unbuttoning my other wrist. I roll both my sleeves up. "So no."

She frowns and sucks on her lip. "Well, I'd like for you to come to Pittsburgh and meet my family." She closes the distance between us, and I feel my breath quicken. But not in a good way.

She traces the crease of my forearm with her finger. "And maybe the Sexiest Man Alive can teach me a thing or two in bed."

It takes all my strength not to buck away from her. That darkness that swarms my brain whenever I have to get intimate with a woman returns, and it feels like I'll never be happy again.

"I'm tired tonight," I say.

She sighs and pulls her hand away. "You're always tired."

I turn to her and put my hands on her shoulder. "How about this," I say. "I come home with you to Pittsburgh this Christmas, and that's when you can unwrap me. I just need some time is all."

She brightens. "I can do that," she says. "I don't mean to push you either. I know you had a rough relationship with Amani."

I let out a sharp laugh. "I guess you could say that."

* * *

Unlike how I failed Michael, I manage to keep my promise to Jessica. Well, so far.

We sit around a large, mahogany table. Her parents sit at either end, and the table is filled her brothers and their wives. Christmas music is playing in the background, and it's snowing in Pittsburgh. Little kids are running around, too excited to sleep but too eager to wait until Christmas morning.

I'm peppered with questions about the season, fellow players, and so on. Her brothers are good men, and their wives are well-rounded. Her parents are charming and thoughtful, and Jessica is an attentive partner.

But it's all still wrong.

This is nothing like Thanksgiving with Michael and my folks. I loved watching Michael get into heated debates with Silas about the best piece of LGBTQ+ fiction. I loved the way my ma doted on Michael, the way that she saw him how I did. How I felt so free, being completely myself around the people I loved.

I can't do that here.

I can't take the man I love up to my room after dinner and fuck my love into him. I can't open my inbox to see Michael's latest draft that he wants me to read and critique. Fuck, I can't even talk to him.

My mom's words echo throughout my mind. Is this really what it means to live with integrity? To live a shadow of the life I really want to live? I feel so small, like I'm trying to fit myself inside a box that wasn't made for me. I feel achy and sad all the time, tired as hell, even though I sleep more than ten hours a night. And being around Jessica so much, the pressure to be intimate constant, the darkness never leaves my brain. Happiness feels like a distant memory. I know my dad didn't like gay people, but would he really want me to stuff my true self down like this? Would he want me to be so sad?

The night wraps up, and all of us go to our separate rooms. And it feels like I'm walking to the gallows to be hanged.

Timmy said that the best way to secure my reputation as a straight man is to get Jessica pregnant. So, in the past week, I've coordinated this with her. She's off birth control, and we're finally going to have sex. Once she's pregnant, we'll announce our wedding date. Sooner rather than later. And when we're finally married, we'll reveal that a little Weaver baby is on the way. The Weaver legacy will finally live on. Just as my father wished.

"Gimme a sec," I say to Jessica just outside the guest room door. "Need to use the bathroom."

"I'll be waiting," she says flirtatiously, but my chest just squeezes hearing her.

I burst into the bathroom, feeling my chest squeeze even harder. The air gets thin around me, and I have trouble breathing.

Inhale for four, I think to myself. *Hold. Exhale for four.* Just like Neeti taught me when the anxiety gets bad. I do that for a while, and then my head feels slightly clearer.

I'm doing this for Dad. I'm carrying on his legacy. This is an honest life. I can do this.

Suddenly, my phone vibrates in a way that I immediately recognize. And my heart picks right back up again, the air thinner than before. I haven't felt this in months, since before I started dating Michael. But I know exactly what it is.

My hands shaking, I reach inside my jean pocket and pull my phone out.

And there it is. The last thing I want to see.

Peter Cummins, aka Michael Cunningham, has posted a new video on OnlyFans.

My knees grow weak, and I lower myself to the tiled ground. My eyes blurry from tears, I open the video and watch. It's some guy I've never seen before. But he's hot. And he's naked with my boyfriend—ex-boyfriend. It feels like someone is slowly stabbing me with a knife, over and over, as I watch this unknown man fuck the man I love more than anyone else. I want to say that Michael looks unhappy, incomplete without me there. But they're get at it with enthusiasm and vigor. He's moved on. Thriving. And here I am, procrastinating my duty to get my soon-to-be wife pregnant.

There's a knock on the bathroom door, and I manage to turn off the video just before I freeze up, dark depression swarming my mind.

"Babe?" Jessica calls out. "Are you alright in there?"

I open my mouth to respond, but nothing comes out. I can't say anything. I don't have any more lies left in me.

"Kyle?" she asks.

I don't respond. I can't. I don't know what to say.

She opens the bathroom door, and when sees me leaning against the bathtub, she rushes in. "Are you okay?" she asks, kneeling next to me. "Are you sick from dinner? What's going on?"

My chest feels like it's caving in on itself, and the air is so thin I feel like I'll pass out.

I start to speak, then stop myself. This is it. I can manage to lie now and keep the future my dad wanted for it, or I can be honest about myself. I remember the question Robyn, the reporter, asked me at the end of our interview: am I playing for my daddy or myself? Up until now, it's been all for him. But I think I'm finally going to do something for myself. I think that's what I can call integrity.

"I..." I take a deep, shaky breath. "I can't do this," I say. "I'm in love with someone else. A man."

My words cause her to physically recoil.

I reach out and gently hold her hand. "Let me explain."

She looks at me skeptically, and then she gives a small nod.

So I tell her the story: how in college, I slept with other football players. And then I tell her everything since. I don't bother keeping any other details out. There's no point in lying about it more. I gave up any future of an NFO career when I told her I loved a man.

"So, do what you will with what I told you," I say. "It doesn't matter. I can't take the lies anymore."

I expect her to get up and storm off. To cry and tell her family, to tell her little matchmaking agency that I forewent the deal, and to tell the world that the I'm the faggot they've all been making me out to be.

But she doesn't. She just keeps holding my hand.

"That's very brave of you to say," she says.

I look up at her like she called me a slur. "Are you serious?"

She nods. "Kyle, I could tell something was off. And this makes sense considering you were the Sexiest Man Alive and yet still didn't have a girlfriend."

I exhale through my nose, some of the darkness in my mind dissipating with my breath. "I know."

"I won't tell," she says. "But you gotta figure out what you're going to do."

Hope floods my chest, and I squeeze her hand. "You have no idea what this means to me."

"Believe me," she says. "I know what it's like to be separated from someone you love." Her voice is heavy, making me think there's a lot about her that she's choosing to keep private. So I'll respect that. But she is on my side.

"Thank you," I say, wiping my eyes.

We both sit there, her against the cabinets, me against the tub, in silence.

"So what now?" she asks. "You'll have to come clean eventually."

I think of the article that Robyn had to write about Amani cheating on me. I think of all the missed calls and messages from Michael, and how the day those stopped was like another heartbreak. Because then I knew he had given up.

"I'll keep this secret as long as you do," she says. "But it can't go past the end of the season."

Plans start to bake in my head, and I feel my body wake from the slothful stupor it's been in for the past month.

"I'll come clean soon," I say. "But first, I need to make some apologies."

Chapter 38

Michael Cunningham

I DRIVE TO WORK on one of those sad, ugly days where the sun hides behind thick, gray clouds. It's been raining on and off but always raining when I need to step outside. The weather in Portland today reflects exactly how I feel: depressed, hopeless, and out of options.

I was epically ghosted by an NFO player with whom I was having the steamiest, most blush-inducing sex of my lifetime. And I've been selling porn for nearly five years. That's saying something.

I also lost my best friend. She was arguably the reason my whole relationship with Kyle imploded in the first place. I can see, though, that expecting her to be a fake-girlfriend for so long, when she was gay herself, was not a fair ask, even if she agreed to it. But neither of us have made the effort to apologize to the other. And with how stubborn we both are, I don't know if we ever will. Skye and Josue, my other writing group friends, have refused to get involved, which has turned into them not speaking to either of us. Or me, at least. I haven't spoken to them in weeks, so I don't know if they've been talking to Amani. I spent my Christmas eve filming porn with some rando I'd never met before. It was hot, but it was empty as it's always been. I've talked with Susan, my sponsor, once and told her what's happened, but I haven't talked to her since. I'm just not ready to dig into it.

An incoming call appears on my dashboard, and my heart skips a beat. But then I remember that literary agents don't cold-call you anymore. They email you first. Not recognizing the number, I decline the call.

I've been querying my first fantasy romance to literary agents for months. Three of them requested to see my full manuscript, but two of them declined me in the past month. The third one has been out for a few months now, and I'm starting to think she's just going to ghost me. But it doesn't matter, anyways. Ever since shit went down with Kyle, I haven't been able to focus on my new novel at all. Maybe this is the sign for me to just give it all up. That was my original goal anyway, right? To give up if I didn't get representation? Maybe it's time to finally throw in the towel.

When I get to work at Rucker's bookstore, I go through my typical tasks: checking inventory, answering customer questions, and handling anything left undone from the night before. But I feel so hollow. I was so grateful when I was offered a job here, thinking that the only job I could stomach besides being a full-time author was working in a bookstore. But now the whole experience feels like ash on my tastebuds. I don't know how I'm going to have the energy or enthusiasm to lead queer book club tonight.

By the time lunch hits, I'm so exhausted that I'm tempted to go home sick. But I need the money. After so many months of producing no videos per Kyle's request—fuck him, by the way—I've had to go about building back up my audience to make what I used to. That takes time, and I'm not quite there yet.

My phone buzzes, and I check the caller. It's that same number. I decline it, then go about my lunch. But then my phone rings again.

I assess the number. The area code is familiar.

And then my stomach sinks. That's the area code of northern Mississippi where Kyle's hometown is located. I know this because Kyle's mom gave me her number before I left Glamour Springs. After unsuccessfully trying to reach him, I blocked Kyle everywhere. He must have gotten a new number to contact me.

And you know what? I'm feeling shitty today. And I'm gonna let him have it.

"You have some fucking nerve calling me," I say. "What the fuck do you want?"

Silence. "Michael?"

My heart skips a beat. That is not Kyle on the other line.

"Uh, yeah," I say, my forehead starting to sweat, sufficiently embarrassed. "Who's this?"

"I'm sorry to keep calling you," the male voice says. "It's Jimmy. Remember me?"

Jimmy. The owner of the diner in Glamour Springs who's like an older brother to Kyle.

"Jimmy," I say. "Nice to hear from you. But Kyle and I aren't exactly together anymore. As you obviously know."

"Yeah," he says. "I know. I had a feeling this would happen. I wanted to reach out for a while to talk to you about it."

"I'm not sure what you could tell me," I say. "Even if Kyle wanted me back, I don't think I'd say yes."

"I wanted to talk because I've been through the same thing," he says. "I wanted to offer my support. You got a few minutes to talk?"

I look around the employee room. Nobody's around, but anyone could walk in. I don't know what Jimmy has to say, but he's a friendly, familiar voice. The only people I've talked to in the past week are customers and the men fucking me.

"Sure," I say, standing up and grabbing my coat. I make my way outside into the cold and put my headphones in. "So what's going on?"

He chuckles. "That's what I wanted to ask you," he says. "How are you holding up since Kyle walked out on you?"

No sugar-coating things I see. "Honestly, pretty bad."

He sighs. "Yeah, sounds about right. That's how it was for me when my ex left."

I start walking down the sidewalk. "This happened to you?"

"Not exactly the same," he says. "But pretty damn similar." He tells me how his ex's insecurity led to him keeping secrets, cheating, and to their eventual falling out.

"And you're saying you told Kyle all this?"

"Yeah," he grunts. "I tried to warn him how vicious internalized homophobia can be. We can obviously see that now. But he thought he'd be okay."

I exhale through my nose, sending steam into the cold air. "Yeah, obviously not."

"But I wanted to share my experience with you. Because I handled it really poorly. And I don't want you to do the same."

My interest is piqued. "How'd you handle it poorly?"

He lets out a long sigh. It sounds like he's still hurt. "I shut everyone out. I blamed everyone I could. I held my anger and bitterness close to my heart. I thought if I let it go, I'd be approving of what Joe did to me. Sending a message to the world that anyone could lie to or cheat on me and that I wouldn't care.

"And I did this for so long. I got depressed. I had to go see a professional. I gained a lot of weight. Still getting over the effects of that. It was bad. But then I learned something that changed my whole perspective."

I reach a street corner and decide to keep walking. "What's that?"

"That I can't do this alone," he says. "In looking for people to blame, I isolated myself. And eventually started blaming myself for everything. I needed to talk to others to get outside myself to get an accurate perspective. To heal. So that's what I did. Kyle's mama was a big inspiration. Silas, Martha, and Llewellyn have been my rocks as well.

"I imagine that someone in your shoes is pissed. I'd be too. But don't let that depression swallow you up. It can do real damage. And from what I know, you're a real good kid. I would hate to see you waste away like I did."

As I walk and listen, something catches my eye. I peer into the glass of the building next to me and spot a bunch of different anime books. Right in front of me is the latest physical volume of One Piece, Amani's favorite anime.

I let out a long sigh, one that I've been holding for what feels like months. "Thank you so much Jimmy," I say. "You're right."

"Just thought I'd pass along the wisdom that was given to me. If Kyle's mama hadn't been there for me, I don't know if I woulda made it."

I remember her, along with my sponsor months ago, telling me to focus on myself. To not try and chase after Kyle. And per Jimmy's advice, I think that means breaking my self-imposed isolation.

"I'm glad you did," I say. "I've been isolating myself hardcore. I think it's time to end that."

"Good," he says. "I didn't want to take too much of your time, but I gotta get back to work."

"Same," I say, searching the manga tome for its price.

"You call me if you ever need anything, okay? Consider me part of your circle. You're a good kid."

My chest warms for the first time in weeks. "I will," I say. "Thanks, Jimmy."

"Take it easy," he says. And hangs up.

I chew on my cold lips, then click my tongue. I open my messages and start drafting a text.

"I've been a huge asshole," I say. "Have time to meet at the anime restaurant tonight? I'm free after book club. Really."

My heart racing, I go inside the store and purchase the very same volume. Last time Amani and I spoke, she had been behind. This might help her catch up. Once I walk out of the store with the tome in hand, my phone buzzes.

"I've been ridiculous too," she says. "Really. I'll see you there."

And for the first time in weeks, I feel hope.

* * *

When I arrive at the restaurant, Amani already has a table, and she's standing there with open arms. I rush to her and wrap my arms around her.

"I've been an idiot," I say, the giant mural of Naruto staring me right in the face.

"Me, too," she says.

I pull away and hand her the giant One-Piece tome that was hidden under my coat.

Her jaw drops, and she beams.

"So you can catch up," I say.

She kisses me on the cheek, then marvels down at the tome again. "Thank you," she says. "I've been dragging my feet now that I'm behind. This will get me all caught up."

We both sit down, and I take a sip of my Diet Coke that Amani already ordered for me.

"I'm just gonna say it," I say. "I put all the blame on you, and that wasn't fair."

She marvels at the giant book one more time before flipping it over so it doesn't distract her. "But you had reason to be angry. I put the whole fake-dating thing at risk when I decided to go on a date with Angie. And it looked like the worst happened."

I sigh. "Yeah, but I miss you, Ams. This situation is complicated, but it's the same as letting our partners get between us. I don't want to be cut off from you anymore. I want to go back to the way it was."

She takes a sip from her straw, and nods. "I don't either. I wish I could go back and undo what I did, but it warms my heart that you're willing to forgive me for it."

"Of course," I say. "And besides, Kyle leaving me is not your fault. It's his. We could have tried to make it work. But he decided to be the asshole and abandon me."

Amani raises her brow. "Yeah, about that..."

"What?" I ask, folding my arms. She knows something about Kyle that I don't. I hate that, even after all this time and all he's done, I need to know about him.

Her eyes bug out. "You haven't heard?"

My heart starts to race. "Heard what?"

But then we're interrupted by the waitress. Amani orders some sushi, and I just order whatever their special bento box is. The waitress catches the spine of the One-Piece tome and then starts fangirling with Amani. Meanwhile, I'm tapping my foot while my blood pressure rises, desperately wanting to hear what she says about Kyle.

Finally, the waitress disappears.

"Tell me," the desperation clear in my voice.

"Here," she says. She pulls out her phone, scrolls for a bit, then hands it to me. She has an article from ESB pulled up. The title reads 'Kyle Weaver Comes Clean about What Happened with Ex'.

I look up at her, deadpan. "Really?"

"Really," she says, invoking our true word. "That's the freaking ESB right there. Just skim it."

I do so begrudgingly, but I find myself surprised by the end. Robyn, the same woman that first leaked that Kyle and Amani were dating, quotes Kyle in saying that Amani did not cheat on him and rather that the relationship ended on mutually respectful terms. He ends the article by saying that any disrespect or slander toward Amani will not be tolerated.

"Is this really true?" I ask.

"Really," she says, and my chest warms. It's so nice to hear her say that again.

"And it's not just that," she continues. "Kyle personally took me out to dinner to apologize.

Butterflies take flight in my stomach. "You saw him?"

She nods. "He took me to this fancy place and apologized to me in person. He asked if there were any personal ramifications from the lies that were spread about me 'cheating on him'. I told him the fallout wasn't as bad as it could have been, especially if I was famous, and that I was fine. He asked me about my writing, how work was going."

I exhale through my nose. "He really said all that?"

She nods. "And it really seemed genuine."

Our food arrives, and we both eat in silence for a bit, which gives me time to process what I've just heard.

Kyle came to Amani and apologized for what he's done. Does that mean I should be expecting to hear from him?

Amani takes a sip of her water. "He also asked about you," she says. "Because he wants to see you."

I nearly spit out the water I'm drinking. "Yeah, right," I say. I put on this indifferent façade, but there's a tingling feeling in my chest now. Part of me wanted to know that Kyle wanted to see me. And I'm relieved that he does.

When Amani doesn't respond, I take the bait.

"What did he say about me?"

"I really don't want to act as the messenger between you two," she says. "I mean, look where that got us."

I chuckle. "Yeah."

"But he said he hasn't been able to reach you."

"Yeah," I say, fiddling with some sushi with my chopsticks. "I blocked him after I never heard back."

"I get it," she says. "I'll share what he said now and leave the rest up to you."

"I appreciate it."

"Kyle wants to talk. In person. To explain himself. To apologize."

I roll my eyes. "Explain what? That I deserved to be ghosted?"

Amani shakes her head. "Like I said, I'm not getting involved more than I am. That's what he said, you can take it or leave it."

I lean back and fold my arms, biting down on my lip. Part of me really wants to see Kyle again, but where would it go? So much of our back in forth has involved him acting out because he's too afraid of being gay, crawling back to me, us working for a while, and then him acting out again. It's a pattern, and I'm tired of it. We've talked enough. He needs to change his actions.

"Shit, I forgot," she says.

I groan. "There's more?"

"Last thing, I promise," she says. "He got us suite tickets to the playoffs in Seattle. Paid for plane tickets and lodging for us as well."

"You're joking."

"Nope," she says, slipping some edamame into her mouth. "He said, if anything, he'd want to see you. Even at one of his games."

I scoff. 'Even at one of his games'. As if it's an honor that he'd consider inviting me.

"Do you want to go?"

I sigh. "Ams, there's no point. I don't want to talk to Kyle. Are you planning on going?"

"To the playoffs? Hell yeah. I don't know about you, but I still love football after watching Kyle play for so long."

I let out a short laugh. Truth be told, I really like it too, but it's not worth the trouble of running into Kyle right now.

"There's two tickets, right?" I ask. "Take Angie with you. Even if she doesn't like football, a suite experience at a playoff game would be crazy fun."

"Really? Alright," she says not without disappointment. "Are you sure?"

"I'm sure," I say.

We finish up the rest of our food, catching up on the rest of our lives. Amani has decided to forgo traditional publication altogether and go the self-publishing route. She details the process, at least what she knows so far, and I'm already overwhelmed. If I decided to no longer try and find a literary agent, there's no way in hell I'd have the energy to do the entire publishing process myself.

"Well, I'm glad you reached out," Amani says after we pay our check.

"Me, too."

"And even though I'm not going to be the mediator between you and Kyle, maybe you could give him a chance. At least unblock him. Maybe talking to him wouldn't hurt."

I bristle at her words. "We'll see."

Chapter 39

Kyle Weaver

It's a snowy day in Seattle, but I'm unfazed. I'm in the locker room with my fellow players, stretching and getting each other hyped up. Today we face off against the Seattle Soldiers in the playoffs. And if we win, it's onto the Championship Game.

Ever since I told Jessica, my girlfriend who is no longer really my girlfriend, everything, football's taken on a new meaning for me. I'm no longer playing out of fear that I'll disappoint my father. I'm finally playing it for me.

But what's got me more excited than anything is that Michael Cunningham, the man I truly love, could be in the stadium watching me right now. After I worked with Robyn to publish an article to dismiss the lie that Amani cheated on me, Amani agreed to meet with me so I could apologize to her in person. And seeing her in the flesh did wonders on my heart. It was so nice to see her smile and laugh again, to hear about her life. And most of all, to get her forgiveness. I'm hoping that today the same can happen with Michael. I miss him so much that my body aches, and it's definitely not just the sex I miss. I miss him—his smile, his voice, his words. He's the best guy a man could ask for. I want him back, and I'm not going to fuck it up this time.

By the time we have to rush onto the field, my heart is racing. But I don't know which is making me more nervous: the game, or the fact that Michael is watching and looking for me right now.

As we jog onto the field, I look up to the booth I rented out for Amani and Michael after memorizing the location like the back of my hand. Close enough to see into, I see Amani and Jessica jumping and waving. I wave back. Next to Amani, I expect to see Michael.

But he's not there.

Maybe I'm wrong. I slow down and try to look closer. Amani is standing next to some woman I don't recognize. She puts her arm around her, and my chest sinks to the ground. Yeah, Michael's not here.

Someone bumps my shoulder. "Come on, man."

It's Ezekiel. I jog just behind him onto the field. It's time to play one of the most important games of my career, but I couldn't be more out of it. What's the point, after all? Michael, the man I wanted to see the most, is not here.

* * *

When the game is over, Tigers players are hugging one another. We're cold and tired, but we won. Next stop: the Championship Game.

But as we rush into the locker room, even the contagious post-game high can't get my mood up. I know I should be happy. I played a game for myself and not my father this time, and we still won. I may have not played my best—no interceptions—but I played damn good defense. So if all this is true, why do I feel like shit?

I slump down in front of my locker and start taking off my clothes. I think I'm disappointed because, in my mind, this was my last chance to make things up to Michael. He's not answering my calls or messages, so I tried to talk to him through Amani. And now that that hasn't worked, I feel I'm out of options. I have no way else to get to Michael.

I feel the back of my eyes heat. The team is supposed to have a little party tonight, then talk about strategy for the Championship Game, honing our plans for if we play the Slayers or the Vanguards. But I don't know if I have the energy for that.

All my gear off, I grab a towel and head to the shower. There has to be another way to get his attention—I don't want to never see him again. I could go to his apartment. But I don't want to creep him out. I don't want to seek him out if he doesn't want to see me.

I bang my fist against the shower tile, hot water warming my snow-chilled body.

Then I remember: there is one woman I know who has been able to help me think clearly, one of the first people I ever came out to. I haven't met with her in a while, but maybe her counsel is just what I need.

Depressed and all but hopeless, I gather a little encouragement from the thought that, at the very least, I'll be able to be fully honest with someone.

* * *

I sit across from Neeti, my old therapist, as she gathers her notes. Her office is in the same condition I remember, and she's even burning the same incense as before—jasmine—bringing back memories of that first session together where I told her about my dad.

"It is so good to see you again, Kyle," she says, her eagerness making her Indian accent a little stronger.

"It's good to see you too," I say, blushing.

"It's been, what, a few months?"

"Something like that," I say, scratching the back of my head.

"Just as we were really working through some issues with your father."

"Yeah," I say, almost embarrassed. "But I have made some headway on my own in terms of what's going on in my head. I can bring you up to speed."

She smiles. "I'd love to hear it."

So I tell her everything, from our last session to me taking Michael to my hometown. To Timmy calling me and telling me the jig was up. To dating Jessica, then to Christmas. And up to now. At least most of the darkness is gone now that Jessica isn't pressuring me to be intimate.

"My, my," she says. "We could make your life a movie."

I laugh, feeling winded from talking for so long. "Yeah."

"So if I can ask," she says, focusing up at a random part of the room. "You are trying to get Michael back?"

"Yes," I say with all the seriousness I can muster.

"Are you sure?"

Something pricks my chest, and I start to get hot. "I'm sure," I say. "Why? Do I not sound convincing?"

"Oh no," she says, shaking her head. "You do sound convincing. The issue is that your past actions are not."

I squint at her. "I beg your pardon?"

She adjusts herself in her seat. "What I'm about to say may be hard to hear."

Now I adjust in my seat, feeling my body heat up further. "Lay it on me," I say. "Not like I have any other options."

"Most sessions you've come in expressing desire to either break free from your father's legacy, or to make things right with Michael. But most of the time, when it matters most, you fall back on what you least want and instead pick what you think you should do. Think about Thanksgiving. You were all but confident that nothing could get in the way of your love for Kyle. And then your agent called."

I let out a heavy sigh. Jimmy was right, after all. When things got hard, I chose to be 'normal' over who I loved.

"Yeah, I'll admit that was not my strongest moment."

"But that's what I'm talking about, Kyle. You've had a couple of really strong moments: your coming out, your decision to date Michael despite the outside pressures. But your own moments of self-sabotage have proved far stronger. It's no wonder that Michael doesn't want to talk to you. He has no reason to believe that your words mean anything."

"Sheesh," I say, wiping my sweaty forehead. "You weren't kidding when said 'hard to hear'."

She scoots her chair closer. "You talk a lot about integrity, how it's important to you."

"Yeah," I say. "I'm trying to have my own integrity. Not live up to my father's."

"Well," Neeti says. "Integrity can mean a lot of things, but I think a clever definition of it is when your words, actions, and beliefs are completely aligned.

Right now, all three are in different places for you. So, Kyle, what do you believe about your sexuality?"

I straighten. "I believe I'm a gay man," I say. I pause. "And I know that I have feelings for Michael Cunningham and him only."

"Okay," she says, nodding. "Now, you express to me that you love him and will do anything to get him back."

"Anything minus going against my morals," I say. "But yes, anything."

"Okay, those are your words," she says. "Now your actions. How can you *show* Michael that you want him back?"

I lean back into the couch and rub my sweaty palms on my jeans.

"And for you, it must be something that is more powerful than all your moments of self-sabotage—a grander gesture than you running away without telling him."

I sit there for a moment, perplexed. The Championship Game is in two weeks, and I've got a shit ton to do before then. Appearances, meetings with reporters. I was barely able to squeeze this session in. If I wanted to prove myself to Michael, I'd have to wait until at least a few days after the Championship Game. Unless...

I nearly jump off the couch with an idea.

"Sounds like you had an insight," she says. "Care to share?"

I suck on my lip, nodding. "It's crazy," I say. "But I think it will be perfect."

Chapter 40

Michael Cunningham

On my day off, I decide to sleep in. I watch the sun rise through the window, and the colors remind me of the Thanksgiving sunset back in Glamour Springs, making my stomach all twisty.

I turn over and face the wall. Amani told me that Kyle wants to see me, but I don't want to see him. I can't. What would be the point? 'Oh, Michael, I love you, and I'll never let you down', and then have him ghost me five minutes after? The man is a freshly out frenetic mess of jumbled nerves who will jump at any opportunity to be 'normal', regardless of the cost. I'm not opening up to somebody who hasn't worked through who he is. I've talked to Susan about this too, and she thinks my logic is sound. I've come too far in my recovery to let some man take advantage of my good will just so he can temporarily get what he wants and then throw me away when he gets too scared of what we have. I'm not doing it anymore. I'm not.

After I lay there for a little longer, my anxiety preventing me from falling back asleep, I decide to roll over and scroll on my phone. I normally hate doing this in the mornings, but fuck it—it's my day off. I check my email, and I see a message at the top that came in just ten minutes ago. It's from a familiar name, but I can't pinpoint how I recognize it. But when I open the email, the memory comes flooding back.

It's the last literary agent who had my full manuscript, the same one I thought ghosted me just like Kyle did.

And she wants to set up a call.

"No fucking way," I say, sitting up in my bed. I reach up and pull my hair up from my scalp to see if I'm dreaming. Thankfully, I'm not. Immediately open up an email to reply. I give her my number and tell her she can call anytime today, and I provide some later times this week as well. I hit send and then sit there, my body lit with excitement. Almost immediately, I receive a reply.

"Great! I'll call around 2PM your time today. Looking forward to it!"

I'm so thrilled that I have to resist screaming and waking my neighbors up. There's usually only one reason why an agent wants to call, and I doubt I'm the exception. I'm about to be an agented author.

I immediately jump out of bed and head for the shower. I want to feel as prepared as possible for this call later. In the shower, I'm singing—fucking singing. I can't remember the last time I was this thrilled. This has been years in the making. God, I've wanted an agent ever since I took that class on the business of publishing in college. And it's finally happening.

After I get out of the shower, I call Amani, and she's squealing so loud through the phone I'm afraid my neighbors will hear.

"You call me immediately after," she says. "I want to know how it goes."

"Will do," I say, sitting down at my desk after I'm all dressed. I hang up and message Skye and Josue, with whom I am again on speaking terms, and I share the news. They offer their congratulations, and the heat of pride warms my chest.

Staring at my computer, I let out one more shout of joy, and then I turn it on. If I'm going to be talking with an agent today, I know she'll ask what else I'm working on. And I can't remember the last time I touched my previous work in progress. I remember it was similar, about two magicians on their way to slay a dragon, but that's about all I have. I'll need to brush up on it, possibly do some edits and more writing, to make sure I know what I'm talking about. So that's what I do. By the time it's lunch time, I've reread the whole thing and added about five pages, confident that my next book isn't total garbage.

I take a break for lunch. When I get back to my desk, I get that post-food drowsiness, and I have to fight to maintain my focus. My train of thought during this period also gets darker too. For whatever reason, at the brightest moments of the day, I get the most depressed. I chuckle to myself, remembering all the times I've been rained on. It's like the weather and I are mortal enemies.

I reread over what I've written today, and then my chest sinks. How could I think this was good? Oh no. This is bad. The dialogue between my characters is cliched and surface level. My worldbuilding is much too obvious and distracting. Oh, and my overall plot? Stupid. Who would want to read about two gay magicians going to slay a dragon? Dumb. Dumb. Dumb.

Exhausted, I collapse my face into my palms and blow a raspberry. I decide to scroll on Instagram to give myself a break. I have been working all morning, after all.

Ads for the Championship Game litter my feed, making my stomach curl into knots. That's where Kyle will be. All hot and sweaty in his uniform. He may be an asshole, but goddamn did God spare no expense when he made that man. He definitely is the Sexiest Man Alive.

Memories of his dick in my asshole pepper my mind, and pretty soon I'm rock hard. When I see an article talking about Kyle's new girlfriend, Jessica, I know it's time to get off social media and get myself off instead. My call with the agent isn't for another thirty.

I slump in my bed and shut off Instagram. I want no reminders of Kyle Weaver. But as I scroll through other videos on OnlyFans, I can't seem to shake him from my mind. Not him, his perfect dick, or his hairy, plump ass.

I huff out a breath. I am *not* jerking off to him. I jump on Twitter, but I keep seeing things about the Championship Game there, too. I groan as I open my internet browser. We're gonna go old school today. Yet even as I scroll through these videos, I can't help but crave the taste of Kyle's cock in my mouth.

Fuck it. I close my eyes and conjure up the Sexiest Man Alive in my head. I have plenty of photos of him, as well as all of the videos I've saved of his commercials. I could easily pull him up, but that feels like I'm conceding something. My pride maybe? I don't know.

But as I'm nearing my climax, the mental image isn't enough. I need him. The true Kyle Weaver.

I pull up my favorite picture of us. It's where were sitting on the back porch of that cabin down in Glamour Springs, the glowing lanterns behind us, right before he walked out on me for good. It's not a *sexy* picture, per se, but it's the one where I think Kyle's the most handsome. His smile shines wide through his thick beard, and his hair's a little overgrown. He has on a windbreaker, and I remember that day he wore the jeans that made his ass perk up.

Looking into his eyes, I think of the man I fell in love with, the one who read my writing and gave me honest feedback. Who helped me love fantasy. Who loved me for who I was, anxious insecurities and all.

And then I fucking cum all over my hairy belly. I look at his picture, and feel my heart skip a beat.

"I hate you so much," I say. "Because I still fucking love you."

I throw my phone down on my bed, and it bounces onto my floor. "Fucking fantastic," I say. I lay there for a second, recollecting the pride I lost with that cumshot. And then my phone starts ringing.

"Shit, shit, shit," I say, standing up. I glance at my bedside clock. I was jerking off to Kyle Weaver for thirty minutes. So much for not still having feelings for hi m.

I quickly roll down my shirt and pull up my pants before I trip and break my nose. I manage reach my phone and answer it before it's too late.

"Hi, this is Michael," I say.

"Michael," a woman says. "This is Lori from Better Books Literary Agency. Is now still a good time?"

I smile, my heart racing with excitement. "Yes, it is."

As we get wrapped up in small talk, I'm tripping over myself, worried I'll say something wrong. But then when I hear her stumbling over her words, I realize that this may be just as nerve-wracking for her as it is for me. She's trying to get a new client!

"Sorry," I say when I manage to trip over my words yet again. "This is just—I've been waiting for this moment for a really long time."

"It's no worries at all," she says. "I can imagine your feelings right now. Let's get right to it then. First of all, I just want to say that your book was phenomenal."

Joy squeezes my chest. "You think so?"

"I know so," she says. "This is just what I've been looking for. Your manuscript perfectly blends that dark, gritty nature of some of these more mature fantasy novels, but it somehow brings the charm of your everyday rom-com. It's so genius, yet so simple. I have high hopes for this book's reception amongst publishers, and I already have a few specific editors in mind that I'll send this to."

'Wow' is all I can say. I can hardly process all this good news. "Jeez. I'm overwhelmed. In a good way, of course."

"Of course," she says. "And I'm getting ahead of myself anyways. I'm calling to say that I would love to represent you. I can give you some time to reach out to other agents have your work, and in the meantime, I can send over my contract for you to review. Do you have any questions for me?"

I sit there, breathing heavily and seeing stars.

This is my dream come true. I've been wanting this for so long. So why does it feel like I'm missing something?

"Sure," I say. "Um, I do have some questions, let me see." I fumble through a notebook where I had written down what questions to ask a literary agent on the representation call. But this was so long ago, when my hopes were high, that I don't remember.

"You know, I'll be honest," I say, still flipping through my journal. "I had been feeling really discouraged these past couple days."

"I'm sorry," she says. "I know how brutal the writing process can be. Let alone querying."

Ennobled by her compassion, I continue. "Exactly." I find the page with some questions, but there is another question burning in my heart.

"I have to ask," I begin. "What was it that drew you into my writing? You mention that the idea was inventive and fresh, but what kept you reading?"

There was a thoughtful pause, and then I heard her take a breath. "Honestly," she says. "It was the romance."

My chest tightens. The word immediately makes me think of Kyle. "The romance. Can you tell me more?"

"Of course," she says. "I just loved how vulnerable these knights were with one another. I mean, hell, they start out in completely different stations, but as they kept doing things for one another, I really saw their romance blossom. I can easily say that some books focus on the sex more than anything else. And don't get me wrong, that's fine sometimes, and the sex you had on the page was great. But it was the intimacy that led to the sex that really kept me going. I was invested in the relationship from the moment the older, more experienced knight took in the poor serf to his retinue. They saw each other. I don't know, it was excellent. And I know other people will love it too."

It's like each of her words pokes tiny holes in my heart, causing me to bleed and drip blood down my chest.

When I first showed Kyle my romance writing, his biggest comment was that the love was superficial—focused and appearance and sex only. Offended that a straight man of all people gave me that advice, I swore that I was going to write the most intimate, thoughtful romance I could, and have the sex be a result, rather than a cause, of said romance. In other words, the intimacy between my characters was a result of Kyle's feedback. And here a literary agent is telling me that this was her favorite part of the book.

"Michael, you still there?"

I shake my head into focus. "Yes, sorry about that. Thanks, writing deep intimacy is really important to me."

"And it shows," she says. "Any other questions?"

I glance down at my notebook and scratch my chest. That's when I realize that my shirt is glued to me as a result of the cum that I didn't clean up earlier. The cumshot that Kyle's stupid smile got out of me.

I ask some of the questions I had written down: her specific vision for the book, what she's done for other clients, her communication style. And it all seems really positive. In talking to her, I realize that she was one of my most preferred agents, so I don't see why I wouldn't sign with her. I will give it some time to think and reach out to the few agents left that have my query, but I think this is the one.

"Great questions," she says. "I have one last one for you."

"Go ahead," I say.

"Tell me what's next," she says. "I wanna know what the next project is!"

I press the spacebar on my computer to wake it up, and I see the blank curser just beneath the words I'd written this morning. At first glance, they don't seem as bad as before, but they definitely don't look as good as I felt writing them. I get the thought to reach out to Kyle to get his thoughts, and my chest aches as I imagine what he would say.

I share the premise with her—gay magicians on a quest to slay a dragon—and I can tell she's intrigued.

"If you sign with me, let's go into greater detail. I have some thoughts. But I like it."

"Thanks," I say, more embarrassed than I should be.

She says she'll look forward to hearing from me, and then the call that's changed my life is over. I sit there—excited, hopeful, afraid, nervous, motivated. But more than anything, there's this grief attached to it all. And now that I'm done talking to the agent, the source of the grief is clear.

I miss Kyle.

I miss him so much.

I know he was a dick to me, and I know I should be angry with him. But he's been trying to reach out to me. To apologize.

If it wasn't for him, I may not have had this phone call. I may have still been writing surface-level romance without deeper intimacy. So this whole thing feels like a sign. Maybe I should keep Kyle in my life—dating, I don't know. But maybe as a friend? I appreciated his insight, so I know he can help me with my writing. But more than anything, having him back in my life feels so right for m e.

So I do something crazy.

I go to my contacts and finally unblock Kyle Weaver's number.

And then I send what feels like the riskiest text of my life.

Chapter 41

Kyle Weaver

"You're gonna be fine, man," Ezekiel says to me. "We got the plan in place. You're not alone." He and two other guys around him nod.

He and I sit at a table on the far side of a large conference room along with several other Tigers players. On the other side, one of the wide receivers for the Vanguards is being interviewed. It's media day, the Monday before the Championship Game. Last year, I nearly outed myself to the whole American public. And this year, I'm fixing to do something even more insane.

"Thanks man," I say. I can hear them wrapping up their questions, which means it's my turn. My heart is already beating outside my chest. I see Ricardo hovering in the crowd of reporters, just waiting to drop some stupid bombshell question. At least this time I'm gonna use him for my own gain.

"You need a beta-blocker or something?" Ezekiel asks. "I know they can help."

"I'll be good," I say, adjusting my hat. When I see the Vanguards player walk off, I stand up. It's time.

I hold out my fist for Ezekiel to fist bump. "Thank you," I say. Then I look up at the rest of my guys. "And thanks to all of you. For everything. You don't have to do this. It means a lot."

"Of course."

"Anything for you, man."

"Love is love."

Ezekiel grins and bumps me back. "Like I said, I would support you no matter what." He lowers his voice. "It doesn't to me which way you swing. I just want you to be happy."

"Fingers crossed that this plan works," I say.

His grin goes wide, and he's almost laughing. "Oh, it will." He rubs his hands together. "I can't wait for it."

Galvanized by Ezekiel, I make my way over to the stand, passing Timmy along the way. He gives me a look that says 'don't fuck this up', and I almost scoff. Boy is he in for a surprise. I sit myself down behind the bouquet of microphones.

Let the games begin.

The questions start out tamer than I would expect—my thoughts on Tigers' defense, my perspective on being nearly undefeated this year, how I feel against playing against the Vanguard's brutal offense. I even get a question about some of the weight I've gained as a result of my depression. But, like as they always do, the questions start to turn silly.

I'm asked whether Jessica and my ex, Amani, get along or fight over me now that Amani and I are publicly friends, to which I respond that that's a sexist question. I see Timmy shift uncomfortably, and I almost laugh. Good. Wait 'til he sees what's up.

There's the inevitable question about being Sexiest Man Alive, which I never know how to answer. Thankfully, someone asks about my charity efforts to kids with cancer, which I gladly expound upon. At least some positive news will come out of this. Then I see Ricardo shimmy is way to the front of the reporters, and I steel myself. Here we go.

"Funny how after I ask if you're gay, you find two girls to date," he says.

Some reporters laugh, but I remain stone-faced.

"That's not a question," I say.

His looks around, his face hardening. "Some are saying that these relationships have been contrived."

Here we go.

"So what if they are?" I respond.

Nearly all the heads whip from Ricardo to me.

"Are you saying that your relationships have been fake?" A woman asks. "Both Amani and Jessica."

Timmy glares at me, his body rigid as a pole. Man, if looks could kill.

"I'm not saying anything," I say. "Just wondering why it matters."

Ricardo pushes himself to the front again. "Because the entire world wants to know if you're gay."

My heart is pounding in my ears, and I have to lean away from the mics so they don't pick up my breathing. And I just know my pit stains are epic right now.

"And if I am?"

The entire crowd of reporters seems to pale a shade lighter, and I see Timmy in my periphery stomping toward me.

"Regardless of who I love, or who anybody loves, I'm here to play some football. We need to stop caring so much about what any of us do in the bedroom."

And with that, I stand up and make my way back to my table of friends. Some reporters peel off to ask me more questions, and Timmy is struggling to break through them so he can reprimand me personally. When he finally does, he grabs my arm.

"What the fuck is wrong with you?" he asks. "Do you have any idea what you've done? Undoing all the work I've done for you?"

I look down at him. My heart is racing wildly, and a year ago I would have thought I was insane for carrying out this plan. But Neeti has been teaching me that the best way to live is to make my beliefs, thoughts, and actions all align. And regardless of what my dad wanted from me, this is what he was really teaching me. So it's what I'm doing.

"Nothing's wrong with me," I say. "And by the way, now that the season's pretty much over, I don't need you anymore. You're fired."

He scoffs and drops his jaw as reporters surround us, hurling questions at us. "I do all this work and you're just throwing me away?"

I sigh through my nose, almost laughing, as I shake my head. "You've been more stress than your worth, Timmy. Have a good life."

And then I walk away, his jaw still agape as reporters swarm him. A life of retirement without Timmy awaits.

As I pass the table of my fellow players, most of them cheer, and Ezekiel holds up a thumbs up. "We're here with you, Kyle," he says.

I lift my hand to him, and one reporter makes her way to me. "Kyle, what are your plans now that you don't have an agent?" she asks.

I stop to answer her question. "I'm doing just what my daddy wanted of me," I say. "I'm living a life of integrity."

By the time I make it to my car, I'm taking deep breaths to slow my heartrate. I know I made the right decision, and everything is going according to plan, but I'm still anxious as hell for what I did. I realize I need more than some breath exercises, so I pull out my phone. Neeti gave me her number to call during this stressful time, so I think I'll utilize her. But then I see a text on my screen, and when I see who it's from, my knees go weak just like they did when I first saw him on my doorstep.

"Hey," Michael says. "I'd like to talk."

Chapter 42

Michael Cunningham

I'M PARKED OUTSIDE THE restaurant where Kyle and I are supposed to meet and talk. And upon arriving, I realize it's the very same place he took me on our first date. I wonder if he's gonna get that secret room for us again. I want a private conversation as much as he would, but I think our reasons are different. I want to talk about what happened, why he really walked out on me—to see if any sort of relationship is still possible. But does he want a private room because he's still too afraid for the world to see us together? Probably.

But as I wait in my car, scrolling through the ESB article that Amani sent me, maybe I'm wrong. The Monday before the Championship Game, the NFO has this big media blitz day where key players are asked all sorts of questions, ranging from their skills to their sex life. Last year, Kyle was asked if he was gay, which ultimately led to us meeting. And this year, Kyle was asked the same question. Except he gave the craziest response. Robyn wrote here that he put the question back on the reporter, likely Ricardo, and openly criticized the public for being so concerned over someone's sexuality. I don't know why he said this or what this means, but this does not sound like the man who would abandon his boyfriend to escape into a life of normalcy. I think he's changed.

Pretty soon, I see Kyle's Cadillac pull up, and my insides immediately twist around themselves. I can do this.

He steps out of the car, and if I wasn't already sitting down, I would have collapsed to the ground. He's wearing a suit I've never seen before: a navy three-piece with a floral tie and light blue pocket square. It's freshly creased, and it fits perfectly. I can see the way his muscles tug on the fabric, wishing to be torn free. His wavy hair effortlessly flows back over his head, and his beard is long, full, and sexy. Yet all I'm wearing is a nice sweater and some slacks.

He looks around, and I lower myself. Which is ridiculous. He knows what my car looks like. But, to my relief, he doesn't spot me and instead walks up to the black façade of the building. An older man comes out of the restaurant and opens the door to the secret hallway, the same way I entered last time. Kyle disappears, and the man stands there. Looks like we're eating in private after all. I still don't know what to make of this whole thing.

My phone buzzes. It's Kyle.

"I'm inside," he says. "Teddy will let you in through side door."

I release the deepest breath I've taken all day, then open my car door. Here goes nothing.

By the time I'm inside, I feel my heart beating in my throat. And when Teddy leads me to my private room with Kyle, my heart nearly tears itself out of my chest when he locks eyes with me and smiles.

He comes to me, quickly but elegantly, and wraps his bear arms around me. I hold onto his shoulder blades and take in the smell of his leathery cologne mixed with his own scent that acts as my very own aphrodisiac. I find myself breathing rapidly, taking in as much of his smell as I can. Melting into him. Nearly tearing up finally being so close to him. God, I've missed him so fucking much.

He pulls away and holds one of his huge hands on my cheek. His thumb strokes me gently, and it takes all my strength not to claim it with my lips and tongue. Behind him, a fire crackles, and tables around us are covered with candles. The lights above are low enough that Kyle's face is the only thing I can see clearly.

"It's so good to see you," he says.

God, his voice.

Then I panic.

This is the same man who walked out on me with no explanation. Who ignored my calls and texts for weeks until I just gave up all together.

I pull away from him. "Hi," I say, wiping my face, getting his touch off me. But his smell still lingers in my nostrils.

He gestures to the table. "Sit with me?"

"That's why I came," I say, scratching my arm.

He pulls out my chair for me, then pushes it in at the exact right time like a gentleman. I will not swoon no matter how swoon worthy he is right now. I can't forget what happened, and I can't forget that words are where he does best. This is what Susan reminded me. Watch their hips, never their lips. It's what he *does* that matters.

"I don't see a point in delaying it," he says, sitting down. He looks me right in the eyes, his hands clasped on the table in front of him. "I am so, so sorry."

The intensity of his gaze, his genuine gaze, makes me squirm.

"You walked out on me, Kyle," I say. "And you never said a word to me after. Do you understand how damaging that is to me? To us?"

Our waiter, Charles, comes out and sets some bread on the table along with an appetizer. Good. At least Kyle's ordered in advance so we won't be interrupted.

"I can't even begin to imagine how damaging it was," Kyle says, shaking his head. "What I did was wrong."

I recall the intense feelings of abandonment that threatened to tear my body in half that night I laid in his mom's kitchen, sobbing into her arms.

"Well," I say, my chest on fire. "You need to imagine it. You have no idea what that was like for me. My parents abandoned me as a child with their neglect. Then time and time again I've had my heart broken by shitty men who didn't know what they wanted. Then I gained some self-respect and started dating out gay men, but even then the same problem persisted. For the life of me, I couldn't find men who were emotionally available.

"So I finally decided to focus on myself and my recovery. And I fucking blossomed. I gained so much confidence in myself, learned so much about who I was. This was when I rediscovered my love for writing for Christ's sake.

"And then you came along. I just so happened to show up on the doorstep of my greatest sexual fantasy. But I kept myself at bay, not letting myself catch feelings. I figured you were straight, and even if you weren't, I knew a closeted man in the NFO would not be emotionally mature enough for a relationship."

Kyle squirms in his seat, anxiously pulling on his beard hairs. I hit the nail on the head there.

"But then you fucking prove me wrong. First, you take an interest in me and what I like to read. Then you like my writing. You help me with it. You show me how sweet you can be. My walls come down. And then you fucking come out to me. Meanwhile, here I am realizing that I don't just think you're hot. You have me realizing that I like you. Then, for the love of God, we have sex, and it's transcendent. We start dating—in secret, of course, but we do.

"And then you pull away. Slowly but surely. Then it's November, and here I am thinking I'm gonna have to break up with you."

By now, tears leak out of my eyes, but I only notice once they cool down my hot cheeks.

"And what do you do? You prove me wrong. Again. On Thanksgiving, you take me into your home. I'm part of your family. I feel safe and loved in ways I haven't in years, maybe ever. And then what do you do?"

Kyle cringes. "I abandon you."

"Yes," I say, thrown off that he took the words out of my mouth. "You abandon me. You throw everything we ever had in the garbage. You leave me to sift through every interaction we've ever had, turning each one over and denying that any of it was ever any good. You leave me to realize that everything you did and said was a lie."

He leans forward. "It wasn't a lie. None of it was."

"Which wasn't a lie, Kyle?" I ask. "You saying you loved me? Or you running away?"

He clenches his fist and chews on his lips. "It's not that simple."

I let out a sharp laugh. "Great. So you invite me here to tell me it's complicated."

"Michael," he says, like a teacher scolding a child. His sternness chills my body.

"What? Didn't want to hear what I have to say?"

"Of course I did," he says, leaning back in his chair. "But I also wanted to talk about how I want to give us another chance. Damnit, Michael. I fucking love you, you know that? I never stopped thinking about you when I ran away. Hell, I couldn't. You stuck to my mind like fucking glue. And when you stopped reaching out, my heart felt like it would burst."

"Then why'd you do it?" I groan. "Why did you just walk away from me? From what we had?"

"Because I was a coward without integrity," he says. "I didn't know what I stood for. But now I do."

I sigh through my nose. "And that is?"

He leans forward and rests his elbow on the table. To our side, another table sits with a bunch of gorgeously expensive looking food that the waiter has been bringing out. Any other day, I'd be seizing the opportunity to eat such delicacies. But I'm the furthest thing from hungry right now.

"Being true to what's inside me," he says. "Not what other people say or want me to be. And that's a man who is attracted to other men. A man who loves you and wants to be with you for the rest of his life."

I slump back in my chair and fold my arms tightly, shaking my head. Charles brings the last of the food out. Plates cover the table next to us, just waiting to be eaten. I hear the crackle of the fireplace, and I can make out the distant conversations from the main restaurant. But were cut off in here. Isolated.

"And what's the rest of this life going to look like?" I ask. "Staying cooped up in your mansion? Eating in private rooms at restaurants so we're not seen? Traveling to places where nobody would recognize us?" I pause for a beat. "Getting you a fake wife so you can live a double life and have everything you want? The semblance of straightness and your gay little fleshlight on the side?"

Kyle almost snarls. "You are so much more to me than a fucking fleshlight. You are everything to me."

"Then fucking treat me like it," I say. "Flaunt me around. Don't just take me to meet your family in private. Take me to a football game. Put your arm around me. *Kiss* me, for Christ's sake. In front of anyone and everyone. Don't just tell me you love me. I'm tired of your words. Show me that you love me. No matter who's watching."

He's looking solemnly down at his hands clasped on the table. Then he meets my eyes. "And if I told you that that's my plan?"

My heart skips a beat. "What?"

"I want you to come to the Championship Game," he says.

"As a friend or boyfriend?" I ask. "Or are you still with your girlfriend Jessica that the media's been talking about?" This is it, the determining answer.

He sucks on his lip and fidgets with the callouses on his palm. It looks like he wants to say something, but can't. Or won't.

"Answer me, Kyle."

"Just come to the Championship Game, okay? Please. I have a plan. I promise I won't disappoint you."

I shake my head, feeling overheated inside my own body. I stand up, tears rushing to my eyes again. "So you are still with Jessica," I say, almost laughing. "I can't take your promises anymore. You've already disappointed me."

I dart straight to our private room's exit.

"Wait," Kyle calls out.

I don't know what possesses me with the strength to stop, because if it were solely up to me, I'd be in my car speeding to the highway by now.

I turn my body sideways to him, looking him in the eye.

He stands up and approaches me but gives a respectable distance. "I'll email you the tickets," he says. "Just please, please come to the Championship Game. It's the only way I can show my love for you."

I sigh, then glance up at him one last time. "You know, I got a literary agent," I say.

Kyle's face goes from solemn to beaming. "Babe, that is so wonderful." He steps closer, but I gesture for him to stop.

"And after I talked with them, I wondered: maybe Kyle's the secret ingredient to my writing. You were what inspired me to write more emotional connection between my characters, after all.

"But after today, I realize that I don't need you. I've just needed myself. Because my whole life, I've pined after men who have never truly loved me back. And today, after this conversation, I think I've finally outgrown this habit."

Kyle sighs, and his shoulders sink. "Please," he says. "Give me this chance."

I shake my head. "Goodbye, Kyle." And then I exit through the private hallway, doing my best to compose myself.

Sometimes it's the hardest things we do that end up for our best.

Chapter 43

Michael Cunningham

I SIT AT THE head of the circle in the Rucker's cafe, surrounded by mostly women but also some men too. Today, I'm leading the discussion of VE Schwab's *The Invisible Life of Addie Larue*. The book was so highly requested and popular that folks from my queer book discussion wanted to join in. Our tiny café is filled way beyond capacity.

As the discussion pops off, great responses to my questions eliciting even more insightful comments from people who've never shared before, pride swells in my chest. When I first came here, I thought I didn't belong. But since then, I've contributed sizably to our book clubs, bringing in more men, both queer and not, as well as queer women. And that's not the only thing.

I'm an agented author! I agreed to start working with the agent who called me last week. And since Amani and I resolved our issues, our writing group started meeting regularly again. It feels like I have that writing community again just like I did in college. But this one is better because we're all seeing success in our own way. I'm agented, Amani is preparing to put her first book up on Kindle Unlimited. Skye has been steadily gaining a following on Patreon with her trans romances, and the money she's seeing is actually substantial. And Josue has finally garnered the courage to query his fantasy novel. We're all successful, thriving, and helping each other. I didn't think I would find a solid community so soon, but now I have one, and I'm on my way to getting published. Everything is just as I wanted it. Yet I can't help but feel a little bit sad.

Talking, and even writing, about romance has made my chest tight in ways it never has before. I don't know why. I finally became strong enough to put off emotionally unavailable men altogether when I rejected Kyle, and it shows in my writing. So why do I feel this way?

"I have a question for the group," Josh, one of our new gay book club goers, says. He looks at me. "Can I ask it?"

"Go right ahead," I say.

He nods. "If your entire life you had been invisible, how would you react to someone who could finally see you? I don't see how you *couldn't* fall in love with them."

Though a simple hypothetical, his question pricks my chest. And it seems to affect others as well because it starts a lively discussion. But as they all discuss, I shrink inside myself. Because the only person I can think of is Kyle.

I did have the experience of being invisible and finally being seen. My whole life, I was seeking people who did not want to be found. Who did not want a relationship. So I closed myself off. But Kyle was the one who went seeking me out. Time and time again. Starting with my writing, seeing it in ways no one else had before. Then taking me on a date and being so present. Then wanting to date me, taking me to his home on Thanksgiving. Yes, he did abandon me. But then he took me out to dinner and said he wanted to make it all up.

By the time the discussion ends and I'm on my way home, I can't stop thinking about him. And I'm honestly confused. This entire time, I've labelled Kyle as emotionally unavailable, someone who says one thing and does another, never really saying what he means. But this dinner we had earlier this week, I think that was a way he was showing his love. But then it was in private? Gah, I don't know.

I pick up my phone and immediately dial Susan. She answers on the second ring. I'm so grateful that she gives up her time to me like this. I need her insight when I get this confused.

"So what's going on?" she asks after some pleasantries, her voice echoing throughout my car.

"I still love Kyle," I say. "Even after everything."

"I don't blame you," she says. "Feelings are hard. And messy."

I sigh, thinking of those Championship Game tickets in my inbox. He got me and my friends a private suite. For the Championship Game! When I saw the price on the receipt, I nearly threw up. We'd be sharing the booth with his girlfriend, Jessica, but still.

"What if I want to give him another chance?" I ask. "Is that bad?"

"If you want to give him a chance, then that's what you want to do. There's nothing wrong with that. It could turn out better than you could imagine, or not. You don't know what you don't know."

"But what he did on Thanksgiving—that's unforgiveable."

"Is it?" she retorts. "What sort of recompense are you expecting?"

I pause, not knowing what to say. "He said he was sorry," she says. "And from what you described about your dinner, it sounds like he's doing everything he can to get you back. Choosing not to forgive only hurts you. But what you do with your boundaries is up to you. You can let him back into your life or let him go. The universe will provide you the lesson you need to learn no matter what you choose."

I want to let him back in, but I feel anxious about it. "But he's all talk," I say. "What if the same thing just happens again? He gets distant and then ghosts me?"

"Ah, the classic 'what if'," she says, laughing. "I'll counter that: what if the two of you live a long, happy, healthy life together?"

The thought of that sends butterflies fluttering all around my torso, and I grip my steering wheel so tight my knuckles go white.

"And you say he's not showing it. Didn't he get you tickets to the Championship Game?"

"Yeah," I say begrudgingly. "But I don't know why. I'm not going as his boyfriend. His girlfriend is going to be there."

"Hmm," she says as if she's onto something. "Maybe there's something else to it. I won't tell you what to do, but I will remind you that sometimes people show love in the ways we least expect it."

"So you think I should go?" I ask.

"I think you should do what feels best for you," she says.

I take a deep breath, and the answer is all but clear. "I think I'm gonna go," I say. "But I'm scared."

"Of course you would be," she says. "But remember: you are not alone. You have me, the universe, your friends."

And maybe after this, Kyle, I think to myself.

"You're right," I say.

"Well, have a great time at the game," she says. "As always, call if you need anything. And give the Tigers all the love you can for me. They've played well this season, but the Vanguards have done even better. They'll need all the luck they can get."

Chapter 44

Kyle Weaver

IT'S SNOWING AT THE Portland stadium today, which would be momentous on its own. But it's also Championship Game Sunday, and the day I prove my love to Michael. The crowd quiets as the two teams huddle around the camera on center field. Ezekiel, our team captain, steps forward and faces the Vanguards' team captain, the referees to our side. Since they're the visiting team, they get to do the coin toss. One of their sponsors comes forward as the head referee says a few words. The Vanguards call tails. The sponsor flips the coin. The coin lands tails up, and the crowd goes wild. That means we're receiving this half.

Ezekiel and I walk next to each other. Since I'm defense, I gotta sit this one out. I pat his back, wishing him luck. He grabs me by the shoulder pads and looks right in my eyes, then offers a solemn nod. A wish of luck. And I know this wish isn't just for the game but for our plan that's been weeks in the making.

Our team lined up, waiting for the kickoff, I can feel my heart pound everywhere in my body. But I don't know which has me more nervous: the fact that this is the most important game that I'm playing for myself rather than my daddy, or the plan to win Michael back for good. I've been too preoccupied to check the suites before the game, so I don't know if he's actually come. I really, really hope he's here. Or else I'll do all this for nothing.

The Vanguards kick the ball, and the game begins. And already, it's like two titans battling it out. The Tigers know how to run a ball, but the Vanguards know how to stop it. I truly don't know who's gonna win this.

Having some time out, I search the suites around the stadium for any hint of Kyle, Amani, Jessica, or any of his friends. In all the commotion of the Championship Game, I've completely forgotten where I sat them. But even if I did remember where I put them, the snow is falling too much now for me to see clearly. I blink the snow out of my eyes, trying to get a better look, but it doesn't matter anymore. Because the Vanguards have already taken possession of the ball, and it's time for me to get out there.

Ezekiel stops me on the field as we swap places. "Give 'em hell," he says.

"One last time," I say, patting him on the shoulder.

Chapter 45

Michael Cunningham

So I'm here. At the Championship Game. And I can't fucking believe it. On the jumbotron, I've seen like fifteen celebrities. And they're all in private suites just like me. This is insane. Amani, her new girlfriend Angie, Skye, Josue and I all sit together, the snow falling outside making us squeeze together for warmth. I thought Ricardo or some other reporters would give Amani shit for showing up to the game as Kyle's ex, but we've not been bothered.

We all watch Kyle, cheering him on. It's 0 – 6, the Vanguards already having scored a touchdown. I'm trying to send as much love to the Tigers as I can. Even as someone who's just recently gotten into football, this is intense.

Jessica, Kyle's girlfriend, is here too. She's sitting separate from us, though, with some other people I don't recognize. I know she and Amani get along, but for obvious reasons, I want nothing to do with her.

As we watch the game, I can't help but think why Kyle wanted me here. Susan mentioned this could be his way of showing his love rather than just saying it, but I'm unsure how. Because what will happen after the game is over? He'll probably be interviewed, regardless of who wins. And then he'll go home with Jessica.

A wave of dread crashes over me. Why the hell did I go through all the trouble of being here?

Amani tugs on my arm. "What's wrong?" she asks. "You got that look."

I shake my head. "I'm just—you know."

"I'm glad you're here," she says. "Kyle really wanted you here too."

"That's what I've been told," I say. "But I don't know why, really."

"Does there need to be a reason?"

I look at her like she called me a slur. "Of course there does. After what's happened to us?"

"I thought you guys talked."

"Yeah," I say. "And not much came of it."

The entire room around us tenses as the Vanguards reach their last down, and Amani and I look down at the field. Tension sucks the noise right out of our room as the Vanguards snap the ball. Their quarterback throws it out to their wide receiver, someone already saw it coming. Kyle, already having broken past their players, jumps up. And he successfully intercepts the ball.

Our suite gets so loud that I want to cover my ears. The stadium is going ballistic. The first Weaver interception of the game.

He's eventually tackled, but he got some yards back to the Tigers, and the ball is now in their possession.

The Vanguards call a timeout, and this is the one thing I hate. Somehow these two minutes turn into something way longer. I'm just surprised that the Vanguards are using theirs so early.

Somebody taps me on the shoulder. I turn and almost recoil when I see Jessica, her perfect blonde hair cascading down from her Tigers beanie. I hate to admit it, but she's even more pretty up close. To think that this woman has slept with Kyle...

"I know how weird this might be," she says.

My stomach jumps. Why would this be weird? She doesn't know about me. My eyes widen. Unless...

"I'm sorry, how do we know each other?" I hate that I'm coming off bitchy, but what am I supposed to say? 'Hey, I fucking hate that you're sleeping with the man I love?'

She laughs and lightly taps her forehead. "Sorry, um," she looks around. "Can we talk outside for a second?"

I glance at the others. Amani is debating with Josue about something, and I can tell Skye is regretting sitting right between them. Her new girlfriend Angie, the one she met at the bar, is unable to contain her laughter. Timeout is still going, so it's not like I'll miss anything.

"Sure," I say slowly.

"Great."

I follow her out in the hallway, my stomach tripping all over itself. What does Jessica want to do with me? Tell me she knows about what happened between me and Kyle and for me to lay off?

Out in the hallway, we're completely alone. Not much traffic in the private suites. She glances down both hallways just to make sure, then looks me dead in the eye.

"I know about you and Kyle," she says.

If I was a cat, I'd be hissing with an arched back, all my hair standing up straight. Well, one of those things is actually true. Goosebumps are making the hair on my arms shoot up.

I scowl at her. "What about me and Kyle?"

She leans in closer, and I step away. Suddenly, one of the suite doors open, and both of us freeze. Then out walk Zendaya and Tom Holland. They smile and say hello as they pass us, and I almost pass out.

Jessica looks back at me, equally stunned, then lets out a laugh. But her laugh is more like a snort, which makes me laugh, too. So pretty soon we're both cracking up in the private suite hallway of the Championship Game.

"I'm sorry," she says, wiping her eyes. "That was fucking amazing."

"Your laugh," I say, still giggling. "I'm sorry."

"Don't be," she says. "It makes every situation funnier."

After that, I'm still angry at her for stealing my man, but I've softened enough to listen.

She sighs. "What I meant to say was that I know about Kyle too. That he's gay."

My chest tightens, and my shoulders tense, still accustomed to always protecting his secret sexuality.

"Don't worry. He told me himself. And for the record, we've never slept together."

My shoulders relax. "Really?"

She nods. "And since he's told me about you. He still really loves you, you know."

I blush and stare at the concrete floor. Then I whip my head up at her. "Wait, then why are you guys still together?"

She smiles. "Because I'm helping him out."

"With what?"

Beyond the walls, cheering begins, and Zendaya and Tom Holland rush back to their suite. I freeze up, not knowing what to say to them, but Jessica lets out an awkward 'hi'.

"Just wait for the half-time show," she says once they're back in their suite. "Someone will come to get you. That's all I can say."

My stomach tumbles over itself again. "Someone's coming to get me? What does that mean?"

Someone opens our suite door—one of Jessica's friends. He gestures for her to come back, and she pushes herself off the wall.

"That's all I can tell you," she says with a shrug.

"What?" I say, confused. But pretty soon she's left me alone in the hallway. After I gather some strength, I return to the suite and sit back down in my seat.

"What was that about?" Amani asks.

"I honestly have no idea," I say.

"Was she mean?" Amani asks, alert.

"No, not at all really," I say. "Just confusing."

Another play begins, and we're sucked back into the game. But I can't stop thinking about the cryptic message that Jessica just left for me. 'Wait until the half-time show', she said. 'Someone will come to get me'. Is that someone Kyle? It can't be. I doubt he'd have that much time to do that. Oh man. This anticipation is going to kill me.

I try to focus on the game, but each passing second only means I'm closer to the half-time show and whatever's happening then. It has to do with Kyle, right? Why else would Jessica be the one giving me the message? And does this have to do with the Kyle's way of showing me he loves me?

While I'm almost hyperventilating, the Tigers manage to score a touchdown, but the Vanguards score one right after and manage to score a safety after their touchdown, giving them two more points. It's now 6 – 14, Vanguards winning. But I would say the mystery happening at half-time is making me substantially more nervous.

But wait. It was Jessica who relayed this message. Who told me she knows all about Kyle being gay and how he loves me still. That means that they're not together in any real way at all. It's all a ruse, just like it was with Amani. But how?

Just before the first half is over, there's a knock on our suite. Two huge, burly security guards open the door. "Is there a Michael Cunningham in here?" the taller one asks.

Oh god. This is it.

I sheepishly raise my hand.

"Will you come with us? We're here to escort you," the shorter one says.

I stand up, and all eyes in the booth are on me. Jessica's watching me with rapt attention. This is what she was preparing me for, after all.

"Escort me where?" I say, stepping up to them.

"Just follow us," the tall one says. "You'll see soon enough."

Not knowing what else to do, I follow the guards into the hallway.

Chapter 46

Kyle Weaver

Jogging off the field for half-time, I should feel relieved—eager to relax and play hard in the next half, especially since we're kicking off to the Vanguards.

But I'm more tense than ever.

This is where all my plans over the last few weeks are coming to fruition. If one thing goes wrong, then this whole thing could blow up in my face. And then I'm not sure if I'll ever get Michael back ever again.

Just before I reach the locker rooms, Ezekiel pulls me off into an industrial hallway filled with dozens of workers with headsets and random equipment that has the vague structure of a stage.

"Kyle," Ezekiel says, taking me around a corner. "I'd like you to meet my friend, Sloane Michaels."

I reach out to shake the all but retired R&B singer's hand. "It's an honor and a pleasure."

He squints at me and shakes my hand. "You're the gay football player I'm helping out?"

I smile and put my hands on my hips. "That's me."

"I'm still reeling that you agreed to do this," Ezekiel says. "And to think this might lead to a new album."

"Hey, no promises," Sloane says, his salt-and-pepper beard widening with a smile.

"Is everything set?" I ask.

Sloane nods. "I've been given full creative control of the half-time show. Those were the only terms I would accept. So, even if you were to run on stage and sing himself, the NFO couldn't do anything as long as I approve. And I definitely approve of two fellow gays getting together."

I laugh. "Thank you so much," I say. "I don't plan on singing though." I pause, my mind beginning to race. "Unless that would persuade Michael…"

"Hey man," Ezekiel says, putting a hand on my shoulder. "The plan's perfect. Let's not change it now."

I pat his hand. "You're right."

"Security will come get you from the locker rooms when it's time," Ezekiel says, putting his hands on his hips. "And then Sloane will give you the signal when it's time to come out."

I nod, recalling the plan in my head. "And they got Michael?"

Ezekiel shrugs. "That was Jessica's part. We've been on the field this whole time, so I don't know."

My stomach flutters, and I start chewing on my lips. If she flaked, or if they didn't get him, then…

"Hey, easy," Ezekiel says. "It's gonna be fine."

"I gotta go," Sloane says as a manager pulls him away. "I'm sticking to the plan!"

"Come on," Ezekiel says. "Before coach starts asking where we are."

The locker room is chaos. Players are scarfing down bananas and chugging water. The majority of us opt in for a fresh change of warm, dry underclothing. It's chilly out there, especially with the snow. The offensive coach pulls offense aside, while the head coach talks to us defense. I'm trying to focus, but it's hard to be in two places at once. Because pretty soon, rather than being in here, I'm gonna be out on the field enacting the final step of the plan.

Out of the corner of my eye, I spot the security guard just outside the locker room gesturing for me to follow. It's time.

All of my fresh gear on, I slip out the locker room. Coach doesn't notice because he's mostly talking to our linemen.

The security guard ushers me into the main hallway, and I can hear Sloane Michaels talking into his mic from here.

"Before I perform," Sloane says. "I have something special to present to you tonight."

The guard walks me out onto the field, and confused cheers echo around me.

"Kyle Weaver," he says from the quickly built stage in the middle of the field. "I believe you have something to tell us."

My heart threatening to break through my shoulder pads, I ascend the stage and take the mic from him.

"Thank you," I say. "And I do."

Chapter 47

Michael Cunningham

"KYLE WEAVER, I BELIEVE you have something to tell us."

My head whips up and I rush to the edge of the concrete opening to peer over the side. My jaw drops as I watch Kyle, in all his football gear, rush up to the stage.

The security guards took me through the labyrinth that is the Portland stadium and have kept me just inside an opening onto the field.

"Kyle's told us to keep you here," the taller security guard says, walking up to my side. "But from here, the choice is yours. You can go to the stage when Kyle calls you up. Or you can choose to leave now. It's up to you."

My breath quickens as I consider what he's saying, but then Kyle starts speaking. I have no time to think. Just listen.

"You know, I've never been very good at this," Kyle says. "But what I'm about to say is completely true and straight from my heart."

I'm worried some NFO official is going to drag him off the stage, but Sloane is just standing by, letting this happen. This was planned. Coordinated. And I think by Kyle. And judging by the way the crowd is cheering, even if some management wanted to take Kyle off stage, it would be a bad idea.

"Over the years, there's been a lot of speculation about me. Specifically, the way that I swing. What my life is like in the bedroom. In short, if I'm straight or gay."

My stomach jumps to my throat as the noise from the crowd intensifies, cheering or jeering I'm not sure. He's not doing what I think he is—he can't be.

"Well," he says, his voice shaky. He pauses to take a breath.

The poor man. I want to hold his hand. But the guards said to wait until he calls me up. So I remain hidden behind the concrete wall, my eyes just peaking above it.

"My whole life, I've tried to make my daddy proud, may he rest in peace," he says. "And that meant becoming a family man so I could live on the family legacy: marry a woman, have kids. But I couldn't do it." He sighs into the microphone. "I just couldn't do it."

"Is Kyle Weaver really coming out right now?" One of the security guards asks as the crowd lets out confused cheers. He looks down at me. "Are you his boyfriend or something?"

The question winds me, but I don't have time to respond.

"So for years, I tried to just put my sexuality in the background. I wasn't straight or gay. I just played football." He pulls away from the mic to clear his throat. "Until I met Michael."

Hearing him say my name for the whole country makes my knees weak, and I hold on to the wall to keep myself standing.

"I met Michael when the Tigers threatened to fire me over my homosexual allegations," he says with a laugh. "Funny how this whole time I actually was."

"No shit," the guard says behind me. "He just came out during the Championship Game half-time show."

"He did," I say, unable to believe it.

"Michael let me be who I was," Kyle says, my stomach turning over itself so much I'm afraid I'll throw up. "He didn't take advantage of me when I came out to him. He helped me keep my sexuality secret, even when it came at great personal expense to him."

My chest tightens, and I feel tears in my eyes.

This is it. This is him *really* apologizing. Instead of just telling me he loves me, he's showing this love by saying it in front of everyone who could judge him for it. This was why he couldn't tell me he wanted me at the game. He wanted his actions to speak for themselves.

"And most importantly," Kyle continues. "He showed me how beautiful romance could be. He's the reason why I'm doing what I am now."

I grip the lip of the concrete wall. "Jesus," I mutter.

"You really are his boyfriend," the guard says.

I shake my head bewildered. "I don't know what I am."

"My dad and I had our differences," Kyle says. "But he did teach me one thing: the importance of integrity." Kyle sighs again, and by now, the crowd has quieted, listening with rapt attention. "But unfortunately, I didn't learn how important integrity was until I really hurt Michael. Before, I thought integrity meant living up to the expectations of other people. But now I know the truth: integrity is making your words, beliefs, and actions align. And I knew there was only one thing I could do to make things right, to show Michael I really loved him instead of just saying it. So, tonight, that's what I'm doing."

Kyle looks my direction, and I duck under the wall.

"Michael, will you come out?"

The crowd breaks into a deafening roar, and I look back at the guards behind me as if they'll tell me what to do. They both just shrug.

"Like I said," the taller one says. "It's up to you."

Chapter 48

Kyle Weaver

My hand is shaking so much that I have to lower the microphone. I asked for Michael to come out, but I don't see him anywhere near the tunnel where I asked security to keep him. The crowd around me is deafening. The snow has stopped falling, but the lights of the stadium blind me. On the edge of the field, I see some pissed NFO officials. They can't do anything to stop this, but the half-time show won't last forever.

Sloane pats me on the shoulder, I lean down to him.

"Don't worry," he says in my ear. "Have faith. It'll work out."

I nod, only slightly reassured. Because if Michael doesn't come out, then this whole thing was for naught.

When I see nothing, I'm tempted to continue my speech a little longer. Maybe I said something wrong. Maybe I didn't say enough. But just as the mic meets my lips, that's when I see him.

Michael comes rushing out of the tunnel, and someone puts a spotlight on him. The crowd goes wild as they see the man who stole the heart of the best linebacker of the 21st century and the Sexiest Man Alive. The man that I love.

By the time Michael reaches the stage, his face is glistening with sweat, and I rush to meet him. He doesn't even take two steps onto the stage before I wrap my arms around him.

The crowd breaks into a roar. Many jeering too, I'm sure. But I don't care. I'm finally with the man that I love. And my integrity is completely intact.

I pull away, but I grab his hand and lift the mic to my mouth. "I was awful to you," I say. "I abandoned you just when I said I loved you the most. Because I was scared of what we had. I was scared of what everyone would think."

I lower the mic, bite my lip, then raise it again. "But I'm here to tell you that the real me—the true Kyle Weaver—loves you from the bottom of his heart. *I* love you, Michael. And I hope you still feel the same for me. Because I want to spend my life with you. Regardless of what my father, the NFO, or anyone else might think."

With this confession, I think the crowd will burst into a riot—fans storming the field to attack the player who just made their favorite game gay.

But that doesn't happen. In fact, the stadium is silent once more. They're waiting for the answer.

My chest heaves as Michael looks into my eyes.

Then he pulls me in for the most passionate kiss he's ever given me. Which is saying something.

And the crowd cheers.

He pulls away and strokes my sweaty face with my thumb. "I love you, too, Kyle Weaver," he says. "And I think I want to spend my life with you too."

A laughter bubbles up inside me—a joyous one born of laughter that is so strong it can't be contained. I kiss him again and then hold my forehead against his, laughing and crying now. And he kisses me back. I raise my first to the crowd, and they break into the most boisterous applause yet.

Sloane taps me on the shoulder. "Alright, he says. "That was beautiful, you two. But I still gotta perform a little."

I pull away from Michael and wipe my eyes. "Right, we'll let you get to it. Thank you again."

Michael and I rush off the stage, my hand on his lower back. And I couldn't be happier.

"Now some love songs for the new lovers," Sloane says, and he begins performing.

I take Michael to his tunnel and hold his hands. "Will you come over after the game?"

He kisses me on the lips and squeezes my hands, and my chest feels like there's a balloon filled with joy inside. "There isn't a place I'd rather be."

I kiss him one last time, then let the wide-eyed security guards take him away. "Hey, even football players can be gay too," I say.

The taller one laughs. "They can," he says. "You're just brave for being one."

I let Michael go and jog back to the locker room. I don't know what the coaches or other players might say, but that doesn't matter anymore. From now on, everything I do is for me.

Chapter 49

Michael Cunningham

THE WALK BACK TO my private suite is the most eventful walk of my life. Even though the guards take me through staff-only corridors and elevators, I'm still stopped by fans whenever they see me. And they're supportive. Kind. Exactly the opposite of what I expected. I do get some dirty looks, but most share about how happy they are that the NFO is finally accepting gay people, and I share my enthusiasm in return.

But that isn't the only reason I'm happy.

Kyle showed me his love, and we're back together.

By the time I reach my private suite, I'm pinching myself. For years, I've thought that it was only possible for me to fall in love with emotionally unavailable men, and that Kyle would be the last string of evidence to prove this curse.

But he didn't.

Instead, in the bravest demonstration I could imagine, he showed me he loved me. In front of millions and millions of people. That's a man who knows what he wants and isn't afraid of it either. In short, an emotionally available man.

When I open my private suite door, Zendaya and Tom Holland pop out of their door to congratulate, and I swear now I have to be dreaming. But when Amani, Skye, and Josue wrap their arms around me, I know that this is indeed sweet reality.

"Congratulations," Amani says, squeezing me tight.

"Okay," Skye says. "But now you need to write something like this. Because I don't know what can top it."

"My thoughts exactly," Josue says.

I pull away from them, both laughing and crying.

Jessica approaches me and gives me a light hug. "I'm happy for you."

I squeeze her hand. "You're a true hero here," I say. "You chose to be so kind to Kyle. And me. Thank you."

She blushes. "He's a nice guy, and you seem like one too. It was the right thing to do."

I squeeze her hand one last time, then take a moment to stand there and bask in the joy, Sloane Michaels singing in the background. Here I am: with friends I call family, now with a boyfriend. And it's so much better than I could have imagined back in college.

"Well," Amani says. "Now all that's left is for the Tigers to win."

My stomach jumps. "Shit. I forgot about that."

"Come on," she says gesturing to our seats. "Let's go cheer on your boyfriend."

I smile at the word. Because now I can actually say out loud that Kyle Weaver is my boyfriend.

Chapter 50

Kyle Weaver

THE SECOND HALF IS about to begin, and we're all lined up outside the locker room to race back onto the field. The Vanguards deferred their choice to the second half, which means we're kicking to them now. It's still 6 – 14 with them in the lead, and they're starting with the advantage.

I shake my head, trying to focus myself on this next half of the game. Coaches are pissed about my little performance, but there's nothing they can do. And like I care. This is my last NFO game ever, and now I can retire with a gorgeous boyfriend in my arms—one that I can publicly say is mine. I just have this last game to get through, and I'm gonna give it my all—not for my daddy or anyone else, but for me.

I pat Ezekiel on the shoulder. "Thanks again, man," I say. "For everything."

He gives me a hug, our shoulder pads and helmets clanging together. "Any time, man. It's a pleasure. And it was awesome to watch."

I blush. "I wasn't cheesy, was I?"

"Oh, you were, but it was perfect," he says, grinning.

But we don't get time to joke for long. It's time. We all rush back out onto the field.

"Bring out that beast," Ezekiel says. "Steal the ball. We're gonna need it this half."

He goes to the sidelines as I get in position with my fellow defensive players. And then, before I know it, we kick the ball, and the game begins.

* * *

We get into position. There's only thirty seconds left on the clock. We managed to score a touchdown, bringing the score to 12 – 14, but we missed our extra point. The Vanguard's have possession of the ball, and it's their second down. If they really pushed it, they could score another touchdown and lock in their win.

Unless I intercept the ball.

But I don't know if I can. I'm exhausted due to both the game and the anxiety from my plan to confess my love to Michael catching up to me. Don't get me wrong, I don't regret it in the slightest. But I could definitely use a hot shower, burger, and nap in that order right now.

The center snaps the ball. I try to break through the line, but their center sees me coming and keeps me in place. The quarterback hands the ball to their running back, and he runs out to the side in what looks like the wide open. No. He's gonna score. But just before he breaks away, one of my guys tackles him to the ground. Thank God.

We quickly get into our next positions. This is their first down, and they're less than twenty yards away from the goal line. This game is all but over.

Hunched down, waiting for them to snap the ball, I spot their quarterback signing something out to their wide receiver. This is the same thing they did last year. They're trying to juke us out.

They snap the ball, and the quarterback rushes back. He cocks his arm back to throw out to the left. Having seen this before, I dart out to the other side of the field. Where I know the ball will be.

And I'm right.

The quarterback throws it to the wide receiver just a few yards from me. Likely anticipating me, the quarterback threw it high. So that means I'm gonna have to jump high to grab it.

As the ball's coming down, I rush to where I see it's going to land.

And then I jump.

My arms stretched high, the ball falls into my arms.

And I land on my two feet.

The crowd roars, but I don't take time to congratulate myself.

I run like hell.

The crowd's roars intensify, now just as loud as they were when I kissed Michael.

When I kissed Michael. My official boyfriend.

I'm running. I manage to stiff arm a guy coming toward me, and I turn my body just out of reach from another. Fifty yards away from the goal line. Then forty.

I see flashes of the Vanguards' red uniform to my right. But I don't focus on them. If I do, I'll slow down. I need to stay fast. Thirty yards now.

I remember that I was exactly here a year ago. So much has changed. But the biggest difference now is that if someone asks me if I'm gay, I can gladly tell them the truth: yes. And I'm in love with a man named Michael Cunningham.

Someone reaches out and nearly grasps my clothing. But they just barely miss. I speed up, and then somehow, miraculously, I pass the goal line.

I go deaf at the sound of the cheering. I don't realize what's happened until all the Tigers are throwing themselves into me, grabbing my shoulder pads and cheering me on.

We did it. We fucking did it.

I won us the Championship Game.

And for the first time, I did it for me.

The next moments blur together. Our team celebrates. We thank the Vanguards for the game. I'm interviewed, but I don't remember what I say. Because now that the game's over, there's only one person I want to see.

In the locker rooms, I don't even shower. I'm too eager to see him. I just change into some nice clothes and grab my phone. Since I forgot where his suite is, I text Michael to meet me in a specific part of the stadium. He says he'll meet me there.

When I see him, he rushes to me, security all around us. He wraps his arms around me, and I press my lips so hard into him I swear I see stars.

"You did it," he says, grabbing both sides of my head.

"I did," I say, still unable to believe it.

We kiss again, and this time everyone around us cheers. And I feel no shame at all.

That night at the after party, some reporters are there, including Robyn, the woman from ESB who first interviewed me about my father.

"How does it feel to be out and with the man you love?" she asks, putting the microphone in front of me. The camera is rolling to my right, and I know this moment is just as important as when I confessed my love in the stadium. Michael is standing by, watching. He gives me an encouraging thumbs up.

I smile at him and look back at Robyn. "I couldn't be happier," I say. "I'm finally being true to myself."

"Do you have any words for your fans out there?"

I pause for a moment, then turn to the camera. "Be yourself," I say. "No matter what other people say. I've found that it's really the best way to live life."

I glance over at Michael and gesture for him to join me. He comes over and I wrap my arm around him. I pull his head to mine and kiss him on the lips, then look back at the camera. "And then you might get as lucky as me," I say. "Because now I have the man of my dreams."

I kiss him one more time, then raise my fist in the air. People cheer around me, my chest burns hot. Not from shame or embarrassment or anxiety like it always has. But from joy.

I thank Robyn for all she's done for me and give her a tight hug. Then I find Jessica.

"Thanks again," I say to her. "You didn't have to do this."

She pats me on the arm. "It was fun," she says. "I hope I find something like what you and Michael have."

I hug her and kiss her on the top of her head. "I think you will."

When the night's over, I take Michael home. To my home. Because we're fucking together now.

We've hardly made it past the laundry room before we're all over each other.

"Careful," I say, pulling away. "I stink."

"Oh, Kyle Weaver," Michael says. "This is a dream come true. Fucking a football player fresh after he wins the Championship Game?"

I smile and kiss him. "I missed you so much."

"I missed you too," he says. He rests his head against my chest while we stand in the kitchen, and I wrap my arms around him.

"Was that enough?" I ask.

He pulls away and gives me a quizzical look.

"Was that whole demonstration enough to show you that I love you?" I ask.

His face relaxes into a calm smile, and I can't stop myself from kissing him again. When I pull away to look in his eyes, I swear I can see his face sparkling with joy.

"I don't think you could have done it better," he says.

"Good," I say. "Because that was my last resort."

He digs his face into my chest and kisses it. "Well now you have me," he says, looking back up at me. "And now it's my turn to show you how much I love you."

My stomach jumps. "Please," I say. "I've been craving the shit out of you."

We can't get to my room fast enough, and thankfully he mentions he's clean sexually so we can get right to it. Michael manages to slip his clothes off in less than three seconds, which is honestly fucking impressive. I'm struggling to get my shirt off because of the sweat.

"Here," Michael says. He helps me take it off, but before I know it, he's got his face buried in my arm pit. I use my other arm to nuzzle him in there.

"God," he says, coming up for air. "You are such a fucking man."

I grab him and kiss him, turned on by my own musk on his face. "I'm your fucking man."

And that turns him into a fucking animal.

He gets off my pants and pushes me onto the bed. He goes down on me, and I swear I've been transported to heaven. I don't want to objectify Michael—he's so much more than that. But the nice thing about dating a pornstar is he there is not one thing he can't do well in the bedroom. And with the passion he brings to everything he does? I'm gonna have to build up my tolerance now that we're officially together. Because it takes some effort not to cum quick.

He releases his hold just before I'm about to release and comes up to kiss me. He collapses into the crook of my arm and wraps himself around me, and I know that I couldn't pull him off me if I tried.

Outside, snow is falling again, and Michael and I lounge here for a minute. Just soaking in the other's presence. He takes in a deep whiff of my armpit, and his ecstatic moan afterwards gets me rock hard again.

"So this is the life we're getting," he says. "This forever?"

I grab and pull him onto me so now he's straddling me. I grab some lube from my nightstand and apply it to myself. Then, grabbing him by the hips, I gently guide him back onto my dick and don't stop until I'm balls deep, his moans and gasps a symphony to my ears.

I grin up at him as he struggles to stay composed. "And there isn't nothing now that's gonna get in between us," I say, slowly beginning to thrust. "I promise you that."

And as we fuck that night, I don't feel any lingering anxiety or dread. Just joy and hope knowing that, while we may struggle like all couples do, he and I are both committed to each other. No matter what.

"I love you so much," I tell him as I hold him close, my dick still inside him after I've given him my third load.

"I love you too," he says, clutching my arms. And as he falls asleep in my arms, I know that I'm the luckiest man in the whole world. Choosing integrity wasn't easy, but with this as the outcome? It was worth all the pain. And I'd do it again for Michael in a heartbeat.

Epilogue One – Six Months Later

Michael Cunningham

I LAY NAKED ON the bed of the very same cabin where Kyle abandoned me. I'm alone and have been for the past hour. But, unlike last time, I know he's coming back.

Dating Kyle has been better than I could have imagined. I was worried that he would slip back into old ways, gradually withholding what was going on inside his head until he would explode with some hurtful behavior, forcing me to reconsider the whole relationship again.

But he hasn't. He's been consistently going to his therapist, coming to understand his relationship with his own sexuality more fully, while also addressing his complicated relationship with his father. It hasn't always been easy for him, and I'm sure challenges will arise in the future, but what's important is that he's honest and true to himself. And that makes any sort of conflict, heartfelt conversation, and even our most intimate moments so much better.

Oh, and speaking of intimate moments, my body is tied up with rope. My arms are pinned to my back, and my legs are tied to the bed frame, forcing me face down with my ass in the air. There's a mirror at the top of the bed, showing how vulnerable of a position I'm in.

Kyle and I have also been experimenting in the bedroom. Since he's had relatively little experience with men—or even women, surprisingly—and since I've had a lot due to my time as a pornstar, Kyle's asked to me to show him the ropes—ha!—on a few things. And since he's *my* Sexiest Man Alive, I happily oblige. That night before he abandoned me, we talked about both of us taking charge equally in bed. And since, we've learned that it's not about who's taking charge but instead how pleasurable what we're doing is. And we've found a lot of things that feel good. So now, every time we make love, it just ratchets up in intensity and pleasure for the both of us. Even as a pornstar, I didn't think sex could be this amazing.

I crane my neck to check the clock. It's past when Kyle said he would be back, but I'm not worried. I trust him now. And besides, we've agreed that stretching the rules a bit makes it fun. We have a safe word and all, but I've hardly needed to use it. It's honestly been perfect.

I hear the cabin door slam, and I feel my hole pucker. My dick is already getting hard against the rope keeping it down. The anticipation of his arrival, paired with not knowing when exactly it would be, has my heart racing and my libido flowing.

The floor creaks as downstairs as he walks around in his boots. I hear him set down the firewood that he was cutting. An hour ago, as he was tying me up, he said he would go do some chores outside. It's a scalding summer day in Mississippi, so I know he's hot and sweaty. Just how I like him.

He turns on the sink, and I let out a low whimper. I need him. Right now. And he's just taking his time, teasing me. When I finally hear him walking up the stairs, I try to spread my legs even further, making sure I'm as open as possible for him.

"Now there's a sight to see," he says, and his deep, Southern drawl sends chills down my spine. From day one—seeing him act all sexy in those commercials or watching one of his post-game interviews—his voice has always made me weak in the knees.

He walks over to the side of the bed, and my dick twitches at the sight of him. He's shirtless with red suspenders keeping his pants up. His entire muscular body glistens with sweat, and I almost pass out when I see a drop of sweat fall from his nipple. Since he retired from the NFO, he's worked hard to keep his workout routine just as rigorous. He likes the way he feels in his huge, beefy body. And I won't complain. I like the way it feels, too.

He lifts his boot on the bed and places it next to my face. "Off," he commands.

Wasting no time, I take my mouth to his laces and carefully undo the knots with my teeth.

He strokes the back of my head, gently pulling on my mullet. "Good piggy," he says.

When I manage to completely undo the knots, he retracts his leg and takes his boot off. He sticks the open shoe in my face, and I sniff in the stink with alacrity.

Poppers are popular in the gay community. It's where people sniff this chemical in a small bottle and get a brief high. For many, it relaxes the muscles, especially in the anus, and increases sensitivity, often bringing with it a quick sense of euphoria.

But I don't need that. I've never been into it, frankly. But Kyle's scent makes me a believer in its potential power. Because Kyle's smell opens me up like a fucking revelation. He's divine.

He pulls away before I can get enough of him, and I whimper.

"Don't worry," he says, putting his other boot on the bed. "You'll be getting plenty of me soon enough."

I get to untying his other boot, this time faster than the other one. And this time, after he takes off his boot, he lets me smell his socked foot directly. But instead of stroking my hair, he strokes my hole with his thumb, gently pushing it in with just enough pressure to alter my breathing.

I moan, the intense euphoria that his smell brings me altering my brain circuits to see him as more safe than before. When I was doing porn, sex with random men felt so lifeless, so distant. But now it's like an exploration, a dynamic plunge into Kyle's being. With each foray into Kyle's body, he feels more like home. And seeing him go crazy for mine, I know he's going through the same experience. Ever since we made up at the Championship Game, which I still can't stop thinking about, he's been opening himself up to me like a perpetual blossom, and the more I find inside him, the more I love him. And boy, do I love him.

"Take it off," he says, gentle but firm.

I slowly raise my head as high as I can to grab hold of the edge of the sock with my teeth. Then I pull. By the time his huge, hairy foot is revealed, I swear I'm worshipping the body of a god himself. But honestly, Achilles has nothing on Kyle.

After I kiss his foot several times, he retracts it. Then he slips his suspenders off his shoulder, and I know I'm in for the time of my life. His pants slip off, revealing tight gray Lycra underwear. He slips them off, and his massive cock whips up after he manages to get the waistband past it. The hair of his bush glistens with sweat, and I want nothing more than to shove my face in it.

And as he gets closer, it looks like that's just what I'm getting.

I open my mouth wider, already salivating, but then Kyle grabs my hair and forces me to look up at him.

"Open your mouth," he says.

I open it like a bird receiving its daily sustenance. And then he spits on my tongue.

"Keep it open," he says when I almost close my mouth to swallow his spit. I need as much of him inside me as I can get.

I expect him to shove his cock in my mouth. I'm ready to show him how much I love him.

But what I get is somehow even better.

He takes his underwear—the Lycra ones he's been wearing all day, the same ones he chopped wood with—bunches them up, and presses them against my nose.

The scent is more intoxicating than I can imagine, and I swear I could cum from this alone. The scent of his dick, his crotch, his gooch, his ass—all so distinct yet perfectly in harmony with one another, a bouquet of scents made especially for me.

"One last big sniff," he commands.

And I obey. I breathe in so hard I see stars. Out of the corner of my eye, I see how rock-hard Kyle is, and I exhale in ecstasy. I love that we both love this, that it's not just my fantasy alone.

"Keep it open," Kyle reminds me. I open my mouth, and he shoves the underwear inside. All of it. Until I can almost feel it against the back of my throat. Anyone else would gag. But not me, especially when it's Kyle inside me.

He leans down and kisses me on the nose, then looks me in the eyes. "I'm gonna fuck your ass so hard you won't be able to walk."

I nod eagerly, warm chills running down my spine and back up again. He takes his place behind me, and I take a deep breath through my nose, preparing myself. As he lubes up his dick and my hole, I watch him through the mirror, taking in every inch of his perfect, manly body. Then, he starts to slide it in.

I lower my head and take a deep breath of the sock he left behind, his scent helping me open my hole even further. And once he's inside, I offer thanks to the universe that this is my life now. Because I didn't know such trust or such joy or such peace could actually be found. And that now I somehow have it. And that it's here to stay.

Kyle's face goes aggressively stoic as he pounds my ass, pulling the rope tight against my body. He stares down at my body as if he's been on a treasure hunt his whole life, and he found my body made of gold. He grunts desperately, thrusting hungrily inside me. His tongue sticks out, and he lets out a little whimper with each thrust, as if now I'm in total control, my asshole bringing the top linebacker of the country to his proverbial knees.

And then he floods me. I breathe the scent from his sock in happily as his entire body jolts with his orgasm. He caresses my back as he breathes heavily, sweat dripping down his face. I gently buck back onto him, squeezing my hole around his dick, sucking every last drop out of my man. With one last breath, he pulls out of me.

With any other guy, I'd be disappointed that it's over. The mood would change now that he's gotten off, and the intimacy we had during sex would evaporate into the air.

But not with Kyle. He is the king of aftercare.

He begins gently untying the rope, caressing and kissing each indent that it leaves in my skin.

"Shoot, sorry, I forgot," he says. He reaches to take the underwear out of my mouth, but I shake my head, and he lets me keep it in. I like having it here, like a pacifier made of his own sweat. And I want it here until I'm completely unbound.

He takes off the rest of the rope and throws it to the side of the bed, and I melt into the soft mattress, finally releasing Kyle's underwear from my mouth and tossing it off the bed. He plops himself next to me and wraps his arms around me. I nuzzle into him and kiss him in between his pecs.

"Ma's having Jimmy and Silas over for dinner tonight," he says.

"Awesome," I say, muffled by his chest hair. When Kyle and I got to Glamour Springs, we just went straight to this cabin that Linda rented for us. "I can't wait to see them."

He kisses me on the head. "Still gotta get you off."

I moan. "Honestly, I could go the rest of my life doing only what we just did."

He laughs. "I never knew anyone could be so creative in bed," he says. "This is better than I could have imagined."

We lay in silence for a while, him stroking the back of my head.

"Come on," he says, letting me go. "You deserve to get off too."

My dick hardens already from the anticipation. "Can we...?"

Without a word, Kyle turns around and swings his massive leg over me, revealing his sweat, hairy hole, after chopping wood outside and fucking me. Kyle then swallows my dick, and I have no choice but to dig in and get his stench all over my face. And Kyle's eager head mixed with my face buried in his ass makes this a quick affair. I cum in less than a minute.

"Alright," Kyle says, unmounting me. He grabs a nearby towel. "Now we really gotta make it to dinner. My mom's been dying to see you."

"Fine," I say. But as I watch him get dressed, my heart just as full as my ass, excited to go hangout with my new family, I smile and stretch my wonderfully sore body. Kyle was right—I might not be able to walk after this.

It turns out I am not only capable of finding an emotionally available man. My life is also filled with others that I love—my reading and writing friends, along with Kyle's family. I finally have that community I've always wanted.

So, as it would also turn out, I *am* capable of loving healthily, and of being loved. I just had to go through a lot to really see it.

Epilogue Two – One Year Later

Kyle Weaver

RUCKERS ISN'T THE SMALLEST bookstore, but Michael's brought in a large enough crowd to fill in every square foot of free space. Kelley, one of the first booksellers that Michael met here, is asking him questions about his debut book as they sit by the front window. I can't help but grin as I remember our argument over whether romance or fantasy was better. Funny how that discussion would lead to this. Jury's still out on the verdict, but I like Michael's solution: put the two together.

The first week that his book hit the shelves, his romantasy about two knights in a disgraced retinue falling in love did better than his publisher expected. So much so that they're now on the second print. But that doesn't surprise me. He worked hard on that book, and he worked even harder marketing it the weeks before its release date. I can't wait for his next book to hit the shelves.

Kelley opens up the discussion for questions from the audience. Nearby, Amani, my former fake-girlfriend, sits with her partner Angie, Skye, Josue, and Ezekiel. I'm still thrilled that he came to support my boyfriend. Next to him sits Michael's sponsor Susan, and she's beaming. I know she's proud of Michael. Don't see how anyone couldn't be.

When I see Michael get nervous, he glances at them, and they try to give supportive gestures without being too conspicuous. But it's not like he really needs it. Back when we first met, he held himself so small when he was nervous, like he was afraid to make a splash. But now he sits tall and answers questions with confidence. The man knows who he is, and he's always the first I think of when it comes to integrity.

And apparently, so many people here are from Kyle's book club and the other Ruckers book clubs. Since he started working here, he's loved every minute, and he's made loads of friends. Now that we're living together, I've told him that I could support him financially so he can work on his books. I'm still doing ads and bringing in a lot of cash, let alone all the money I saved as a single man in the NFO. But he said he wants to keep working here. Says it helps him with his writing, and he loves the community. So I won't get in the way of that.

But as I lean here against a bookshelf, behind the main crowd, I'm getting a little nervous myself. Not because I'm out in public with my boyfriend, afraid that people will see us together. Not at all. I'm proud to call Michael my own. I'm nervous because I have a little stunt planned, not unlike what I pulled at the Championship Game a year and a half ago. And I'm hoping it goes just right.

When Kelley says she has room for one more question, I raise my hand, and she calls on me, just as we planned. When Michael sees it's me, a smile forms on his face as his brow furrows, which looks cute as hell on him. He has no idea what I'm about to do.

"I understand that this bookstore is how you and I met," I say.

All eyes turn on me, and some gasp. Since I'm standing in the back, not many have seen me until now. But now the sound of hushed whispers fills the store. Some even pull out their phones to film me. Before I decided to live a life of integrity, this would have terrified me. I wouldn't have wanted people to see me showing affection toward another man. But now it fills me with joy because the whole world gets to see what I'm about to do.

"Yeah," Michael says, almost laughing. "It is." He doesn't say more, and I can tell he's waiting for me to ask my question. He likely thinks I'll ask about how the bookstore brought us together so he has an excuse to tell everyone our story, but I got something much better in mind.

I start making my way to where Michael and Kelley are sitting on their stools. When I'm halfway there, his eyes widen, and I think he's realizing what's going on. I hear Amani squeal to my left as she takes out her phone.

I go down on one knee, and everyone in the bookstore gasps. Now everyone's taking out their phone to film me. But my eyes are locked on the man that I love.

Michael's covering his mouth with his hand as he gets off the stool. He slowly steps toward me, tears welling in his eyes. "You're not…"

"I am," I say, pulling out a little black box from my back pocket. "Michael Cunningham, I've put you through hell."

Michael laughs and wipes his eyes.

"But I've worked real hard to make our life what it is now, and it's my aim to only make it better. But that only works if we're committed. For life."

The bookstore is so quiet that I can hear the little black box creak open. Inside is a thick gold band.

"So I ask you," I say, trying not to let my voice shake. "Will you marry me?"

Michael lets out a noise that's half-laugh and half sob, then reaches out to me. "Yes, I would love to."

I stand up and wrap my arms around him as our lips press together. Everyone's standing and filming us now. As I kiss him, I think about what this could mean for other gay men like me. After my stunt at the Championship Game, so many officials were pissed. But what it did was show not only the organization, but also the fans, that there are gay men like me who play and want to play football. Since I retired, I honestly don't know what life will be like for a gay football player in the NFO. But I'm hoping that what I've done can show my fellow gay players that it's not only okay but also beautiful to be true to ourselves. And that NFO teams will still draft them even when they are their authentic gay selves.

Michael and I pull away from each other and smile, oblivious to those around us.

"I love you," he says.

"I love you, too," I say, loud enough for the whole room to hear.

* * *

Kelley sets up a table for Michael to sign copies of his book after the whole proposal is done. He sits down to sign, and I step off to the side. The first woman comes up and greets Michael.

"Thanks," she says, once he does. "But I was also wondering... can he sign it to?" She's pointing at me.

Michael gives me a look that says I totally should.

"I didn't write the book," I say.

"Okay," Michael says. "But you are kinda the reason the book exists—helping me write better, inspiring me with all your fantasy books. Besides, you're like still famous. I don't see why people wouldn't want your signature."

I let out a laugh. "Alright," I say, sitting down at the table. And now Michael and I are both signing hardcover copies of his book. I thought this would be tiring at first, but seeing all the different people who have already read Michaels' book greeting him like he's the Pope—I am enlivened by the unique energy that each person brings.

As the signing line gets shorter, the store gets quieter, and some of the book-sellers begin their closing routine. Ezekiel and Susan are talking to Michael's friends about what they write, and he's eating it up. And at the far end of the line, I think I spot someone familiar, though I can't tell from here. But when it's finally his turn, my stomach jumps to my throat.

"Tanner Bash," I say, standing up to hug the man.

Michael flashes me a curious look. *From Miss U?* He mouths.

I nod to him. Yes, that Tanner—one of the players I fucked on and off in college. But I don't have any feelings for the guy now. We've seen each other enough over the years for me to know we're just friends. And Michael knows enough about him not to be jealous. Plus, it's Michael. I don't know anyone who's worked harder to have a level head.

I put my hands on my hips. "What are you doing here, big guy?"

He laughs shyly, scratching the back of his head.

He was a center at Miss U, and now he's playing for the San Diego Seals. He's an inch shorter than me, standing at 6'4". He's wider, but, dare I say, he's gotten more muscular since I last saw him. Almost more muscular than me. He's blonde with a boyishly handsome face that's only grown more rugged over the last ten years.

He looks at us, then around at the people left. It's just us, our friends, and the booksellers.

"Congrats on your proposal," he says to both of us. "And that stunt you pulled at the Championship Game—that was awesome."

"Thanks, man," I say. "It's good to see you."

He nods, then looks around again, more nervously this time.

"You okay?" I ask.

"Do you two have time to talk to me?" he asks, looking between me and Michael. "I—I'm—" He clears his throat.

Michael watches him intently. I think I know what's coming next, but it looks like Michael's certain. It's like he pulls these confessions out of people. I mean, look how he did it to me.

"I think I'm gay," he says in the most intense whisper I've heard. "And I don't know what to do about it. I have one year left in the NFO. I need help—someone to talk to."

There's a million things I want to say, ask, and do right now, all things I've been learning in therapy. But while I'm paralyzed by all the things I could do, Michael just stands up, walks around the table, and wraps my old friend in a bear hug. When I hear Tanner sniffling, I know that Michael made the right move. And I can't think of someone better for Tanner to trust just as he's coming out. I'm still impressed by the respect Michael showed me when I did.

Michael pulls away from him and looks at me, asking a question with his eyes only. We've gotten good at communicating with no words. I nod.

"We'd love to talk more," Michael says. "Why don't you join us at our house tonight? We'll make you dinner."

Our house. God, hearing him call it that makes my chest tingle. Because it is our house. And seeing how kind and tender he is with someone he could easily dismiss if he was jealous, there is no one I'd rather share it with.

Tanner nods and wipes his red eyes. "I'd like that," he says. "Thanks guys."

"It's an honor," I say, putting my arm around my old friend. "Come on, I'll take you there. Let's give you some of the peace that I've found."

What's next?

Thank you so much for reading. Please don't forget to leave a review for *Catching Kyle*! It would mean the world.

Want to read about Jimmy and Tanner's story? Read *Tackling Tanner* now!

Still want to stick with Michael and Kyle? Type in this link (https://dl.bookfunnel.com/bqrzrnbygt) to gain exclusive access to a bonus short story about them after their engagement. You'll also gain free access to my Football Heartthrobs prequel novella, *Downing Dominic*, in the newsletter welcome email.

Acknowledgements

I WILL DO MY very best to account for everyone, but if I miss someone, know that you were meant to be included here and my human brain forgot to include you.

To my very own sponsor Bev, thank you for encouraging me to see that my writing was part of my own recovery and for always giving the encouragement and support I knew I needed, as well as the ample encouragement and support I never even knew I needed until I had it. I don't think I would be here without you.

A special thanks to my mom and dad who supported me in innumerable ways since the beginning of this novel.

And a warm thanks to my beta readers and critique partners—Naomi, James, Taylor, Madi, Alyse, and all my writing group friends.

A special thank you to James who spent countless hours enlightening me on how the hell professional football works. This novel wouldn't be what it is without you! I'm glad that paintgate never got in the way of our friendship.

And thanks to you, dear reader, for taking the time to read my novel. It means more to me than you could ever know.